Prize Stories 2001

THE O. HENRY AWARDS

PRIZE STORIES 2001

The O. Henry Awards

Edited and with an Introduction
by Larry Dark

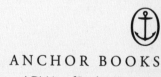

ANCHOR BOOKS
A Division of Random House, Inc.
New York

AN ANCHOR ORIGINAL, SEPTEMBER 2001

Copyright © 2001 by Anchor Books, a division of Random House, Inc.

Library of Congress Cataloging-in-Publication Data
Prize stories 2001 : the O. Henry awards / edited with an introduction by Larry Dark.
p.   cm.
ISBN: 0-385-49878-0
1. Short Stories, American.   I. Dark, Larry.
PS648.S5 P73   2001
813'.0108054—dc21
2001031593

www.anchorbooks.com

Printed in the United States of America

10   9   8   7   6   5   4   3   2   1

Publisher's Note

WILLIAM SYDNEY PORTER, who wrote under the pen name O. Henry, was born in North Carolina in 1862. He started writing stories while in prison for embezzlement, a crime for which he was convicted in 1898 (it is uncertain if he actually committed the crime). His writing career was short and started late, but O. Henry proved himself a prolific and widely read short story writer in the twelve years he devoted to the craft, and his name has become synonymous with the American short story.

His years in Texas inspired many lively Westerns, but it was New York City that galvanized his creative powers, and his New York stories became his claim to fame. Loved for their ironic plot twists, which made for pleasing surprise endings, his highly entertaining tales appeared weekly in Joseph Pulitzer's *New York World*.

His best known story, "The Gift of the Magi," was written for the *World* in 1905 and has become an American treasure. Dashed off past deadline in a matter of hours, it is the story of a man who sells his watch to buy a set of hair combs as a Christmas present for his wife, who in the meantime has sold her luxurious locks to buy him a watch chain. "The Last Leaf" is another O. Henry favorite. It is the story of a woman who falls ill with pneumonia and pronounces that she will die when the last leaf of ivy she sees outside her Greenwich Village window falls away. She hangs on with the last stubborn leaf, which gives her the resolve to recover. She eventually learns that her inspirational leaf wasn't a real leaf at all, but rather a painting of a leaf. Her neighbor, who has always dreamed of painting a masterpiece, painted it on the wall and caught pneumonia in the process.

His work made him famous, but O. Henry was an extremely private man who, sadly, preferred to spend his time and money on drink, and ultimately it was the bottle that did him in. He died alone and penniless in 1910. O. Henry's legacy and his popularization of the short story was such that in 1918 Doubleday, in conjunction with the Society of Arts and Sciences, established the O. Henry Awards, an annual anthology of short stories, in his honor. Anchor Books is proud, with the eighty-first edition of the series, to continue the tradition of publishing this much beloved collection of outstanding short stories in O. Henry's name.

The seventeen stories included in *Prize Stories 2001: The O. Henry Awards* were chosen by the series editor, Larry Dark, from among the three thousand or so short stories published during the course of the previous year in the magazines consulted for the series and listed on page 415. Blind copies of these seventeen stories, that is, copies with the names of the authors and magazines omitted, were then sent to the prize jury members. Each juror was instructed to vote for his or her top three choices, and the first-, second-, and third-prize winners were determined as a result of these votes. The jurors for the 2001 volume were Michael Chabon, Mary Gordon, and Mona Simpson. An introduction by one of the three jurors precedes each of the top-prize stories selected.

A shortlist of fifty other stories given serious consideration for *Prize Stories 2001: The O. Henry Awards,* along with brief summaries of each, can be found on page 402.

The Magazine Award is given to the magazine publishing the best fiction during the course of the previous year, as determined by the number of stories selected for *Prize Stories: The O. Henry Awards,* the placement of stories among the top-prize winners, and the number of short-listed stories. The Magazine Award winner for 2001 is *The New Yorker.* A citation for this award is provided on page 413.

Acknowledgments

Thanks to Jenny Minton, Adam Pringle, and Jen Marshall at Vintage
Anchor and, for their assistance, to Augustine Chan and Denise Delgado.

Contents

INTRODUCTION • xv
   Larry Dark

THE DEEP • 1
FIRST PRIZE
   Mary Swan
   The Malahat Review, No. 131
   Introduced by Mary Gordon

BIG ME • 57
SECOND PRIZE
   Dan Chaon
   The Gettysburg Review, Vol. 13, No. 2
   Introduced by Michael Chabon

FLOATING BRIDGE • 81
THIRD PRIZE
SPECIAL AWARD FOR CONTINUING ACHIEVEMENT
   Alice Munro
   The New Yorker, July 31, 2000
   Introduced by Mona Simpson

THAT WINTER • 106
   Fred G. Leebron
   TriQuarterly, Nos. 107/8

THE LOVE OF MY LIFE • 117
    T. Coraghessan Boyle
    The New Yorker, March 6, 2000

THE GIRL WITH THE BLACKENED EYE • 134
    Joyce Carol Oates
    Witness, Vol. XIV, No. 2

THE SMOKER • 145
    David Schickler
    The New Yorker, June 19 & 26, 2000

FEMALE TROUBLE • 166
    Antonya Nelson
    Epoch, Vol. 49, No. 1

THE MOURNING DOOR • 191
    Elizabeth Graver
    Ploughshares, Vol. 26, Nos. 2 & 3

ZOG-19: A SCIENTIFIC ROMANCE • 200
    Pinckney Benedict
    Zoetrope: All-Story, Vol. 4, No. 1

AT THE JIM BRIDGER • 223
    Ron Carlson
    Esquire, May 2000

REVIVAL ROAD • 239
    Louise Erdrich
    The New Yorker, April 17, 2000

THE PAPERHANGER • 254
    William Gay
    Harper's Magazine, February 2000

BLISS • 270
Dale Peck
Zoetrope: All-Story, Vol. 4, No. 2

BOW DOWN • 288
Murad Kalam
Harper's Magazine, October 2000

PASTORALIA • 299
George Saunders
The New Yorker, April 3, 2000

SERVANTS OF THE MAP • 344
Andrea Barrett
Salmagundi, Nos. 124 & 125

CONTRIBUTORS' NOTES • 391

JURORS • 400

SHORT-LISTED STORIES • 402

2001 MAGAZINE AWARD: *The New Yorker* • 413

MAGAZINES CONSULTED • 415

PERMISSIONS ACKNOWLEDGMENTS • 441

Introduction

THE JOB of choosing twenty or so short stories out of more than three thousand published during the course of a year requires that an editor be receptive, even somewhat passive. You have to wait for the stories to come to you, keep an open mind, and be prepared to find the unexpected in unexpected places. At the same time, it also helps to be actively looking for certain kinds of stories. While the purpose of *Prize Stories: The O. Henry Awards* is to present the reader with a core representation of the year's most interesting and accomplished short fiction, an editorial focus can illuminate and sharpen a collection. Of course, no single idea can sweep up all of the work selected for a single edition of *The O. Henry Awards*. To impose one would result in excluding some of the year's best stories, whose excellence most often depends on their originality. Nonetheless, in the course of reading a huge volume of work in a given year, connections emerge. Certain ideas are simply out there at any time, part of a collective consciousness that writers and editors tap into, knowingly or not.

One trend that I found to be prevalent when reading for this volume was the publication of more long stories or novellas than I had previously encountered. The first one I came across was Andrea Barrett's "Servants of the Map," published in *Salmagundi*. At forty-five pages, I first thought it might be too long to put in *The O. Henry Awards*, but I found myself engrossed by the story of a young Englishman on a mapping expedition of the Himalayas in the 1860s. In the end, I not only concluded that it was possible to include a novella-length story but also began to look for other long stories to group with it.

Because there's a limit to the length of a given volume of *The O. Henry Awards,* I decided that I would have to take out one story for every long story or novella I chose to include. I settled on a plan of three long pieces, with a total of seventeen stories in the book rather than the customary twenty—provided I could find other long stories that were good enough. This was a difficult commitment to make because I know that inclusion in a volume of *Prize Stories: The O. Henry Awards* can provide a boost to an author or a magazine, but I felt that what was gained balanced out what was lost. Long stories allow for a fuller exploration of ideas, a larger plot trajectory, and a richer, more novelistic sense of detail. Including such stories, I hope, will expose readers to the possibilities for the story form toward the longer end of the spectrum, while also reflecting a strong recent trend in fiction writing.

As it happened, it wasn't difficult to find more good long stories. Rather, I discovered, it was difficult to narrow down the field. Among the other notable novella-length stories I read during 2000 were Junot Díaz's "The Brief Wondrous Life of Oscar Wao," from *The New Yorker;* Mary Helen Stefaniak's "The Turk and My Mother," from *Epoch;* and John Updike's "Nelson and Annabelle," a sequel to his Rabbit cycle of novels, published in two parts in *The New Yorker.* The second long story that became a serious contender for the collection, however, was George Saunders's sharply satirical "Pastoralia," from *The New Yorker.* Viewing length as a virtue rather than a limitation, I consulted the longer version, which is the title story of Saunders's collection, and decided to run it in this form.

The story I chose as the third long piece for the collection turned out to be this year's first-prize winner, Mary Swan's "The Deep." If I hadn't specifically been looking for long stories, this vivid, accomplished story set during World War I may have escaped my notice. Over the years, I have come to accept the fact that three thousand or so stories is too much for any single reader to keep up with and devote full attention to, so I've enlisted sharp-eyed assistants to do some of the preliminary reading—for this volume, Augustine Chan and Denise Delgado. As part of our frequent discussions over the course of the year, I told each to be on the lookout for good long stories. It was Denise who first read "The Deep" in *The Malahat Review,* late in the year, and recommended that I consider it for one of the long story slots. Mary Gordon discusses what makes this such a remarkable piece of writing in her citation for "The Deep" (page 3).

A second element common to *Prize Stories 2001: The O. Henry Awards* is that crime plays an important part in several of the stories. In Joyce Carol Oates's "The Girl with the Blackened Eye," a teenage girl is abducted and brutalized. In William Gay's "The Paperhanger," a young child disappears and the mystery is grimly resolved some time later. "Bow Down," by Murad Kalam, concerns an enterprising inner-city youth who takes over an abandoned house in a poor Phoenix neighborhood and turns it into a haven for drug dealers and junkies, pimps and whores. In "Bliss," by Dale Peck, a man takes home the paroled murderer of his mother, in an effort to bring closure to the childhood trauma he endured. And T. Coraghessan Boyle's "The Love of My Life" offers a fictional interpretation of a tragic, much-publicized real-life event.

I come across stories concerned with crime and violence every year, so I wouldn't say these subjects were uniquely characteristic of the fiction I encountered in 2000. Unlike my inclusion of long stories, this was not a theme I deliberately pursued; this focus only became apparent to me after I'd made my final choices. Crime and violence are an unavoidable part of the world we live in, and serious literary writers can't avoid the subject altogether, nor should they. A criminal act is inherently dramatic—either something definitive occurs that has an immediate impact on characters or it is the culmination of other events in the story. The trick in keeping the story from crossing the line—and it can be a fine line—into a more lurid genre of fiction is to steer clear of exploiting tragedy for entertainment's sake and to avoid seeking to titillate readers gratuitously. One way to handle this is to explore the aftermath of a violent act, the moral and psychological consequences, without describing in detail the act itself. Another path, chosen by some of the authors of the stories in this collection, is to take an unflinching look at a violent crime itself, to take the measure of its physical and psychological impact when it happens, center stage. The risks to this approach can be great, but the results can be powerful and accomplished, eye-opening and thought-provoking.

There are other common elements to the stories collected here, and interesting, odd little connections among them. For instance, in both this year's second-prize winner, "Big Me," by Dan Chaon, and Kalam's "Bow Down," young protagonists break into neighbor's houses. In "Big Me," the twist is that the child illegally enters the house of a man who he fantasizes is his future self. Michael Chabon's introduction (page 59) goes into more detail on the inventiveness and subtlety of Chaon's story. An even odder connection is that in both Swan's "The Deep" and Elizabeth Graver's "The Mourning Door," a character finds the hand of a child. In "The Deep," the hand is discovered in the middle of a road "lying palm up in the dust," a desolate symbol of the senseless destruction of war. In "The Mourning Door," a woman hoping to become pregnant finds a "walnut-sized hand" in her bed. One child's hand represents the end of life, the other the beginning—an elegant opposition no editor could plan.

In addition to these small coincidences, certain larger themes and common subjects are likely to be represented in any distillation of a given year's work. Cancer plays a part in this year's third-prize winner, Alice Munro's "Floating Bridge," as well as in Fred G. Leebron's "That Winter," which links a man's midlife crisis to his sister's fatal illness. A broad, humorous tone is shared by Saunders's "Pastoralia" and Pinckney Benedict's "Zog-19: A Scientific Romance," a story with Kurt Vonnegut–like sci-fi overtones that is also about the waning of the American family farm. The romance at the heart of Benedict's story connects it to stories in this collection that concern love and the complexity of human relationships: for example, David Schickler's charming "The Smoker" and Antonya Nelson's witty and observant "Female Trouble." Romantic relationships also figure strongly in "At the Jim Bridger," by Ron Carlson, which, like Leebron's story, grapples with a male protagonist in the throes of a midlife crisis. "Revival Road," by Louise Erdrich, touches on the theme of love and involves car theft and a police chase, connecting it to the stories in which crime plays a part. It also shares star-crossed young lovers with Boyle's "The Love of My Life."

The contributors' notes (page 391) reveal another interesting and unanticipated link. Chaon's "Big Me," Barrett's "Servants of the Map," Erdrich's "Revival Road," and Swan's "The Deep" are all, by their authors' accounts, stories that were several years in the making. I can't recall another volume in which so many contributors discussed working at a single story for such a long time. That might be something else that was in the air last year: a long-awaited coming to fruition of difficult and complex work.

This is the fourth volume for which I have asked each prize juror—for 2001, Michael Chabon, Mary Gordon, and Mona Simpson—to introduce his or her favorite work. These concise, intelligent, and insightful essays have become an essential part of each collection, one that greatly adds to the pleasure of reading the top-prize-winning stories. O. Henry Awards jury duty involves reading blind copies of the complete set of stories I choose for the collection and voting for first-, second-, and third-prize winners. The introductions to these stories offer the astute observations of accomplished authors and often provide an inside perspective on the current state of fiction. Because the jurors are primarily fiction writers and sophisticated readers of fiction, these essays also lay out emotional connections to the work. I'm grateful to the fifteen writers who in the last five years have given so generously of themselves and their valuable writing time to serve this function.

One curious result of the outcome of the jury process is that a single author, Alice Munro, one of the most important short story writers of our time, has three times been named a third-prize winner in the past four volumes of the series and never placed first or second. I think it's because, even reading blind, writers know a Munro story when they read one. Most are long-time admirers of her work and have favorite Munro stories against which they weigh any new story of hers that they read, so that Munro is not just competing against the other stories in the collection but also against her reputation and her own best work.

This year, when I read "Floating Bridge" and another story by Alice Munro not included in this collection, "Post and Beam," both in *The New Yorker,* I found myself faced with a difficult choice. It was so difficult that I briefly considered including both. This didn't prove to be practical, but it occurred to me that Munro was deserving of special praise for her brilliant work in the short story form. In compiling a complete list of O. Henry Award winners since the inception of the series in 1919,[1] I found that the previous series editor, William Abrahams, had four times bestowed a Special Award for Continuing Achievement—to Joyce Carol Oates in 1970 and 1986, to John Updike in 1976, and to Alice Adams in 1982—and I decided to resurrect the award for Alice Munro. Of all the writers currently publishing short stories who have not thus far achieved this honor, none is more deserving than she. "Floating Bridge" marks her

[1]Available on the Web at www.boldtype.com/Ohenry

fourth appearance in this series. But it wasn't until 1997 that Canadian authors were made eligible for inclusion in *The O. Henry Awards*. Who knows how many times Munro's stories would have been chosen had they been considered from the start? By way of a citation for this special honor and an introduction to the third-prize-winning story, I will leave it to Mona Simpson to introduce "Floating Bridge" and discuss the impact of Munro's work, which she does with passion and eloquence (page 83).

And though I need hardly justify honoring one of the world's greatest living writers, I can't help but profess great admiration for Alice Munro's writing. It has that magical quality of drawing the reader in and presenting a deep and vivid experience, yet it does so without over-specifying. There are mysteries in every Munro story that invite the reader's participation, mysteries that never can be entirely solved. She often presents a great sweep of time in a single story and bounds over many years in the telling. Munro's protagonists are usually women, and their struggles are in most cases with or against their marriages, the choices they have made and those they haven't, accommodations they have come to regret or one day will. Still, the stories she writes are of near universal appeal and moral relevance. Her writing is traditional in its scope, yet often experimental in its use of time and narrative structure. I would call her a feminist, but her work is always illustrative and never didactic. Her stories are well worth reading for anyone trying to learn how to write short fiction, and yet they are so idiosyncratic and often so fully realized that her writing remains beyond imitation. Most of all, I think of an Alice Munro story as working on several levels and plumbing the depths of experience with great artistry and humanity.

It's my pleasure to bestow upon Alice Munro this Special Award for Continuing Achievement. As the name implies, this is an award for writers with impressive bodies of short story work behind them but still at the height of their powers. As the name also implies, this is an award that will be given judiciously and on an irregular basis in the years ahead. The short story is not an easy form, and greatness is difficult to attain in any artistic endeavor. Nonetheless, on the basis of the work I read every year and the fiction collected here, I can't help but feel optimistic.

LARRY DARK, 2001

Prize Stories 2001

THE O. HENRY AWARDS

The Deep

By Mary Swan

INTRODUCED BY MARY GORDON

Prose fiction is the bastard child of poetry and journalism. If we, arbitrarily perhaps, but perhaps not, name poetry as the mother, and journalism the father, it seems to me that current prose fiction suffers as a child who takes too much nourishment from its father's hand, an insufficient amount from its mother's. But "The Deep" triumphantly insists on fiction's kinship with poetry. Its greatest strength lies in its creation of image and atmosphere: the pen that leaks into the servant's pocket at the news of the mother of the house's death, the identical scars on the legs of the identical twins, the scars not quite identical because in incising the scars, the twins sat with their feet touching and the scars are therefore mirror images. "The Deep" marks the deep strangeness of the project of being alive. It begins with the inherently uncanny phenomenon of twinship: the other self that is simultaneously the self and other. It includes the darkness of family hatred, family coldness. It rescues the past—a particular slice of the past, the frequently limned period of the First World War—from the dead life of a museum piece. It touches on the limitations and frustrations of the existence of privileged young women, and points to their resilience in the face of genteel oppression. At the same time, the story has a strong, clear narrative line, an unlooked-for climax that in retrospect seems inevitable, so perfectly connected is it to all the elements that make up the story. In these few pages, a thick and shapely world is presented, and the author has risked the unfashionable in many bold, sure strokes. I chose this story as first among so many strong others because of its utter originality, its daring to assert the primacy of complexity and mystery, its avoidance of the current appetite for ironic anomie and thinness. It flowers entirely on its own terms, and the terms are rich and strange.

—MARY GORDON

Mary Swan

The Deep

From *The Malahat Review*

AFTER

HERE THERE are two tall windows, very tall, many-paned, and the gauzy white curtains swirl in the breeze, lift and fall like a breath, like a sigh. There is a faint, sweet smell, like blossoms; perhaps it is spring. The leaves on the trees also lift and sigh, all that can be seen through those windows. Sounds reach us from the street, wheels turning and hard shoes and sometimes a voice raised, calling out something, but they are muffled, all these sounds. Distant. Father told us once about the Queen's funeral, straw laid in the street to mute the sound. It is like that, and we wonder if someone has died.

HOW TO BEGIN

Has it ever happened to you, that you have wakened suddenly from a long, deep sleep, that it takes some time for you to realize who you are, where you are? Familiar objects, even faces become mysterious, remote. You stumble about, trailing the fog of sleep into the waking world, and nothing makes sense. Just a few, fuddled moments, if you're lucky. Until you splash your face with cold water and recognize it again, in the mirror above the basin. Until you drink a cup of tea, breathe fresh air, let routine tasks draw you back. Where do we go, in such a sleep, what is the world that we enter?

It may be France, in 1918.

SURVIVAL SUIT

How to explain it, what it was like? The interview, and then the notice that we were accepted, the official look of it, and then the date for sailing, ten days on. A sudden twinge of panic, of dismay—ten days, such an imaginable length of time. So many things to do, to gather together, the momentum of that carried us for a while. The vaccinations and the endless lists. Blankets and heavy stockings and high boots. Coats, thermos bottles, sewing case, flannel nightgowns. Knife. Two closely written pages listing essential equipment, with a note at the bottom reminding us that it was our patriotic duty to bring as little luggage as possible.

We laughed about that when we went to dine with Miss Reilly, and she told us how envious she was, how she wished she were setting off too. We talked about the brave boys who had given their lives, James, and the friends and brothers of people we knew. And of course we reminisced about our European journey, spoke of the spirit of France, of Belgium, of how much we had learned. That time we stood in the little church of San Maurizio, tears streaming down our faces, and how no one thought it strange. Miss Reilly gave us each a slim black pen that evening when we left, so that we would remember to write her everything.

The next day, Father took us to lunch. Someone had told him that the crossing was more dangerous than anything we'd be close to in France, and so after we had eaten he insisted on going with us to try on lifesaving suits. We saw the flicker in his eye when the woman said that one suit could support fourteen additional people hanging on to it. But then it was gone and he said very firmly that we would require two suits. To make him happy we tried them on all afternoon, although it all seemed quite ridiculous. The heavy rubber suits, lined with cork, the snapping steel clamps at chest and ankle, buckling on the headgear. The woman showed us the special pockets, designed to hold bread and a flask of whiskey, and assured us that along with the fourteen hangers-on, the suit would support the person wearing it for forty-eight hours in a standing position, submerged only to just above the waist. "Ophelia!" we said together when we heard this, remembering the doll we had once. The flowers we braided in her long stiff hair and how we tried to float her in the shallow stream. How she kept bobbing up to stand, petals falling everywhere, until we finally tied our heavy wet stockings around her neck and then she did float, but face down. The trouble from Nan when she found us, not because of the stockings but because we'd been at the stream, and she hadn't known.

We left the store with two bulky parcels, and Father seemed quite relieved that he had been able to purchase what was required to keep us safe.

THE CASTLE

Our mother was a sad woman lying on a couch, on a bed, or very occasionally wrapped in shawls and blankets in a chair on the veranda. We killed her, of course; everyone knew that.

We saw her every day, almost every day, though sometimes it was just a glimpse from the doorway. Her hazy face, eyes, amid the pillows in the darkened room. Nan holding our hands tightly, holding us back. Our mother's pale face shifting, swimming toward us through the gloom as she whispered, "Hello my darlings."

"Hello, my darlings," we mocked sometimes, laughing ourselves silly as we rolled in the soft grass, collecting stains that Nan would scold us for. And we whispered it at night, lying in our narrow beds, holding hands across the gulf between us. Goodnight, my daring. Goodnight, my darling.

Our mother had a smell, something flowery over something heavier, a little sweet. We recognized it in France, or something very like it. The smell of fear, of despair, of things slowly rotting.

Our brothers said that she had been beautiful. Tall with shining dark hair that she sometimes wore unpinned, and long silk dresses the color of every flower in the garden. When they came home from school every few months they spent hours in her room, talking or reading to her; we heard their voices going on and on, with pauses where we imagined her own slipping in. They were much older than we were, down already forming on their upper lips, and it seemed a different world they described. Picnics and music and parties with candlelight, a cake shaped like a Swiss mountain and mounds of strawberries. These things they told us when we were older. When we were very small they despised us, could not be left alone with us, Nan said, for fear of what might happen.

Once we performed for our mother, turning somersaults and something we called cartwheels all over the front lawn. And as we spun and rolled we heard a sound we didn't recognize; we stood, finally, looking up at the veranda, panting a little and brushing the hair out of our eyes. In her chair, from the midst of her blankets and shawls, our mother was laughing. She laughed until she cried, until she could hardly catch her breath, and then we stood, resting our heads near her lap, and she stroked our hair and said, "Oh my dears, it wasn't meant to be this way."

So we understood that we were all under a spell. Crawling through the tangled vines in the kitchen garden we imagined them growing and growing, twining round the big stone house, blotting out the sun, growing thick and fast over the windows of the room where the princess lay sleeping for a hundred years. Jameson roared when we started to hack our way through, so we became more cautious, sitting in a sunny corner popping pods of stolen peas and imagining the prince, the white horse he would ride upon. How he would sweep Jameson aside and slash his way through the jungle with his sharp sword and ride through the big front door, up the curving stairs, leave his horse grazing in the hallway while he rescued the sleeping princess. Then there would be a feast with a thousand candles blazing; she would wear a long sea-green gown shot with silver, and laugh and dance with the prince until morning.

The prince had blue eyes and long fair hair. Years later we found a photograph of our father as a very young man; the face was exactly what we had imagined and we were amazed, for we would never have cast our father as the prince. Or would we? Had we, perhaps, been shown that picture before, and what did that mean? We talked about that for hours, warming our toes before the stove while a dark rain slashed at the windows, but we reached no conclusion.

Our father also had a smell; he brought it with him from the city. Cigars and dust and ashes. As children we grew prickly in his presence, longing to hurl things about, to stick out our tongues, to do something shocking. But terrified too, of saying the wrong thing.

We saw him in his study usually, before we went to bed. The shadowed room, his face lit strangely from the lamp on the desk, the piles of papers and folders and a thin curl of cigar smoke. We assumed that he blamed us too, and wished we had never been. He asked us if we had been good, if we had done all our lessons, and of course we said yes. And then he called us to him, we walked around the sides of the desk and he circled an arm about our shoulders, planted a kiss on our foreheads, first one, then the other, the scratchy tickle of his mustache. He never called us by our names and we never tried to fool him as we did everyone else. It would have been pointless, for we were sure he didn't know or care which was which.

When we talked about it later, those long nights when the guns went on and on, we wondered if it was just that he didn't know quite what to do with us. He had no sister, no other daughters; he may have been just ill at ease. And busy, of course. Certainly when we were older he would talk to us, ask us what we were reading or studying, he seemed to know things which, looking back through a rainy night, suggested that he watched us, thought about us. If our mother had been there perhaps—but of course that was the whole point.

THE CORPORAL REMEMBERS

They made me think of horses—well, they would, wouldn't they? Skittish white horses, dream horses, maybe. You know how they raise their hooves, their legs, holding them in the air, trying so hard to become weightless, not touch the ground. I can't explain. But that's what they made me think of. That's all.

THE FOUNTAIN

There is a portrait of our mother; it hangs in our father's study, a dark room, even on the brightest of days. The artist stayed in our house while he worked on it, and Nan still talks with some surprise about how he made her laugh. And there is another picture, done at the same time. A quick, light sketch in soft colors that used to hang by the fire, until our father let Marcus take it away to his own house.

In this second picture our mother wears a pale yellow dress and sits on the edge of a fountain. James and Marcus are two young boys in shades of blue, sitting on either side, all of them looking down at something she holds in her lap. From the position, from the shape of her mouth, her half-parted lips, it looks as if she is reading them a story, though it seems a strange place to do that. We used to love that picture when we were young, used to stare and stare at it. The grass so exactly the color of rich, late spring grass and the way he painted the spray from the fountain, a glistening in the air. It hung on the wall by the fire like a window to another world and it seemed quite possible that by staring hard enough we could step right through.

There is a signature in the bottom corner of that painting, and a date. When we were older we realized from that date that we were already growing, beneath the pale yellow dress, getting ready to smash that world to pieces.

The fountain doesn't exist any longer; the space where it stood holds a circular bed of flowers that change with the seasons. We caused that too. When we were very small, two at the most, the silly girl who helped care for us fell asleep beneath a shady tree. We don't remember her; they say we can't remember any of it, we were far too young. But we do remember, we are certain that we do. The prismed spray of the fountain, the sound and feel of it. Like the feeling, not just the thought, of being hand in hand. The way the water was neither hot nor cold but just the temperature to welcome us in. It wasn't deep, but we were very small and it was deep enough to close over our heads. And we remember the magic of underwater, the absolute silence and peace. It's not likely there were fish in that fountain, but we remember the color, darting streaks of light.

We must somehow have pulled each other out, though when we think of how it was inside, we wonder why. Clambered back over the side and began to walk, walking ahead of our wet footprints toward the big house where a door was already opening, a white shape running. Walking hand in hand toward everything that came after.

This happened on a bright day in June. We know that; we've been told. So why do we have another picture in our minds, just as clear? The grass brown and dead, trees bare except for a few withered curls of leaf that rattle when the wind comes. Two people, large and dark, with dark heavy feet, carry two small bodies, held forward in their arms like an offering about to be deposited on a stone. Water drips from the sky, and from the sodden bundles, and there is a vast silence.

MRS. MOORE

They were angels. And by that I don't just mean they were good, although they were that. Kind and hardworking, generous with their time and their money. Not minding what they did. I had my doubts, when I first met them. Even bedraggled as they were from the journey, it was clear they'd not done a hard day's work in their lives. And we'd had a few like that—not many, but a few who couldn't take it. Who had some vision of themselves passing plates of cucumber sandwiches or wheeling some handsome boy about the garden. Garden! And there were some, of course, who were there for a good time—well, why not, I said. As long as they did their work, as long as they were there when I needed them, what business of mine was it?

Listen to me now—I would have shocked myself speechless a few years ago. But those poor boys, the look in their eyes and their poor broken bodies, the way they twitched and jumped, but always ready with a joke, with a smile. And some of the women—well, they wouldn't have much of a chance would they, otherwise, if I tell the truth. Which makes you wonder, doesn't it, just what it takes for a fellow to overlook thick ankles, a crossed eye. Like I said, as long as I could count on them to be where they should, to do their work, as long as they didn't get themselves diseased or worse and become a problem—well, who am I to say they shouldn't take some pleasure while they could?

Not that the twins were like that, nothing like. If anything, they were a bit too much the other way. Too serious, you know, and I don't think they'd had much to do with men in their lives. Not romantically, I mean. There was a young fellow they went around with, for a while. I don't know what was in it, just friendly, I would imagine. My friend Dr. Thomas told me the boy was having a course of treatment—you know. Like so many. Although usually it was the French girls to blame for that and this boy didn't look—well, he didn't look like he'd ever be looking for companionship, if you know what I mean. He looked like he could be choosy. Though the way things were over there I suppose that's no guarantee. Not if half the things my friend the Colonel says are true.

So this boy—I can't think of his name right now, but he was a devil all right. And such a joker—he had a gift for that. No matter what kind of mood you were in when you ran into him, you'd be laughing by the time he moved on. He wasn't in our camp too long, a couple of weeks, maybe. Though he'd pop up every once in a while after, to see the twins. And that charm of his worked on them too, you could tell. They were lighter, some-how, when he was around. Like I say though, I don't know what was in it. I'd never really known any twins, not really known, until I met Esther and Ruth. And they were just like you'd imagine twins to be, if you had to imagine. Same voice, same expressions, moved the same way. And always *we*—I'd forgotten that, I guess I got so used to it. We did this, we think that, never *I*. After a time they started wearing different-colored ribbons around their wrists, so people could tell them apart, but I always had the feeling they used to switch those around every once in a while, like some private little joke. Or maybe it just didn't matter to them. I used to won-der sometimes—I mean it's bad enough if two friends fall for the same young man, especially if he's a bit of a scoundrel like that one. It seems I heard he was wounded, just at the end of the war, or had some trouble, but I don't remember just what it was. Ah well, it's all water under the bridge—oh Lordy, I didn't mean to say that.

THE HEADMISTRESS—I

There will be those who think it is somehow my fault. Not say it, perhaps, but think it. Their father may. He came to see me in my office, sat in the green chair, refused a cup of tea. And asked me to persuade them not to go, and never to tell them that he had asked. "You have influence," he said. "They would listen to you, to what you say."

At the time I told him I had no right to do that. That they were grown women, twenty-six years old, that they had to make their own decisions. I pretended, and I see now that it was pretending, that I didn't know what he meant by *influence*. As if I'd never said any of the things I've said, lived the life I've lived. He recognized the pretense, that showed for a moment, behind his gold spectacles. But all he said was, "Very well." And we talked of general things until he left. We have always just missed saying things to each other, their father and I.

It is cold out tonight and a vicious sleet smashes against the window. But I sit here by the fire, quite warm and dry, a tray close at hand, my books, my pen. And it comes to me that all the things I've said and done, all the battles fought have been from this position of warmth and comfort. This morning at the school I looked down on those rows of upturned faces and thought that they receive my message from the same position of comfort. No fault of theirs, but what about mine?

I believed I was sending them into the world well-equipped, year after year, a generation of women proud of their minds, secure in their worth, who believed in truth, in beauty, who would spread that belief by their very existence. I believed that the world would have to become a better place, that they would see to that. Perhaps I should have given them armor. Taught them to think but not to feel, taught them to save themselves. I say this in all seriousness.

I have said that we always seemed to just miss saying things, their father and I. Now I have to stop and think about that. I met him first almost fifteen years ago; I have known him longer than I knew my own parents. We were interviewing each other, I suppose, about the possibility of the girls attending the school. I had been to a meeting outside and was taking the tram back through an unfamiliar part of the city. I remember that I was a little worried about being late, that I was in that state of heightened awareness that comes when your surroundings are strange, when you must actually use your eyes and ears. The streets, the houses we skimmed by were like those I knew, and yet not. The people getting on and off like that too. As if a glass had shifted to distort, ever so slightly. Like those moments in a dream when little things are just odd enough to make you wonder if you *are* dreaming. It was summer, the trees in full dark leaf, and a steady rain fell from a sky that was a vast, washed gray. The tram was a little cocoon moving through it, and the people who pulled themselves on from outside were giddy with the rain, but gently so. Some soaked to the skin, wiping water from their hands and cheeks. A middle-aged woman scattering droplets from her black umbrella as she closed it, laughing as she caught her breath and saying things to herself that would have had us looking carefully away at any other time or place. But it was clear, there, that it was rain madness, nothing more. We were all touched with it.

That was what I came from, the day I first met their father. Still worried about the time, I remember that I hurried down the corridor to my new office, lit the lamps, sent for tea. I was expecting the tea when the soft tap at the door came, and was quite taken aback when a gray-haired man walked into my room. He looked like what he was, a successful man of business, yet there was something hesitant about the way he crossed the threshold, something that made me want immediately to put him at ease. I remember that he told me right away that his wife was dead. I knew that, of course, and knew that she had been for a number of years, and I thought it strange that he would mention it like that. But then I remembered who he was, his reputation in the world of business, and realized that it was probably deliberate, some kind of tactic. First words, after all, can be just as calculated as the clothing we put on, the faces we compose to meet someone or to face the world.

Mr. A. went on to tell me that his sons had gone away to school from the beginning, but that he had always wished to keep his daughters, then eleven, at home. That from all he had found out it seemed that my school would provide the type of education he wished for them to have, with the added advantage of being only a short train ride from their home, so that they could attend as day pupils. "They're clever girls," he said, "but a little—"

There was another tap at the door, really the tea this time, and we fussed about with cups and tiny spoons. He drank his clear, as I usually did, but for some reason that day I added milk and sugar to my cup. The lights pushed the rain-colored air to the corners of the room and I remember thinking that it was another cocoon, like the tram. This circle of light where we sat, the music of silver spoons.

"They don't really know other children," he said, after lifting his cup to his lips. "We live a very quiet life where we are. And they seem quite content, but I've been thinking. . . . Also, they are growing up, you see. . . ." "Of course," I said, and then he said, "I was born a twin myself, but my brother didn't survive," and while I was wondering what to say to that he took off his glasses and rubbed at his left eye, saying, "How strange, I don't think I've ever told anyone that."

I didn't believe him, thinking it was another part of some peculiar strategy. The same way he showed his face, vulnerable without the spectacles.

As it happened, at that particular time we were rather desperate for new pupils, but I had learned a few tricks myself. I suggested that he come back with the girls, bringing a sample of the work they were currently doing. Told him that although we usually had a long waiting list, there was a possibility that we could accept them both for the fall term.

How much of it is my fault? Or because of my influence, which comes to the same thing. Those letters they wrote, my responses. Before they stopped writing. You see, I thought what they needed was reassurance. That they were doing the right thing, that it was all worthwhile. And I believed that it was, it's not that I lied. But reading their letters again I can't believe that I was so blind; my whole being cringes when I think of the letters I wrote back.

Am I too hard on myself? It's true that it's only now that so many have returned, telling their stories, now that we see who has become rich, or richer, what the world is still like, only now that it's all so clear. But I failed them, there's no escaping that. What they told me was not what I myself believed, and instead of listening I tried to nudge them back to my way. So much for all those fine words about confidence and identity. I failed them, and now they're dead.

Many years ago I knew a young man who died of a fever in Africa. If I had agreed to marry him he would not have gone to Africa, would not have caught the fever, would not have died. But I did not agree, because I was already taking the first steps along what I believed was my proper path. Because in marrying him I believed that I would have lost control of my life, and even though I still believe that would have been true, I am no longer so certain that it would have been the worst thing. After the death of my parents I was raised by an aunt and uncle. They were ignorant people; things happened in that house that I have not told a soul. My parents had left a little money for my education, and I understood that this would be my means of escape, my way of saving myself. I know that I didn't kill him, that earnest young man whose face I can no longer recall. A fever killed him. But it can't be denied that I played a part. As with Ruth and Esther. I remember that first day when their father took off his glasses and rubbed at his eye, and I realize suddenly that I could talk to him about this, that he is perhaps the only person I could talk to about this. Except for the fact that he is the last person in the world I could talk to about this.

SAILING

We stood at the railing, looking down at the mass of people, and just as we spotted our father he took off his hat and waved it frantically in the air. We had never known him to do such a thing. We were too far away to see anything more than the dark overcoat, the pale blob that was his face, his hand clutching the waving black hat. But we were struck by an astonishing thought. It was as if we were really seeing him. Over that distance, in the midst of all the noise and confusion, we saw something completely unexpected. Our father moved slowly always, deliberately, and we realized that we pictured him motionless, like a photograph. Sitting at his desk in a pool of light, or at the dinner table. Even at the wheel of his new motor car, he was somehow still while the machine hurtled through space. We remembered how he ran up the stairs the day our mother died, how we had no idea he could move so fast. The very air, after he had rushed past, was shivering and charged. The same thing now, in the frenzied waving of his hat. As if something had burst from him, alone in the crowd on the dock.

A girl stood beside us at the rail, a girl with very blue eyes and pale hair tucked under a funny little hat, made from the same material as her coat. When our eyes met she gave a little smile and said, "I don't know why I'm looking down, there's no one here to say good-bye." Then she turned and walked quickly away, leaving us wondering whether we should follow. But then the ship began to move, and we watched the land fall away, imagining, long after it was possible, that we still saw the black speck of our father's waving hat.

We told ourselves that it was no different from any other crossing. There were uniforms, of course, and a disproportionate number of young people on board, but we had been to Europe twice before; it was not, we said, as if we were going into something completely unfamiliar. What can have been in our minds?

The girl's name was Elizabeth; we shared a table with her at dinner that first night, and came to know her well on the voyage. It was not difficult to know her well; we had never met a person who talked so freely, so openly. We learned very quickly that she was going overseas to find her brother. Arthur, his name was. Art. He was nineteen, just a little more than two years younger than she was, and he had gone over as an ambulance driver just after his eighteenth birthday. They hadn't heard from him in five or six months and her mother was terribly worried. And she had enough to worry about without that, poor Mother, with Elizabeth's father being so sick and four younger ones at home, such a little bit of money to live on. So they held a family meeting one night in the kitchen, and decided that Elizabeth should volunteer, so she could be over there and find out where he was, how he was. Her mother was tormented by the thought that he was in a hospital somewhere, alone and suffering, missing them. The other possibility she didn't allow anyone to mention.

Elizabeth had already taken a nursing course; she got interested when her father became ill, so she was accepted without any problem. Someone had told her not to mention Art when she went to be interviewed, so she didn't, although she felt terrible keeping it back. Somehow her mother found the money to get most of the things she needed to take with her, and she made her a new coat and hat out of an overcoat that her father wouldn't wear again. But there was nothing left over for anyone to travel with her to the city, so she had to say good-bye at the station and she missed them all so; she'd never spent a night away from home before.

We pictured it all as Elizabeth talked, pictured it as a scene from a sentimental novel, so removed from our own experience. The scrubbed table in the warm kitchen, the dishes cleared away and the kettle simmering on the stovetop. All of them there except Father, whose coughing could be heard from upstairs. Mother looking so tired, her hands swollen and chapped. Young Bob, who was trying desperately to grow a mustache. He thought he should be the one to go, thought he could just lie about his age, but Mother said absolutely not, and besides, she needed him so much at home. Bob was fourteen and growing almost as quickly as he thought he was. Nessie thought she should go too, so Elizabeth wouldn't be all alone, but they needed the money she brought in, and she didn't have the nursing course so they didn't think she'd have much luck trying to go along. Peter and Amy were too young but they were there, Amy sitting on her red cushion, watching and listening. When it was all decided Elizabeth and her mother went upstairs to tell Father, but he fell asleep before they'd finished.

We didn't tell Elizabeth much about our own family, talking instead about things we'd heard about the war, about our European journeys, about France, the last time we saw it. About red-roofed villages and the quiet of the countryside, small cobbled squares. The food in Paris, the gardens and museums and the galleries. We told all this to Elizabeth, who cheerfully said that she didn't know a thing about art, but perhaps she'd have a chance to learn. What else could we have told Elizabeth that would not have seemed grotesque to her? That we'd heard our mother laugh once? That our father bought us rubber suits and waved his hat as we sailed away? That our brother Marcus didn't see us off, not because he couldn't afford to, but because he had a business luncheon. We couldn't tell her about James, for obvious reasons, but even if we had, she couldn't have understood how it was. Perhaps it was because our brothers were so much older, because they went away to school, because they were cruel to us when we were young. Perhaps that was why they didn't seem connected to us, like the most casual of acquaintances. When we heard that James had been killed we were sad, but in a strangely abstract way. Like hearing about the brother of someone you went to school with, or met at a dance. It was different for Marcus, of course, and for our father. The light burning in his study until morning, a smell of whiskey on occasion.

After James enlisted he came home to collect some things and we were alone in the house one afternoon. Rain fell outside the tall windows and the rooms were chill; we had a fire lit and sat reading beside it. And James came in, restless, pacing about the room. Touching pictures, the vase on the mantle, a dish on the table. He was a little stocky, James, his oiled hair thinning already, his chin very square and his eyes pale. We saw suddenly that he would look very like our father, when he reached his age.

Finally James stopped pacing and drew another chair closer to the fire, sat drumming the fingers of his right hand on his knee. We closed our books and asked him something—when he would sail, likely, or if he had everything he needed. And he answered, and then began to talk about others he knew who were going at the same time, or had already sailed. How he couldn't wait to be there in the thick of it, whipping the Hun, all those phrases that came so easily to everyone's lips in those days. "Poor Marcus," he said. "He'll miss all the fun."

And then, being James, he went on and on about what a lot of fools the generals were, how they were doing it all wrong, how what was needed was—well, we didn't really listen, we'd heard it all before. He got up to put another log on the fire and burned his finger arranging it. We looked up at his exclamation and saw him put his finger in his mouth for a moment and we noticed, at the same moment, that his eyes were glistening in the firelight, that there were tears in his pale eyes. And one of us said, "Are you afraid, James?"; it was a moment to ask and be answered, and he took his finger from his mouth, looked at it and said, "Oh yes."

That was all; the next moment he strode over to draw the heavy curtains against the fading day, and left the room. Then back to camp, then onto a ship, then marching down a dark, rutted road on the way to the trenches for the first time. The scream of a shell, and nothing more.

We tell ourselves that it is too easy to call a moment by a crackling fire the true moment. To say that the glint of tears was more real than the childhood cruelty, the adult arrogance and bluster. Our brother James was not particularly likable, meant little to us, nor we to him. Our sadness when he died was more because that was so. A moment in a rainy room just one of the things we remember, should we happen to think of him. We knew that this would have been incomprehensible to Elizabeth, perhaps appalling.

But is it true, what we've said about James? What we felt, what we didn't feel? Is it possible that it was really like that, all our life before? So removed. Or does it just seem so from here? Here where things are so different, where what we think about is just the cocoa, will it hold out? And where we can get some eggs. How much our feet hurt, the long soak we will give them, if we can get hot water. Will our headache ever go, can we stand it another hour, two, the noise and the heat and the pounding. Will this one ever come back, or that one.

Walking back to the hut one gray afternoon, boards over mud that was almost frozen and so quiet, suddenly, the canteen left behind. The sky heavy, air cold and dense with the rain that had fallen, would fall again. By the tree that we called the last tree in Europe, Hugh sat writing. He had a wooden chair he'd scrounged somewhere, a couple of boards laid over some empty tins. He was wearing a gray sweater, the color of dense smoke, pearled with moisture from the air, holes in one elbow. Black pipe clenched between his teeth, smoke, more gray, wisping up. We were on our way to sleep a little, thinking of nothing but the chill in our bones, how wonderful it was to walk through such silence to a damp cot, to wrap the blankets tight, close eyes. We were happy with that, at that moment.

Wanted nothing more from life, and the sight of Hugh in his smoke-colored sweater became all entwined with that moment of perfect contentment.

THE HEADMISTRESS—II

Mr. A. brought the girls to meet me a week later. I was sleeping better by then; the day was sunny and warm and I felt calm and quite like myself, none of the eeriness surrounding our first meeting. It's difficult—I came to know them well over many years, or thought I did, and so it's difficult to look back to that first meeting, clear of any of the knowledge or familiarity that came later. What struck me first, I think, was their calmness. They were not especially beautiful children, but there was something very appealing about them. Their long hair tied back neatly and although they weren't dressed identically, that was somehow the impression they gave. When they were not responding to one of my questions they both looked down at their polished shoes, the toes just brushing the floor. This did not seem like shyness, or deference. Rather it was as if they returned to some serious and self-contained contemplation. They replied politely to anything I asked, whichever one answered speaking in the plural. I'd quite forgotten that, but I remember how it struck me at the time. The way they never spoke together, but there was no hesitation, no collision, conversation flowing easily from one or the other so that the effect was of talking to a single person.

It's an interesting exercise, this recollection, the way it makes you remember more and more. Like opening a door, having no control over who walks through. Since I heard the news I've been looking at photographs. Ones from that European trip, several that they sent me from Paris, in their uniforms. But it wasn't until after the memorial service that I made myself bring out the oldest. I suppose it was seeing everyone there, all the old pupils. A year or two after they came to the school we received an unexpected bequest, and decided to use part of it to make a proper photographic record, of the rooms, of the teachers and pupils. At the end of the year I gave each one a small, individual portrait in a soft leather folder.

The photographer we hired was a very talented young man, several years younger than myself. Jones, his name was, and he had a soft Welsh voice to go with it. He went west later and I don't know what happened to him. But we had several long conversations about art, about photography and painting. I would have thought, if I had thought about it at all, that photography was a scientific process, a way of recording reality, would have thought that was the marvel of it. But Mr. Jones made me see it differently. He said, for example, that while a painter has all kinds of tricks at his disposal—different materials, different brushes and brushstrokes, all the colors of the rainbow—a photographer works only with light and shadow. This particular conversation took place in an empty classroom; there was a wild blue sky through the tall windows, the tops of flame-colored trees.

"This moment," Mr. Jones said, "were I to photograph it—the record of reality would be a man and a woman talking in an empty room. Now if I were a painter, of course, I could add things. The color of that sky, the leaves, and I could pick up that color at the throat of your dress, perhaps a touch on your cheekbones. I could change your expression slightly, or my own, the curve of your lips, and the painting would not be about an empty room.

"But what can I do?" Mr. Jones said. "What can I do with my camera? Oh, there are some tricks of course. Those photographs for your booklet—there are ways to make rooms look bigger, the view more enticing. But how do I photograph a moment, this moment say, and have it clear that the leaves outside the window are not the soft green of spring, that the year is dying and not beginning. I must pull out the truth of it, of a person or a place. If there is to be anything real, I must draw out the heart."

I don't remember what happened next, but there was truth in what he said, and the photographs are the proof. I have them all together in a folder, a record of a particular year of my life.

Mr. Jones spent a great deal of time in the school that autumn. He was clearly an artist and not a businessman, for he was paid one price to provide photographs of each teacher and pupil, yet he took some again and again until he was satisfied, going away with the plates and coming back to try once more. In his studio he showed me the different attempts, laying them out on a round table covered with a rich blue cloth, and I understood what he meant.

Of course, he had more tricks than he admitted. I observed all the individual sittings; it would not have been proper otherwise, even in 1905. I saw the way he arranged the light or the folds of a dress, positioned the arms. The way the sitter submitted totally, becoming somehow inanimate while he moved limbs, smoothed the hair, turned the chin just a fraction. Called for different props—a book, a flute, a flower. But the end result, trick or not, was as he had said. Some essence of the women and girls I knew captured in a way that was quite astounding. In the end it was only the twins who gave him trouble. He came back for them again and again, all through that cold, dark December, until finally he admitted defeat and posed them together.

My own photograph from that time both pleases and disturbs me. I remember every sitting vividly, at the school and in his studio, yet I can't imagine a moment when I looked like this. I know I faced the camera straight on, unafraid, yet my eyes somehow slide off, away from it. My hair is dressed as I have always worn it, yet it seems to be struggling to escape. Wisps worked free to dance along my cheek, to wave in the soft light about my head. My hands are folded as I remember, but there is a tension in the fingers, and the bottom hand is slightly blurred, as if caught in a sudden movement. And I am certain my mouth has never looked like this. The photograph pleases me, as a work of art might; it invites one to understand certain things about the woman in it. But I have never recognized it as myself.

LETTER

Dear Father,

Thank you so much for your latest package, which arrived safely two days ago. We are greedily devouring the books and chocolate, and the stockings are a Godsend. Please thank Janet—we assume she bought them—and tell her how glad we are to get them, as what we brought is much be-darned. We were very sorry to hear about John Tupper.

You ask where we are—of course we can't say exactly, but can tell you that we are fairly close to the front, but not in any danger. This is a sort of interim camp, for men on their way to or from the front. Sometimes they go from here to a real rest camp, or sometimes right back up to the line. When we first came here we stayed in a tent pitched on the stubble field behind the camp. Very damp and cold. But just last week we moved into a room made from an old storeroom in the end of the canteen hut. Small, but it seems like a palace to us after the tent. We have just enough room for our two cots with their now-dry straw mattresses and our trunks, and one of the boys pounded some nails into the walls so we can hang up our tin hats, gas masks and clothes. We also have a little stove, but don't need to use it much now that the nights are not so cold. The hills round about are covered with wildflowers this time of year, and in our free time if we are not sleeping—which we seem to do a great deal of—we have lovely long walks.

As you see, we are well settled in and the routine of our days no longer seems at all strange. We generally mess with the officers, and the food is plentiful, though not particularly satisfying. Mornings we spend washing hundreds of mugs from the previous night in the canteen, and preparing sandwiches and sometimes cakes and sweets for the afternoon and evening. Two little French boys keep us supplied with wood for the small stove, which is all we have to heat the huge kettles of cocoa and coffee that we go through each day. In addition to ourselves and Mrs. Moore, who is in charge, a woman named Berthe from the nearby village helps out. She speaks no English and as Mrs. Moore knows no French we do a great deal of translating and thank heaven for those classes at Miss Reilly's. We had a letter from her last week and she mentioned that she saw you at dinner at the Barretts. It is so strange sometimes to think of life going on at home, just like before. You would be amazed at the life we have settled into here, but settled in we have. The work is hard and might be seen as monotonous, but we know it's important, the boys so appreciative of any little thing we do for them. There are always a few who can barely read or write, and if there's time we often write letters to their dictation. And mend torn shirts or sew on stripes or badges. All kinds of little things that mean a great deal over here. We can't, as we said, tell you where we are, but we are close enough to hear the guns. Don't worry though, we have been assured that the camp will move if the fighting draws much closer.

There is a large hospital in a beautiful old chateau a few miles from here, and on our free day we usually go there to do what we can to help out. We read to the soldiers or write more letters, help feed those that need help. The nurses are wonderful but so busy; they are always glad to see us. So you see our days are very full and we really have no time to miss home, so you mustn't worry about that. We must close now as it is very late and we will be rising with the sun.

STAIN

When our mother actually died, you would have thought we would all have been prepared for it. Living her half-life for years. Off in her upstairs room the last long time, just a hint of recognition in her sunken eyes, and that only sometimes. You would have thought that we would have gotten on with our lives, that she would have been a sad, fixed point outside our orbit. What we would have thought at the time, if we had to explain it. For our father too, who rarely saw her, as far as we knew, who inquired after her health, her day, when the nurse sat down to eat with us, as one would of a mutual acquaintance.

It was Sunday morning. Early June, that time of year when the sky is blue every time you open your eyes, when the lilac blossoms fill the air. The night nurse was having a cup of tea in the kitchen, talking about carrots and peas, and we were just coming through the door, blinking after the light outside, our shoes wet with dew.

And then someone cried out, and we ran too; ahead of us the door of the study flung open, our father with his shirt sleeves caught up, running up the stairs, we'd never seen him move like that. The gold pen falling from his hand to roll and rattle, a small distinct noise amid the calls, the sound of thumping feet. Mrs. B. coming after, stooping to pick it up automatically, not even looking, slipping it into her apron pocket where it continued to ooze. The dark, spreading stain on her apron pocket—it seemed that stain spread out slowly to cover our whole lives.

MARCUS

They were always strange, always trouble. From the very beginning, when they took our mother away. We were called home from school to see her before she died, although as it happened her dying took years. But those days we were home when the house was hushed and strange we would hear their thin squalling in the night. James thought we should kill them, and we tried a few times, I don't remember how, childish things I'm sure, but someone always stopped us. In the end we were glad to go back to school.

As they grew up they stopped squalling of course, and took to whispering, heads together. The sound of a couple of snakes. They had their own language for a while, a lot of nonsense words that they seemed to understand completely. The day of Mother's funeral they sliced themselves up with broken glass and had to be carried upstairs, screaming and kicking and getting blood everywhere. And how glad James and I were to hear them screaming even louder while Nan and Mrs. B. scrubbed their wounds with alcohol. When Father sent us up to the nursery later they were sitting up in bed with their legs all bandaged, eating cake, looking pale and oh so smug.

THE WAR BOOK

It began to seem, after a time, that everyone had something. Had one thing that they'd seen or heard, that they couldn't shake off, that they carried, would carry forever, like a hard, dull stone in the heart. Not obvious things, not blood and mayhem, for that was everywhere and there was nothing exceptional about that. But it might be the shell of a house, seen through a train window. A little place, in what was left of a village they passed by, part of two walls left standing and a mess of rubble inside. It might lead to an obsessive need to discover—or maybe just to wonder—what was the name of the village, and who had lived in that house, what had happened, what *exactly* had happened to them. Or it might be a rope swing, still hanging from a blasted tree, the line of a little girl's neck in an echoing black station, one half of a beautiful bowl. A woman in black whacking the backside of a crying child all along a deserted street. Why was the child crying? Not that there weren't reasons enough to cry but what was it, at just that moment? Or a creased photograph found somewhere, no way to know anything about the people in it, not even what side they were on. A white cat sleeping in a patch of sunlight, a piece of music heard in a most unlikely place. We thought if we could gather those things together we would call it *The War Book*. And that would be the only way to communicate it, to give someone an idea of how it was.

Hugh's story concerned his friend Tom, the one he grew up with, joined up with. They'd stayed together, against all the odds, and one frosty morning they were standing together on the fire step and Hugh saw something glittering in the frozen mud at his feet. He bent to pick it up; his fingers were numb and he fumbled at it, cursed. "What?" Tom said, turning his head, looking down at the spot where Hugh crouched. And then with a thud he was lying with his dead eyes looking *up* at the spot where Hugh crouched, the glittering object between his fingers, and Hugh remembers looking at it, seeing that it was only a jagged bit of wood, something that could never have glittered at all.

So Hugh's story is about mathematics, about physics, about how he tried to work it all out. The chances of the sniper's bullet finding that exact spot at the base of Tom's ear. The distance to the other side, and if the bullet had already left the gun when Hugh suddenly crouched. He drew diagrams, tried to work out exactly where the other had been, how tall he was, what he looked like. Did he squeeze the trigger slowly, or with a sudden burst of excitement? He called on everything he'd learned in that school a world away, smell of chalk dust in his nostrils, the way it looked, floating in the sunlight through the high windows, the creak of his desk chair, the oiled floor. He knew he hadn't paid enough attention—he'd usually copied Tom's assignments, after all. But he thought he could learn what he needed to know.

And he thought about all the things that could have made a difference. If he hadn't seen the glittering thing that couldn't possibly have glittered, he and Tom would have remained standing exactly as they were, the bullet would have thumped into the wall of the trench behind them, between them, or maybe not come at all. Or the sniper himself—if he'd had to scratch his nose suddenly, if someone had called to him, some noise had made him look away, only for an instant. If he'd had a cut on his finger, making it a little stiff, if his eyelashes had been longer, his vision blurred for an instant.

When that kind of thinking drove him mad, he would think instead about the bullet. The place where it was made—gloomy, he pictured it, and very noisy. Heat and sparks flying. The long journey it made even to get to the fingers that loaded it into the gun. All the things that could have changed it, even then. The temperature that morning, so clear and cold and no wind, but what if there had been? Or not even a wind but some shift, some tiny shift in the currents of air, the last breath of some storm that whirled around a mountain somewhere, the disturbance of someone running, even a cough. If someone had coughed in Paris—one of us, say, we were there. If one of us had coughed in Paris at exactly the right moment, would Tom still be alive?

RAIN

So tired tonight, too tired to do anything, even to order scattered thoughts. Silent except for the rain that splatters against the window, against the flimsy walls of the hut, splatters fitfully, as if tossed by a bored child. Think of the rain falling here, how it must be falling all over the country, all the way to the coast, to the grim Atlantic. Roiling there, a tumbled picture in black and white, the winds that toss those waves driving the rain on. Only in that deep, wintry zone far beneath is everything still and silent, suspended in dark green light. But up above the rain sweeps on, rolls over another shore. Splatters like this against the windows of our old room, but the room is empty, we are not there. And even if we were to return it would be empty; quite impossible, now, for us to be there.

IN HIS STUDY THE FATHER CLOSES HIS EYES

And thinks about what he has lost. It is very quiet and, although his children were never noisy, he knows that this is the silence of their absence, that it will be like this for the rest of his life.

He will sell the house, of course. The big house in the country, bought with the first of his money. The place where the happy life was to be lived. How can it be that they're all gone? Alice. James. Esther and Ruth. His daughters brushed his cheek with their cool lips, first one and then the other. First Esther, with the slightly higher arch to her eyebrow, and then Ruth. The ship waited, a big, hard lump of the inevitable. He waved like a madman, swept off his hat and waved that too, long after it began to move away. Thinking that if he stopped at all he would snap the fragile thread, that they would lose sight of the place they must come back to and gently drift away forever. His shoulder ached for days, and he welcomed it.

Marcus is not gone, of course. Marcus is still alive. In his rooms in the city, surrounded by furniture no longer needed in the big house, and by his own things when he was a boy. The painting of the happy life hangs near Marcus' bed, where the father need never see it. Marcus is still alive, still in the business, still making money. And he might still marry, have children who will run and jump and tumble, the juice of different fruits smeared on their chins.

Could they belong to Marcus, these ghost children who flicker behind his eyes? Marcus, the pale second son, the one who was always there, just there, two steps behind James, even when he grew to be the taller. What does Marcus feel, suddenly an only child? They meet in the office or outside it, with sheaves of paper or without, and there is an amazing harmony, the way they think about the business, the way it lives for them, what they see in its future. The war years have been good for them, very good, and the father wonders if Marcus also feels guilty at the way he can't help being pleased with that. Excited by that. Distracted from his grief.

Perhaps they do belong to Marcus, the ghost children whose running footsteps patter along the floors above his head. Perhaps Marcus will meet the right woman and find himself a completely different life. But the father remembers that he himself found the right woman, that it guaranteed nothing but this long night alone in the creaking house.

And there was Anne Reilly, the girls' headmistress. A handsome woman, intelligent and witty. Comfortable with children. She would have looked just right, through candlelight, at the end of the table. In all his encounters with her over the years there had been this flutter of possibility. But he could never get to it, through the thicket of their first meeting. He had been expecting an older woman, although she was, at the time, older than he first assumed. When he opened the door she was reaching to secure a hairpin and she completed the movement before she spoke, without any hint of awkwardness. The hem of her dress was damp; he could tell by the way it moved as she came around the desk toward him, saying something about the weather. And he wondered what she had been doing, out in the rain, and realized that he would have believed anything at all. Posting a letter or riding a white horse or dancing around a pagan altar.

As he settled into a chair he was astonished to hear himself say, "My wife has died." And it terrified him, the way she had so effortlessly drawn those words from his very heart, words he hadn't even realized were lurking there. He wondered if she was at all aware of this power, and many years later he still wondered. From that moment he was always somehow on guard with her, he couldn't help it, for she was someone who could lay you bare in an instant. Just once, when the girls showed him the official letter, when they quietly went about gathering up the things they would need, just then did he try to speak, to enlist her help. She pretended she didn't know what he meant, pretended they were just two people, talking about two other people. He had left as quickly as he could, numbed by another loss.

And later in the shop his heart was sick, watching them try things on. The heavy rubber, the ridiculous headgear, and all he could see was the two of them, bobbing alone in the vast gray waste of some ocean.

SOLDIERS—I

Hugh told us this story, about a man named Baker. Known as Silly Sam when he worked as a comedian, before. One day he was blown up; they dug him out quite quickly and he seemed to be all right. They were due to be relieved in a few days anyway and they'd lost so many men they couldn't spare him, so he stayed in the line. But as it happened there was a push somewhere and their relief didn't come for nearly two weeks, and Baker had to be sent back before that, because he started to cry. Slowly at first, a few tears splashing onto his muddy knees where he crouched, trying to eat a chunk of bread. The concussion, they all thought, it does funny things to your body. But it got worse. *This makes no sense,* Baker would say, *I'm the happiest man in France!* It stopped when he was sleeping, but they had little time for that, and the moment he opened his eyes the tears began to well up, to roll down his cheeks, splash on his tunic front. So thick and fast he had to wipe his cheeks constantly, and in the end he was so busy doing that that he couldn't even hold his rifle. Then they sent him back.

SOLDIERS—II

There was a pig of a man named Smythe. Little pale eyes, flicking like a snake's. In the canteen, when the cigarettes were gone, the battered cauldrons of cocoa empty. "Let me help you with that," lifting the heavy pot from the fire. Then an arm about the waist, squeezing, his breath foul, stained teeth beneath the mustache and stubbly chin rubbing, and then a voice said, "That's enough," and he was gone, scuttering out the back door. That was how we first met Hugh.

SOLDIERS—III

It was only a trick of the Paris traffic that had us pause behind them. The woman's face turned to look behind. Nothing in her expression, just the fact that she was looking back. It was a staff car, we could see the dark shape of the driver's head, looking straight in front. And we thought—for this is how we've changed or learned—well, maybe she'll get a decent meal out of it, maybe he'll take her somewhere where the cutlery sparkles and nothing is in short supply, the officer belonging to the scratchy-uniformed arm that rested on the seat behind her. And just as we thought that, his large white hand splayed on the back of her head, forcing it down.

And we remembered Neufchateau, the Hotel Agriculture in the afternoon. Waiting in that dingy, smoky lobby for someone to get us out of there. Across the street a few tables barely fit on the narrow sidewalk, and we went there, finally, to drink a cup of coffee. Beside us, two soldiers and a boy of ten or eleven. They were giving him tumblers of wine to drink, and chocolate from their pockets. He didn't speak any English, but they kept putting their hands on his shoulders, saying, "Friends, *oui?* Friends."

These men are also dying in the trenches—can it be right to think that less of a tragedy? The cowards, the liars, the bullies, and worse. They are also fighting for their country.

THINKING ABOUT HOME

Everyone did it. Talked about it. *Say, these toy trains wouldn't get you anywhere back home, would they?* Or, *They do have funny notions about break-fast here, don't they, nothing like back home.* After all, what was there to talk about here? The dead, the rain, the rotten food. Rumors, of course. Germans here and there, we were smashing them, no we weren't. It was a balance, thinking about home; it was necessary. To remind yourself, keep on reminding yourself who you were. That you had not always gone for three days without combing your hair. That there was another kind of life, that you had lived it.

No one talked much about going back after; there was a superstitious reluctance to do that. But stories, memories, most of us young enough to have school pranks fresh in our minds. It was something to hold on to, too.

Try to imagine this. A refugee train unloading at a station, the noise and the smell and the smoke swirling and rising, drawing your eyes for a moment to the cavernous dark roof, girders and blackness and malevolent foggy steam—don't want to look there, like looking into a nightmare under a child's bed. Now say you look down again and see a young girl, nine or ten maybe, who looks around and around but seems to be alone in that crowd. She is wearing a dress that might once have been blue, might once have had a pattern, tiny white flowers maybe. You know that some-one must have made her this dress, that it was a pretty thing; you know from the age of the girl that she probably loved it, tried it on and twirled around a warm kitchen. Probably there was a swing outside, and you can see her swinging on it, see her toes pointing in neat black shoes. What's on her feet now may be shoes, tied round and round with string to hold them. Her legs are streaked with mud and dried blood, as is every bit of her that you can see. She's clutching a baby in her arms, wrapped in bits of someone's coat; a green button winks for a moment as it catches a stray bit of light. What you can see of the baby's head is also bloody and muddy; it is very still, and you hope that it is sleeping.

The child scans the crowd, her head moves back and forth, her eyes flick here and there, but you can tell from those eyes that she doesn't expect to recognize anyone. So as you make your way to her, as you bend down so that she can hear you, as you bend down to take a closer look at the bundle she is carrying, which is now making tiny mewling sounds, as you, still stooping, put an arm about her narrow shoulders and feel what you couldn't see, the way her whole body trembles as if it will never stop, as you move her with her sleepwalker's stumble toward the big red cross and whatever can be done—as you do all that, you find you are remembering a doll you had once, after Ophelia, the way you took it everywhere with you, fed it and talked to it just like a real baby. And that makes you remember green grass and the feeling of sunlight on your skin, someone's voice singing, a host of things. If you couldn't do that, it's hard to know what would happen. Probably you would just die for sorrow.

It's different, of course, for those who have children at home, or obligations. Mrs. Moore frets and frets about her married daughter, who is having her first baby soon. How she never liked vegetables and probably isn't watching her diet, how even a scraped knee would make her howl like the end of the world. The men show pictures and read out bits of letters they've received, all the clever and naughty things going on in a home they can walk through every time they close their eyes. Even the horrible Smythe has three little Smythes and their mother folded in his front pocket. Or for some there are worries about a business, is it being run all right, will the right decisions be made while they're away. So that even if they don't speak about *after*, it's always there, and home is something to go back to.

It's not the same for us. Once, on a hospital visit, there was a boy with no hands. He'd been reaching for something or someone when the shell came; he was not too badly hurt, except for that. But he needed someone to write letters for him, of course, and someone to hold his cigarettes. He had beautiful hair, that boy, thick and dark and very curly. It kept tumbling over his forehead and he kept trying to lift his arms, to brush it back. "You should get someone to cut it," we said as we smoothed it back again and again. "Oh, my girl would never forgive me for that," he said. "She loves to do just what you're doing." When we held the cigarette to his lips, he seemed to kiss our fingertips.

In another bed in that ward there was a boy who was not expected to live. He was getting huge doses of morphine, but even when he was asleep his lips would twitch. And when he was—not awake, he was never that—but semiconscious, he repeated a list of words over and over. Oak, beech, ash, elm, maple, oak beech ash elm maple. The boy with the beautiful hair said at first they thought he was just naming trees, but then someone heard *Main* and someone heard *Water* and they guessed that he was reciting the names of streets, the names of streets in whatever town he came from. His company had been hit hard; those that survived had been moved on and no one in the hospital knew yet what town it was. Some of the men in the ward thought it was a small place, that he was naming every street in the town. But most of them thought it was a route he was walking. Oak-

Beech-Ash-Elm-Maple-Main-Water. The way to school, maybe, or the way to his girlfriend's house. The way to his own house from the station. Over and over he walked it, Oak-Beech-Ash-Elm-Maple-Main-Water, and after a while we could see it ourselves. See the tall trees leaning over the sidewalks, the shady verandas, the storefronts on Main Street, the cooler air on Water. If it was evening, we could smell the blossoms.

As the morphine wore off his voice got louder and louder, and after he'd had the next shot he'd sometimes stop in the middle, even in the middle of a word. And someone else would finish for him—-ple, Main, Water—and we realized that along with everything else they were doing, or saying, or thinking, every man on that ward was walking along with him.

Our own thinking about home had that obsessive quality. Things we went over and over, trying to get the truth of. Maybe that was the difference, between us and Mrs. Moore, the men with their pockets full of photographs. Home for us was not exactly something to hold on to, it was something to figure out, to understand. So many things seemed strange, there in France. It did not seem possible that our life was as we remembered it. But we both remembered it, so wasn't that some kind of proof? We were not together every minute of our childhood, every minute of our lives, although most, perhaps. But there must have been times when one of us was in a room but not the other. When only one of us saw something, heard something, was spoken to. But we don't remember anything like that. This is something you have to understand, if you are to understand anything. The things we talked about in the wet tent, in the wooden room at Chalons—we shared them all. And if there was a split second, the tiniest of moments, briefer than the blink of an eye, when one of us said something—then in that briefest of moments the other had the memory, could hear, feel, taste it.

INTERVIEW

The journalist was fresh from home, and his questions made us realize how far away that was. The last thing he asked was for one thing, one experience, that would give his readers—the folks, he called them—an idea of what it was really like. So we told him about traveling a road near Ancerville, where the bombardment had been heavy a few days before.

How we stopped to stretch our legs for a moment. And found a small, perfect child's hand, lying palm up in the dust.

NAN

I don't see so well now; perhaps that's why the memory pictures are so clear. Know what I mean by memory pictures? Of course you do; everybody's got them. I've been thinking about it ever since I heard. Seeing it clear as day. The path that led off the kitchen garden and down to the river. The two of them running ahead of me, trees overhanging and sunlight falling through and their feet kicking up behind them. And I thought *Run girls, keep running. Run right out of this.* So maybe I always knew.

I was going to leave service long ago; that was my plan. My sister had a cottage in a little place by the sea, and I was going to go and live there with her. Before I got too old to walk along the sand, to really live there. We grew up on an island, you see, and I always missed it. That clean wind blowing, the smell of it. So I was going to see her through the birthing, stay just until they got someone else settled in. I owed them that; they'd been so generous to me. Not *owed* exactly, but anyway that's what I agreed to. I'd been with Miss Alice since she was a girl, and when she asked me I couldn't say no. But one thing I've learned is that this life always has surprises in store, and most of them aren't the kind to make you jump for joy. It was the two of them that did her in. She'd never been strong, Miss Alice, but she was so lively. It was a happy house, before. Break your heart to see it happen. So of course I couldn't just walk away. Stayed until the girls were grown, did my best. My sister died and I never did get to that cottage by the sea, but it's not so bad here. It took her so long to die, poor soul, but it was written on her face from before the birth. Things changed overnight, it seemed, like the heart went out of that house, leaving nothing but a lot of echoing rooms. Even the boys changed, became sly and sad. I had to keep a sharp eye when the girls were small, even though I couldn't believe they would really harm them. There was that business with the fountain—we never did get to the truth of that. Everyone so busy blaming that useless Susan for falling asleep.

What were they like as children? Like children, of course. They learned to walk and talk, they had tea parties for their dolls and played on the lawns. Perhaps more serious than most but that's not surprising, the house being the way it was and the Mister never what you could call a warm man. I used to fancy I could tell them apart, though if you asked me I couldn't say how. Alike as two peas in a pod they were, and if one had a stomachache the other would too, without fail. When they were small, four or five maybe, they had a special language they spoke to each other. A lot of made-up words that they seemed to understand. *Brimble* meant cake; I remember I figured that out, but for the rest I had no idea. It used to make me a little cross, if I tell the truth, the way they would sit whispering nonsense together as if no one else mattered at all. But there, they only had each other all those years. I thought it would be good for them when they went off to Miss Reilly's school, thought they would somehow open, make lots of new friends. They did bring girls home once in a while, but not often. Still they were good girls, never a moment's trouble. Except for the way they used to go to the river; many's the time I've scolded them for that. And the day of Miss Alice's funeral, poor little mites. They adored that Miss Reilly; she has a lot to answer for, in my opinion. Always going on about the state of the world, about hunger and injustice. "Miss Reilly says women can change the world," they told me more than once. Now I don't deny this world needs some changing, but why should it be my poor girls to do it? I used to be delighted when they'd accept an invitation to a dance or a party. I'd wait up for them with a pot of cocoa and we'd sit around the kitchen table like we used to when they were small. "Thank heavens that's over," they always said. "The silliness, Nan, you just wouldn't believe." Talking to them was like talking to one person, always was, the way they started and finished each other's sentences. I used to wonder how they would ever get married and have a normal life; it was impossible to imagine them separated like that.

They came to see me before they went away. I'd left the house of course, but they still came to visit me often, always brought some of that shortbread I like. They were wearing their uniforms, and very smart they looked. Sort of a greenish whipcord with blue ties and little blue hats with the brims curved down. They said there were also heavy long capes, so I didn't have to worry about them being cold. They didn't stay long; their eyes were bright as they told me about all the things they still had to gather up. I could see it was no use but I tried anyway, told them there was plenty of war work right here at home. Told them to think of their father, with James gone and only Marcus for company. They'd thought of all that, well of course they had. But they were convinced that they were meant to do their bit overseas. When they left I watched them from my window, walking side by side away down the street. And I felt it in my bones, and it turns out I was right; I knew I'd never see them again.

IN THE CELLAR

We met Elizabeth in the cellar of the Hotel Terminus, during an *alerte*. It was not so crowded that night. Two small children curled against their mother, so tired that only the loudest bangs made them flinch. An old woman with a maid and an ugly little dog. Several others who were just huddled shapes under blankets—the staff, perhaps, who often slept in the cellar to avoid having their sleep interrupted by the journey, night after night.

It was surprising that we recognized Elizabeth, for she was very changed. But we were too, so perhaps that gave us eyes to recognize each other. She was fully dressed; she said that she'd been in Paris a week, waiting to be moved out again, that she'd spent so many nights shivering in her dressing gown that she'd finally decided just to sleep in her clothes. We talked for a long time, speaking softly, for the children's mother had finally fallen asleep too. There was something about their pale faces, the way they breathed in unison, that broke your heart, there in the cellar.

Elizabeth was terribly thin; she said she'd had the flu, although she was much better. She said that in her last hospital there'd been a nurse who'd come across on a ship struck by flu. Like the worst nightmare, Elizabeth said. Like a ghost ship, people dead all over it, scores of them, and barely enough left standing to sail the ship. And then we talked of our own crossing, of the time the handsome officer asked Elizabeth to dance and she vomited all down the front of his uniform, how she thought she'd die of shame. "Strange, isn't it," she said, "the things that mattered then." And we knew what she meant.

We were afraid to ask about Art, but then she told us that her mother had received word the very day we all arrived in France. Now she was trying to find the place where he was buried. "I have to do that, at least," Elizabeth said. "I can't go home and face them unless I've done that." She'd even bought a little camera, so she could take pictures of the spot when she found it.

"I don't know how I can go home anyway," Elizabeth said. "Do you? How can we do it, how can we go back to our own table, our own beds, as if we were the same people?" "I feel broken," Elizabeth said, in the flickering candlelight in the cellar of the Hotel Terminus. "Something is broken in me. It's all just a horrible mess, and there's no meaning in any of it."

Was it right or wrong, what we did then? Holding Elizabeth's hands and telling her it was all worthwhile. That it did have meaning, that we were right to be where we were, doing what we were doing. That the world would be different, after. A better place. Was it right or wrong, at that moment, to tell Elizabeth things we no longer believed?

When the bugle sounded we made our way back up to our rooms; there was still enough of the night left to make sleep possible, if there wasn't another *alerte*. We arranged to meet for breakfast the next day, but in the morning Elizabeth was gone and we didn't see her again.

THE SEA KING

We know, of course we know, that it's just a story Nan told. Spun out of her Irish dreams and taking hold in ours. Those nights of soft rain a long time ago, in a sloping room at the top of the fragile house. But we live in a world where everything we know has been proved wrong, a world gone completely mad. If this world can exist, then anything is possible.

Nan said the Sea King lived at the deepest bottom, where only the drowned men go. He had power over the oceans and the rivers, and all things that moved upon them. And the schools of swimming fish were his spies and messengers, bringing back news from the farthest reaches of his kingdom. He was fierce and angry and the gates of his palace were built from dead men's bones. A mound of skulls guarded his treasure room, chests filled with gold and jewels from ships he had caused to sink. Sometimes a chest broke open as it spiraled slowly down to the depths, and the sea floor for miles around the palace was littered with precious stones that glowed in the greenish light. The Sea King's children played games with those gems, and arranged them in intricate patterns that could sometimes be glimpsed if you looked down through clear water on a still, sunny day. There were also beautiful necklaces that had lain around the necks of drowned women, and they floated gently down to that quiet place.

In Nan's stories the Sea King brought nothing but storms and death, his rage against the world. But in a world gone mad, a world where everything had been proved wrong, we wondered if that was too. Perhaps his kingdom was a beautiful, gentle place, his wrath really sorrow, pining for lost children who had disappeared into the world of men. Perhaps that's who we are, perhaps we really are the Sea King's beautiful daughters. Lost, long lost, wandering ill at ease through the world of foggy air.

CLASSMATES

We ran into them in Paris, the way you ran into people you knew in the war. Sitting at a table outside the Café de la Paix, across from the Opera. Weren't we surprised to see them there, with their hair cut short, just like ours. Though when I think of it, back home they used to help out in soup kitchens and raise money for things, so perhaps it was not so strange that they came to the war. They only had three nights in Paris and they'd already spent two down in the Gare du Nord, helping with refugee trains and feeding soldiers. We went on to Rumpelmayer's for tea and ice cream—very watery, as usual—and then they came back to The Hive for the evening. Marjorie played her funny little piano a bit, and Jess and Molly from across the hall popped in and we had a grand old time, talking about old friends. It was quite astonishing how many had turned up in Paris at one time or another.

They were the same as always, maybe a little more so. Quiet, I mean. How I envied them, being up close to the front. Marjorie and I worked at the refugee center, and it's not that that wasn't important. Finding clothes for the poor things and a place to stay, whatever bits of furniture we could lay our hands on. Scrambling always to find *essence* for the old car we drove around in. But somehow it didn't feel like really being in the war—I don't know why. It certainly looked like it—soldiers everywhere and all the statues sandbagged, shop windows taped. The dark streets at night, only an occasional dim blue light. No hot water except on Saturday, no coffee, no meat most days. But all the restaurants and cafes were open, shows at night, people filling the streets—it was all such *fun*. Even when the big gun boomed, you would see people flinch, then shrug and carry on, maybe checking their watch to see how long before the next shell. We were all mad to go to the front, just to see it, and we hoped to arrange an excursion. I remember how they looked when we said that. It reminded me of the old school days, how they always seemed a little too good for the world. Not snobbish, I don't mean that at all. But you know how when you get a couple of hundred girls together there are always rivalries and tiffs and dramas. Well they were never drawn into any of that; I don't remember a single time. They always kept themselves apart; they always seemed to have a certain standard of behavior. I've often thought that this world must have been a constant disappointment to them.

YELLOW LEAVES

We weren't expecting the noise. Could have had no idea how it would be. Not the guns and explosions when near the front; that's a particular agony. And even when far away, an undertone. But more the constant ruckus, living in a large group of people. The shouting in the camp, the singing and sounds of hammering. Horses and motors and airplanes if they're near. The racket in the canteen or mess hall, always something. There's no place for contemplation, no space for it, every waking moment, and even sleeping ones, filled up with sound.

On our last morning at home we woke early and went to sit in the silence on the kitchen porch. A cold morning, the grass rimed with frost that was just beginning to glisten as the sun touched it. The distant line of silent, colored hills. We didn't speak, just tried to take it in, our stomachs in nagging, queasy knots that eased a little, as the sun reached the spot where we sat. It was completely still, no sound from the sleeping house behind us, no bird or animal.

But then there *was* a sound, we gradually became aware of it, a wrenching, tearing, rattling sound, becoming louder and more constant as we began to listen to it. It sounded like—something, and yet like nothing we'd ever heard before. And then we saw a flicker of movement, and understood what was happening. As the sun warmed the frosted yellow maples that ringed the back garden the leaves began to detach with a snap, fall with an icy clatter. First one, then another, then more and more, a shower. On our last morning we realized that we had been living in a silence so absolute that we could hear the sound each leaf makes as it falls.

It can never be like that again. This is the sound of the modern world, the world we are fighting for. The tramp tramp tramp of a thousand feet marching, the jingle of harnesses and medals. The shriek of train whistles, the rattle of a clean gun being assembled, the howls of men in pain.

LETTER

Dear Anne,

Thank you for your last letter, and all the news of home. It's good to be reminded; we feel so far away in this new life we are living. As you see, the black pen is working beautifully—it's a pity the paper doesn't do it justice.

We were glad to hear that Father was well when last you saw him. He writes that the business is booming, and to tell you the truth we are dismayed that someone so close to us is growing rich out of all this suffering. Father would say that's the way of the world, but surely that's what we are fighting to change.

We are just back from a few days' leave in Paris—you wouldn't recognize the place. Soldiers and sandbags everywhere, shop windows taped up. Taxis charge exorbitant rates after dark, and it's very difficult to find your way at night, with only the blue lights marking the shelters. But the cafes and restaurants are full, and life goes on, even though every second person you see is dressed in mourning. We met up with Jane and Marjorie and spent a pleasant evening in their apartment, which they call The Hive because they've painted everything yellow and black. They are working very hard at one of the refugee centers, but still having a grand time—you remember they were such jolly girls. It must be very gratifying to know that so many of your old girls are here, doing their bit with the same spirit that carried us through all those marches and rallies. Let anyone who still doubts women's capabilities just see what we are doing, over here and at home, in this time of crisis.

We sometimes wonder if we could better serve helping with the refugees, who number in the thousands, pitiful souls, often with nothing more than the clothes on their backs. Or in a hospital—the work the you're taking pins from your hair. Touch your cheeks together, yes, that's good. Stay like that. Now touch each other's cheeks, but slowly, very slowly."

His tongue came out to lick his bottom lip. The record needle had come to the end of the long, long trail and hissed and scratched, and that seemed to be the only sound. "Now," he said, and we wondered why we had thought him a boy when the look in his mismatched eyes was ancient. "Now——" And we said, "Time's up," and turned away, busying ourselves with things behind the counter, laughing as if it had all been harmless.

Willows grew on the farther bank and dappled the light on the surface of the river. It was marvelous to be swimming, and we laughed and splashed and ducked each other and Hugh swam beneath us and tickled the soles of our feet. And we stayed in the water after he climbed out, and he watched us, lying on the grassy bank, smoking a cigarette and looking completely contented. We floated on our backs, on our stomachs, arms and legs played, and dived down to see if we could reach the bottom. And there was something magical in that pale green underwater light, in the fronded reeds that waved and beckoned us down. It was deeper than we thought; our hair floated free behind us, and we reached out a hand to each other, fingertips skimmed, and missed.

And there was, suddenly, a moment of cold panic. Cold, as if the water itself had chilled and darkened, inexplicable. We kicked to the surface, boiled our way to the bank where Hugh lounged, felt the sun begin to warm us again, our racing hearts slow down. We didn't speak of it.

"So kids," Hugh said, squinting his eyes against the smoke rising from his cigarette, "how did you get those scars?" And we surprised ourselves by telling him. It was one of those things we didn't talk about, except to each other. From a time we didn't talk about, either, except to each other. The summer our mother died, the day our brothers were allowed to go to the bay, and we were not. We prowled the garden in a rage, hitting at things with sticks and stones, and shattered a pane of glass that guarded the tomatoes and then shattered more, the sound became intoxicating. And some time later we sat on the grass facing each other, toe to toe, and drew our skin with a shard of that glass, copying the moves exactly. Blood running down to pool in our folded stockings. Oh what a fuss when Nan

nurses and doctors are doing is nothing short of heroic. We constantly feel that there should be more we can do. But we know that our work is important too. It was explained to us on our first day that we are here to provide a civilizing influence in the camp, an alternative to the filthy *estaminets* and the women who appear wherever soldiers are gathered. And the men appreciate what we do for them. We get to know some; they tell us about their lives back home, and we wonder what happens to them when they leave. It is horrible to think that many will have been wounded or killed. The front is moving closer; we often hear the guns and think of the men out there fighting. The camp is on standby, ready to move at a moment's notice, and this is very hard on the nerves.

We have just received word that there is to be a dance tonight; of all our duties this is the most onerous. The dances are held every few weeks in a nearby camp, and though canteen workers and sometimes nurses are brought in from miles around there are never nearly enough women for the hundreds of men who come to them. The room is bright and rather hot and smelly from all the bodies packed in. Usually there's a Victrola, or sometimes a real band. A whistle blows every two minutes to change partners, and sometimes there are terrible fights. All for two minutes' shuffle around the floor with a woman in your arms. For that's what we are at these times, Women, and not ourselves at all. It is a most disheartening experience, and no matter how many times we are assured that it is important for morale we can't help thinking, as we pull our aching heads and feet into the truck for the ride home, that it's not at all what we came to France for.

Two weeks ago we saw our first Germans, wounded prisoners in the hospital where we help out on our free day. And the strange thing was they were just like our boys, frightened and in pain. So young. They were so excited that we spoke some German, for they speak no English and only one knows a little French. We helped one write a letter to his mother—heaven knows if she'll ever receive it—and you know, it was so much like the letters we write for our boys, full of the same concerns and reassurances. Many of the men say that they hate the generals who run the war far more than the "enemy." Oh, sometimes this war seems like a terrible machine, carried along by its own momentum. Chewing up lives and spitting them out. We do our work day by day and try not to think about the enormity of it. The destruction, the horror, the waste. And it seems like it will go on and on, until there are no young men left in the world. We wonder then if we did the right thing by coming here, by being part of it.

SAINTE GERMAINE

In Bar-Sur-Aube we asked Hugh what it was like.

"Boring," he said. "If it wasn't for the terror, we'd all be bored to death." "It's hard to explain," he said. "Like a dream, it's something like a dream. I don't mean like a nightmare, not just that. But things have their own logic, things operate by their own rules, and it makes some kind of sense, at the front, although it would make none at all in the real world."

We were sitting at a little table, on a narrow white-walled street. Hugh had persuaded us that we needed an outing, on our free day, that we needed to get right away from the war. He said he would organize everything. We had stopped asking, or even wondering, how Hugh was always able to lay his hands on things. Old cars or bicycles or new bars of soap. Something very close to real coffee, day passes. He just seemed to manage, that's how it was with him.

The little street was just off the shady town square, where three or four women chatted by the ancient well; now and then they would shake their heads, hand on cheek.

"This should be what's real," Hugh said. "What's been forever, what will go on, long after we're gone."

Another woman had come to the well, was drawing up water, and we knew he was thinking of the deep grooves we'd noticed in the gray stone, how many hundreds of years it had taken bucket ropes to make them. But what we also noticed was the way the chatting group seemed to register the other's presence, without pausing in their conversation or turning their heads. To our eyes, she looked like one of them. About the same age, dressed in much the same way. Nothing, to our eyes, that would explain why the little group turned away from her, without actually moving. The way she seemed oblivious, yet the set of her back, walking away, showed she was not. And we thought how Hugh's words meant this as well.

We went a few miles out of the town to swim, to a place where the river eddied in a deep green pool. We changed in the trees, thankful for that

frivolous impulse, long ago and far away, that made us squeeze our swimming costumes into our bulging trunks. When we emerged from the tr Hugh said, "Good God, even the scars match," and we looked dowr our pale legs, the paler web of lines. We might have shown him then the scars didn't quite match, but he turned away quickly, embarrassed supposed, to be looking.

It was one of the things we liked about Hugh, the way he didn' play that tedious game of trying to tell us apart. Most people did, ar done all our lives. As if together we were too much for them, as if th way they could deal with us was to divide, to diminish us. But Hu always accepted us just as we were, just as we were with each other

Soldiers loved to play the guessing game. Our first day at the Mrs. Moore gave us a little talk. "Girls," she said, "you mus remember that these boys don't expect to see their old age, and them won't. So we have to make some—allowances. Of cour mean that anyone has to put up with any real unpleasantnes must try not to be shocked if their behavior, their conversat always what we would demand in our own parlours."

Dear Mrs. Moore, with her friend Dr. Thomas, who cam calling, and Colonel McAndrew not so long after the doc home. But we remembered her words, we consciously mad those first weeks, before we grew our skin. But one night ther in the canteen. An edge to the laughter, to the tone of the vc the men were going up to the line the next day and drifted twenty or thirty lingered, playing our two records over and them were standing about near our counter, and one of th and said, "My friends don't believe I can tell you apart, w out?"

And we said all right, and smiled when we said it, Moore and thinking that, though we were heartily sick of little enough to do for this poor boy, on what migh evening on earth. He had a mess of short reddish hair, pale eyelashes. One eye seemed noticeably smaller tha dark brown mole on his cheek beneath it. He didn't shave, but there was a pale, reddish stubble on his chir

His friends drew closer as he gave us directions. " right round. Now turn back, look at me. Smile. Frow

found us. It hurt then, and later, but the wounds healed quickly, leaving identical scars. Identical but reversed, of course, from sitting toe to toe.

"What's it like?" Hugh asked later. It was so peaceful there in the sunlight. The only sound the wind through the trees, a bell far away.

"It's safe," we said. "No matter what happens you're not alone," we said.

"Isn't that supposed to be God?" he said.

And then Hugh said that of everyone over here he maybe felt sorriest for the chaplains, and then he told us about the old aunt who'd raised him, the widow of his father's brother, and how he had scars himself, from the whippings. She used a switch, willow maybe, and they had to pray on their knees before and after. But he said he never could hold it against her. Because after a whipping she'd go to her room and he'd hear her. Muffled, like her face was in a pillow, which it probably was. Sobbing as if her heart would break.

"She wasn't a cruel woman," Hugh said. "She was doing what she truly believed had to be done. And it tormented her."

We asked about his parents, but he said he didn't know much about them, had never even seen a picture. His aunt told him they had just died, but he never quite believed her. He threw himself back, hands beneath his head, and spoke to the sky, to the overhanging trees.

"I was five or six when I came to her, and I don't remember anything at all before that. Strange, isn't it? Five or six years is a long time, you'd think there'd be something. Their faces, looking at me, the sound of their voices."

Once he heard his aunt telling a woman from the church that he'd lived just like a gypsy, and he got the idea that his parents really were gypsies, that they'd somehow misplaced him and that one day they'd look around and realize he was missing, come back for him. And they'd all drive away together in a brightly painted caravan, pulled by a horse named Old Joe.

"And every morning, early, I'd hear the milkman's horse and think— well, you know," Hugh said. "Her husband was a parson, and after he died she must have thought that her life would go a certain way. But she took me in, and so it went another way. What was that like for her? She knew nothing about children, she had no—imagination. And I was a handful, no question. I fought her all the way. It wasn't easy.

"Time we were going," Hugh said in his poshest voice. "We have reservations at a charming little inn nearby."

When he sat up we saw the marks on his back and without thinking we reached out to touch them. His skin shuddered beneath our fingers, and we snatched them back. And asked how he could be so understanding.

"Oh, there was my friend Tom," he said. "I met him very soon after I came there, in this dusty little laneway behind our houses. He laughed at the clothes she'd put me in, but then he said I could share his parents, as I didn't have my own. That's the kind of fellow Tom was, even then. And I suppose I did share his family, in a way. Certainly his house always felt more like home to me. They were a grand bunch—well, they still are, of course. So much laughter. So I was lucky, you see. I always had that to balance things, to show me there was another way. Otherwise—well, who knows."

Hugh really did know of an inn nearby; we sat outside on the edge of a great cliff with the fan-shaped Aube valley spread out below us. The small square fields in shades of green and yellow and the white road snaking north. And there were omelets and sausages, salad, and it all tasted wonderful, in a way you could only understand if you'd spent time picking lumps of gristle from a mess tin. We all grew a little giddy on the local champagne and looked down the valley as the light began to fade.

Hugh said the place was the cliff of Sainte Germaine, and he told us the story, though not how he'd learned it. How long ago the conqueror Attila was camped on top of the cliff, right where we were now giggling and eating. And he sent word down to the town of Bar to send their prettiest girl up to him, or he would destroy them all. So a beautiful girl named Germaine came up the steep path, slowly and steadily, but when she reached the top, before anyone could stop her or even guess what was in her mind, she broke and ran, threw herself over the cliff to the valley far below.

It was easy to imagine it in that place, as the light began to fade and ancient shadows appeared. The girl climbing through them, her breath coming a little harder as she went. Hearing the sound of the camp as she came nearer, probably not so different from the sounds of a modern army camp at rest. Knowing that this was happening to her simply because she was a girl, because she was pleasing to look at, which should not have been a bad thing. The flames of the torches, as she drew nearer, the bellowing of animals. The escape.

We talked then about whether it took more courage to live or to die, in such a situation. And argued a little; Hugh said one should always choose life, that was the only way for the human spirit to triumph.

"Otherwise," he said, "The bravest and the best are dying every day. Otherwise there'll only be scoundrels like me left to run the world."

As we stood to go, we asked Hugh if there was some kind of stone or marker at the place where Sainte Germaine leapt.

"No idea," he said. "Maybe I made it all up."

And we chased him all the way back to the motor.

On the drive we slept; it was completely dark. I woke once and the two of them were laughing at something I hadn't heard.

HUGH

And what did Hugh want? It should have been a simple thing. He wanted a quiet place, that was all. A place where he didn't have to do anything, be anything, a place where he could just lay his head down. He wanted to be close to something soft and human.

He thought of Tom's older sisters sometimes, the way he ran in and out of their lives all his childhood, the way they always made a space for him. Stopped whatever they were doing to smile, to say "Hello Hugh," sometimes a big hug when he was smaller. The wonder of what they had to give him.

There was a girl back home who tried. Wrote letters about missing him, asked questions he couldn't possibly answer. She wanted to know what it was like, she wanted to be able to imagine him, day by day. How could he tell her anything at all? It wasn't the thought of the censors that stopped him, it was the fact that she would have to be there to even begin to imagine it, and even then she couldn't have believed it. He couldn't believe it himself. He knew there must have been stages; it didn't all happen at once. He and Tom sitting in their secret place on the riverbank, the cave they'd made when they were boys, from shrubs and low hanging branches. There was still a rotting bit of mat on the ground, and he remembered how at one time they'd rolled it up and hidden it in a hole they'd dug beneath an old log, how they carefully wiped out their footprints with a fanned branch kept for that purpose. They went there, alone or together, through their childhood, eating sweet things filched from Tom's house, making fishing poles and lures, carving bits of wood with the knives they were not allowed to have. It filled him with wonder, always, that people could pass by and not notice the little notch in the tree trunk, that they would assume, if they thought about it at all, that the log had fallen just so, that the fanned branch was just like any other. That, if you didn't know what to expect, you would never think to look for it.

The afternoon he and Tom decided to join up they sat outside the cave, drinking bottles of beer, too big now to be comfortable hunched inside. They accused each other of leaving the mat out, the mat he had taken from his aunt's spare room and never even been questioned about, for she would never imagine he would want such a thing. It had been years since either one had been there; neither would admit to being the last. Hugh wondered sometimes if other boys had found the place, would wonder themselves about that bit of cloth and who had brought it there. But he knew it was already earth-colored, already rotted to nothing.

And he knew that there must have been stages, between that afternoon and this. The crisp autumn sky above them, the sound of the river, so close yet only glimpsed from where they sat. He couldn't have gone straight from that to this, become this creature in the line who was just so incredibly weary. The rank smell of himself that he no longer noticed, but assumed. The thick taste in his mouth, the itching and grime all over his body, his hands thickened and scarred, fingernails blackened from bangs and injuries he hadn't even noticed. The girl at home knit him warm stockings and thick pullovers the color of smoke. He wiggled and yanked the boots from his foul, soupy feet, peeled or sometimes cut off the old socks and pulled on the new. He thought of her fleetingly then, thought that whatever she imagined, stitch by stitch in the lamp glow, it could never be this, could never come close to this.

All he wanted was something simple, and he thought for a while he'd found it. The first night in camp he went to the canteen, not wanting, suddenly, to spend another evening in an *estaminet,* with rough wine and bragging soldiers' talk. The canteen was crowded, thick with smoke and mugs of cocoa, a record playing, gingham curtains at the windows. He found himself a corner with a pile of old magazines and tried to settle himself to read, but there was a restlessness in him, a twitching, and he thought maybe a glass of wine after all. And then he saw them behind the counter, just standing side by side, and in the same instant they each raised an arm, brushed the hair from their foreheads with the back of a hand, and something in that paired gesture brought a great peace to settle on him, as if it was something he'd been waiting to see all his life.

When the canteen closed a couple of men stayed behind to help tidy up and he stayed too, and when all the chairs were straightened, the dirty mugs collected, they all sat around in the little kitchen area, perched on chairs and crates, talking about nothing in particular. He lay down to sleep that night feeling cleaner than he had in years. And that became the pattern of his evenings. The camp was in a little dip, surrounded by low hills, and after supper he would walk a particular path, sit down on a particular rock, smoke a cigarette and watch the light fade from the untouched hills. Sometimes he could hear the guns faintly, but that only made it more peaceful. Then back down to the canteen and always, after the men drifted away, the three of them left talking.

When he went back up to the line they were in a quiet sector, only firing over the top once in a while to remind themselves there was a war on, and he thought, for his aunt must have had some influence, that it was because he'd been living so purely. He thought that if he'd seen one woman raise a hand to her forehead it would have been the same old story, but it was all different because they were two. He found he even looked around in a different way, storing up things to tell them about the next time he went back. He loved to make them laugh, but he also loved the melancholy that was part of their containment, part of the seriousness that made him feel that when they spoke together they were really talking, not just exchanging words. He told them things about himself that he might have told other people, but in a different way entirely, and he thought it was the same for them. When the Armistice came he was far away, and then he was sent to Germany, and that was where he saw the old newspaper. And he wasn't exactly surprised, but it still broke his heart.

ABOUT THE SENTRY

He was never quite the same. Not that it changed his life, not that it made him crazy or restless or morose. Or not any more than he already was. But of all the things he'd seen—and he'd seen enough to give the whole world nightmares—it was the thing that stayed with him. Not the thing that he talked about, over a jug or, more rarely, lying in the dark with his wife, but the thing that stayed with him. The thing that he couldn't shake, the thing that was on his mind when his eyes snapped open, heart pounding. One minute he was hiding a smoke in his cupped hand, stamping his feet as he walked and thinking only that he was cold, that he'd be glad to get down below to the steamy light. And then nothing was ever the same again.

He blamed himself. He'd seen it time and again, some fellow with days or hours to go who let his breath out a little, started to think he'd made it. Let himself think about a chair by the fire, soft hands, loved faces. And then *wham* and home all right, but in a shape no one would recognize. So he blamed himself, but who could have known that it would come like that, the thing that would do for him? Not that it changed his life. But how could he know? When he first saw the woman who would be his wife she was wearing a long dark dress that billowed in a cold wind.

He never talked about it, though there were times when he was close. And he thought the worst part was the way they looked right past him. Changed his life and never even noticed he was there.

NEAR THE FIELD OF CROSSES

We all have those pictures in our heads. Those moments of memory caught and held, for some reason, and perhaps if we could string them all together they would make some sense of our lives. Not for anyone else, but for ourselves, for of course the moments we hold would have been passed by anyone else, on their way to their own collection. Little things. The way the light fell on a certain wall, the dappled shadow dancing there. Drops of dew glistening on a blowsy orange flower. The way the wind shifts before a storm, exposing the pale undersides of leaves, the way the lamplight strikes a particular face or the intense, wonderful melancholy of certain notes on a piano. Each cross in this field marks a nest of those kind of memories, along with whatever is left of the person who enclosed it. And no one could ever guess, not even the closest person, just what those moments would be. Should that be chilling, or liberating?

Once, you see, I would have known that ours were shared. How can you imagine what this sudden uncertainty is like? There is a memory that

I know is mine alone. Waking suddenly in a dark car, and she and Hugh were laughing, together.

IN THE EVENING

I went to meet Hugh. Such a simple thing to say, five little words. But oh, the chasm that opened up. I went to meet Hugh and nothing was ever the same. I can't even say why I went, what I expected. Only that it seemed a way to end the turmoil. When we drove back from the place of Sainte Germaine it was very dark, and Hugh had to drive slowly and carefully. Ruth fell asleep in the back, and maybe it was the champagne, I don't know, I don't have much experience of champagne. We were talking, Hugh and I, in a little dark bubble moving through a dark sea of night, and suddenly I felt such a great opening up. And I realized, I think right then I realized, that it was because Hugh was talking to *me*. I don't think I can explain what that was like.

I knew the way he walked, each evening after supper; I had watched him. I waited until Ruth uncapped her pen, straightened the notepaper on the writing board, and then I said, "I think I'll go for a bit of a stroll." She raised her eyes, faintly puzzled; perhaps my voice sounded as strange as it did to my own ears. And then I was outside and then I was walking the path that led up, out of the camp, and my thoughts wheeled like a flock of startled birds. I settled myself to wait by the big rock that splits the path in two, and I waited and waited, but he didn't come.

It was nearly dark when I came down, the canteen already bustling. "Sorry, I lost track of time," I said, and the lie lay, an ugly thing between us. Hugh didn't appear that night, but we saw him with his kit the next morning. His eyes were red and there was a big discolored swelling high on one cheek. "Knew I shouldn't have gone to Papa George's," he said. And then with a wave of his hand he was gone, falling in with a line of marching men, marching down the rutted road and out of our lives. Leaving me with a broken thing to try to put together.

ARMISTICE

And then suddenly it was all over. A cold, misty day like so many others, breaking up packing cases to feed the fire. All morning the guns roared without pause; eleven o'clock came and went and we thought it had just been another rumor. But then gradually, so gradually, they stopped, and then there was silence. Berthe paused in her stirring and said, *"C'est fini?"* Then she sank to the ground with her apron covering her eyes and huge sobs shaking her shoulders.

Later we bounced into town in a truck filled with laughing soldiers, riding up front with Corporal Easton. Every so often he would bang the steering wheel with the heel of his hand, give his shoulders a twitch and say, "It's over, it's really over."

The main square was still thronged with people, some crying, some dancing. There were uniforms everywhere, and women in black, and children darting through the crowd playing tag. All the windows around the square were open, and in each open window was a row of lighted candles. We had thought to treat ourselves to a meal, but every cafe was filled with drunken soldiers, singing and crashing glasses and bottles. A group had commandeered the town's only taxi and was screeching through the narrow streets, whooping and firing revolvers in the air. Others staggered by, their arms around local girls or around each other. It was not a place for us, and we finally managed to find a ride back to camp. We thought at least we would sleep, really sleep, but our dreams were filled with dead men.

TEACUP

When our papers came we didn't know what to think. Now it was over, really over. We were no longer necessary; we were about to be spun loose. Into what, we wondered, and couldn't imagine. Since the Armistice we had been moved from camp to camp as they closed down, and that was part of the strangeness. We missed Berthe's humming, little Albert's grin as he dumped a stack of kindling on the kitchen floor. The faces of men we'd come to know. The work was the same, the big kettles of cocoa, of coffee, the piles of cigarettes and chocolate bars. But the mood was different, the men restless and eager to be gone. They chafed at the regulations they were still forced to live by, cursed the drilling that filled up their days. There were always fights. Men who had fought side by side now ploughed their fists into each other at the slightest excuse. Was this the new world?

And between ourselves there was a strangeness, and that was the worst part. Since I went to meet Hugh, since I lied. Once Mrs. Moore got a letter saying that her father had suffered a stroke, and Dr. Thomas explained it over lunch. He said it was like a severing in the brain, and that was what this felt like. An emptiness and a terrible thrumming panic. We were no longer whole; we couldn't imagine how we would ever be whole again. We thought of Nan's favorite teacup, the one with the little blue flowers around the rim. She dropped it once and it split in two, and she spent an evening with a pot of glue and a matchstick, putting it back together. She still used it after—it still held tea—but you could always see the join.

JOURNEY

The little train stood in the station, the few freight cars still bearing the legend *40 hommes 8 chevaux*. The platform was crowded—soldiers with their heavy packs, people with bags and bundles. And perhaps we felt it as we put our foot on the step, pulled a little with tired arms, but everyone was laughing and waving and pushing and there was no time to say *Stop. Wait.* No way to turn back against the bodies behind, to say *No, we won't go.* Pushed into our seat. The final click of the doors, our shoulders bumping hard, and the knowledge dawning with our exhaled breath that we were caught up in another thing, by another thing. The signs were still posted in the carriage. *Taisez-vous, mefiez-vous, les oreilles enemies vous ecoutent.* We spoke in whispers, if we spoke at all.

So hot on the train, no air. Crammed together, the smells rising from all those bodies, wet wool and worse, much worse. Impossible to open a window, impossible even to see through a window while the rain slashed down. Cold, hard rain. There was a time in our life when it was wonderful to sit in a window seat and watch the rain. Books in our laps, the feel of paper at our fingertips and raising our eyes again and again to look through to the dripping trees, the garden. It was possible then to imagine any hero appearing, water dripping from his cape, his wide-brimmed hat, as he looked up at our white shapes in the window. It was possible then to spend an entire day with the fire hissing, the gentle rain falling, the gray light slowly deepening. Dreaming. On the train we understood that there were no heroes, that that life could not possibly be ours.

The journey took two days. The train crawled slowly, sometimes reversing for miles, sometimes sitting motionless for an hour or more. We passed through villages blasted to piles of rubble, we passed the burned-out shells of trucks, the splintered remains of horse-drawn carts. The roads we could see were filled with lines of people, walking with heads down, shoulders hunched against the rain. They had the look of people who had been walking forever, who would never reach their destination.

There was a soldier sitting beside us; he named the battlefields we passed near. His foot was bandaged, crutches leaning against the seat.

"I hurt it playing football yesterday," he said. "My only war wound, can you believe it?"

He showed us photographs of his girlfriend, of his parents and younger brother. We saw our own hands reaching out to take them, heard our own voices, but all the time there was a terrible pounding in our heads.

Toward evening of the first day the rain stopped and the train moved into the night. And it was like that, moving *into* night, as if it were a strange new country. We had dinner tickets but we let them fall to the muddy floor, the bright green paper soon an unrecognizable mass. When the soldier came back he fell asleep, his head lolling back, his mouth open. Dreaming, no doubt, of his girlfriend's soft arms, his mother's apple pie. Soon everyone was asleep, the carriage filled with exhaled breath while we watched through the window.

"What can we do?" I whispered to our reflections. "What can we ever do?"

Ruth reached for my hand and we held on to each other as we moved through the country called night.

The next day the countryside was untouched by war, but still dead and colorless beneath a lowering sky. When we finally reached Bordeaux everything speeded up around us, the crowds at the station, the docks. Faces looming and receding—a woman's fat cheeks, her mouth opening and closing soundlessly, a man's bushy eyebrows, the red lines on the back of the taxi driver's neck. We were swept along, our feet so heavy we could barely put one in front of the other. The ship rearing up, impossibly huge, our hands on the grimy rope of the gangway.

DR. MAITLAND

Someone told me they needed my attention, and when they didn't appear at dinner I went looking, knocked at their cabin door. They were very agitated when I entered. One—I don't know which—was pacing back and forth, her hands in her hair. One was sitting at the tiny writing desk, scribbling on pieces of paper which fell to the floor as I closed the door behind me. I introduced myself, and the pacing one sat down on the edge of the bunk, folding her hands in her lap. I asked how they were and they said they were very tired, that they hadn't slept for the two days it took the train to reach Bordeaux. They said there was a terrible racket in their heads, that if they could just sleep maybe it would stop. They asked if I knew when the ship would sail, and I said that I understood that it would be within the hour. I gave them a mild sedative and said that I would come back in the morning. I've thought about it since, and I don't think there's any way I could have known. You can't imagine what it was like, the stress we'd all been living under. To be suddenly on the verge of a normal life. The cruel limbo of the sea voyage. Everyone on that ship was in distress, and I couldn't have known what they would do.

THE DEEP

Without each other we are in pieces, we are scattered to the wide winds. These past weeks we are put together like the broken teacup. In the train our shoulders bumped and we felt those rough edges grating. Nothing feels as it did; we have to find a way back.

There is a terrible racket in our heads. In the cabin we pace and pace, and our hearts beat loudly, thrumming to our fingertips. We are the same age our mother was, when we were born.

The doctor comes with soothing powders, but we are beyond that. She says with a smile that in a few days we'll be home again, as if that should mean something. We pace and pace, holding ourselves together. Bits of us straining to break loose; we will be scattered.

The ship moves off with a lurch and we pace and pace; we are trapped now, there's a terrible pounding in our heads. The lighthouse sends its beam through the cabin, a darting streak of light, and we know, suddenly, what we have to do.

TESTIMONY OF THE SENTRY

Walter Allingham, 339th Field Artillery, was stationed in the bow on Sunday night. He saw two young women walking along the deck toward him at about 7 o'clock. It was so dark he could not see what they wore, except what appeared to be big cloaks which blew out in the wind. They were talking to each other and stopped when they reached the bow on the port side. Suddenly one of them placed her foot on the rail and scrambled over it, jumped into the water. The other followed almost immediately. Neither screamed or made any noise, and the splash when they struck the water was drowned by the noise of the tide rushing along the ship's sides.

AFTER

Here there are two tall windows and the gauzy white curtains lift and fall like a breath, like a sigh. The sounds that reach us are muffled, and we wonder if someone has died.

SECOND PRIZE

Big Me

By Dan Chaon

INTRODUCED BY MICHAEL CHABON

I'll confess it; I'm kind of tired of short stories. Maybe it has something to do with the fact of my having just, for the purposes of this venerable prize, ploughed through seventeen of them in three days. But a sense of dissatisfaction or impatience with the genre, at least in its current state, has been growing in me for some time. This discontent, I hasten to add, extends to (it may, in fact, derive from and ultimately pertain only to) most of my own work in the form. The short story form has, pretty much from the time of its invention, afforded a convenient and capable staging ground for the operations of the baleful, the jaundiced, the severe, the caustic, the unremitting, the bleak, the dyspeptic, and the harsh view of things. And my faith in the value of taking one or another such a view of things—or all of them at once—in particular during yet another age of lies, brutality, and compromise, remains more or less unshaken, I suppose. But I think that—with a few brilliant exceptions, some of whom you will encounter in this volume—short story writers, or all of us, seem to have lost the sense of mystery, of the Mystery that redeems the whole sad production. The short story, they say, began with Poe or de Maupassant; in both writers, at their best, a sense of mystery is omnipresent, at times almost oppressive. And I'm certain that the tale, from which the early masters and ultimately the whole genre derive, arose in some earlier age of lies, brutality, and compromise as an attempt to locate the evanescent, glowing heart of it all. I guess what I'm trying to say is that, while it's probably just a coincidence, we seem (to me—only to me!) to have arrived at a point where both the sense of mystery and the ancestral tale, constructed around equal parts of incident and wonder, have been left far, far behind. What remains, primarily, is the psychological element that Poe introduced and Joyce pushed to the foreground, and the writer's voice, unmoored, unhinged, and wildly riffing, to cope with the overwhelming darkness of the visible world.

"Big Me" is, almost secretly, a tale of the supernatural. It has the bones of a ghost story, clothed in the tatters of a more conventional story of malaise, retrospection, and family collapse. Readers who shy from such fare are hereby reassured that in it, no physical laws are violated nor occult forces invoked. And yet it tells the amazing story of a man who is haunted—haunted, in fact, at both ends of his life: at this end by the oddly fractured memory of the boy he once was; at that end, more chillingly, by the mystery of the man he will one *day become. It has all the modern virtues: mordancy, rue, anomie, and dark humor. It never strains credulity, or offends the contemporary sensibility. And yet it proceeds with a confidence in the inherent interest of the story to be told and a matter-of-fact apprehension of the barely hidden wonder of the world that recalls the ancestral roots of the genre. The horror at its heart—the strange, retrospective certainty that one has become, in the eyes of one's childhood self, a dreadful thing, that one may have, without remarking it, wandered into the wrong life with no hope of escape—is revealed in a way that gives us a fresh look at the great modern theme of failure and offers a kind of timeless, delicious thrill that hearkens all the way back to Hoffman or Ewers. With a story like this one by the marvelous writer Dan Chaon, I am confronted not only with an unfathomable mystery such as that of the endurance of a single human identity over time but also with new proof, if such proof were ever wanting, of the enduring value of telling tales in the ongoing struggle to understand those mysteries when, intangible as they may be, we brush unmistakably against them.*

—MICHAEL CHABON

Dan Chaon

Big Me

From *The Gettysburg Review*

I T ALL started when I was twelve years old. Before that, everything was a peaceful blur of childhood, growing up in the small town of Beck, Nebraska. A "town," we called it. Really, the population was just under two hundred, and it was one of those dots along Highway 30 that people didn't usually even slow down for, though strangers sometimes stopped at the little gas station near the grain elevator or ate at the café. My mother and father owned a bar called The Crossroads, at the edge of town. We lived in a little house behind it, and behind our house was the junkyard, and beyond that were wheat fields, which ran all the way to a line of bluffs and barren hills, full of yucca and rattlesnakes.

Back then I spent a lot of time in my mind, building a city up toward those hills. This imaginary place was also called Beck, but it was a metropolis of a million people. The wise though cowardly mayor lived in a mansion in the hills above the interstate, as did the bullish, Teddy Roosevelt–like police commissioner, Winthrop Golding. There were other members of the rich and powerful who lived in enormous old Victorian houses along the bluffs, and many of them harbored dreadful secrets or were involved in one way or another with the powerful Beck underworld. One wealthy, respectable citizen, Mr. Karaffa, turned out to be a lycanthrope who preyed on the lovely, virginal junior high school girls, mutilating them beyond recognition, until I shot him with a silver bullet. I was the city Detective, though I was often underappreciated and, because of my radical notions, in danger of being fired by the cowardly mayor. The police commissioner always defended me, even when he was exasperated by my unorthodox methods. He respected my integrity.

I don't know how many of my childhood years took place in this imaginary city. By the age of eight I had become the Detective, and shortly thereafter I began drawing maps of the metropolis. By the time we left Beck, I had a folder six inches thick, full of street guides and architecture and subway schedules. In the real town, I was known as the strange kid who wandered around talking to himself. Old people would find me in their backyard gardens and come out and yell at me. Children would see me playing on their swing sets, and when they came out to challenge me, I would run away. I trapped people's cats and bound their arms and legs, harshly forcing confessions from them. Since no one locked their doors, I went into people's houses and stole things, which I pretended were clues to the mystery I was trying to solve.

Everyone real also played a secret role in my city. My parents, for example, were the landlord and his wife, who lived downstairs from my modest one-room apartment. They were well-meaning but unimaginative people, and I was polite to them. There were a number of comic episodes in which the nosy landlady had to be tricked and defeated. My brother, Mark, was the district attorney, my nemesis. My younger sister, Kathy, was my secretary, Miss Kathy, whom I sometimes loved. I would have married her if I weren't such a lone wolf.

My family thought of me as a certain person, a role I knew well enough to perform from time to time. Now that they are far away, it sometimes hurts to think that we knew so little of one another. Sometimes I think if no one knows you, then you are no one.

In the spring of my twelfth year, a man moved into a house at the end of my block. The house had belonged to an old woman who had died and left her home fully furnished but tenantless for years, until her heir had finally gotten around to having the estate liquidated, the old furniture sold, the place cleared out and put up for sale. This was the house I had taken cats to, the hideout where I had extracted their yowling confessions. Then finally the house was emptied, and the man took up residence.

I first saw the man in what must have been late May. The lilac bush in his front yard was in full bloom, thick with spade-shaped leaves and clusters of perfumed flowers. The man was mowing the lawn as I passed, and I stopped to stare.

It immediately struck me that there was something familiar about him—the wavy dark hair and gloomy eyes, the round face and dimpled chin. At first I thought he looked like someone I'd seen on TV. And then I realized: he looked like me! Or rather, he looked like an older version of me—me grown up. As he got closer with his push lawnmower, I was aware that our eyes were the same odd, pale shade of gray, that we had the same map of freckles across the bridge of our noses, the same stubby fingers. He lifted his hand solemnly as he reached the edge of his lawn, and I lifted my opposite hand, so that for a moment we were mirror images of one another. I felt terribly worked up and hurried home.

That night, considering the encounter, I wondered whether the man actually *was* me. I thought about all that I'd heard about time travel, and considered the possibility that my older self had come back for some unknown purpose—perhaps to save me from some mistake I was about to make or to warn me. Maybe he was fleeing some future disaster and hoped to change the course of things.

I suppose this tells you a lot about what I was like as a boy, but these were among the first ideas I considered. I believed wholeheartedly in the notion that time travel would soon be a reality, just as I believed in UFOs and ESP and Bigfoot. I used to worry, in all seriousness, whether humanity would last as long as the dinosaurs had lasted. What if we were just a brief, passing phase on the planet? I felt strongly that we needed to explore other solar systems and establish colonies. The survival of the human species was very important to me.

Perhaps it was because of this that I began to keep a journal. I had recently read *The Diary of Anne Frank* and had been deeply moved by the idea that a piece of you, words on a page, could live on after you were dead. I imagined that, after a nuclear holocaust, an extraterrestrial boy might find my journal, floating among some bits of meteorite and pieces of buildings and furniture that had once been Earth. The extraterrestrial boy would translate my diary, and it would become a bestseller on his planet. Eventually, the aliens would be so stirred by my story that they would call off the intergalactic war they were waging and make a truce.

In these journals I would frequently write messages to myself, a person whom I addressed as "Big Me," or "The Future Me." Rereading these entries as the addressee, I try not to be insulted, since my former self admonishes me frequently. "I hope you are not a failure," he says. "I hope you are happy," he says. It gives me pause.

I'm trying to remember what was going on in the world when I was twelve. My brother, Mark, says it was the worst year of his life. He remembers it as a year of terrible fights between my parents. "They were drunk every night, up till three and four in the morning, screaming at each other. Do you remember the night Mom drove the car into the tree?"

I don't. In my mind, they seemed happy together, in the bantering, ironic manner of sitcom couples, and their arguments seemed full of comedy, as if a laugh track might ring out after their best put-down lines. I don't recall them drunk so much as expansive, and the bar seemed a cheerful, popular place, always full, though they would go bankrupt not long after I turned thirteen.

Mark says that was the year he tried to commit suicide, and I don't recall that either, though I do remember he was in the hospital for a few days. Mostly, I think of him reclining on the couch, looking regal and dissipated, reading books like *I'm Okay, You're Okay*, and filling out questionnaires that told him whether or not he was normal.

The truth is, I mostly recall the Detective. He had taken an interest in the mysterious stranger who had moved in down the block. The Stranger, it turned out, would be teaching seventh grade science; he would be replacing the renowned girl's basketball coach and science teacher, Mr. Karaffa, who'd had a heart attack and died right after a big game. The Stranger was named Louis Mickleson, and he'd moved to Beck from a big city: Chicago or maybe Omaha. "He seems like a lonely type of guy," my mother commented once.

"A weirdo, you mean?" said my father.

I knew how to get into Mickleson's house. It had been my hideout, and there were a number of secret entrances: loose windows, the cellar door, the back door lock that could be dislodged with the thin, laminated edge of my library card.

He was not a very orderly person, Mr. Mickleson, or perhaps he was simply uncertain. The house was full of boxes, packed and unpacked, and the furniture was placed randomly about the house, as if he'd simply left things where the moving men had set them down. In various corners of the house were projects he'd begun and then abandoned—tilting towers of stacked books next to an empty bookcase, silverware organized in rows along the kitchen counter, a pile of winter coats left on the floor near a closet. The boxes seemed to be carefully classified. Near his bed, for example, were socks, underwear, white T-shirts—each in a separate box, neatly folded near a drawerless dresser. The drawers themselves lay on the floor and contained reams of magazines: *Popular Science* in one, *Azimov's Science Fiction* in another, and *Playboy* in yet another, though the dirty pictures had all been fastidiously scissored out.

You can imagine what a cave of wonders this was for me, piled high with riches and clues; each box almost trembled with mystery. There was a collection of costume jewelry, old coins, and keys. Here were his old lesson plans and grade books, the names of former students penciled in alongside their attendance records and grades and small comments ("messy," "lazy," "shows potential!") racked up in columns. Here were photos and letters: a gold mine!

One afternoon I was kneeling before his box of letters when I heard the front door open. Naturally, I was very still. I heard the front door close, and then Mr. Mickleson muttering to himself. I tensed as he said, "Okay, well, never mind," and read aloud from a bit of junk mail he'd gotten, using a nasal, theatrical voice: "'A special gift for you enclosed!' How lovely!" I crouched there over his cardboard box, looking at a boyhood photo of him and what must have been his sister, circa 1952, sitting in the lap of an artificially bearded Santa. I heard him chuckling as he opened the freezer and took something out. Then he turned on the TV in the living room, and other voices leapt out at me.

It never felt like danger. I was convinced of my own powers of stealth and invisibility. He would not see me because that was not part of the story I was telling myself: I was the Detective! I sensed a cool, hollow spot in my stomach, and I could glide easily behind him as he sat in his La-Z-Boy recliner, staring at the blue glow of the television, watching the news. He didn't shudder as the dark shape of me passed behind him. He couldn't see me unless I chose to be seen.

I had my first blackout that day I left Mickleson's house, not long after I'd sneaked behind him and crept out the back door. I don't know whether

blackout is the best term, with its redolence of alcoholic excess and cata-
tonic states, but I'm not sure what else to call it. I stepped into the backyard and remember walking cautiously along a line of weedy flowerbeds
toward the gate that led to the alley. I had taken the Santa photo, and I
stared at it. Yes, it could have been a photograph of me when I was five,
and I shuddered at the eerie similarity. An obese calico cat hurried down
the alley in front of me, disappearing into a hedge that bordered someone
else's backyard.

A few seconds later, I found myself at the kitchen table, eating dinner
with my family. I was in the process of bringing an ear of buttered corn to
my mouth, and it felt something like waking up, only faster, as if I'd been
transported in a blink from one place to another. My family had not
seemed to notice that I was gone. They were all eating silently, grimly, as if
everything were normal. My father was cutting his meat, his jaw firmly
locked, and my mother's eyes were on her plate, as if she were watching a
small round television. No one seemed surprised by my sudden appearance.

It was kind of alarming. At first, it just seemed odd—like, "Oh, how
did I get here?" But then, the more I thought about it, the more my skin
crawled. I looked up at the clock on the kitchen wall, a grinning black cat
with a clock face for a belly and a pendulum tail and eyes that shifted from
left to right with each tick. I had somehow lost a considerable amount of
time—at least half an hour, maybe forty-five minutes. The last thing I
clearly recalled was staring at that photo—Mr. Mickleson, or myself, sitting on Santa's knee. And then, somehow, I had left my body. Where had I
gone? I sat there, thinking, but there wasn't even a blur of memory. There
was only a blank spot.

Once, I tried to explain it to my wife.

"A *blank* spot?" she said, and her voice grew stiff and concerned, as if
I'd found a lump beneath my skin. "Do you mean a blackout? You have
blackouts?"

"No, no," I said and tried to smile reassuringly. "Not exactly."

"What do you mean?" she said. "Listen, Andy," she said. "If I told you
that I had periods when I . . . lost time . . . wouldn't you be concerned?
Wouldn't you want me to see a doctor?"

"You're blowing this all out of proportion," I said. "It's nothing like
that." And I wanted to tell her about the things that the Detective had

read about in the weeks and months following the first incident—about trances and transcendental states, about astral projection and out-of-body travel. But I didn't.

"There's nothing wrong with me," I said and stretched my arms luxuriously. "I feel great," I said. "It's more like daydreaming. Only—a little different."

But she still looked concerned. "You don't have to hide anything from me," she said. "I just care about you, that's all."

"I know," I said, and I smiled as her eyes scoped my face. "It's nothing," I said, "just one of those little quirks!" And that is what I truly believe. Though my loved ones sometimes tease me about my distractedness, my forgetfulness, they do so affectionately. There haven't been any major incidents, and the only times that really worry me are when I am alone, when I am driving down one street and wake up on another. And even then, I am sure that nothing terrible has happened. I sometimes rub my hands against the steering wheel. I am always intact. It's just one of those things! There are no screams or sirens in the distance.

But back then, that first time, I was frightened. I remember asking my mother how a person would know if he had a brain tumor.

"You don't have a brain tumor," she said irritably. "It's time for bed."

A little later, perhaps feeling guilty, she came up to my room with aspirin and water.

"Do you have a headache, honey?" she said

I shook my head as she turned off my bedside lamp. "Too much reading of comic books," she said and smiled at me exaggeratedly, as she sometimes did, pretending I was still a baby. "It would make anybody's head feel funny, Little Man!" She touched my forehead with the cold, dry pads of her fingertips, looking down into my eyes, heavily. She looked sad and for a moment lost her balance as she reached down to run a palm across my cheek. "Nothing is wrong," she whispered. "It will all seem better in the morning."

That night, I sat up writing in my diary, writing to Big Me. "I hope you are alive," I wrote. "I hope that I don't die before you are able to read this."

That particular diary entry always makes me feel philosophical. I'm not entirely sure of the person he is writing to, the future person he was imagining. I don't know whether that person is alive or not. There are so many people we could become, and we leave such a trail of bodies through our teens and twenties that it's hard to tell which one is us. How many versions do we abandon over the years? How many end up nearly forgotten, mumbling and gasping for air in some tenement room of our consciousness, like elderly relatives suffering some fatal lung disease?

Like the Detective. As I wander through my big suburban house at night, I can hear his wheezing breath in the background, still muttering about secrets that can't be named. Still hanging in there.

My wife is curled up on the sofa, sipping hot chocolate, reading, and when she looks up she smiles shyly. "What are you staring at?" she says. She is used to this sort of thing by now—finds it endearing, I think. She is a pleasant, practical woman, and I doubt that she would find much of interest in the many former selves that tap against my head, like moths.

She opens her robe. "See anything you like?" she says, and I smile back at her.

"Just peeking," I say brightly. My younger self wouldn't recognize me, I'm sure of that.

Which makes me wonder: what did I see in Mickleson, beyond the striking resemblance? I can't quite remember my train of thought, though it's clear from the diary that I latched wholeheartedly onto the idea. Some of it is obviously playacting, making drama for myself, but some of it isn't. Something about Mickleson struck a chord.

Maybe it was simply this—July 13: "If Mickleson is your future, then you took a wrong turn somewhere. Something is sinister about him! He could be a criminal on the lam! He is crazy. You have to change your life now! Don't ever think bad thoughts about Mom, Dad, or even Mark. Do a good deed every day."

I had been going to his house fairly frequently by that time. I had a notebook, into which I had pasted the Santa photo, and a sample of his handwriting, and a bit of hair from a comb. I tried to write down everything that seemed potentially significant: clues, evidence, but evidence of what, I don't know. There was the crowd of beer cans on his kitchen counter, sometimes arranged in geometric patterns. There were the boxes, unpacked then packed again. There were letters: "I am tired, unbelievably tired, of going around in circles with you," a woman who signed herself

"Sandi" had written. "As far as I can see, there is no point in going on. Why can't you just make a decision and stick to it?" I had copied this down in my detective's notebook.

In his living room, there was a little plaque hanging on the wall. It was a rectangular piece of dark wood; a piece of parchment paper, burned around the edges, had been lacquered to it. On the parchment paper, in careful calligraphy, was written:

I wear
the chain
I forged
in life.

This seemed like a possible secret message. I thought maybe he'd escaped from jail.

From a distance, behind a hedge, I watched Mickleson's house. He wouldn't usually appear before ten in the morning. He would pop out of his front door in his bathrobe, glancing quickly around as if he sensed someone watching, and then he would snatch up the newspaper on his doorstep. At times, he seemed aware of my eyes.

I knew I had to be cautious. Mickleson must not guess that he was being investigated, and I tried to take precautions. I stopped wearing my favorite detective hat, to avoid calling attention to myself. When I went through his garbage, I did it in the early morning, while I was fairly certain he was still asleep. Even so, one July morning I was forced to crawl under a thick hedge when Mickleson's back door unexpectedly opened at eight in the morning, and he shuffled out the alley to dump a bag into his trash can. Luckily I was wearing brown and green, so I blended in with the shrubbery. I lay there, prone against the dirt, staring at his bare feet and hairy ankles. He was wearing nothing but boxer shorts, so I could see that his clothes had been concealing a large quantity of dark, vaguely sickening body hair; there was even some on his back! I had recently read a Classics Illustrated comic book version of *Dr. Jekyll and Mr. Hyde,* and I recalled the description of Hyde as "something troglodytic," which was a word I had looked up in the dictionary and now applied as Mickleson dumped his bag into the trash can. I had just begun to grow a few hairs on my own body and was chilled to think I might end up like this. I heard the clank of beer cans, then he walked away. I lay still, feeling uneasy.

At home, after dinner, I would sit in my bedroom, reading through my notes, puzzling. I would flip through my lists, trying to find clues I could link together. I'd sift through the cigar box full of things I'd taken from his home: photographs, keys, a Swiss army knife, a check stub with his signature, which I'd compared against my own. But nothing seemed to fit. All I knew was that he was mysterious. He had some secret.

Late one night that summer, I thought I heard my parents talking about me. I was reading, and their conversation had been mere background, rising and falling, until I heard my name. "Andrew . . . how he's turning out . . . not fair to anybody!" Then, loudly: "What will happen to him?"

I sat up straight, my heart beating heavily, because it seemed that something must have happened, that they must have discovered something. I felt certain I was about to be exposed: my spying, my breaking and entering, my stealing. I was quiet, frightened, and then after a while, I got up and crept downstairs.

My mother and father were at the kitchen table, speaking softly, staring at the full ashtray that sat between them. My mother looked up when I came in and clenched her teeth. "Oh, for God's sake," she said. "Andy, it's two-thirty in the morning! What are you doing up?"

I stood there in the doorway, uncertainly. I wished that I were a little kid again, that I could tell her I was scared. But I just hovered there. "I couldn't sleep," I said.

My mother frowned. "Well, try harder, God damn it," she said.

I stood there a moment longer. "Mom?" I said.

"Go to bed!" She glared.

"I thought I heard you guys saying something about that man that just moved in down the block. He didn't say anything about me, did he?"

"Listen to me, Andrew," she said. Her look darkened. "I don't want you up there listening to our conversations. This is grown-up talk, and I don't want you up there snooping."

"He's going to be the new science teacher," I said.

"I know," she said, but my father raised his eyebrows.

"Who's this?" my father said, raising his glass to his lips. "That weirdo is supposed to be a teacher? That's a laugh."

"Oh, don't start!" my mother said. "At least he's a customer! You'd better God damn not pick a fight with him. You've driven enough people away as it is, the way you are. It's no wonder we don't have any friends!" Then she turned on me. "I thought I told you to go to bed. Don't just stand there gaping when I tell you to do something! My God, I can't get a minute's peace!"

Back in my bedroom, I tried to forget what my parents had said—it didn't matter, I thought, as long as they didn't know anything about me. I was safe! And I sat there, relieved, slowly forgetting the fact that I was really just a strange twelve-year-old boy, a kid with no real playmates, an outsider even in his own family. I didn't like being that person, and I sat by the window, awake, listening to my parents' slow, arguing voices downstairs, smelling the smoke that hung in a thick, rippling cloud over their heads. Outside, the lights of Beck melted into the dark fields; the hills were heavy, huddled shapes against the sky. I closed my eyes, wishing hard, trying to will my imaginary city into life, envisioning roads and streetlights suddenly sprouting up through the prairie grass. And tall buildings. And freeways. And people.

It has been almost twenty years since I last saw Beck. We left the town the summer before eighth grade, after my parents had gone bankrupt, and in the succeeding years we moved through a blur of ugly states—Wyoming, Montana; Panic, Despair—while my parents' marriage dissolved.

Now we are all scattered. My sister, Kathy, suffered brain damage in a car accident when she was nineteen, out driving with her friends. She now lives in a group home in Denver, where she and the others spend their days making Native American jewelry, which is sold at truck stops. My brother, Mark, is a physical therapist who lives on a houseboat in Marina Del Rey, California. He spends his free time reading books about childhood trauma, and every time I talk to him, he has a series of complaints about our old misery: at the very least, surely I remember the night that my father was going to kill us all with his gun, how he and Kathy and I ran into the junkyard and hid in an old refrigerator box? I think he's exaggerating, but Mark is always threatening to have me hypnotized, so I'll remember.

We have all lost touch with my mother. The last anyone heard, she was living in Puerto Vallarta, married to a man who apparently has something to do with real estate development. The last time I talked to her, she didn't sound like herself: a foreign-accented lilt had crept into her voice. She laughed harshly, then began to cough, when I mentioned old times.

For a time before he died, I was closest to my father. He was working as a bartender in a small town in Idaho, and he used to call me when I was in law school. Like me, he remembered Beck fondly: the happiest time of his life, he said. "If only we could have held on a little bit longer," he told me, "it would have been a different story. A different story entirely."

Then he'd sigh. "Well, anyway," he'd say. "How are things going with Katrina?"

"Fine," I'd say. "Just the usual. She's been a little distant lately. She's very busy with her classes. I think med school takes a lot out of her."

I remember shifting silently, because the truth was, I didn't really have a girlfriend named Katrina. I didn't have a girlfriend, period. I made Katrina up one evening, on the spur of the moment, to keep my dad from worrying so much. It helped him to think that I had a woman looking after me, that I was heading into a normal life: marriage, children, a house, etcetera. Now that I have such things, I feel a bit guilty. He died not knowing the truth. He died waiting to meet her, enmeshed in my made-up drama—in the last six months of his life, Katrina and I came close to breaking up, got back together, discussed marriage, worried that we were not spending enough time together. The conversations that my father and I had about Katrina were some of the best we ever had.

I don't remember much about my father from that summer when I was twelve. We certainly weren't having conversations that I can recall, and I don't ever remember that he pursued me with a gun. He was just there; I would walk past him in the morning as he sat, sipping coffee, preparing to go to work. I'd go into the bar, and he would pour me a glass of Coke with bitters, "to put hair on my chest." I'd sit there on the barstool, stroking Suds, the bar's tomcat, in my lap, murmuring quietly to him as I imagined my detective story. My father had a bit part in my imagination, barely a speaking role.

But it was at the bar that I saw Mr. Mickleson again. I had been at his house that morning, working through a box of letters, and then I'd been out at the junkyard behind our house. In those unenlightened times, it was called The Dump. People drove out and pitched their garbage over the edge of a ravine, which had become encrusted with a layer of beer cans, broken toys, bedsprings, car parts, broken glass. It was a magical place, and I'd spent a few hours in the driver's seat of a rusted-out Studebaker, fiddling with the various dashboard knobs, pretending to drive it, to stalk suspects, to become involved in a thrilling high-speed chase. At last I had come to the bar to unwind, to drink my Coke and bitters and re-create the day in my imagination. Occasionally my father would speak to me, and I would be forced to disengage myself from the Detective, who was brooding over a glass of bourbon. He had become hardened and cynical, but he would not give up his fight for justice.

I was repeating these stirring lines in my mind when Mr. Mickleson came into the bar. I felt a little thrum when he entered. My grip tightened on Suds the cat, who struggled and sprang from my lap.

Having spent time in The Crossroads, I recognized drunkenness. I was immediately aware of Mickleson's flopping gait, the way he settled heavily against the lip of the bar. "Okay, okay," he muttered to himself, then chuckled. "No, just forget it, never mind," he said cheerfully. Then he sighed and tapped his hand against the bar. "Shot o' rum," he said. "Captain Morgan, if you have it. No ice." I watched as my father served him, then flicked my glance away when Mickleson looked warily in my direction. He leveled his gaze at me, his eyes heavy with some meaning I couldn't decipher. It was part friendly, that look, but part threatening, too, in a particularly intimate way—as if he recognized me.

"Oh, hello," Mr. Mickleson said. "If it isn't the staring boy! Hello, Staring Boy!" He grinned at me, and my father gave him a stern look. "I believe I know you," Mr. Mickleson said jauntily. "I've seen you around, haven't I?"

I just sat there, blushing. It occurred to me that perhaps, despite my precautions, Mr. Mickleson had seen me after all. "Staring Boy," he said, and I tried to think of when he might have caught me staring. How many times? I saw myself from a distance, watching his house but now also being watched, and the idea set up a panic in me that was difficult to quell. I was grateful that my father came over and called me *son*. "Son," he said, "why don't you go on outside and find something to do? You may as well enjoy some of that summer sunshine before school starts."

"All right," I said. I saw that Mickleson was still grinning at me expectantly, his eyes blank and unblinking, and I realized that he was doing an imitation of my own expression—Staring Boy, meet Staring Man. I tried to step casually off the barstool, but instead I stumbled and nearly fell. "Oopsie-daisy!" Mr. Mickleson said, and my father gave him a hard look, a careful glare that checked Mr. Mickleson's grin. He shrugged.

"Ah, children, children," he said confidingly to my father, as I hurried quickly to the door. I heard my father start to speak sharply as I left, but I didn't have the nerve to stick around to hear what was said.

Instead, I crept along the outside of the bar; I staked out Mickleson's old Volkswagen and found it locked. There were no windows into the bar, so I pressed myself against the wall, trying to listen. I tried to think what I would write in my notebook: that look he'd given me, his grinning mimicry of my stare. "I believe I know you," he said. What, exactly, did he know?

And then I had a terrible thought. Where was the notebook? I imagined, for a moment, that I had left it there, on the bar, next to my drink. I had the dreadful image of Mr. Mickleson's eyes falling on it, the theme book cover, which was decorated with stylized question marks, and on which I'd written: Andy O'Day Mystery Series #67: The Detective Meets the Dreadful Double! I saw him smiling at it, opening it, his eyes narrowing as he saw his photo pasted there on the first page.

But it wasn't in the bar. I was sure it wasn't, because I remembered not having it when I went in. I didn't have it with me, I knew, and I began to backtrack, step by step, from the Studebaker to lunchtime to my bedroom, and then I saw it, with the kind of perfect clarity my memory has always been capable of, despite everything.

I saw myself in Mickleson's living room, on my knees in front of a box of his letters. I had copied something in the notebook and put it down on the floor. It was right there, next to the box. I could see it as if through a window, and I stood there observing the image in my mind's eye, as my mother came around the corner, into the parking lot.

"Andy!" she said. "I've been calling for you! Where the hell have you been?"

She was in one of her moods. "I am so sick of this!" she said and gave me a hard shake as she grabbed my arm. "You God damned lazy kids just think you can do as you please, all the God damn day long! The house is a pig sty, and not a one of you will bend a finger to pick up your filthy clothes or even wash a dish." She gritted her teeth, her voice trembling, and slammed into the house, where Mark was scrubbing the floor and Kathy was standing at the sink, washing dishes. Mark glared up at me, his eyes red with crying and self-pity and hatred. I knew he was going to hit me as soon as she left. "Clean, you brats!" my mother cried. "I'm going to work, and when I get home I want this house to shine!" She was in the frilly blouse and makeup she wore when she tended bar, beautiful and flushed, her eyes hard. "I'm not going to live like this anymore. I'm not going to live this kind of life!"

"She was a toxic parent," Mark says now, in one of our rare phone conversations. "A real psycho. It haunts me, you know, the shit that we went through. It was like living in a house of terror, you know? Like, you know, a dictatorship or something. You never knew what was next, and that was the scariest part. There was a point, I think, where I really just couldn't take it anymore. I really wanted to die." I listen as he draws on his cigarette and then exhales, containing the fussy spitefulness that's creeping into his voice. "Not that you'd remember. It always fell on me, whatever it was. They thought you were so cute and spacey; you were always checked out in La-La Land while I got the brunt of everything."

I listen but don't listen. I'm on the deck behind my house, with my cell phone, reclining, watching my daughters jump through the sprinkler. Everything is green and full of sunlight, and I might as well be watching an actor portraying me in the happy ending of a movie of my life. I've never told him about my blackouts, and I don't now, though they have been bothering me again lately. I can imagine what he would come up with: fugue states, repressed memories, multiple personalities. Ridiculous stuff.

"It all seems very far away to me," I tell Mark, which is not true exactly, but it's part of the role I've been playing for many years now. "I don't really think much about it."

This much is true: I barely remember what happened that night. I wasn't even there, among the mundane details of children squabbling and cleaning and my mother's ordinary unhappiness. I was the Detective!—driving my sleek Studebaker through the streets of Beck, nervous though not panicked, edgy and white-knuckled but still planning with steely determination: the notebook! The notebook must be retrieved! Nothing else was really happening, and when I left the house, I was in a state of focused intensity.

It must have been about eleven o'clock. Mark had been especially evil and watchful, and it wasn't until he'd settled down in front of the television with a big bowl of ice cream that I could pretend, at last, to go to bed.

Outside, out the door, down the alley: it seems to me that I should have been frightened, but mostly I recall the heave of adrenaline and determination, the necessity of the notebook, the absolute need for it. It was my story.

The lights were on at Mickleson's house, a bad sign, but I moved forward anyway, into the dense and dripping shadows of his yard, the crickets singing thickly, my hand already extended to touch the knob of his back door.

It wasn't locked. It didn't even have to be jimmied; it gave under the pressure of my hand, a little electrical jolt across my skin, the door opening smooth and uncreaking, and I passed like a shadow into the narrow back foyer that led to the kitchen. There was a silence in the house, and for a moment I felt certain that Mickleson was asleep. Still, I moved cautiously. The kitchen was brightly fluorescent and full of dirty dishes and beer cans. I slid my feet along the tile, inching along the wall. Silence, and then Mickleson's voice drifted up suddenly, a low mumble and then a firmer one, as if he were contradicting himself. My heart shrank. *Now what?* I thought as I came to the edge of the living room.

Mickleson was sitting in his chair, slumping, his foot jiggling with irritation. I heard the sail-like snap of a turning page, and I didn't even have to look to know that the notebook was in his hands. He murmured again as I stood there. I felt lightheaded. *The notebook!* I thought and leaned against the wall. I felt my head bump against something, and Mr. Mickleson's plaque tilted, then fell. I fumbled for a moment before I caught it.

But the sound made him turn. There I was, dumbly holding the slice of wood, and his eyes rested on me. His expression seemed to flicker with surprise, then terror, then annoyance, before settling on a kind of blank amusement. He cleared his throat.

"I believe I see a little person in my house," he said, and I might have fainted. I could feel the Detective leaving me, shriveling up and slumping to the floor, a suit of old clothes; the city of Beck disintegrated in the distance, streets drying up like old creek beds, skyscrapers sinking like ocean liners into the wheat fields. I was very still, his gaze pinning me. "A ghostly little person," he said, with satisfaction. He stood up for a moment, wavering, and then stumbled back against the chair for support, a look of affronted dignity freezing on his face. I didn't move.

"Well, well," he said. "Do I dare assume that I am in the presence of the author of this"—he waved my notebook vaguely—"this document?" He paused, thumbing through it with an exaggerated, mime-like gesture. "Hmm," he murmured, almost crooning. "So—imaginative! And—there's a certain—charm—about it—I think." And then he leaned toward me. "And so at last we meet, Detective O'Day!" he said, in a deep voice. "You may call me Professor Moriarty!" He made a strange shape with his mouth and laughed softly—it wasn't sinister exactly, but musing, as if he'd just told himself a good joke, and I was somehow in on it.

"Why so quiet?" he exclaimed and waggled the notebook at me. "Haven't you come to find your future, young Detective?" I watched as he pressed his fingers to his temples, like a stage medium. "Hmm," he said and began to wave his arms and fingers in a seaweed-like floating motion, as if casting a magic spell or performing a hula dance. "Looking for his future," he said. "What lies in wait for Andy O'Day? I ask myself that question frequently. Will he grow up to be . . ."—and here he read aloud from my journal—". . . 'troglodytic' and 'sinister'? Will he ever escape the sad and lonely life of a Detective, or will he wander till the end of his days through the grim and withering streets of Beck?"

He paused then and looked up from my journal. I thought for a moment that if I leapt out, I could snatch it from him, even though the things I had written now seemed dirty and pathetic. I thought to say, "Give me back my notebook!" But I didn't really want it anymore. I just stood there, watching him finger the pages, and he leaned toward me, wavering, his eyes not exactly focused on me, but on some part of my fore-head or shoulder or hair. He smiled, made another small effort to stand, then changed his mind. "What will happen to Andy O'Day?" he said again, thoughtfully. "It's such a compelling question, a very lovely question, and I can tell you the answer. Because, you see, I've come through my time machine to warn you! I have a special message for you from the future. Do you want to know what it is?"

"No," I said at last, my voice thick and uncertain.

"Oh, Andy," he said, as if very disappointed. "Andy, Andy. Look! Here I am!" He held his arms out wide, as if I'd run toward them. "Your Dreadful Double!" I watched as he straightened himself, correcting the slow tilt of his body. "I know you," Mr. Mickleson said. His head drooped, but he kept one eye on me. "You must be coming to me—for something?"

I shook my head. I didn't know. I couldn't even begin to imagine, and yet I felt—not for the last time—that I was standing in a desolate and empty prairie, the fields unraveling away from me in all directions, and the long winds running through my hair.

"Don't you want to know a secret?" he said. "Come over here, I'll whisper in your ear."

And it seemed to me, then, that he did know a secret. It seemed to me that he would tell me something terrible, something I didn't want to hear. I watched as he closed my notebook and placed it neatly on the coffee table, next to the *TV Guide.* He balanced himself on two feet, lifting up and lurching toward me. "Hold still," he murmured. "I'll whisper."

I turned and ran.

I once tried to explain this incident to my wife, but it didn't make much sense to her. She nodded, as if it were merely strange, merely puzzling. "Hmmm," she said, and I thought that perhaps it *was* odd to remember this time so vividly, when I remembered so little else. It *was* a little ridiculous that I should find Mr. Mickleson on my mind so frequently.

"He was just a drunk," my wife said. "A little crazy, maybe, but. . . ." And she looked into my face, her lips pursing. "He didn't . . . *do* anything to you, did he?" she said, awkwardly, and I shook my head.

"No—no," I said. And I explained to her that I never saw Mr. Mickleson again. I avoided the house after that night, of course, and when school started he wasn't teaching Science 7. We were told, casually, that he had had an "emergency," that he had been called away, and when, after a few weeks, he still didn't return, he was replaced without comment by an elderly lady substitute, who read to us from the textbook—*The World of Living Things*—in a lilting storybook voice, and who whispered, "My God," as she watched us, later, dissecting earthworms, pinning them to corkboard and exposing their many hearts. We never found out where Mr. Mickleson had gone.

"He was probably in rehab," my wife said sensibly. "Or institutionalized. Your father was right. He was just a weirdo. It doesn't seem that mysterious to me."

Yes. I nodded a little, ready to drop the subject. I couldn't very well explain the empty longing I had felt, the eager dread that would wash over me, going into the classroom and thinking that he might be sitting there behind the desk, waiting. It didn't make sense, I thought, and I couldn't explain it, any more than I could explain why he remained in my mind as I crisscrossed the country with my family, any more than I could explain why he seemed to be there when I thought of them, even now: Mark, fat and paranoid, on his houseboat; my mother in Mexico, nodding over a cocktail; Kathy, staring at a spider in the corner of her room in the group home, her eyes dull; my father, frightened, calling me on the phone as his liver failed him, his body decomposing in a tiny grave in Idaho that I'd never visited. How could I explain that Mickleson seemed to preside over these thoughts, hovering at the edge of them like a stage director at the back of my mind, smiling as if he'd done me a favor?

I didn't know why he came into my mind as I thought of them, just as I didn't know why he seemed to appear whenever I told lies. It was just that I could sense him. *Yes,* he whispered as I told my college friends that my father was an archaeologist living in Peru, that my mother was a former actress; *yes,* he murmured when I lied to my father about Katrina; *yes,* as I make excuses to my wife, when I say I am having dinner with a client when in fact I am tracing another path entirely—following a young family as they stroll through the park, or a whistling old man who might be my father, if he'd gotten away, or a small, brisk-paced woman who looks like Katrina might, if Katrina weren't made up. How can I explain that I walk behind this Katrina woman for many blocks, living a different life, whistling my old man tune?

I can't. I can't explain it, no more than I can admit that I still have Mickleson's plaque, just as he probably still has my notebook; no more than I can explain why I take the plaque out of the bottom drawer of my desk and unwrap the tissue paper I've folded it in, reading the inscription over, like a secret message: "I wear the chains I forged in life." I know it's just a cheap Dickens allusion, but it still seems important. I can hear him say, "Hold still. I'll whisper."

"Hmmm," my wife would say, puzzled and perhaps a bit disturbed. She's a practical woman, and so I say nothing. It's probably best that she doesn't think any more about it, and I keep to myself the private warmth I feel when I sense a blackout coming, the darkness clasping its hands over my eyes. It's better this way—we're all happy. I'm glad that my wife will be there when I awake, and my normal life, and my beautiful daughters, looking at me, wide-eyed, staring.

"Hello?" my wife will say, and I'll smile as she nudges me. "Are you there?" she'll say. "Are you all right?" she'll whisper.

SPECIAL AWARD FOR CONTINUING ACHIEVEMENT

Floating Bridge

By Alice Munro

INTRODUCED BY MONA SIMPSON

Writers love Alice Munro for her ability, like Chekhov's, to compress whole lives, long marriages, without miniaturizing. We feel we've read a novel in twenty pages.

She understands class and shows us a world's nuanced social hierarchies. To some readers, it may seem that Alice Munro's people are all of one class. But to themselves, of course, they are not. And we learn, through such stories as "A Real Life" and "Floating Bridge," how class is built, phrase by phrase, invitation by lapsed invitation. She renders the universal elements of human nature that crave distinction.

It's a great pleasure, reading, to recognize something one knows personally, even privately. Alice Munro has an uncanny knack for mining and showing us emotional positions (the internal equivalent of Degas's woman leaning over a bathtub to dry her legs) we understand from life but have never before found captured in language, in a book. This experience seems to enlarge the reader, even to embolden the reader, to instill his or her own sensibility with more importance by carving into words what he or she has felt before, perhaps fleeting, but never told anyone.

In the stories of the last two volumes, Alice Munro ambitiously extends the realm of her material to encompass a kind of intuition that is as close as an American writer has come to an organic, homegrown supernaturalism or surrealism. When I consider all of the scenes in which a character sees into the past or future (the package on the stairs, for example, or the hand on the stove) I would venture a guess that Alice Munro herself "believes" them. They are that earned.

Alice Munro jars us. In "Floating Bridge," the way she mentions Neal's infatuations ("It would be over some boy at the school. . . . A mushy look, an apologetic yet somehow defiant bit of giggling.") while we, the readers, feel his palpable crush on a girl from the smile he can't seem to keep off his face assumes and somehow proves the easy existence of bisexuality.

More than any other contemporary writer, Alice Munro excavates packed and resonant expressions of North American vocal English. Her ear resurrects phrases, words, even pronunciations that chime with the feeling of a particular time and place, like "Don't be scairt" in "Floating Bridge."

Usually, when we say we admire a writer for his or her linguistic gift, we think fancy. Piled similes, overlapping metaphors, late James, middle to late Joyce. But Munro is a poet in her use of repetition, transposition, a kind of prose rhyme. "Floating Bridge" begins with an inside-out fairy tale. "One time, *she had left him.*" But in this once upon a time, our heroine came back. She was unsure of her anger ("perhaps it was petty?"). Later, she'd asked Neal if he would have thought to come looking for her. He'd answered, "Of course. Given time." In the story's last paragraph (I'm tempted to write "stanza") Jinny felt "a rain of compassion, almost like laughter. A swish of tender hilarity, getting the better of her sores and hollows, for the time given." The story is about given time, the difference between Neal's conditional "given time," with its implicit "if" and "enough" and the final "time given" by life or God or whomever reprieves. There is a physical manifestation of divine reprieve: a young man, who, like Jinny, doesn't ever wear watches, but nonetheless understands time enough to give her a kiss that is much more complex than the prelude to a sequence the word "kiss" usually suggests.

Munro's humanity sounds most often in the generosity characterized by surprise. This seems to be a story about resistance, in which Life forces a character to a hard point of recognition that may necessitate action, an action that she, the character, dreads. The difficult realizations all register, put into stark relief by the kindness, courteous and crude, of extra, peripheral men. But with the arrival of the final character, a laughter bubbles up and our heroine feels suffused with forgiveness.

Great stories endure use, opening sometimes to the reader on the tenth or eleventh turn, much the way language may refine and blossom for the writer in later drafts. I return to Alice Munro's stories to find ways into "the world beneath the world," as James Merrill wrote. I've read "Floating Bridge" a dozen times already. With each round, my understanding deepens. I know I will reread "Floating Bridge."

—MONA SIMPSON

Alice Munro

Floating Bridge

From *The New Yorker*

ONE TIME, she had left him. The immediate reason was fairly trivial. He had joined a couple of the Young Offenders ("Yo-yos" was what he called them) in gobbling up a gingerbread cake she had just made, and had been intending to serve after a meeting that evening. Unobserved—at least by Neal and the Yo-yos—she had left the house and gone to sit in a three-sided shelter on the main street, where the city bus stopped twice a day. She had never been in there before, and she had a couple of hours to wait. She sat and read everything that had been written on or cut into those wooden walls. Various initials loved each other 4 ever. Laurie G. sucked cock. Dunk Cultis was a fag. So was Mr. Garner (Math).

Eat Shit. H.W. Gange rules. God hates filth. Kevin S. Is Dead meat. Amanda W is beautiful and sweet and I wish they did not put her in jail because I miss her with all my heart. I want to fuck V.P. Ladies have to sit here and read this disgusting dirty things what you write. Fuck them.

Looking at this barrage of human messages—and puzzling in particular over the heartfelt, very neatly written sentence concerning Amanda W—Jinny wondered if people were alone when they wrote such things. And she went on to imagine herself sitting here or in some similar place, waiting for a bus, alone as she would surely be if she went ahead with the plan she was set on now. Would she be compelled to make statements on public walls?

She felt herself connected at present to those people who had had to write certain things down—connected by her feelings of anger and petty outrage (perhaps it was petty?), and by her excitement at what she was doing to Neal, to pay him back. It occurred to her that the life she was carrying herself into might not give her anybody to be effectively angry at, or anybody who owed her anything, who could possibly be rewarded or punished or truly affected by what she might do. She was not, after all, somebody people flocked to. And yet she was choosy, in her own way.

The bus was still not in sight when she got up and walked home. Neal was not there. He was returning the boys to the school, and by the time he got back, somebody had already arrived for the meeting. She told Neal what she'd done, but only when she was well over it and it could be turned into a joke. In fact, it became a joke she told in company—leaving out or just describing in a general way the things she'd read on the walls.

"Would you ever have thought to come after me?" she said to Neal.

"Of course. Given time."

The oncologist had a priestly demeanor and even wore a black turtleneck shirt under a white smock—an outfit that suggested he had just come from some ceremonial mixing and dosing. His skin was young and smooth—it looked like butterscotch. On the dome of his head, there was just a faint black growth of hair, a delicate sprouting, very like the fuzz Jinny was sporting herself, though hers was brownish-gray, like mouse fur. At first, Jinny had wondered if he could possibly be a patient as well as a doctor. Then, whether he had adopted this style to make the patients more comfortable. More likely it was a transplant. Or just the way he liked to wear his hair.

You couldn't ask him. He came from Syria or Jordan—someplace where doctors kept their dignity. His courtesies were frigid.

"Now," he said, "I do not wish to give a wrong impression."

She went out of the air-conditioned building into the stunning glare of a late afternoon, in August, in Ontario. Sometimes the sun burned through, sometimes it stayed behind thin clouds—it was just as hot either way. She saw the car detach itself from its place at the curb and make its way down the street to pick her up. It was a light-blue, shimmery, sickening color. Lighter blue where the rust spots had been painted over. Its stickers said, "I Know I Drive a Wreck But You Should See My House," and "Honor Thy Mother—Earth," and (this was more recent) "Use Pesticide—Kill Weeds, Promote Cancer."

Neal came around to help her.

"She's in the car," he said. There was an eager note in his voice which registered vaguely as a warning or a plea. A buzz around him, a tension, that told Jinny it wasn't time to give him her news, if "news" was what you'd call it. When Neal was around other people, even one person other than Jinny, his behavior changed, becoming more animated, enthusiastic, ingratiating. Jinny was not bothered by that anymore—they had been together for twenty-one years. And she herself changed—as a reaction, she used to think—becoming more reserved and slightly ironic. Some masquerades were necessary, or just too habitual to be dropped. Like Neal's antique appearance—the bandanna headband, the rough gray ponytail, the little gold earring that caught the light like the gold rims around his teeth, and his shaggy outlaw clothes.

While Jinny had been seeing the doctor, Neal had been picking up the girl who was going to help them with their life now. He knew her from the Correctional Institute for Young Offenders, where he was a teacher and she had worked in the kitchen. The Correctional Institute was just outside the town where they lived, about thirty miles away. The girl had quit her kitchen job a few months ago and taken a job looking after a farm household where the mother was sick. Luckily she was now free.

"What happened to the woman?" Jinny had said. "Did she die?"

Neal said, "She went into the hospital."

"Same deal."

Neal had spent nearly all his spare time, in the years Jinny had been with him, organizing and carrying out campaigns. Not just political campaigns (those, too) but efforts to preserve historic buildings and bridges and cemeteries, to keep trees from being cut down both along the town streets and in isolated patches of old forest, to save rivers from poisonous runoff and choice land from developers and the local population from casinos. Letters and petitions were always being written, government departments lobbied, posters distributed, protests organized. The front room of their house had been the scene of rages of indignation (which gave people a lot of satisfaction, Jinny thought) and of confused propositions and arguments, and Neal's nervy buoyancy. Now it was suddenly emptied. The front room would become the sickroom. It made her think of when she first walked into the house, straight from her parents' split-level with the swag curtains, and imagined all those shelves filled with books, wooden shutters on the windows, and those beautiful Middle Eastern rugs she always forgot the name of, on the varnished floor. On the one bare wall, the Canaletto print she had bought for her room at college—Lord Mayor's Day on the Thames. She had actually put that up, though she never noticed it anymore.

They rented a hospital bed—they didn't really need it yet, but it was better to get one while you could, because they were often in short supply. Neal thought of everything. He hung up some heavy curtains that were discards from a friend's family room. Jinny thought them very ugly, but she knew now that there comes a time when ugly and beautiful serve pretty much the same purpose, when anything you look at is just a peg to hang the unruly sensations of your body on.

Jinny was forty-two, and until recently she had looked younger than her age. Neal was sixteen years older than she was. So she had thought that in the natural course of things she would be in the position he was in now, and she had sometimes worried about how she would manage it. Once, when she was holding his hand in bed before they went to sleep, his warm and present hand, she had thought that she would hold or touch this hand, at least once, when he was dead. And no matter how long she had foreseen this, she would not be able to credit it. To think of his not having some knowledge of this moment and of her brought on a kind of emotional vertigo, the sense of a horrid drop.

And yet—an excitement. The unspeakable excitement you feel when a galloping disaster promises to release you from all responsibility for your own life. Then from shame you must compose yourself, and stay very quiet.

"Where are you going?" he had said, when she withdrew her hand.

"No place. Just turning over."

She didn't know if Neal had any such feeling, now that it had turned out to be her. She had asked him if he was used to the idea yet. He shook his head.

She said, "Me neither."

Then she said, "Just don't let the Grief Counsellors in. They could be hanging around already. Wanting to make a preëmptive strike."

"Don't harrow me," he said, in a voice of rare anger.

"Sorry."

"You don't always have to take the lighter view."

"I know," she said. But the fact was that, with so much going on and present events grabbing so much of her attention, she found it hard to take any view at all.

"This is Helen," Neal said. "This is who is going to look after us from now on. She won't stand for any nonsense, either."

"Good for her," said Jinny. She put out her hand, once she was settled in the car. But the girl might not have seen it, low down between the two front seats.

Or she might not have known what to do. Neal had said that she came from an unbelievable situation, an absolutely barbaric family. Things had gone on that you could not imagine going on in this day and age. An isolated farm, a widower—a tyrannical, deranged, incestuous old man—with a mentally deficient daughter and the two girl children. Helen, the older one, who had run away at the age of fourteen after beating up on the old man, had been sheltered by a neighbor, who phoned the police. And then the police had come and got the younger sister and made both children wards of the Children's Aid. The old man and his daughter—that is, the children's father and their mother—were both placed in a psychiatric hospital. Foster parents took Helen and her sister, who were mentally and physically normal. They were sent to school and had a miserable time there, having to start first grade in their teens. But they both learned enough to be employable.

When Neal had started the car up, the girl decided to speak.

"You picked a hot enough day to be out in," she said. It was the sort of thing she might have heard people say, to start a conversation. She spoke in a hard, flat tone of antagonism and distrust, but even that, Jinny knew by now, should not be taken personally. It was just the way some people sounded—particularly country people—in this part of the world.

"If you're hot, you can turn the air-conditioner on," Neal said. "We've got the old-fashioned kind—just roll down all the windows."

The turn they made at the next corner was one Jinny had not expected. "We have to go to the hospital," Neal said. "Helen's sister works there, and she's got something Helen wants to pick up. Isn't that right, Helen?"

Helen said, "Yeah. My good shoes."

"Helen's good shoes." Neal looked up at the mirror. "Miss Helen Rosie's good shoes."

"My name's not Helen Rosie," said Helen. It seemed as if it was not the first time she had said this.

"I just call you that because you have such a rosy face," Neal said.

"I have not."

"You do. Doesn't she, Jinny? Jinny agrees with me—you've got a rosy face. Miss Helen Rosie-Face."

The girl did have tender pink skin. Jinny had also noticed her nearly white lashes and eyebrows, her blond baby-wool hair, and her mouth, which had an oddly naked look, not just the normal look of a mouth without lipstick. A fresh-out-of-the-egg look was what she had, as if one layer of skin were still missing, one final growth of coarser, grown-up hair. She must be susceptible to rashes and infections, quick to show scrapes and bruises, to get sores around the mouth and sties between her white lashes, Jinny thought. Yet she didn't look frail. Her shoulders were broad, she was lean but big-boned. She didn't look stupid, either, though she had a head-on expression like a calf's or a deer's. Everything must be right on the surface with her, her attention and the whole of her personality coming straight at you, with an innocent and—to Jinny—a disagreeable power.

They drove up to the main doors of the hospital, then, following Helen's directions, swung around to the back. People in hospital dressing gowns, some trailing their I.V.s, had come outside to smoke.

"Helen's sister works in the laundry," Neal said. "What's her name, Helen? What's your sister's name?"

"Muriel," said Helen. "Stop here. O.K. Here."

They were in a parking lot at the back of a wing of the hospital. There were no doors on the ground floor except a loading door, shut tight. Helen was getting out of the car.

"You know how to find your way in?" Neal said.

"Easy."

The fire escape stopped four or five feet above the ground, but she was able to grab hold of the railing and swing herself up, maybe wedging a foot against a loose brick, in a matter of seconds. Neal was laughing.

"Go get 'em, girl!" he said.

"Isn't there any other way?" said Jinny.

Helen had run up to the third floor and disappeared.

"If there is, she ain't a-gonna use it," Neal said.

"Full of gumption," said Jinny, with an effort.

"Otherwise she'd never have broken out," he said. "She needed all the gumption she could get."

Jinny was wearing a wide-brimmed straw hat. She took it off and began to fan herself.

Neal said, "Sorry. There doesn't seem to be any shade to park in."

"Do I look too startling?" Jinny said. He was used to her asking that.

"You're fine. There's nobody around here anyway."

"The doctor I saw today wasn't the same one I'd seen before. I thin this one was more important. The funny thing was he had a scalp th looked about like mine. Maybe he does it to put the patients at ease."

She meant to go on and tell him what the doctor had said, but the f ning took up most of her energy. He watched the building.

"I hope to Christ they didn't haul her up for getting in the wrong w he said. "She is just not a gal for whom the rules were made."

After several minutes, he let out a whistle.

"Here she comes now. Here-she-comes. Headin' down the h stretch. Will she, will she, will she have enough sense to stop befo jumps? Look before she leaps? Will she, will she—nope. Nope. Unh

Helen had no shoes in her hands. She got into the car and bang door shut and said, "Stupid idiots. First I get up there and this assh in my way. Where's your tag? You gotta have a tag. I seen you com the fire escape, you can't do that. O.K., O.K., I gotta see my sis can't see her now, she's not on her break. I know that. That's why I off the fire escape. I just need to pick something up. I don't want her. I'm not goin' to take up her time. I just gotta pick something you can't. Well, I can. Well, you can't. And then I start to holle *Muriel.* All their machines goin'. It's two hundred degrees in the know where she is, can she hear me or not. But she comes tearii as soon as she sees me—Oh, shit. Oh, shit, she says, I went and forgot. I phoned her up last night and reminded her, but there she forgot. I could've beat her up. Now you get out, he says stairs and out. Not by the fire escape, because it's illegal. Piss o

Neal was laughing and laughing and shaking his head.

Jinny said, "Could we just start driving now and get som think fanning is doing a lot of good."

"Fine," said Neal, and started the car and backed and turned around, and once more they were passing the familiar front of the hospital, with the same or different smokers parading by in their dreary hospital clothes with their I.V.s. "Helen will just have to tell us where to go."

He called into the back seat, "Helen."

"What?"

"Which way do we turn now to get to where your sister lives? Where your shoes are."

"We're not goin' to their place, so I'm not telling you. You done me one favor and that's enough." Helen sat as far forward as she could, pushing her head between Neal's seat and Jinny's.

They slowed down, turned into a side street. "That's silly," Neal said. "You're going thirty miles away, and you might not get back here for a while. You might need those shoes." No answer. He tried again. "Or don't you know the way? Don't you know the way from here?"

"I know it, but I'm not telling."

"So we're just going to have to drive around and around till you get ready to tell us."

They were driving through a part of town that Jinny had not seen before. They drove very slowly and made frequent turns, so that hardly any breeze went through the car. A boarded-up factory, discount stores, pawnshops. "Cash, Cash, Cash," said a flashing sign above barred windows. But there were houses, disreputable-looking old duplexes, and the sort of single wooden houses that were put up quickly, during the Second World War. In front of a corner store, some children were sucking on Popsicles.

Helen spoke to Neal. "You're just wasting your gas."

"North of town?" Neal said. "South of town? North, south, east, west, Helen, tell us which is best." On Neal's face there was an expression of conscious, helpless silliness. His whole being was invaded. He was brimming with foolish bliss.

"You're just stubborn," Helen said.

"You'll see how stubborn."

"I am, too. I'm just as stubborn as what you are."

It seemed to Jinny that she could feel the blaze of Helen's cheek, which was so close to hers. And she could certainly hear the girl's breathing, hoarse and thick with excitement and showing some trace of asthma.

The sun had burned through the clouds again. It was still high and brassy in the sky. Neal swung the car onto a street lined with heavy old trees, and somewhat more respectable houses.

"Better here?" he said to Jinny. "More shade for you?" He spoke in a lowered, confidential tone, as if what was going on in the car could be set aside for a moment. It was all nonsense.

"Taking the scenic route," he said, pitching his voice again toward the back seat. "Taking the scenic route today, courtesy of Miss Helen Rosie-Face."

"Maybe we ought to just go on," Jinny said. "Maybe we ought to just go on home."

Helen broke in, almost shouting. "I don't want to stop nobody from getting home."

"Then you can just give me some directions," Neal said. He was trying hard to get his voice under control, to get some ordinary sobriety into it. And to banish the smile, which kept slipping back in place no matter how often he swallowed it.

Half a slow block more, and Helen groaned. "If I got to, I guess I got to," she said.

It was not very far that they had to go. They passed a subdivision, and Neal, speaking again to Jinny said, "No creek that I can see. No estates either."

Jinny said, "What?"

"Amber Creek Estates. On the sign. They don't care what they say anymore. Nobody even expects them to explain it."

"Turn," said Helen.

"Left or right?"

"At the wrecker's."

They went past a wrecking yard, with the car bodies only partly hidden by a sagging tin fence. Then up a hill, and past the gates to a gravel pit, which was a great cavity in the center of the hill.

"That's them. That's their mailbox up ahead," Helen called out with some importance, and when they got close enough, she read out the name. "Matt and June Bergson. That's them."

A couple of dogs came barking down the short drive. One was large and black and one small and tan-colored, puppylike. They bumbled around at the wheels and Neal sounded the horn. Then another dog—this one more sly and purposeful, with a slick coat and bluish spots—slid out of the long grass.

Helen called to them to shut up, to lie down, to piss off. "You don't need to bother about any of them but Pinto," she said. "Them other two's just cowards."

They stopped in a wide, ill-defined space, where some gravel had been laid down. On one side was a barn or implement shed, tin covered, and over to one side of it, on the edge of a cornfield, an abandoned farmhouse. The house inhabited nowadays was a trailer, nicely fixed up with a deck and an awning, and a flower garden behind what looked like a toy fence. The trailer and its garden looked proper and tidy, while the rest of the property was littered with things that might have a purpose or might just have been left around to rust or rot.

Helen had jumped out and was cuffing the dogs. But they kept on running past her, and jumping and barking at the car, until a man came out of the shed and called to them. The threats and names he called were not intelligible to Jinny, but the dogs quieted down.

Jinny put on her hat. All this time, she had been holding it in her hand.

"They just got to show off," said Helen. Neal had got out, too, and was negotiating with the dogs in a resolute way. The man from the shed came toward them. He wore a purple T-shirt that was wet with sweat, clinging to his chest and stomach. He was fat enough to have breasts, and you could see his navel pushing out like a pregnant woman's.

Neal went to meet him with his hand out. The man slapped his own hand on his work pants, laughed, and shook Neal's. Jinny could not hear what they said. A woman came out of the trailer and opened the toy gate and latched it behind her.

"Muriel went and forgot she was supposed to bring my shoes," Helen called to her. "I phoned her up and everything, but she went and forgot anyway, so Mr. Lockley brought me out to get them."

The woman was fat, too, though not as fat as her husband. She wore a pink muumuu with Aztec suns on it, and her hair was streaked with gold. She moved across the gravel with a composed and hospitable air. Neal turned and introduced himself, then brought her to the car and introduced Jinny.

"Glad to meet you," the woman said. "You're the lady that isn't very well?"

"I'm O.K.," said Jinny.

"Well, now you're here, you better come inside. Come in out of this heat."

The man had come closer. "We got the air-conditioning in there," he said. He was inspecting the car, and his expression was genial but disparaging.

"We just came to pick up the shoes," Jinny said.

"You got to do more than that, now you're here," said the woman, June, laughing as if the idea of their not coming in was a scandalous joke. "You come in and rest yourselves."

"We wouldn't like to disturb your supper," Neal said.

"We had it already," said Matt. "We eat early."

"But there's all kinds of chili left," said June. "You have to come in and help clean up that chili."

Jinny said, "Oh, thank you. But I don't think I could eat anything. I don't feel like eating anything when it's this hot."

"Then you better drink something, instead," June said. "We got ginger ale, Coke. We got peach schnapps."

"Beer," Matt said to Neal. "You like a Blue?"

Jinny waved at Neal, asking him to come close to her window. "I can't do it," she said. "Just tell them I can't."

"You know you'll hurt their feelings," he whispered. "They're trying to be nice."

"But I can't."

He bent closer. "You know what it looks like if you don't."

"You go."

"You'd be O.K. once you got inside. The air-conditioning really would do you good."

Jinny just shook her head.

Neal straightened up.

"Jinny thinks she better just stay in the car and rest here in the shade," Neal said. "But I wouldn't mind a Blue, actually."

He turned back to Jinny with a hard smile. He seemed to her desolate and angry. "You sure you'll be O.K.?" he said for the others to hear. "Sure? You don't mind if I go in for a little while?"

"I'll be fine," said Jinny.

He put one hand on Helen's shoulder and one on June's shoulder, walking them companionably toward the trailer. Matt smiled at Jinny curiously, and followed. This time, when he called the dogs to come after him, Jinny could make out their names.

Goober. Sally. Pinto.

The car was parked under a row of willow trees. These trees were big and old, but their leaves were thin and gave a wavering shade. Still, to be alone was a great relief.

Earlier today, driving along the highway from the town where they lived, they had stopped at a roadside stand and bought some early apples. Jinny got one out of the bag at her feet and took a small bite—more or less to see if she could taste and swallow it and hold it in her stomach. It was all right. The apple was firm and tart, but not too tart, and if she took small bites and chewed seriously she could manage it.

She'd seen Neal like this—or something like this—a few times before. It would be over some boy at the school. A mention of the name in an off-hand, even belittling way. A mushy look, an apologetic yet somehow defiant bit of giggling. But that was never anybody she had to have around the house, and it could never come to anything. The boy's time would be up, he'd go away.

So would this time be up. It shouldn't matter. She had to wonder if it would have mattered less yesterday than it did today.

She got out of the car, leaving the door open so that she could hang on to the inside handle. Anything on the outside was too hot to hang on to for any length of time. She had to see if she was steady. Then she walked a little, in the shade. Some of the willow leaves were already going yellow. Some were already lying on the ground. She looked out from the shade at all the things in the yard.

A dented delivery van with both headlights gone and the name on the side painted out. A baby's stroller that the dogs had chewed the seat out of, a load of firewood dumped but not stacked, a pile of huge tires, a great number of plastic jugs and some oil cans and pieces of old lumber and a couple of orange plastic tarpaulins crumpled up by the wall of the shed. What a lot of things people could find themselves in charge of. As Jinny had been in charge of all those photographs, official letters, minutes of meetings, newspaper clippings, a thousand categories that she had devised and had been putting on disk when she had to go into chemo and everything got taken away. All those things might end up being thrown out. As all this might, if Matt died.

The cornfield was the place she wanted to get to. The corn was higher than her head now, maybe higher than Neal's head—she wanted to get into the shade of it. She made her way across the yard with this one thought in mind. The dogs, thank God, must have been taken inside.

There was no fence. The cornfield just petered out into the yard. She walked straight ahead into it, onto the narrow path between two rows. The leaves flapped in her face and against her arms like streamers of oil-cloth. She had to remove her hat, so they would not knock it off. Each stalk had its cob, like a baby in a shroud. There was a strong, almost sick-ening smell of vegetable growth, of green starch and hot sap.

What she had intended to do, once she got in there, was lie down. Lie down in the shade of these large, coarse leaves and not come out till she heard Neal calling her. Perhaps not even then. But the rows were too close together to permit that, and she was too busy thinking to take the trouble. She was too angry.

It was not about anything that had happened recently. She was remem-bering how a group of people had been sitting around one evening on the floor of her living room—or meeting room—playing one of those serious psychological games. One of those games that were supposed to make a person more honest and resilient. You had to say just what came into your mind as you looked at each of the others. And a white-haired woman named Addie Norton, a friend of Neal's, had said, "I hate to tell you this, Jinny, but whenever I look at you, all I can think of is—Nice Nelly."

Other people had said kinder things to her. "Flower child" or "Madonna of the Springs." She happened to know that whoever said that meant "Manon of the Springs," but she offered no correction. She was outraged at having to sit there and listen to people's opinions of her.

Everyone was wrong. She was not timid or acquiescent or natural or pure. When you died, of course, these wrong opinions were all that was left.

While this was going through her mind, she had done the easiest thing you can do in a cornfield—got lost. She had stepped over one row and then another, and probably got turned around. She tried going back the way she had come, but it obviously wasn't the right way. There were clouds over the sun again, so she couldn't tell where west was. And she had not checked which direction she was going when she entered the field, anyway, so that would not have helped. She stood still and heard nothing but the corn whispering away, and some distant traffic.

Her heart was pounding just like any heart that had years and years of life ahead of it.

Then a door opened, she heard the dogs barking and Matt yelling, and the door slammed shut. She pushed her way through stalks and leaves, in the direction of that noise. It turned out that she had not gone far at all. She had been stumbling around in one small corner of the field, the whole time.

Matt waved at her and warned off the dogs.

"Don't be scairt of them, don't be scairt," he called. He was going toward the car just as she was, though from another direction. As they got closer to each other, he spoke in a lower, perhaps more intimate, voice.

"You shoulda come and knocked on the door." He thought that she had gone into the corn to have a pee. "I just told your husband I'd come out and make sure you're O.K."

Jinny said, "I'm fine. Thank you." She got into the car but left the door open. He might be insulted if she closed it. Also, she felt too weak.

"He was sure hungry for that chili."

Who was he talking about?

Neal.

She was trembling and sweating and there was a hum in her head, as if a wire were strung between her ears.

"I could bring you some out if you'd like it."

She shook her head, smiling. He lifted up the bottle of beer in his hand—he seemed to be saluting her.

"Drink?"

She shook her head again, still smiling.

"Not even a drink of water? We got good water here."

"No, thanks." If she turned her head and looked at his purple navel, she would gag.

"You hear about this fellow going out the door with a jar of horseradish in his hand?" he said in a changed voice. "And his dad says to him, 'Where you goin' with that horseradish?'

"'Going to get a horse,' he says.

"Dad says, 'You're not goin' to catch a horse with no horseradish.'

"Fellow comes back next morning. Nice big horse on a halter. Puts it in the barn.

"Next day Dad sees him goin' out, bunch of branches in his hand.

"'What's them branches in your hand?'

"'Them's pussy willows—'"

"What are you telling me this for?" Jinny said, almost shaking. "I don't want to hear it. It's too much."

"What's the matter now?" Matt said. "All it is is a joke."

Jinny was shaking her head, squeezing her hand over her mouth.

"Never mind," he said. "I won't take no more of your time."

He turned his back on her, not even bothering to call to the dogs.

"I do not wish to give the wrong impression or get carried away with optimism." The doctor had spoken in a studious, almost mechanical way. "But it looks as if we have a significant shrinkage. What we hoped for, of course. But frankly, we did not expect it. I do not mean that the battle is over. But we can be to a certain extent optimistic and proceed with the next course of chemo and see how things look then."

What are you telling me this for? I don't want to hear it. It's too much.

Jinny had not said anything like that to the doctor. Why should she? Why should she behave in such an unsatisfactory and ungrateful way, turning his news on its head? Nothing was his fault. But it was true that what he had said made everything harder. It made her have to go back and start this year all over again. It removed a certain low-grade freedom. A dull, protecting membrane that she had not even known was there had been pulled away and left her raw.

Matt's thinking she had gone into the cornfield to pee had made her realize that she actually wanted to. Jinny got out of the car, stood cautiously, and spread her legs and lifted her wide cotton skirt. She had taken to wearing big skirts and no panties this summer, because her bladder was no longer under perfect control.

A dark stream trickled away from her through the gravel. The sun was down now. Evening was coming on, and there was a clear sky overhead. The clouds were gone.

One of the dogs barked halfheartedly, to say that somebody was coming but somebody they knew. They had not come over to bother her when she got out of the car—they were used to her now. They went running out to meet whoever it was, without any alarm or excitement.

It was a boy, a young man, riding a bicycle. He swerved toward the car and Jinny went round to meet him, a hand on the warm fender to support herself. When he spoke to her, she did not want it to be across her puddle. And maybe to distract him from even looking on the ground for such a thing, she spoke first. She said, "Hello. Are you delivering something?"

He laughed, springing off the bike and dropping it to the ground, all in one motion.

"I live here," he said. "I'm just getting home from work."

She thought that she should explain who she was, tell him how she came to be here and for how long. But all this was too difficult. Hanging on to the car like this, she must look like somebody who had just come out of a wreck.

"Yeah, I live here," he said. "But I work in a restaurant in town. I work at Sammy's."

A waiter. The bright-white shirt and black pants were waiters' clothes. And he had a waiter's air of patience and alertness.

"I'm Jinny Lockley," she said. "Helen. Helen is—"

"O.K., I know," he said. "You're who Helen's going to work for. Where's Helen?"

"In the house."

"Didn't nobody ask you in, then?"

He was about Helen's age, she thought. Seventeen or eighteen. Slim and graceful and cocky, with an ingenuous enthusiasm that would probably not get him as far as he hoped. Jinny had seen a few like that who ended up as Young Offenders. He seemed to understand things, though. He seemed to understand that she was exhausted and in some kind of muddle.

"June in there, too?" he said. "June's my mom."

His hair was colored like June's, gold streaks over dark. He wore it rather long, and parted in the middle, flopping off to either side.

"Matt, too?" he said.

"And my husband. Yes."

"That's a shame."

"Oh, no," she said. "They asked me. I said I'd rather wait out here."

Neal used sometimes to bring home a couple of his Yo-yos, to be supervised doing lawn work or painting or basic carpentry. He thought it was good for them, to be accepted into somebody's home. Jinny had flirted with them occasionally, in a way that she could never be blamed for. Just a gentle tone, a way of making them aware of her soft skirts and her scent of apple soap. That wasn't why Neal had stopped bringing them. He had been told it was out of order.

"So how long have you been waiting?"

"I don't know," Jinny said. "I don't wear a watch."

"Is that right?" he said. "I don't, either. I don't hardly ever meet another person that doesn't wear a watch. Did you never wear one?"

She said, "No. Never."

"Me neither. Never, ever. I just never wanted to. I don't know why. Never, ever wanted to. Like, I always just seem to know what time it is anyway. Within a couple minutes. Five minutes at the most. Sometimes one of the diners asks me, 'Do you know the time,' and I just tell them. They don't even notice I'm not wearing a watch. I go and check as soon as I can, clock in the kitchen. But I never once had to go in there and tell them any different."

"I've been able to do that, too, once in a while," Jinny said. "I guess you do develop a sense, if you never wear a watch."

"Yeah, you really do."

"So what time do you think it is now?"

He laughed. He looked at the sky.

"Getting close to eight. Six, seven minutes to eight? I got an advantage, though. I know when I got off of work, and then I went to get some cigarettes at the 7-Eleven, and then I talked to some guys a couple of minutes, and then I biked home. You don't live in town, do you?"

Jinny said no.

"So, where do you live?"

She told him.

"You getting tired? You want to go home? You want me to go in and tell your husband you want to go home?"

"No. Don't do that," she said.

"O.K. O.K. I won't. June's probably telling their fortunes in there anyway. She can read hands."

"Can she?"

"Sure. She goes in the restaurant a couple of times a week. Tea, too. Tea leaves."

He picked up his bike and wheeled it out of the way of the car. Then he looked in, through the driver's window.

"Keys in the car," he said. "So—you want me to drive you home or what? Your husband can get Matt to drive him and Helen when they get ready. And he can bring me back from your place. Or if it don't look like Matt can, June can. June's my mom, but Matt's not my dad. You don't drive, do you?"

"No," said Jinny. She had not driven for months.

"No. I didn't think so. O.K. then? You want me to? O.K.?"

"This is just a road I know. It'll get you there as soon as the highway."

They had not driven past the subdivision. In fact, they had headed the other way, taking a road that seemed to circle the gravel pit. At least they were going west now, toward the brightest part of the sky. Ricky—that was what he'd told her his name was—had not yet turned the car lights on.

"No danger meeting anybody," he said. "I don't think I ever met a single car on this road, ever. See—not so many people even know this road is here. And if I was to turn the lights on, then the sky would go dark, and everything would go dark, and you wouldn't be able to see where you were. We just give it a little while more, so then when it gets dark, we can see the stars, that's when we turn the lights on."

The sky was like very faintly colored glass—red or yellow or green or blue glass, depending on which part of it you looked at. The bushes and trees would turn black, once the lights were on. There would just be black clumps along the road and the black mass of trees crowding in behind them, instead of, as now, the individual, still identifiable, spruce and cedar and feathery tamarack, and the jewelweed with its flowers like winking bits of fire. It seemed close enough to touch, and they were going slowly. She put her hand out.

Not quite. But close. The road seemed hardly wider than the car.

She thought she saw the gleam of a full ditch ahead. "Is there water down there?" she said.

"Down there?" said Ricky. "Down there and everywhere. There's water to both sides of us and lots of places, water underneath us. Want to see?"

He slowed the car down and stopped. "Look down your side," he said. "Open the door and look down."

When she did that, she saw that they were on a bridge. A little bridge, no more than ten feet long, of crosswise-laid planks. No railings. And motionless water.

"Bridges all along here," he said. "And where it's not bridges it's culverts. 'Cause it's always flowing back and forth under the road. Or just laying there and not flowing."

"How deep?" she said.

"Not deep. Not this time of year. Not till we get to the big pond—it's deeper. And then, in spring, it's all over the road, you can't drive here, it's deep then. This road goes flat for miles and miles, and it goes from one end to the other. There isn't even any road that cuts across it. This is the only road I know of through the Borneo Swamp."

Jinny said, "Borneo Swamp? There is an island called Borneo. It's halfway round the world."

"I don't know about that. All I ever heard of was just the Borneo Swamp."

There was a strip of dark grass now, growing down the middle of the road.

"Time for the lights," he said. He switched them on, and they were in a tunnel in the sudden night. "Once I turned the lights on like that, and there was this porcupine. It was just sitting there in the middle of the road, sitting up on its hind legs, and looking right at me. Like some little tiny old man. It was scared to death and it couldn't move. I could see its little old teeth chattering."

Jinny thought, This is where he brings his girls.

"So what do I do? I tried beeping the horn, and it still didn't do anything. I didn't feel like getting out and chasing it. He was scared, but he still was a porcupine and he could let fly. So I just parked there. I had time. When I turned the lights on again, he was gone." Now the branches really did reach the car and brush against the door, but if there were flowers she could not see them.

"I am going to show you something," he said. "I'm going to show you something like I bet you never seen before."

If this had been happening back in her old, normal life, it's possible that she might now have begun to be frightened. If she were back in her old, normal life she would not be here at all.

"You're going to show me a porcupine," she said.

"Nope. Not that."

A few miles farther on, he turned off the lights. "See the stars?" he said. He stopped the car. Everywhere, there was at first a deep silence. Then this silence was filled in, at the edges, by some kind of humming that could have been faraway traffic, and little noises that passed before you properly heard them, that could have been made by birds or bats or night-feeding animals.

"Come in here in the springtime," he said, "you wouldn't hear nothing but the frogs. You'd think you were going deaf with the frogs." He opened the door on his side.

"Now. Get out and walk a ways with me."

She did as she was told. She walked in one of the wheel tracks, he in the other. The sky seemed to be lighter ahead, and there was a different sound—something like mild and rhythmical conversation. The road turned to wood and the trees on either side were gone.

"Walk out on it," he said. "Go on."

He came close and touched her waist, guiding her. Then he took his hand away, left her to walk on these planks, which were like the deck of a boat. Like the deck of a boat, they rose and fell. But it wasn't a movement of waves, it was their footsteps, his and hers, that caused this rising and falling of the boards beneath them. "Now do you know where you are?" he said.

"On a dock?" she said.

"On a bridge. This is a floating bridge."

Now she could make it out—the plank roadway just a few inches above the still water. He drew her over to the side, and they looked down. There were stars riding on the water.

"It's dark all the time," he said proudly. "That's because it's a swamp. It's got the same stuff in it tea has got, and it looks like black tea."

She could see the shoreline, and the reed beds. Water in the reeds, lapping water, was what was making that sound.

"Tannin," she said.

The slight movement of the bridge made her imagine that all the trees and the reed beds were set on saucers of earth and the road was a floating ribbon of earth and underneath it all was water.

It was at this moment that she realized she didn't have her hat. She not only didn't have it on, she hadn't had it with her in the car. She had not been wearing it when she got out of the car to pee and when she began to talk to Ricky. She had not been wearing it when she sat in the car with her head back against the seat and her eyes closed, when Matt was telling his joke. She must have dropped it in the cornfield, and in her panic left it there.

While she had been scared of seeing the mound of Matt's navel with the purple shirt plastered over it, he had been looking at her bleak knob.

"It's too bad the moon isn't up yet," Ricky said. "It's really nice here when the moon is up."

"It's nice now, too."

He slipped his arms around her as if there were no question at all about what he was doing and he could take all the time he wanted to do it. He kissed her mouth. It seemed to her that this was the first time that she had ever participated in a kiss that was an event in itself. The whole story, all by itself. A tender prologue, an efficient pressure, a wholehearted probing and receiving, a lingering thanks, and a drawing away satisfied.

"Oh," he said. "Oh."

He turned her around, and they walked back the way they had come.

"So was that the first you ever been on a floating bridge?"

She said yes, it was.

He took her hand and swung it as if he would like to toss it.

"And that's the first time I ever kissed a married woman."

"You'll probably kiss a lot more of them," she said. "Before you're done."

He sighed. "Yeah," he said. "Yeah, I probably will."

Amazed, sobered, by the thought of his future.

She had a sudden thought of Neal, back on dry land. Neal also startled by the thought of the future, giddy and besotted and disbelieving, as he opened his hand to the gaze of the woman with bright streaks in her hair.

Jinny felt a rain of compassion, almost like laughter. A swish of tender hilarity, getting the better of her sores and hollows, for the time given.

Fred G. Leebron

That Winter

From *TriQuarterly*

I T WAS the winter that once again he did not reach into the upper rack of year-end bonuses, the winter that his dad suffered through prostate cancer and his sister discovered that she was going to die, the winter that returning from seeing her in New York he endured three flat tires within ninety minutes. Three flat tires, his friends said. How could that be? And he would patiently explain the crummy patching job from the guy in Liberty Corners, the underinflated donut that blew after only a mile, the rain pouring down through the fog as he sat on the shoulder of 78 in the eight-year-old Civic wagon with his wife and their five-year-old and one-year-old and waited for help, for rescue. It was the winter of inch after inch of rainwater in the basement of their new home, it was the first winter of his new job in a new town, it was the winter when he woke every morning feeling oppressed and paranoid only to discover that by the end of each day his presentiments were justified. It was the winter when questions of death and life became so paramount for him that he actually tried to address them himself, that he spent evenings with his wife pondering aloud whether anyone should ever judge anyone else and yet wasn't a person's judgment what made him that particular person, the winter that he wondered if people denied the fact of their death even as they irreversibly slid toward it, the winter that he and his wife bandied about words like grace and mercy and debated just what the fuck they meant. It was a winter when he fought his rage and tried to titrate it as if it were an analgesic, the winter that his sister's doctor told him that for pain management he liked to go to narcotics early on in the process, and they both understood to what process he referred. It was the winter of death, a lot of imminent death, a lot of rain that had nothing to do with growth and everything to do with being buried, the winter that his kids astonished him with their resilience and obliviousness. It was the winter that he understood that everyone sat at a window, the window between what they were and what they could be, what they had and what they wanted, their own nature and the nature of an ongoing world.

It began with a phone call after a business trip, or perhaps it began years before, at the first opalescence inside his sister, that grew along her spine in prickly metastases, or even before then, within the unknown gland the name of which even an autopsy might fail to reveal, when the cells split, when her life divided. But that Saturday he sat managing his kids while his wife worked at the office. And the phone rang. Sylvie was building Tinker Toys. Henry wrestled the cat into the fridge. Wearily he rose from the step where he sat surveying them and retrieved the receiver.

"Hello," he said flatly, not hiding the fatigue, the annoyance, the it's-a-Saturday-leave-me-alone tone.

"Hey, Sweetie."

His mind backed up, not quite recognizing. "Hey."

"It's Elizabeth."

His middle sister. Of course. "Oh, hi. How are you?"

"Good, good. How was your trip? You sell a lot?"

"Never enough," he admitted.

"Isn't that how it is?"

"Oh yes." The small talk irritated him, but he stuck with it. She didn't call that often, she lived in London. For years they'd been close. But the distance had brought distance, though she'd come for the last family Thanksgiving.

"Is your lovely wife around?"

He marveled at the Anglo inflection. "No. She's at the office since I've been gone all week."

"And you're stuck with the kids."

"I wouldn't say stuck." He glanced at their perfect little heads. How beautifully they were playing. In that week of hotels he'd missed them, missed the way they smelled, how they crawled over him and drooled on him, how they laughed. "How'd your tests go?"

She'd been troubled by muscle stiffness and back pain for seven months. She'd visited an osteopath and a chiropractor, and at Thanksgiving an American doctor had recommended a battery of evaluations. They suspected something chronic, was what he recalled.

"Well, actually," she said, "that's why I'm calling. They didn't go so well."

"Oh," he said. He'd sat again on the step, the kids partially in view in the living room. He felt something odd going up inside his mind.

"I have advanced cancer," she said. "It's not curable."

"What," he said. "What does that mean?"

"He said it's two or three years on, moving slowly."

"Well," he said. He was struggling. He saw what was rising inside him and it was some kind of brick wall trying to shut her out, saying she lived far away, she lived in London, she was sick, he wasn't, his kids weren't, his wife wasn't, that his side of the brick wall was okay, that he could keep it okay. "Can they manage it?" he managed. "I mean, what are you saying?"

"It was the bone scan," she said clearly. "They said I've got something like forty tumors on my spine. Beyond that, I don't know."

"How's Richard?" he struggled to ask, feeling his forehead, how real and foreign it seemed at the same time.

"Richard is shattered," she said.

"Oh," he said again. In his mind, right inside his head, to his horror he saw the solidity of the brick wall. "What happens next?"

"A biopsy." God she was in control. "More tests. We'll get some results maybe Wednesday. They want to find the primary. Although," she paused, "and this is kind of odd, they said the fact that it was already in the bone meant that the original source may already be healed."

"Weird," he said.

"I'm sorry I had to tell you last. I called everyone else Thursday, when I knew, but I heard you were out of town and didn't want to lay this all on your wife."

"That was kind of you." What else could he say? That Thursday night he was out drinking beer with a new road buddy and doing a bit of Percodan.

"So," she said. "I guess I should be going."

"I'll call you after the doctor's appointment," he said. "I love you."

"I love you, too."

She hung up. He dialed his wife at the office.

"When are you coming home," he tried, his voice eroding.

"Well, I thought I'd—"

"—Come home," he said.

"What is it?"

"Just come home," he cried.

It was Chanukah. It was Christmas. It was a lot of gifts under the tree in a lot of different homes up and down the east coast. It was New Year's and sharing a half bottle of champagne and pouring the rest down the sink before turning in at eleven. It was long mornings that started at four or three and lasted five hours before he could pry himself from bed while his wife handled the children. It was gently cajoling, cajoling gently his sister back to the East, to New York, for a second opinion at the famously aggressive Tomkins Morrow Cancer Center while the rest of the family battered her about British passivity and incompetence. It was turgid phone calls with his mother, his other sisters, his brother, each of them preaching to the already converted on the need for Elizabeth to return to live in the States, where the care was better, where they could be with her. Tiredly he listened as they took her reluctance as personal rejection. He felt he knew what it was. That she didn't want to give into the cancer, that she didn't want it to change her life. And he thought, somewhere in his mind where the brick wall could have been, that she'd have to come to them, that she'd have to cross whatever barrier there was so they could face whatever there was to face together. How he dreaded and wanted that to happen.

It was New York, in the first shopping week of January, he and his wife and the kids staying at a buddy's apartment in Chelsea while the buddy stayed with his girlfriend in the Village and Elizabeth and Richard stayed uptown near Columbia where their brother worked, and the other sisters trained in from D.C. and Philadelphia, the family gathering as if for a funeral.

The day of the appointment he took his sister for a morning swim at the 92nd Street Y. Within a chlorinated vault he sat in a short balcony and watched her swim. There were a dozen other sickly looking swimmers, most in their sixties or seventies, and he wondered if they had cancer, too. She side-stroked facing him, and he tried to study her, the ringed eyes, the pale face. Was she really, truly dying? Could you die at forty having exercised every day, eaten right, done nothing to excess? Their mother was searching for blame, for fault. She complained there was something environmental wrong with London or the computers at his sister's office. The cancer books said you had to surrender your wrath. The cancer books said you had to live one day at a time, drink eight glasses of water, research the clinical trials, stay positive, acquire and strengthen your faith. They were written by survivors, people who had been handed death sentences yet had kept on living five, ten, fifteen, endless years. You wanted to believe them. You had to believe them. There were doctors who could do all the research for you, doctors who would charge $20,000 for their specially tailored cures, doctors who weren't even doctors. She swam with water cloaking her face.

In the lobby afterwards she walked slightly stooped.

"Do you have my wallet?" she said.

"I thought you had it."

"No, I gave it to you."

He ran back to the pool. The lifeguard waved to him as soon as he saw him. She'd entrusted him with her wallet and he'd nearly blown it. As he thanked the lifeguard he was trembling with gratitude and self-loathing.

Driving toward Columbia, each pothole jarred her pain loose and she moaned. I'm sorry, he kept saying. I'm sorry. He wondered how many people in New York had cancer. He'd done enough browsing in bookstores and clicking through the internet to rattle off that men had a one in x chance to getting it in a lifetime, women a one in y, the average life expectancy with cancer of an unknown primary was z and occurred in anywhere between a and b of all diagnosed cancers. Blah, blah, blah. She didn't want to hear the statistics. She hadn't wanted to come for this fancy second opinion. Ignorance could give her strength. Their family history was prostate cancer, he'd told one Tomkins Morrow screener. Well, the guy remarked drily, we can rule that out. It took him a short while to learn why that was. He was dumb and he was smart. He just wanted to be smart.

Upstairs in his brother's apartment, the children ran up and down the long hallway. His father sagged in a chair, his jowled face looking sad and exhausted. What they said about his own cancer was newly formulaic—that he would die of other shortcomings (his weight, his heart, his kidneys) before it could kill him. Twenty years before he had sat with his father in a car in late spring, while his sister and his mother shopped at a chaotic county flea market, and his father had sighed deeply and with tired eyes looked at him in the rearview mirror. "You know," he said, "I'm at the winter of my life." "You're fifty-one," his son had said, "what do you mean?" "I mean," he'd said, "I'm on my way out." For twenty years now, he'd been in this state of surrender and yet kept on living. The cancer authors wouldn't know what to make of the success of his defeatism.

In the hall his wife hid a look of mild harassment. His sister lay silent on a white couch.

"Can I get you anything?" he asked. She shook her head. "A glass of water?" She assented. They had to leave in twenty minutes for the appointment that had taken him two weeks of phone calls to schedule. He fed his sister sips of water, as if nursing her for the next performance. The children skittered and shrieked in the hallway. His wife kept coming in, quietly reminding them of the time. In a back room, his sister's husband fed e-mail to his London office. His sister drank a little more water. He *really* didn't want to hurry her.

"Okay." She winced as she rose from the couch. "I'm ready."

The line into the parking garage under Tomkins Morrow lasted twenty minutes, and along the corridors to their designated office suite were waiting room after waiting room packed like bus stations at Thanksgiving. Apparently, there were two kinds of people: those who had cancer, and those who were going to get it. At Tomkins Morrow the "cure" rate was well into double digits, and one thing was certain: even if you were essentially alone, sometimes it could be pretty hard to feel that way.

After an hour's wait beyond the scheduled appointment, the four of them—his mother, his sister, her husband, and he—were shown to an examining room. A nurse came in, thoughtful, smiling, and issued a warm and heartfelt greeting. She was like some kind of stewardess on a plane into the stratosphere of world-renowned oncological care. A quarter hour later came the Fellow, Eastern European. He interrogated Elizabeth in a friendly fashion, drew the curtain around her, examined her, and then informed them that shortly the Boss would come. Evidently the Boss was a cross between a rock star and the service manager at an auto repair center, a guy who didn't get his hands dirty but told you what the problem was and how much it was going to cost. Within ten minutes he arrived, tall, clipped brown hair fringed with gray. He looked at the ground as he walked. He strode right up to Elizabeth, snapped the curtain around her, felt in unknown places, whipped the curtain open, and pronounced himself ready to talk. At that point his pager beeped. He plucked up the desk phone, spoke briefly, rang off.

"That was what I was afraid of," he said. "I have a conference call. We'll move you all to another room and I'll be in as soon as I can."

In a corner office five stories up, overlooking a fruit stand and a hot dog cart, they talked giddily about how hungry they should be and how they could all hold off eating. The busy hum of people and machines sounded hopeful and American. At a certain point Elizabeth dialed another hospital and proceeded to try to schedule a third opinion. In the hallway they heard the Boss preparing to enter. Behind him trailed the Fellow.

The six of them sat at a small round table.

"I've reviewed all the results," the Boss said, crisply, matter-of-factly. "I think the physician in London did an excellent job working you up, and I confirm the diagnosis."

There followed a thirty minute Q and A where the Boss looked at his watch only once and everyone tiptoed around prognosis, choosing to land on issues of chemotherapy, hormone therapy, and the fact that searching for the primary rarely identifies it. Finally, Elizabeth's mother could wait no longer. She wanted to know: Where would the care be best?

"Wherever home is," the Boss said. "London is as good as New York in all aspects of treatment. In some ways, they're even ahead of us."

The brother was stunned. Tomkins Morrow was saying it was no better, Tomkins Morrow was declining to pursue. He looked long at the Boss. He was writing her off. Her case had no hope. The brother was devastated.

As he drove Elizabeth and Richard uptown, they forced shreds of conversation.

"I'm glad he said the care in London was excellent," Elizabeth said.

"That justifies the whole trip," said Richard.

By this time the brother understood that chemotherapy could kill you or make you stronger, that it was a complicated choice, that it was the only chance—and the most minute chance at that—for cure.

"Is there any roast turkey back at the apartment?" Elizabeth asked.

He nodded his head. She needed to keep her weight up. She needed to drink eight glasses of water a day. And sometime within the next three weeks, she needed to make a decision. There'd be radiation for pain. Beyond that, he could see nothing good. The books said you had to project yourself into that small surviving percentile. You had to lead the fight against your own disease. Elizabeth called it dis-ease. Once, when he was trying to arrange return tickets for them and they wanted the cheapest rate, he told her that the conditions weren't appropriate for sick people. "I am not sick," she said. "I'm sorry," he said, "I just don't think you can fly standby." "Oh," she said quietly, "that *is* right."

Back in their brother's apartment, he looked secretly at his wife and shook his head. His sister lay again on the white couch. The care in London was good. The big deal doctor had confirmed the diagnosis. Everything was fine.

Weeks and weeks. Months that could not quite make a season. Checks written for $275, $1800, to various alternative programs. The brother recalled the story of a movie star stricken with cancer, who traveled wherever he'd heard of a cure. Coffee enemas in Mexico, shark cartilage in Cuba, protein injections in the Bahamas. He died within the allotted time. Everybody dies, the brother consoled himself. I believe that the mind is merciful, his wife said. That she'll accept it with peace. At night, sometimes, he heard his wife talking on the phone to her sister about his sister, about her state of mind or her ovaries, and he wanted to rip the phone from her hand and scream, *that's my sister you're talking about.* Privacy, dignity—these were only abstractions. Did he get on the phone to his brother about her sister's wily boyfriend or her last dysplastic pap smear? He couldn't say anything to her. She flew with him on grueling trips to London, she sat with him in his sister's feng shui'd bedroom and talked about all the trivial things his sister yearned to discuss—celebrity weddings, interior design. On the flights home she reached across the armrest and held his hand and wouldn't let go. He needed her. He loved her. He just didn't want anyone judging his sister. What she tried. What she thought. What she wanted.

He wrote letters to various companies about the three blown tires and waited for checks in the mail. He tried to quit drinking. He tried to reach eight glasses of water a day. In the evening he mopped the basement and marveled how anyone had missed the fact that the sump pump did not occupy the lowest point in the floor. He e-mailed Elizabeth. She believed in God. She believed that God was everywhere. He told her about making Cajun meatloaf or shrimp with portabello mushrooms. He gossiped with her about his more successful colleagues. He signed every e-mail, I love you. She e-mailed, I love you, too.

He was offended by people who would ask if she had any children, as if that would make her illness that more unearned. He understood it was almost utilitarian—how many would be left behind, how many would be inconsolable? It was just weeks ago that he'd felt enraged by the year-end magazine features, Fifty Who Made a Difference, Twenty-five Who Have Left Us Bereft, as if only so few mattered in the annual summed obituaries. Again, it was utilitarian—how many lives had the lost lives diminished? In New York he had been harmed most by his buddy's girlfriend's clear-eyed pronouncement, as she crossed her legs, lit a cigarette, and looked him squarely in the heart: that perhaps this struggle was the reason his sister was brought to her life in the first place. The facts were these: she had no children, her job was in middle-tier investment banking. Why else should she be alive, but to face some form of the unspeakable?

He hated most the sense of the future, that for the world beyond his window there was always next week, next month, next year. Sometimes he found himself wishing for the mobs at Tomkins Morrow. How silent and polite they were, the only waiting room he'd ever been in where people actually moved so that families could sit together. Like Auschwitz, a friend told him.

Each morning he woke groping for an exit from this dream. They used to shoplift Lifesavers together from the Acme on Woodbine, when he was six and she was ten. In the dark room over the garage she practiced kissing on him before she pursued it with the sixth-grade boys—how he curled into her arms in the loud Naugahyde chair and she kept kissing him and kissing him, her pursed lips sloppily finding his face in the darkness. Ten years later they planned an elaborate tour of Europe together. They took a train all the way from Germany to Greece, boarded a ferry to an island, climbed steps to a white villa, purchased rooftop accommodations for fifty cents each. The next morning she awoke covered in hives or bites, scratching furiously. They tried to ignore and outlast the bumps, but within a day they multiplied like chicken pox and spread she said even to her genitals, and just a week after their trip had begun they had to bail out all the way back home to the States. When he was in college in New Jersey, he visited her once every few weeks in New York, where they ate and drank in tapas bars and he pretended that he liked her friends from work. One New Year's Eve they dressed up and went to all the parties, told everyone they were each other's dates. That kind of crap.

Before he was born, an uncle whom he would be named after lay dying of cancer, his brain growing mismashed. Close the Venetian blinds, he'd ask, when he meant, Turn off the television. His wife, sweet-faced, utterly gentle, attended him. They were childless. "A man as sick as I am," he managed to say once, quite clearly, "does not tell his wife his thoughts." What did that mean, Elizabeth's brother now wondered. Regret? Bitterness? Hatred? If life were the continuous pressure to understand—why do I love her, why does she love me, why do I hate my job, why do I love my children, why, why, why—then what did it mean to know it was going to end? He did not believe that you could take that understanding with you. What would be left between them when he stood beside her that last time in London? Was the purpose of accrued memory something like mercy, as his wife suggested? Or was mercy the release from exhaustion and pain? Couldn't denial—the instinct that even as you slipped under you still might emerge again—be merciful? Was grace acceptance or wishful thinking? He wanted to *know*. He couldn't know.

"We're all going to die," his New York buddy had said. "Isn't that wild? I mean, all of us are going to die."

It was the only solace he could find, that kind of universality. One's love could endure, one's work—a day, a week, a month, a year, a decade. One Hundred Who Made the Millennium—would be the next headline. He did not think that anyone he knew would be among them. Wasn't there comfort in that, in the essentially cozy, futile, hermetic quality of everyone's life? In eighth grade, a cranky Ukranian classmate, the skin of his stomach doubled into two belly-buttons by some past barbaric surgery, turned to him and sneered. "How many people do you think *really* care about you, really know you? What do you say, 100, 150?" He snickered. "I don't think so. You know what I think?" And the brother shrugged, wide-eyed. "I think twenty, max, if that. That's what I think."

"Sweetie," his sister called across the ocean past Valentine's Day, nearer the Millennium. "It all matters. Everything matters."

"I can't believe you haven't turned to God yet," a colleague said, studying him, the pointy chin of her face pointed at him. "Everybody turns to God in some form at times like these. Everybody."

He couldn't find God. He didn't have the impulse to look.

"Up until now," his brother said, "we've all been pretty lucky." Five siblings around their forties, two parents nearing their seventies. It was easy to see what he meant. The first wretchedness.

"You have to keep on living." Now who was saying that? Some idiot. He looked at his children and knew it to be true. He wanted to live. He looked at his wife and knew that there was so much more between them, unexplored, unknown, that he needed to reach, that he wanted to reach. He wanted her, he wanted the children.

"I hope you're finding a way to release your anxiety," Elizabeth wrote in an e-mail. "I don't want you to stress out about this."

She was dying, oh God she was dying. It was the winter that death was everywhere, that he woke every morning and could not escape it, that he kept feeling he was missing everybody, that he had to keep living, that death descended, that it was descending, that it hadn't yet arrived. It was the winter that death was everywhere. He never wanted it to end.

T. Coraghessan Boyle

The Love of My Life

From *The New Yorker*

T HEY WORE each other like a pair of socks. He was at her house, she was at his. Everywhere they went—to the mall, to the game, to movies and shops and the classes that structured their days like a new kind of chronology—their fingers were entwined, their shoulders touching, their hips joined in the slow triumphant sashay of love. He drove her car, slept on the couch in the family room at her parents' house, played tennis and watched football with her father on the big, thirty-six-inch TV in the kitchen. She went shopping with his mother and hers, a triumvirate of tastes, and she would have played tennis with his father, if it came to it, but his father was dead. "I love you," he told her, because he did, because there was no feeling like this, no triumph, no high—it was like being immortal and unconquerable, like floating. And a hundred times a day she said it, too: "I love you. I love you."

They were together at his house one night when the rain froze on the streets and sheathed the trees in glass. It was her idea to take a walk and feel it in their hair and on the glistening shoulders of their parkas, an otherworldly drumming of pellets flung down out of the troposphere, alien and familiar at the same time, and they glided the length of the front walk and watched the way the power lines bellied and swayed. He built a fire when they got back, while she towelled her hair and made hot chocolate laced with Jack Daniel's. They'd rented a pair of slasher movies for the ritualized comfort of them—"Teens have sex," he said, "and then they pay for it in body parts"—and the maniac had just climbed out of the heating vent, with a meat hook dangling from the recesses of his empty sleeve, when the phone rang.

It was his mother, calling from the hotel room in Boston where she was curled up—shacked up?—for the weekend with the man she'd been dating. He tried to picture her, but he couldn't. He even closed his eyes a minute, to concentrate, but there was nothing there. Was everything all right? she wanted to know. With the storm and all? No, it hadn't hit Boston yet, but she saw on the Weather Channel that it was on its way. Two seconds after he hung up—before she could even hit the Start button on the VCR—the phone rang again, and this time it was her mother. Her mother had been drinking. She was calling from the restaurant, and China could hear a clamor of voices in the background. "Just stay put," her mother shouted into the phone. "The streets are like a skating rink. Don't you even think of getting in that car."

Well, she wasn't thinking of it. She was thinking of having Jeremy to herself, all night, in the big bed in his mother's room. They'd been having sex ever since they started going together at the end of their junior year, but it was always sex in the car or sex on a blanket or the lawn, hurried sex, nothing like she wanted it to be. She kept thinking of the way it was in the movies, where the stars ambushed each other on beds the size of small planets and then did it again and again until they lay nestled in a heap of pillows and blankets, her head on his chest, his arm flung over her shoulder, the music fading away to individual notes plucked softly on a guitar and everything in the frame glowing as if it had been sprayed with liquid gold. That was how it was supposed to be. That was how it was going to be. At least for tonight.

She'd been wandering around the kitchen as she talked, dancing with the phone in an idle slow saraband, watching the frost sketch a design on the window over the sink, no sound but the soft hiss of the ice pellets on the roof, and now she pulled open the freezer door and extracted a pint box of ice cream. She was in her socks, socks so thick they were like slippers, and a pair of black leggings under an oversize sweater. Beneath her feet, the polished floorboards were as slick as the sidewalk outside, and she liked the feel of that, skating indoors in her big socks. "Uh-huh," she said into the phone. "Uh-huh. Yeah, we're watching a movie." She dug a finger into the ice cream and stuck it in her mouth.

"Come on," Jeremy called from the living room, where the maniac rippled menacingly over the Pause button. "You're going to miss the best part."

"O.K., Mom, O.K.," she said into the phone, parting words, and then she hung up. "You want ice cream?" she called, licking her finger.

Jeremy's voice came back at her, a voice in the middle range, with a congenital scratch in it, the voice of a nice guy, a very nice guy who could be the star of a TV show about nice guys: "What kind?" He had a pair of shoulders and pumped-up biceps, too, a smile that jumped from his lips to his eyes, and close-cropped hair that stood up straight off the crown of his head. And he was always singing—she loved that—his voice so true he could do any song, and there was no lyric he didn't know, even on the oldies station. She scooped ice cream and saw him in a scene from last summer, one hand draped casually over the wheel of his car, the radio throbbing, his voice raised in perfect synch with Billy Corgan's, and the night standing still at the end of a long dark street overhung with maples.

"Chocolate. Swiss-chocolate almond."

"O.K.," he said, and then he was wondering if there was any whipped cream, or maybe hot fudge—he was sure his mother had a jar stashed away somewhere, *Look behind the mayonnaise on the top row*—and when she turned around he was standing in the doorway.

She kissed him—they kissed whenever they met, no matter where or when, even if one of them had just stepped out of the room, because that was love, that was the way love was—and then they took two bowls of ice cream into the living room and, with a flick of the remote, set the maniac back in motion.

It was an early spring that year, the world gone green overnight, the thermometer twice hitting the low eighties in the first week of March. Teachers were holding sessions outside. The whole school, even the halls and the cafeteria, smelled of fresh-mowed grass and the unfolding blossoms of the fruit trees in the development across the street, and students— especially seniors—were cutting class to go out to the quarry or the reservoir or to just drive the backstreets with the sunroof and the windows open wide. But not China. She was hitting the books, studying late, putting everything in its place like pegs in a board, even love, even that. Jeremy didn't get it. "Look, you've already been accepted at your first-choice school, you're going to wind up in the top ten G.P.A.-wise, and you've got four years of tests and term papers ahead of you, and grad school after that. You'll only be a high-school senior once in your life. Relax. Enjoy it. Or at least *experience* it."

He'd been accepted at Brown, his father's alma mater, and his own G.P.A. would put him in the top ten per cent of their graduating class, and he was content with that, skating through his final semester, no math, no science, taking art and music, the things he'd always wanted to take but never had time for—and Lit., of course, A.P. History, and Spanish 5. *"Tú eres el amor de mi vida,"* he would tell her when they met at her locker or at lunch or when he picked her up for a movie on Saturday nights.

"Y tú también," she would say, "or is it *'yo también'*?"—French was her language. "But I keep telling you it really matters to me, because I know I'll never catch Margery Yu or Christian Davenport, I mean they're a lock for val and salut, but it'll kill me if people like Kerry Sharp or Jalapy Seegrand finish ahead of me—you should know that, you of all people—"

It amazed him that she actually brought her books along when they went backpacking over spring break. They'd planned the trip all winter and through the long wind tunnel that was February, packing away freeze-dried entrées, PowerBars, Gore-Tex windbreakers, and matching sweatshirts, weighing each item on a handheld scale with a dangling hook at the bottom of it. They were going up into the Catskills, to a lake he'd found on a map, and they were going to be together, without interruption, without telephones, automobiles, parents, teachers, friends, relatives, and pets, for five full days. They were going to cook over an open fire, they were going to read to each other and burrow into the double sleeping bag with the connubial zipper up the seam he'd found in his mother's closet, a relic of her own time in the lap of nature. It smelled of her, of his mother, a vague scent of her perfume that had lingered there dormant all these years, and maybe there was the faintest whiff of his father, too, though his father had been gone so long he didn't even remember what he looked like, let alone what he might have smelled like. Five days. And it wasn't going to rain, not a drop. He didn't even bring his fishing rod, and that was love.

When the last bell rang down the curtain on Honors Math, Jeremy was waiting at the curb in his mother's Volvo station wagon, grinning up at China through the windshield while the rest of the school swept past with no thought for anything but release. There were shouts and curses, T-shirts in motion, slashing legs, horns bleating from the seniors' lot, the school buses lined up like armored vehicles awaiting the invasion—chaos, sweet chaos—and she stood there a moment to savor it. "Your mother's car?" she said, slipping in beside him and laying both arms over his shoulders to pull him to her for a kiss. He'd brought her jeans and hiking boots along, and she was going to change as they drove, no need to go home, no more circumvention and delay, a stop at McDonald's, maybe, or Burger King, and then it was the sun and the wind and the moon and the stars. Five days. Five whole days.

"Yeah," he said, in answer to her question, "my mother said she didn't want to have to worry about us breaking down in the middle of nowhere—"

"So she's got your car? She's going to sell real estate in your car?"

He just shrugged and smiled. "Free at last," he said, pitching his voice down low till it was exactly like Martin Luther King's. "Thank God Almighty, we are free at last."

It was dark by the time they got to the trailhead, and they wound up camping just off the road in a rocky tumble of brush, no place on earth less likely or less comfortable, but they were together, and they held each other through the damp whispering hours of the night and hardly slept at all. They made the lake by noon the next day, the trees just coming into leaf, the air sweet with the smell of the sun in the pines. She insisted on setting up the tent, just in case—it could rain, you never knew—but all he wanted to do was stretch out on a gray neoprene pad and feel the sun on his face. Eventually, they both fell asleep in the sun, and when they woke they made love right there, beneath the trees, and with the wide blue expanse of the lake giving back the blue of the sky. For dinner, it was étouffée and rice, out of the foil pouch, washed down with hot chocolate and a few squirts of red wine from Jeremy's bota bag.

The next day, the whole day through, they didn't bother with clothes at all. They couldn't swim, of course—the lake was too cold for that—but they could bask and explore and feel the breeze out of the south on their bare legs and the places where no breeze had touched before. She would remember that always, the feel of that, the intensity of her motions, the simple unrefined pleasure of living in the moment. Wood smoke. Duelling flashlights in the night. The look on Jeremy's face when he presented her with the bag of finger-size crayfish he'd spent all morning collecting.

What else? The rain, of course. It came midway through the third day, clouds the color of iron filings, the lake hammered to iron, too, and the storm that crashed through the trees and beat at their tent with a thousand angry fists. They huddled in the sleeping bag, sharing the wine and a bag of trail mix, reading to each other from a book of Donne's love poems (she was writing a paper for Mrs. Masterson called "Ocular Imagery in the Poetry of John Donne") and the last third of a vampire novel that weighed eighteen-point-one ounces.

And the sex. They were careful, always careful—*I will never, never be like those breeders that bring their puffed-up squalling little red-faced babies to class,* she told him, and he agreed, got adamant about it, even, until it became a running theme in their relationship, the breeders overpopulating an overpopulated world and ruining their own lives in the process—but she had forgotten to pack her pills and he had only two condoms with him, and it wasn't as if there were a drugstore around the corner.

In the fall—or the end of August, actually—they packed their cars separately and left for college, he to Providence and she to Binghamton. They were separated by three hundred miles, but there was the telephone, there was E-mail, and for the first month or so there were Saturday nights in a motel in Danbury, but that was a haul, it really was, and they both agreed that they should focus on their course work and cut back to every second or maybe third week. On the day they'd left—and no, she didn't want her parents driving her up there, she was an adult and she could take care of herself—Jeremy followed her as far as the Bear Mountain Bridge and they pulled off the road and held each other till the sun fell down into the trees. She had a poem for him, a Donne poem, the saddest thing he'd ever heard. It was something about the moon. *More than moon,* that was it, lovers parting and their tears swelling like an ocean till the girl—the woman, the female—had more power to raise the tides than the moon itself, or some such. More than moon. That's what he called her after that, because she was white and round and getting rounder, and it was no joke, and it was no term of endearment.

She was pregnant. Pregnant, they figured, since the camping trip, and it was their secret, a new constant in their lives, a fact, an inescapable fact that never varied no matter how many home-pregnancy kits they went through. Baggy clothes, that was the key, all in black, cargo pants, flowing dresses, a jacket even in summer. They went to a store in the city where nobody knew them and she got a girdle, and then she went away to school in Binghamton and he went to Providence. "You've got to get rid of it," he told her in the motel room that had become a prison. "Go to a clinic," he told her for the hundredth time, and outside it was raining—or, no, it was clear and cold that night, a foretaste of winter. "I'll find the money—you know I will."

She wouldn't respond. Wouldn't even look at him. One of the "Star Wars" movies was on TV, great flat thundering planes of metal roaring across the screen, and she was just sitting there on the edge of the bed, her shoulders hunched and hair hanging limp. Someone slammed a car door—two doors in rapid succession—and a child's voice shouted, "Me! Me first!"

"China," he said. "Are you listening to me?"

"I can't," she murmured, and she was talking to her lap, to the bed, to the floor. "I'm scared. I'm so scared." There were footsteps in the room next door, ponderous and heavy, then the quick tattoo of the child's feet and a sudden thump against the wall. "I don't want anyone to know," she said.

He could have held her, could have squeezed in beside her and wrapped her in his arms, but something flared in him. He couldn't understand it. He just couldn't. "What are you thinking? Nobody'll know. He's a doctor, for Christ's sake, sworn to secrecy, the doctor-patient compact and all that. What are you going to do, keep it? Huh? Just show up for English 101 with a baby on your lap and say, 'Hi, I'm the Virgin Mary'?"

She was crying. He could see it in the way her shoulders suddenly crumpled and now he could hear it, too, a soft nasal complaint that went right through him. She lifted her face to him and held out her arms and he was there beside her, rocking her back and forth in his arms. He could feel the heat of her face against the hard fibre of his chest, a wetness there, fluids, her fluids. "I don't want a doctor," she said.

And that colored everything, that simple negative: life in the dorms, roommates, bars, bullshit sessions, the smell of burning leaves and the way the light fell across campus in great wide smoking bands just before dinner, the unofficial skateboard club, films, lectures, pep rallies, football— none of it mattered. He couldn't have a life. Couldn't be a freshman. Couldn't wake up in the morning and tumble into the slow steady current of the world. All he could think of was her. Or not simply her—her and him, and what had come between them. Because they argued now, they wrangled and fought and debated, and it was no pleasure to see her in that motel room with the queen-size bed and the big color TV and the soaps and shampoos they made off with as if they were treasure. She was pig-headed, stubborn, irrational. She was spoiled, he could see that now, spoiled by her parents and their standard of living and the socioeconomic expectations of her class—of his class—and the promise of life as you like it, an unscrolling vista of pleasure and acquisition. He loved her. He didn't want to turn his back on her. He would be there for her no matter what, but why did she have to be so *stupid?*

Big sweats, huge sweats, sweats that drowned and engulfed her, that was her campus life, sweats and the dining hall. Her dorm mates didn't know her, and so what if she was putting on weight? Everybody did. How could you shovel down all those carbohydrates, all that sugar and grease and the puddings and nachos and all the rest, without putting on ten or fifteen pounds the first semester alone? Half the girls in the dorm were waddling around like the Doughboy, their faces bloated and blotched with acne, with crusting pimples and whiteheads fed on fat. So she was putting on weight. Big deal. "There's more of me to love," she told her roommate, "and Jeremy likes it that way. And, really, he's the only one that matters." She was careful to shower alone, in the early morning, long before the light had begun to bump up against the windows.

On the night her water broke—it was mid-December, almost nine months, as best as she could figure—it was raining. Raining hard. All week she'd been having tense rasping sotto-voce debates with Jeremy on the phone—arguments, fights—and she told him that she would die, creep out into the woods like some animal and bleed to death, before she'd go to a hospital. "And what am I supposed to do?" he demanded in a high childish whine, as if he were the one who'd been knocked up, and she didn't want to hear it, she didn't.

"Do you love me?" she whispered. There was a long hesitation, a pause you could have poured all the affirmation of the world into.

"Yes," he said finally, his voice so soft and reluctant it was like the last gasp of a dying old man.

"Then you're going to have to rent the motel."

"And then what?"

"Then—I don't know." The door was open, her roommate framed there in the hall, a burst of rock and roll coming at her like an assault. "I guess you'll have to get a book or something."

By eight, the rain had turned to ice and every branch of every tree was coated with it, the highway littered with glistening black sticks, no moon, no stars, the tires sliding out from under her, and she felt heavy, big as a sumo wrestler, heavy and loose at the same time. She'd taken a towel from the dorm and put it under her, on the seat, but it was a mess, everything was a mess. She was cramping. Fidgeting with her hair. She tried the radio, but it was no help, nothing but songs she hated, singers that were worse. Twenty-two miles to Danbury and the first of the contractions came like a seizure, like a knife blade thrust into her spine. Her world narrowed to what the headlights would show her.

Jeremy was waiting for her at the door to the room, the light behind him a pale rinse of nothing, no smile on his face, no human expression at all. They didn't kiss—they didn't even touch—and then she was on the bed, on her back, her face clenched like a fist. She heard the rattle of the sleet at the window, the murmur of TV: *I can't let you go like this,* a man protested, and she could picture him, angular and tall, a man in a hat and overcoat in a black-and-white world that might have been another planet, *I just can't.* "Are you—?" Jeremy's voice drifted into the mix, and then stalled. "Are you ready? I mean, is it time? Is it coming now?"

She said one thing then, one thing only, her voice as pinched and hollow as the sound of the wind in the gutters: "Get it out of me."

It took a moment, and then she could feel his hands fumbling with her sweats.

Later, hours later, when nothing had happened but pain, a parade of pain with drum majors and brass bands and penitents crawling on their hands and knees till the streets were stained with their blood, she cried out and cried out again. "It's like 'Alien,'" she gasped, "like that thing in 'Alien' when it, it—"

"It's O.K.," he kept telling her, "it's O.K.," but his face betrayed him. He looked scared, looked as if he'd been drained of blood in some evil experiment in yet another movie, and a part of her wanted to be sorry for him, but another part, the part that was so commanding and fierce it overrode everything else, couldn't begin to be.

He was useless, and he knew it. He'd never been so purely sick at heart and terrified in all his life, but he tried to be there for her, tried to do his best, and when the baby came out, the baby girl all slick with blood and mucus and the lumped white stuff that was like something spilled at the bottom of a garbage can, he was thinking of the ninth grade and how close he'd come to fainting while the teacher went around the room to prick their fingers one by one so they each could smear a drop of blood across a slide. He didn't faint now. But he was close to it, so close he could feel the room dodging away under his feet. And then her voice, the first intelligible thing she'd said in an hour: "Get rid of it. Just get rid of it."

Of the drive back to Binghamton he remembered nothing. Or practically nothing. They took towels from the motel and spread them across the seat of her car, he could remember that much . . . and the blood, how could he forget the blood? It soaked through her sweats and the towels and even the thick cotton bathmat and into the worn fabric of the seat itself. And it all came from inside her, all of it, tissue and mucus and the shining bright fluid, no end to it, as if she'd been turned inside out. He wanted to ask her about that, if that was normal, but she was asleep the minute she slid out from under his arm and dropped into the seat. If he focused, if he really concentrated, he could remember the way her head lolled against the doorframe while the engine whined and the car rocked and the slush threw a dark blanket over the windshield every time a truck shot past in the opposite direction. That and the exhaustion. He'd never been so tired, his head on a string, shoulders slumped, his arms like two pillars of concrete. And what if he'd nodded off? What if he'd gone into a skid and hurtled over an embankment into the filthy gray accumulation of the worst day of his life? What then?

She made it into the dorm under her own power, nobody even looked at her, and, no, she didn't need his help. "Call me," she whispered, and they kissed, her lips so cold it was like kissing a steak through the plastic wrap, and then he parked her car in the student lot and walked to the bus station. He made Danbury late that night, caught a ride out to the motel, and walked right through the "Do Not Disturb" sign on the door. Fifteen minutes. That was all it took. He bundled up everything, every trace, left the key in the box at the desk, and stood scraping the ice off the windshield of his car while the night opened up above him to a black glitter of sky. He never gave a thought to what lay discarded in the Dumpster out back, itself wrapped in plastic, so much meat, so much cold meat.

. . .

He was at the very pinnacle of his dream, the river dressed in its currents, the deep hole under the cutbank, and the fish like silver bullets swarming to his bait, when they woke him—when Rob woke him, Rob Greiner, his roommate, Rob with a face of crumbling stone and two policemen there at the door behind him and the roar of the dorm falling away to a whisper. And that was strange, policemen, a real anomaly in that setting, and at first—for the first thirty seconds, at least—he had no idea what they were doing there. Parking tickets? Could that be it? But then they asked him his name, just to confirm it, joined his hands together behind his back, and fitted two loops of naked metal over his wrists, and he began to understand. He saw McCaffrey and Tuttle from across the hall staring at him as if he were Jeffrey Dahmer or something, and the rest of them, all the rest, every head poking out of every door up and down the corridor, as the police led him away.

"What's all this about?" he kept saying, the cruiser nosing through the dark streets to the station house, the man at the wheel and the man beside him as incapable of speech as the seats or the wire mesh or the gleaming black dashboard that dragged them forward into the night. And then it was up the steps and into an explosion of light, more men in uniform, stand here, give me your hand, now the other one, and then the cage and the questions. Only then did he think of that thing in the garbage sack and the sound it had made—its body had made—when he flung it into the Dumpster like a sack of flour and the lid slammed down on it. He stared at the walls, and this was a movie, too. He'd never been in trouble before, never been inside a police station, but he knew his role well enough, because he'd seen it played out a thousand times on the tube: deny everything. Even as the two detectives settled in across from him at the bare wooden table in the little box of the overlit room he was telling himself just that: *Deny it, deny it all.*

The first detective leaned forward and set his hands on the table as if he'd come for a manicure. He was in his thirties, or maybe his forties, a tired-looking man with the scars of the turmoil he'd witnessed gouged into the flesh under his eyes. He didn't offer a cigarette ("I don't smoke," Jeremy was prepared to say, giving them that much at least), and he didn't smile or soften his eyes. And when he spoke his voice carried no freight at all, not outrage or threat or cajolery—it was just a voice, flat and tired. "Do you know a China Berkowitz?" he said.

And she. She was in the community hospital, where the ambulance had deposited her after her roommate had called 911 in a voice that was like a bone stuck in the back of her throat, and it was raining again. Her parents were there, her mother red-eyed and sniffling, her father looking like an actor who has forgotten his lines, and there was another woman there, too, a policewoman. The policewoman sat in an orange plastic chair in the corner, dipping her head to the knitting in her lap. At first, China's mother had tried to be pleasant to the woman, but pleasant wasn't what the circumstances called for, and now she ignored her, because the very unpleasant fact was that China was being taken into custody as soon as she was released from the hospital.

For a long while no one said anything—everything had already been said, over and over, one long flood of hurt and recrimination—and the antiseptic silence of the hospital held them in its grip while the rain beat at the windows and the machines at the foot of the bed counted off numbers. From down the hall came a snatch of TV dialogue, and for a minute China opened her eyes and thought she was back in the dorm. "Honey," her mother said, raising a purgatorial face to her, "are you all right? Can I get you anything?"

"I need to—I think I need to pee."

"Why?" her father demanded, and it was the perfect non sequitur. He was up out of the chair, standing over her, his eyes liked cracked porcelain. "Why didn't you tell us, or at least tell your mother—or Dr. Fredman? Dr. Fredman, at least. He's been—he's like a family member, you know that, and he could have, or he would have . . . What were you *thinking*, for Christ's sake?"

Thinking? She wasn't thinking anything, not then and not now. All she wanted—and she didn't care what they did to her, beat her, torture her, drag her weeping through the streets in a dirty white dress with "Baby Killer" stitched over her breast in scarlet letters—was to see Jeremy. Just that. Because what really mattered was what he was thinking.

The food at the Sarah Barnes Cooper Women's Correctional Institute was exactly what they served at the dining hall in college, heavy on the sugars, starches, and bad cholesterol, and that would have struck her as ironic if she'd been there under other circumstances—doing community outreach, say, or researching a paper for sociology class. But given the fact that she'd been locked up for more than a month now, the object of the other girls' threats, scorn, and just plain *nastiness,* given the fact that her life was ruined beyond any hope of redemption, and every newspaper in the country had her shrunken white face plastered across its front page under a headline that screamed "MOTEL MOM," she didn't have much use for irony. She was scared twenty-four hours a day. Scared of the present, scared of the future, scared of the reporters waiting for the judge to set bail so that they could swarm all over her the minute she stepped out the door. She couldn't concentrate on the books and magazines her mother brought her, or even on the TV in the rec room. She sat in her room—it was a room, just like a dorm room, except that they locked you in at night—and stared at the walls, eating peanuts, M&M's, sunflower seeds by the handful, chewing for the pure animal gratification of it. She was putting on more weight, and what did it matter?

Jeremy was different. He'd lost everything—his walk, his smile, the muscles of his upper arms and shoulders. Even his hair lay flat now, as if he couldn't bother with a tube of gel and a comb. When she saw him at the arraignment, saw him for the first time since she'd climbed out of the car and limped into the dorm with the blood wet on her legs, he looked like a refugee, like a ghost. The room they were in—the courtroom—seemed to have grown up around them, walls, windows, benches, lights, and radiators already in place, along with the judge, the American flag, and the ready-made spectators. It was hot. People coughed into their fists and shuffled their feet, every sound magnified. The judge presided, his arms like bones twirled in a bag, his eyes searching and opaque as he peered over the top of his reading glasses.

China's lawyer didn't like Jeremy's lawyer, that much was evident, and the state prosecutor didn't like anybody. She watched him—Jeremy, only him—as the reporters held their collective breath and the judge read off the charges and her mother bowed her head and sobbed into the bucket of her hands. And Jeremy was watching her, too, his eyes locked on hers as if he defied them all, as if nothing mattered in the world but her, and when the judge said *First-degree murder* and *Murder by abuse or neglect* he never flinched.

She sent him a note that day—"I love you, will always love you no matter what, More than Moon"—and in the hallway, afterward, while their lawyers fended off the reporters and the bailiffs tugged impatiently at them, they had a minute, just a minute, to themselves. "What did you tell them?" he whispered. His voice was a rasp, almost a growl; she looked at him, inches away, and hardly recognized him.

"I told them it was dead."

"My lawyer—Mrs. Teagues?—she says they're saying it was alive when we, when we put it in the bag." His face was composed, but his eyes were darting like insects trapped inside his head.

"It was dead."

"It looked dead," he said, and already he was pulling away from her and some callous shit with a camera kept annihilating them with flash after flash of light, "and we certainly didn't—I mean, we didn't slap it or anything to get it breathing. . . ."

And then the last thing he said to her, just as they were pulled apart, and it was nothing she wanted to hear, nothing that had any love in it, or even the hint of love: "You told me to get rid of it."

There was no elaborate name for the place where they were keeping him. It was known as Drum Hill Prison, period. No reform-minded notions here, no verbal gestures toward rehabilitation or behavior modification, no benefactors, mayors, or role models to lend the place their family names, but then who in his right mind would want a prison named after him anyway? At least they kept him separated from the other prisoners, the gangbangers and dope dealers and sexual predators and the like. He was no longer a freshman at Brown, not officially, but he had his books and his course notes and he tried to keep up as best he could. Still, when the screams echoed through the cell block at night and the walls dripped with the accumulated breath of eight and a half thousand terminally angry sociopaths, he had to admit it wasn't the sort of college experience he'd bargained for.

And what had he done to deserve it? He still couldn't understand. That thing in the Dumpster—and he refused to call it human, let alone a baby—was nobody's business but his and China's. That's what he'd told his attorney, Mrs. Teagues, and his mother and her boyfriend, Howard, and he'd told them over and over again: *I didn't do anything wrong.* Even if it was alive, and it was, he knew in his heart that it was, even before the state prosecutor presented evidence of blunt-force trauma and death by asphyxiation and exposure, it didn't matter, or shouldn't have mattered. There was no baby. There was nothing but a mistake, a mistake clothed in blood and mucus. When he really thought about it, thought it through on its merits and dissected all his mother's pathetic arguments about where he'd be today if she'd felt as he did when she was pregnant herself, he hardened like a rock, like sand turning to stone under all the pressure the planet can bring to bear. Another unwanted child in an overpopulated world? They should have given him a medal.

It was the end of January before bail was set—three hundred and fifty thousand dollars his mother didn't have—and he was released to house arrest. He wore a plastic anklet that set off an alarm if he went out the door, and so did she, so did China, imprisoned like some fairy-tale princess at her parents' house. At first, she called him every day, but mostly what she did was cry—"I want to see it," she sobbed. "I want to see our daughter's *grave*." That froze him inside. He tried to picture her—her now, China, the love of his life—and he couldn't. What did she look like? What was her face like, her nose, her hair, her eyes and breasts and the slit between her legs? He drew a blank. There was no way to summon her the way she used to be or even the way she was in court, because all he could remember was the thing that had come out of her, four limbs and the equipment of a female, shoulders rigid and eyes shut tight, as if she were a mummy in a tomb . . . and the breath, the shuddering long gasping rattle of a breath he could feel ringing inside her even as the black plastic bag closed over her face and the lid of the Dumpster opened like a mouth.

He was in the den, watching basketball, a drink in his hand (7UP mixed with Jack Daniel's in a ceramic mug, so no one would know he was getting shit-faced at two o'clock on a Sunday afternoon), when the phone rang. It was Sarah Teagues. "Listen, Jeremy," she said in her crisp, equitable tones, "I thought you ought to know—the Berkowitzes are filing a motion to have the case against China dropped."

His mother's voice on the portable, too loud, a blast of amplified breath and static: "On what grounds?"

"She never saw the baby, that's what they're saying. She thought she had a miscarriage."

"Yeah, right," his mother said.

Sarah Teagues was right there, her voice as clear and present as his mother's. "Jeremy's the one that threw it in the Dumpster, and they're saying he acted alone. She took a polygraph test day before yesterday."

He could feel his heart pounding like it used to when he plodded up that last agonizing ridge behind the school with the cross-country team, his legs sapped, no more breath left in his body. He didn't say a word. Didn't even breathe.

"She's going to testify against him."

Outside was the world, puddles of ice clinging to the lawn under a weak afternoon sun, all the trees stripped bare, the grass dead, the azalea under the window reduced to an armload of dead brown twigs. She wouldn't have wanted to go out today anyway. This was the time of year she hated most, the long interval between the holidays and spring break, when nothing grew and nothing changed—it didn't even seem to snow much anymore. What was out there for her anyway? They wouldn't let her see Jeremy, wouldn't even let her talk to him on the phone or write him anymore, and she wouldn't be able to show her face at the mall or even the movie theater without somebody shouting out her name as if she were a freak, as if she were another Monica Lewinsky or Heidi Fleiss. She wasn't China Berkowitz, honor student, not anymore—she was the punch line to a joke, a footnote to history.

She wouldn't mind going for a drive, though—that was something she missed, just following the curves out to the reservoir to watch the way the ice cupped the shore, or up to the turnout on Route 9 to look out over the river where it oozed through the mountains in a shimmering coil of light. Or to take a walk in the woods, just that. She was in her room, on her bed, posters of bands she'd outgrown staring down from the walls, her high-school books on two shelves in the corner, the closet door flung open on all the clothes she'd once wanted so desperately she could have died for each individual pair of boots or the cashmere sweaters that felt so good against her skin. At the bottom of her left leg, down there at the foot of the bed, was the anklet she wore now, the plastic anklet with the transmitter inside, no different, she supposed, than the collars they put on wolves to track them across all those miles of barren tundra or the bears sleeping in their dens. Except that hers had an alarm on it.

For a long while she just lay there gazing out the window, watching the rinsed-out sun slip down into the sky that had no more color in it than a TV tuned to an unsubscribed channel, and then she found herself picturing things the way they were an eon ago, when everything was green. She saw the azalea bush in bloom, the leaves knifing out of the trees, butterflies—or were they cabbage moths?—hovering over the flowers. Deep green. That was the color of the world. And she was remembering a night, summer before last, just after she and Jeremy started going together, the crickets thrumming, the air thick with humidity, and him singing along with the car radio, his voice so sweet and pure it was as if he'd written the song himself, just for her. And when they got to where they were going, at the end of that dark lane overhung with trees, to a place where it was private and hushed and the night fell in on itself as if it couldn't support the weight of the stars, he was as nervous as she was. She moved into his arms and they kissed, his lips groping for hers in the dark, his fingers trembling over the thin yielding silk of her blouse. He was Jeremy. He was the love of her life. And she closed her eyes and clung to him as if that were all that mattered.

Joyce Carol Oates

The Girl with the Blackened Eye

From *Witness*

THIS BLACK eye I had, once! Like a clown's eye painted on. Both my eyes were bruised and ugly but the right eye was swollen almost shut, people must've seen me and I wonder what they were thinking, I mean you have to wonder. Nobody said a word—didn't want to get involved, I guess. You have to wonder what went through their minds, though.

Sometimes now I see myself in a mirror, like in the middle of the night getting up to use the bathroom, I see a blurred face, a woman's face I don't recognize. And I see that eye.

Twenty-seven years.

In America, that's a lifetime.

This weird thing that happened to me, fifteen years old and a sophomore at Menlo Park High, living with my family in Menlo Park, California, where Dad was a dental surgeon (which was lucky: I'd need dental and gum surgery, to repair the damage to my mouth). Weird, and wild. Ugly. I've never told anyone who knows me now. Especially my daughters. My husband doesn't know, he couldn't have handled it. We were in our late twenties when we met, no need to drag up the past. I never do. I'm not one of those. I left California forever when I went to college in Vermont. My family moved, too. They live in Seattle now. There's a stiffness between us, we never talk about that time. Never say that man's name. So it's like it never did happen.

Or, if it did, it happened to someone else. A high school girl in the 1970s. A silly little girl who wore tank tops and jeans so tight she had to lie down on her bed to wriggle into them, and teased her hair into a mane. That girl.

When they found me, my hair was wild and tangled like broom sage. It couldn't be combed through, had to be cut from my head in clumps. Something sticky like cobwebs was in it. I'd been wearing it long since ninth grade and after that I kept it cut short for years. Like a guy's hair, the back of my neck shaved and my ears showing.

I'd been forcibly abducted at the age of fifteen. It was something that could happen to you, from the outside, *forcibly abducted,* like being in a plane crash, or struck by lightning. There wouldn't be any human agent, almost. The human agent wouldn't have a name. I'd been walking through the mall parking lot to the bus stop, about 5:30 p.m., a weekday, I'd come to the mall after school with some kids, now I was headed home, and somehow it happened, don't ask me how, a guy was asking me questions, or saying something, mainly I registered he was an adult my dad's age possibly, every adult man looked like my dad's age except obviously old white-haired men. I hadn't any clear impression of this guy except afterward I would recall rings on his fingers which would've caused me to glance up at his face with interest except at that instant something slammed into the back of my head behind my ear, knocking me forward, and down, like he'd thrown a hook at me from in front, I was on my face on the sun-heated vinyl upholstery of a car, or a van, and another blow or blows knocked me out. Like anesthesia, it was. You're out.

This was the *forcible abduction.* How it might be described by a witness who was there, who was also the victim. But who hadn't any memory of what happened because it happened so fast, and she hadn't been personally involved.

It's like they say. You are there, and not-there. He drove to this place in the Sonoma Mountains, I would afterward learn, this cabin it would be called, and he raped me, beat me, and shocked me with electrical cords and he stubbed cigarette butts on my stomach and breasts, and he said things to me like he knew me, he knew all my secrets, what a dirty-minded girl I was, what a nasty girl, and selfish, like everyone of my *privi-*

leged class as he called it. I'm saying these things were done to me but in fact they were done to my body mostly. Like the cabin was in the Sonoma Mountains north of Healdsburg but it was just anywhere for those eight days, and I was anywhere, I was holding on to being alive the way you would hold on to a straw you could breathe through, lying at the bottom of deep water. And that water opaque, you can't see through to the surface.

He was gone, and he came back. He left me tied in the bed, it was a cot with a thin mattress, very dirty. There were only two windows in the cabin and there were blinds over them drawn tight. It was hot during what I guessed was the day. It was cool, and it was very quiet, at night. The lower parts of me were raw and throbbing with pain and other parts of me were in a haze of pain so I wasn't able to think, and I wasn't awake most of the time, not what you'd call actual wakefulness, with a personality.

What you call your personality, you know?—it's not the actual bones, or teeth, something solid. It's more like a flame. A flame can be upright, and a flame can flicker in the wind, a flame can be extinguished so there's no sign of it, like it had never been.

My eyes had been hurt, he'd mashed his fists into my eyes. The eyelids were puffy, I couldn't see very well. It was like I didn't try to see, I was saving my eyesight for when I was stronger. I had not seen the man's face actually. I had felt him but I had not seen him, I could not have identified him. Anymore than you could identify yourself if you had never seen yourself in a mirror or in any likeness.

In one of my dreams I was saying to my family I would not be seeing them for a while, I was going away. *I'm going away, I want to say good-bye.* Their faces were blurred. My sister, I was closer to than my parents, she's two years older than me and I adored her, my sister was crying, her face was blurred with tears. She asked where I was going and I said I didn't know, but I wanted to say good-bye, and I wanted to say *I love you.* And this was so vivid it would seem to me to have happened actually, and was more real than other things that happened to me during that time I would learn afterward was eight days.

It might've been the same day repeated, or it might've been eighty days. It was a place, not a day. Like a dimension you could slip into, or be sucked into, by an undertow. And it's there, but no one is aware of it. Until you're in it, you don't know; but when you're in it, it's all that you know. So you have no way of speaking of it except like this. Stammering, and ignorant.

. . .

Why he brought me water and food, why he decided to let me live, would never be clear. The others he'd killed after a few days. They went stale on him, you have to suppose. One of the bodies was buried in the woods a few hundred yards behind the cabin, others were dumped along Route 101 as far north as Crescent City. And possibly there were others never known, never located or identified. These facts, if they are facts, I would learn later, as I would learn that the other girls and women had been older than me, the oldest was thirty, and the youngest he'd been on record as killing was eighteen. So it was speculated he had mercy on me because he hadn't realized, abducting me in the parking lot, that I was so young, and in my battered condition in the cabin, when I'd started losing weight, I must've looked to him like a child. I was crying a lot, and calling *Mommy! Mom-my!*

Like my own kids, grown, would call *Mom-my!* in some nightmare they were trapped in. But I never think of such things.

The man with the rings on his fingers, saying, There's some reason I don't know yet, that you have been spared.

Later I would look back and think, there was a turn, a shifting of fortune, when he first allowed me to wash. To wash! He could see I was ashamed, I was a naturally shy, clean girl. He allowed this. He might have assisted me, a little. He picked ticks out of my skin where they were invisible and gorged with blood. He hated ticks! They disgusted him. He went away, and came back with food and Hires Diet Root Beer. We ate together sitting on the edge of the cot. And once when he allowed me out into the clearing at dusk. Like a picnic. His greasy fingers, and mine. Fried chicken, french fries and runny cole slaw, my hands started shaking and my mouth was on fire. And my stomach convulsing with hunger, cramps that doubled me over like he'd sunk a knife into my guts and twisted. Still, I was able to eat some things, in little bites. I did not starve. Seeing the colour come back into my face, he was impressed, stirred. He said, in mild reproach, Hey, a butterfly could eat more'n you.

I would remember these pale-yellow butterflies around the cabin. A swarm of them. And jays screaming, waiting to swoop down to snatch up food.

I guess I was pretty sick. Delirious. My gums were infected. Four of my teeth were broken. Blood kept leaking to the back of my mouth, making me sick, gagging. But I could walk to the car leaning against him, I was able to sit up normally in the passenger's seat, buckled in, he always made sure to buckle me in, and a wire wound tight around my ankles. Driving then out of the forest, and the foothills I could not have identified as the Sonoma hills, and the sun high and gauzy in the sky, and I lost track of time, lapsing in and out of time but noticing that highway traffic was changing to suburban, more traffic lights, we were cruising through parking lots so vast you couldn't see to the edge of them, sun-blinded spaces and rows of glittering cars like grave markers: I saw them suddenly in a cemetery that went on forever.

He wanted me with him all the time now, he said. Keep an eye on you, girl. Maybe I was his trophy? The only female in his abducting/raping/ killing spree of an estimated seventeen months to be publicly displayed. Not beaten, strangled, raped to death, kicked to death and buried like animal carrion. (This I would learn later.) Or maybe I was meant to signal to the world, if the world glanced through the windshield of his car, his daughter. A sign of—what? *Hey, I'm normal. I'm a nice guy, see.*

Except the daughter's hair was wild and matted, her eyes were bruised and one of them swollen almost shut. Her mouth was a slack puffy wound. Bruises on her face and throat and arms and her ribs were cracked, skinny body was covered in pus-leaking burns and sores. Yet he'd allowed me to wash, and he'd allowed me to wash out my clothes, I was less filthy now. He'd given me a T-shirt too big for me, already soiled but I was grateful for it. Through acres of parking lots we cruised like sharks seeking prey. I was aware of people glancing into the car, just by accident, seeing me, or maybe not seeing me, there were reflections in the windshield (weren't there?) because of the sun, so maybe they didn't see me, or didn't see me clearly. Yet others, seeing me, looked away. It did not occur to me at the time that there must be a search for me, my face in the papers, on TV. My face as it had been. At the time I'd stopped thinking of that other world. Mostly I'd stopped thinking. It was like anesthesia, you give in to it, there's peace in it, almost. As cruising the parking lots with the man whistling to himself, humming, talking in a low affable monotone, I understood that he wasn't thinking either, as a predator fish would not be thinking cruising beneath the surface of the ocean. The silent gliding of sharks, that never cease their motion. I was concerned mostly with sitting right: my head balanced on my neck, which isn't easy to do, and the wire wound tight around my ankles cutting off circulation. I knew of gangrene, I knew of toes and entire feet going black with rot. From my father I knew of tooth-rot, gum-rot. I was trying not to think of those strangers who must've seen me, sure they saw me, and turned away, uncertain what they'd seen but knowing it was trouble, not wanting to know more.

Just a girl with a blackened eye, you figure she maybe deserved it.

He said: There must be some reason you are spared.

He said, in my daddy's voice from a long time ago, Know what, girl?—you're not like the others. That's why.

They would say he was insane, these were the acts of an insane person. And I would not disagree. Though I knew it was not so.

The red-haired woman in the khaki jacket and matching pants. Eventually she would have a name but it was not a name I would wish to know, none of them were. This was a woman, not a girl. He'd put me in the back seat of his car now, so the passenger's seat was empty. He'd buckled me safely in. O.K., girl? You be good, now. We cruised the giant parking lot at dusk. When the lights first come on. (Where was this? Ukiah. Where I'd never been. Except for the red-haired woman I would have no memory of Ukiah.)

He'd removed his rings. He was wearing a white baseball cap.

There came this red-haired woman beside him smiling, talking like they were friends. I stared, I was astonished. They were coming toward the car. Never could I imagine what those two were talking about! I thought *He will trade me for her* and I was frightened. The man in the baseball cap wearing shiny dark glasses asking the red-haired woman—what? Directions? Yet he had the power to make her smile, there was a sexual ease between them. She was a mature woman with a shapely body, breasts I could envy and hips in the tight-fitting khaki pants that were stylish pants, with a drawstring waist. I felt a rush of anger for this woman, contempt, disgust, how stupid she was, unsuspecting, bending to peer at me where possibly she'd been told the man's daughter was sitting, maybe he'd said his daughter had a question for her? needed an adult female's advice? and in an instant she would find herself shoved forward onto the front seat of the car, down on her face, her chest, helpless, as fast as you might snap your fingers, too fast for her to cry out. So fast, you understand it had happened many times before. The girl in the back seat blinking and staring and unable to speak though she wasn't gagged, no more able to scream for help than the woman struggling for her life a few inches away. She shuddered in sympathy, she moaned as the man pounded the woman with his fists. Furious, grunting! His eyes bulged. Were there no witnesses? No one to see? Deftly he wrapped a blanket around the woman, who'd gone limp, wrapping it tight around her head and chest, he shoved her legs inside the car and shut the door and climbed into the driver's seat and drove away humming, happy. In the back seat the girl was crying. If she'd had tears she would have cried.

Weird how your mind works: I was thinking I was that woman, in the front seat wrapped in the blanket, so the rest of it had not yet happened.

It was that time, I think, I saw my mom. In the parking lot. There were shoppers, mostly women. And my mom was one of them. I knew it couldn't be her, so far from home, I knew I was hundreds of miles from home, so it couldn't be, but I saw her, Mom crossing in front of the car, walking briskly to the entrance of Lord & Taylor.

Yet I couldn't wave to her, my arm was heavy as lead.

Yes. In the cabin I was made to witness what he did to the red-haired woman. I saw now that this was my importance to him: I would be a witness to his fury, his indignation, his disgust. Tying the woman's wrists to the iron rails of the bed, spreading her legs and tying her ankles. Naked, the red-haired woman had no power. There was no sexual ease to her now, no confidence. You would not envy her now. You would scorn her now. You would not wish to be her now. She'd become a chicken on a spit.

I had to watch, I could not close my eyes or look away.

For it had happened already, it was completed. There was certitude in this, and peace in certitude. When there is no escape, for what is happening has already happened. Not once but many times.

When you give up struggle, there's a kind of love.

The red-haired woman did not know this, in her terror. But I was the witness, I knew.

They would ask me about him. I saw only parts of him. Like jigsaw puzzle parts. Like quick camera jumps and cuts. His back was pale and flaccid at the waist, more muscular at the shoulders. It was a broad pimply sweating back. It was a part of a man, like my dad, I would not see. Not in this way. Not straining, tensing. And the smell of a man's hair, like congealed oil. His hair was stiff, dark, threaded with silver hairs like wires, at the crown of his head you could see the scalp beneath. On his torso and legs hairs grew in dense waves and rivulets like water or grasses. He was grunting, he was making a high-pitched moaning sound. When he turned, I saw a fierce blurred face, I didn't recognize that face. And the nipples of a man's breasts, wine-colored like berries. Between his thighs the angry thing swung like the length of rubber, slick and darkened with blood.

I would recall, yes, he had tattoos. Smudged-looking like ink blots. Never did I see them clearly. Never did I see him clearly. I would not have dared as you would not look into the sun in terror of being blinded.

He kept us there together for three days. I mean, the red-haired woman was there for three days, unconscious most of the time. There was a mercy in this. You learn to take note of small mercies and be grateful for them. Nor would he kill her in the cabin. When he was finished with her, disgusted with her, he half-carried her out to the car. I was alone, and frightened. But then he returned and said, O.K., girl, goin for a ride. I was able to walk, just barely. I was very dizzy. I would ride in the back seat of the car like a big rag doll, boneless and unresisting.

He'd shoved the woman down beside him, hidden by a blanket wrapped around her head and upper body. She was not struggling now, her body was limp and unresisting for she, too, had weakened in the cabin, she'd lost weight. You learned to be weak to please him for you did not want to displease him in even the smallest things. Yet the woman managed to speak, this small choked begging voice. Don't kill me, please. I won't tell anybody. I won't tell anybody don't kill me. I have a little daughter, please don't kill me. Please, God. Please.

I wasn't sure if this voice was (somehow) a made-up voice. A voice of my imagination. Or like on TV. Or my own voice, if I'd been older and had a daughter. *Please don't kill me. Please, God.*

For always it's this voice when you're alone and silent you hear it.

Afterward they would speculate that he'd panicked. Seeing TV spot announcements, the photographs of his "victims." When last seen and where, Menlo Park, Ukiah. There were witnesses' descriptions of *the abductor* and a police sketch of his face, coarser and uglier and older than his face which was now disguised by dark glasses. In the drawing he was clean-shaven but now his jaws were covered in several days' beard, a stubbly beard, his hair was tied in a ponytail and the baseball cap pulled low on his head. Yet you could recognize him in the drawing, that looked as if it had been executed by a blind man. So he'd panicked.

The first car he'd been driving he left at the cabin, he was driving another, a stolen car with switched license plates. You came to see that his life was such maneuvers. He was tireless in invention as a willful child and would seem to have had no purpose beyond such maneuvers and when afterward I would learn details of his background, his family life in San Jose, his early incarcerations as a juvenile, as a youth, as an adult "offender" now on parole from Bakersfield maximum security prison, I would block off such information as not related to me, not related to the man who'd existed exclusively for me as, for a brief while, I'd existed exclusively for him. I was contemptuous of "facts" for I came to know that no accumulation of facts constitutes knowledge, and no impersonal knowledge constitutes the intimacy of knowing.

Know what, girl? You're not like the others. You're special. That's the reason.

Driving fast, farther into the foothills. The road was even narrower and bumpier. There were few vehicles on the road, all of them mini-vans or campers. He never spoke to the red-haired woman moaning and whimpering beside him but to me in the back seat, looking at me in the rearview mirror, the way my dad used to do when I rode in the back seat, and Mom was up front with him. He said, How ya doin, girl?

O.K.

Doing O.K., huh?

Yes.

I'm gonna let you go, girl, you know that, huh? Gonna give you your freedom.

To this I could not reply. My swollen lips moved in a kind of smile as you smile out of politeness.

Less you want to trade? With her?

Again I could not reply. I wasn't certain what the question was. My smile ached in my face but it was a sincere smile.

He parked the car on an unpaved lane off the road. He waited, no vehicles approaching. There were no aircraft overhead. It was very quiet except for birds. He said, C'mon, help me, girl. So I moved my legs that were stiff, my legs that felt strange and skinny to me, I climbed out of the car and fought off dizziness helping him with the bound woman, he'd pulled the blanket off her, her discolored swollen face, her face that wasn't attractive now, scabby mouth and panicked eyes, brown eyes they were, I would remember those eyes pleading. For they were my own, but in one who was doomed as I was not. He said then, so strangely: Stay here, girl. Watch the car. Somebody shows up, honk the horn. Two-three times. Got it?

I whispered yes. I was staring at the crumbly earth.

I could not look at the woman now. I would not watch them move away into the woods.

Maybe it was a test, he'd left the key in the ignition. It was to make me think I could drive the car away from there, I could drive to get help, or I could run out onto the road and get help. Maybe I could get help. He had a gun, and he had knives, but I could have driven away. But the sun was beating on my head, I couldn't move. My legs were heavy like lead. My eye was swollen shut and throbbing. I believed it was a test but I wasn't certain. Afterward they would ask if I'd had any chance to escape in those days he kept me captive and always I said no, no I did not have a chance to escape. Because that was so. That was how it was to me, that I could not explain.

Yet I remember the keys in the ignition, and I remember that the road was close by. He would strangle the woman, that was his way of killing and this I seemed to know. It would require some minutes. It was not an easy way of killing. I could run, I could run along the road and hope that someone would come along, or I could hide, and he wouldn't find me in all that wilderness, if he called me I would not answer. But I stood there beside the car because I could not do these things. He trusted me, and I could not betray that trust. Even if he would kill me, I could not betray him.

Yes, I heard her screams in the woods. I think I heard. It might have been jays. It might have been my own screams I heard. But I heard them.

A few days later he would be dead. He would be shot down by police in a motel parking lot in Petaluma. Why he was there, in that place, about fifty miles from the cabin, I don't know. He'd left me in the cabin chained to the bed. It was filthy, flies and ants. The chain was long enough for me to use the toilet. But the toilet was backed up. Blinds were drawn on the windows. I did not dare to take them down or break the window panes but I looked out, I saw just the clearing, a haze of green. Overhead there were small planes sometimes. A helicopter. I wanted to think that somebody would rescue me but I knew better, I knew nobody would find me.

But they did find me.

He told them where the cabin was, when he was dying. He did that for me. He drew a rough map and I have that map!—not the actual piece of paper but a copy. He would never see me again, and I would have trouble recalling his face for I never truly saw it.

Photographs of him were not accurate. Even his name, printed out, is misleading. For it could be anyone's name and not *his*.

In my present life I never speak of these things. I have never told anyone. There would be no point to it. Why I've told you, I don't know: you might write about me but you would respect my privacy.

Because if you wrote about me, these things that happened to me so long ago, no one would know it was me. And you would disguise it so that no one could guess, that's why I trust you.

My life afterward is what's unreal. The life then, those eight days, was very real. The two don't seem to be connected, do they? I learned you don't discover the evidence of any cause in its result. Philosophers debate over that but if you know, you know. There is no connection though people wish to think so. When I was recovered I went back to Menlo Park High and I graduated with my class and I went to college in Vermont, I met my husband in New York a few years later and married him and had my babies and none of my life would be different in any way, I believe, if I had not been "abducted" when I was fifteen.

Sure, I see him sometimes. More often lately. On the street, in a passing car. In profile, I see him. In his shiny dark glasses and white baseball cap. A man's forearm, a thick pelt of hair on it, a tattoo, I see him. The shock of it is, he's only thirty-two.

That's so young now. Your life all before you, almost.

David Schickler

The Smoker

From *The New Yorker*

Douglas Kerchek taught twelfth-grade advanced-placement English at St. Agnes High School on West Ninety-seventh and Broadway, and Nicole Bonner was the standout in his class. She was the tallest, at five feet ten, the oldest, at nineteen, and the smartest, with a flawless A. She wasn't the prettiest, Douglas thought—not beside the spunky nose of Rhonda Phelps or Meredith Beckermann's heart-shaped derrière—but Nicole was dangerously alluring. She had a chopped black Cleopatra haircut and wise blue eyes, and her recent essay on "Othello" had ended with this note:

Dear Mr Kerchek:
Last night in bed I read Fear + Loathing in L.V. It is puerile, self-involved gamesmanship. I suppose I don't love drugs enough, although my parents make me drink brandy with them every night. They consider it a gesture of affection.

I saw you yesterday, outside the locker room, changing your shoes to go running, and your ankle looked quite blue. What did you bang it on?

Respectfully
Nicole Bonner

This note caused Douglas some concern. He, too, disliked Hunter S. Thompson, but Nicole had also written "in bed" and mentioned his bruise. It was Nicole's habit to do this, to call out random, intimate specifics from the world around her and bring them to Douglas's attention. She'd done it that day in class.

"Iago is filled with lust, Mr Kerchek," said Jill Eckhard.

"He's a Machiavellian bastard," said Rhonda Phelps.

"You know what's an excellent word to say out loud repeatedly?" Nicole Bonner chewed her hair. "'Rinse.' Think about it, Mr Kerchek. Rinse. *Rinse.*"

That evening, as always, Douglas walked home to his shabby studio apartment. Douglas was thirty-one. He lived alone, five blocks north of St. Agnes, in an apartment building filled with Mexican men who drank Pabst and held boisterous, high-stakes poker games every night in the lobby outside Douglas's first-floor apartment. They were amiable, violent men, and their nickname for Douglas was Uno, because whenever he sat with them he had one quiet beer, then bowed out.

"Uno," cackled the Mexicans. "Come take our money, Uno."

"Fuck us up, Uno."

A twelve-year-old boy named Chiapas rattled a beer can. "Come get your medicine, Uno."

Douglas grinned wanly, waved them off, and opened his door.

Rinse, he thought, frowning. Rinse. *Rinse.*

After a quick sandwich, Douglas corrected essays. He was a fastidious, tough grader. Also, he had short black sideburns with streaks of gray in them, a boxer's build, a Ph.D. in English literature from Harvard, and no wife or girlfriend. These qualities made Douglas a font of intrigue for the all-female population of St. Agnes—both the lay faculty and the students—but in truth Douglas led a sedentary life. He loved books, he was a passionate, solitary filmgoer, and he got his hair cut every four weeks by Chiapas, whose father ran a barbershop down the block. All told, Douglas was a quiet and, he thought, happy man. He was also the only male teacher at St. Agnes. Cheryl, Audrey, and Katya, the three single women on the faculty, would have taken up the crusade of dating him, but he wasn't drawn to his coworkers. Cheryl wore electric shades of suède that confused him, Audrey had two cops for ex-husbands, and Katya, despite her long legs and Lithuanian accent, was cruel to the girls. So Douglas spent his nights alone seeing films, correcting essays, and occasionally chatting with Chiapas and company. On this particular night, Douglas was barely into his stack of essays when the phone rang.

"Hello?" sighed Douglas. He expected it to be his mother, who called weekly from Pennsylvania to see if her son had become miraculously engaged.

"Good evening, Mr Kerchek,"

Douglas frowned. "Nicole?"

"Yes, sir."

"How did you get this number?"

"Off the Rolodex in the principal's office. How's your ankle?"

Douglas sneezed, twice. He did this instinctively when he didn't know what to say.

"God bless you," said Nicole.

"Thank you," said Douglas. He glanced around, as if expecting his apartment suddenly to fill with students.

"How's your ankle?"

"It's . . . it's all right. I banged it on my radiator."

"Really?"

The truth was, Douglas had slipped in his shower, like an elderly person.

"Yes, really. Nicole—"

"Do you know what's happening to *my* ankle as we converse?"

"No."

"John Stapleton is licking it. He likes to nibble my toes, too."

Douglas blinked several times.

"John Stapleton is a domestic shorthair. Sometimes he licks, other times he nibbles."

"I see," said Douglas. There was a substantial pause.

"John Stapleton is a cat," said Nicole.

"Of course," agreed Douglas.

"Do you enjoy gnocchi?"

Douglas set his essays on the couch beside him. "Pardon?"

"Gnocchi. Italian potato dumplings. We had them for dinner tonight. Father makes them by hand every Thursday. It's the only thing Father knows how to cook, but he's good at it."

Douglas crossed his ankle over his knee.

"So, do you enjoy them?" said Nicole.

"Gnocchi?"

"Yes."

"Yes."

"Yes meaning you enjoy them, or yes meaning you understood what I was asking?"

"Yes. I mean yes, I like them."

Nicole Bonner laughed.

"When should I start hearing from colleges?" she asked. "It's nearly April."

Douglas was relieved at the topic. "Any week now. But you'll get in everywhere. It's all about what you want."

"I want Princeton."

Douglas imagined Nicole sitting on a dorm bed, reading, sipping soup. He imagined baggy sweater sleeves covering her wrists.

"Fitzgerald went there," said Nicole.

"Yes," said Douglas.

"He was a career alcoholic."

"Yes."

"Did you know that John Stapleton is toilet trained?"

Douglas laughed out loud, once. This usually happened only at the movies, if he was alone and the film was absurd.

"Toilet trained. Meaning what?"

"Meaning that he uses the toilet, like a human being. He crouches on the rim of the bowl and does his business and presses his paw on the flusher afterward. He's very tidy."

"Nicole," said Douglas.

"It's the truth, sir. It took Father aeons to train him, but he did it. We don't even have a litter box. Father was a marine."

Douglas checked his watch. "John Stapleton's an unusual name for a cat."

"He's an unusual cat," said Nicole.

"I think maybe I should hang up now, Nicole. Why don't we talk in school tomorrow?"

"All right. I don't want to inconvenience you in your evening time."

"It's all right."

"Really?"

"Well," said Douglas. "What I mean is, it's no problem. But, um, we'll talk in school tomorrow."

"Inevitably," said Nicole.

. . .

Douglas had written Nicole a letter of recommendation for Princeton. In the letter he'd said this:

> Whether she's tearing across the field-hockey grass, debunking Whitman, or lecturing me about Woody Allen films, Nicole exudes an irrepressible spirit and a generous, unguarded tenacity. She reads an entire novel every night, not to impress anyone but because she loves to do it. She is organized, clever, and kindhearted, and once she knows what she wants she will pursue a thing—a line of argument, a hockey ball, a band to hire for the prom—with a charmingly ruthless will.

Douglas prided himself on his recommendations, on making his students shine on paper. It was one of the few vanities he allowed himself. When it came to crafting words, Douglas felt that he'd been blessed with a knack for always knowing what to say. That was why, the morning after the call from Nicole, Douglas awoke feeling flummoxed. He'd spent ten minutes on the phone with a nineteen-year-old girl and tripped over his tongue like a schoolboy the whole time. During the night, he'd also dreamed he'd been walking barefoot down a beach with Nicole. In the dream, she wore a lowrider black bikini and a lovely blue scarf in her hair like Jackie Kennedy. Douglas, meanwhile, wore green Toughskins jeans and a shirt made of burlap. Every time the waves washed over their feet, Douglas scampered back and yelled, "Beware of the manatees!"

Ridiculous, thought Douglas. Embarrassing. He put on a smart coat and tie, and decided to give the girls a pop quiz.

At school, in the faculty lounge, he forced himself to make small talk with Cheryl, the suède-clad mathematician. When the bell rang for his class, Douglas strode into the classroom with confidence.

"Mr Kerchek." Meredith Beckermann jumped from her desk. "Jill's going to ask you to come watch softball today, but you promised to see our Forensics meet against Regis, remember?"

"I remember," said Douglas.

"Suckup," Jill told Meredith.

Meredith glared at Jill. "Avaunt, and quit my sight," she sniffed.

Douglas set his satchel on his desk, surveyed the room. His advanced-placement class consisted of six girls, the brightest lights in the St. Agnes senior class. There were Meredith and Jill, the arguers; Rhonda Phelps, the bombshell achiever; Kelly DeMeer, the agnostic; Nancy Huck, who was always on vacation; and Nicole Bonner, who sat by the window.

"Where's Nancy?" asked Douglas.

"Bermuda," said Rhonda. "Snorkeling, with her aunt."

Jill tapped her copy of "Othello." "Can we discuss the last act?"

"Desdemona's a dipshit," said Meredith.

"Meredith," Douglas warned. He glanced at Nicole, then at Kelly. They spoke the least of the six, Kelly because she was cultivating spiritual fatigue and Nicole because . . . Well, thought Douglas, because she was Nicole. The look in her eyes when she stared out the window reminded Douglas of when he was a boy and he would gaze at his mother's dressing-room mirror, wondering who lived on the other side.

"Vocab quiz," said Douglas.

The girls cleared their desks. They whipped out pens and blank pieces of paper.

"Three synonyms, from Latin roots, for 'bellicose.'" Douglas thought out loud. "Two antonyms for 'abstruse.' One example of synecdoche. Extra credit, list four books by Melville. You have five minutes."

The girls began writing immediately. Douglas watched them with fondness. They were gifted young women, and they would all conquer this class and every literature class in their future. He passed among them, staring at their bent heads, at the roots of their hair and their earlobes, wondering how many had prom dates, how many might end up teachers, how quickly Rhonda would marry. He rolled his eyes at Meredith's and Jill's papers: each of them already had seven synonyms for "bellicose." Kelly had finished in three minutes, and was now drawing hangman nooses—her trademark—on all of her "T"s. Then Douglas looked over Nicole's shoulder. Her paper was in a band of sunlight, and on it she had written no vocabulary words whatsoever. She was, however, busily churning out sentences. Douglas watched, then caught his breath. Nicole had written verbatim, from memory, the entire first page of "Moby-Dick," and was still going. Douglas waited to see if she would run out of steam or turn her head to look at him, but she didn't.

Douglas leaned down. He could smell Nicole's raspberry shampoo. He scribbled in the margin of her paper, "This isn't what I asked for."

Without glancing up, Nicole crossed out what he'd set down and wrote, "It is a far, far better thing that I do."

"Pens down," said Douglas.

After school, he performed his daily regimen, half an hour of free weights followed by a three-mile run in Central Park. He got back to St. Agnes with just enough time for a shower before the Forensics match. Outside the locker room, lounging on her back on a windowsill eight feet off the ground, was Nicole Bonner.

"How'd you get up there?" panted Douglas. He was winded from his run.

"Flew." Nicole sat up, studied her teacher. Douglas had a privileged view of her ankles, which were crossed and not at all blue. She wore low black pumps.

"What'd you read last night?" he asked.

"'The Moviegoer.' Walker Percy. Did you know, Mr Kerchek, that thousands of runners die every year from heart attacks in mid-workout?"

"I don't think I run fast enough to induce cardiac trauma, Nicole."

The girl on the ledge didn't swish her legs. Even when she chewed her hair, Douglas thought, she didn't do it nervously. She made it seem correct.

"'Trauma' is an excellent word to say out loud repeatedly. Trauma. Trauma."

"I should shower," said Douglas.

Nicole pointed at him. "Give me one good reason why I should go to college at all."

"Tons of reading time," said Douglas.

Nicole jumped off the ledge, landed lightly on her feet a yard from Douglas.

"I'll accept that," she said, and off she walked.

It was three weeks later, on a rainy Tuesday morning in mid-April, that Douglas received the invitation. Just before chapel, Nicole Bonner poked her head into the faculty lounge, where Douglas and Katya Zarov sat beside each other on the couch. Douglas was reading the paper, and Katya had just noticed a run in her stocking.

"Mr Kerchek," said Nicole.

Douglas and Katya looked up.

"No students in here," said Katya.

"Mr Kerchek, I need to speak to you privately." Nicole stood with her hands behind her back like a butler.

Douglas stood. Katya Zarov made a little snort.

Out in the hall, Nicole flashed Douglas a smile.

"Princeton's taking me," she said.

Douglas had a fleeting image of hugging his student. He patted her once on the shoulder.

"That's wonderful," he said. "Congratulations."

Nicole nodded sharply. She had a Bible under one arm, which surprised Douglas.

"As a thank-you for your letter of recommendation, my parents and I would like you to join us for dinner this Thursday at our home."

"Well," said Douglas, "that's very kind, but there's no need."

"We'll be serving gnocchi that Father will have prepared by hand. I've assured Father that you enjoy gnocchi."

"Nicole," began Douglas.

The bell for chapel rang.

"You told me that you enjoy gnocchi, Mr Kerchek."

"Oh, I do," said Douglas quickly. "But— Listen, Nicole, I'm very proud that you've gotten into Princeton, but you don't have to—"

"I'm reading the Book of Revelation." Nicole tapped the Bible. "In case you were wondering."

Girls surged past Douglas and Nicole, chattering, chapel-bound.

"Come on, Nicky," said Rhonda Phelps.

"Good morning, Mr Kerchek," said Audrey Little, the horny health teacher.

Nicole cocked her head to one side. "Did you know, Mr Kerchek, that there are creatures in the Book of Revelation covered entirely with eyeballs?"

Douglas shook his head. He felt slightly dizzy, in need of ibuprofen.

"My parents and I will expect you at seven on Thursday." Nicole stepped backward. "We live in the Preëmption apartment building, West Eighty-second and Riverside."

"Preëmption?" called Douglas, but Nicole Bonner had turned away.

On Thursday afternoon, Douglas got his hair cut at the corner barbershop. Chiapas, who wasn't yet five feet tall, stood on a milk crate, moving an electric razor over Douglas's sideburns, grinning at him in the mirror.

"You a week early, Uno. Hot date tonight?"

Douglas smirked. "Yeah, right."

Chiapas whistled a tune Douglas didn't know. Because Chiapas was only an apprentice, Douglas got his haircuts for free, but, in what he recognized as a ridiculous instinct, Douglas felt he was keeping the boy out of trouble.

"Bet you got a date, Uno. Bet you and Grace Kelly going out for langostino."

"Uh-huh."

Chiapas knew Douglas's movie addictions.

"Ow." Douglas flinched, and Chiapas pulled the razor away. Douglas turned his head. Two inches below his part, the razor had bitten his hair down to the scalp.

"Whoops." Chiapas shrugged. "Sorry, Uno."

Douglas fingered the gash. "Chiapas. Today of all days."

The boy's eyes lit up. "You do got a date."

Douglas blushed. "I do not."

Chiapas inspected Douglas's head. The cutaway hair was in the shape of a question mark without the period. "Don't worry, Uno. It's cool. She'll love it."

"There is no she," insisted Douglas.

At 7 P.M., Douglas arrived at the Preëmption. He wore a camel's-hair sports coat, and he carried a German chocolate cake from Café Mozart. He'd thought first to bring wine, then decided it was inappropriate, since Nicole was his student.

In the lobby, Douglas was met by a tall black doorman with an oval scar on his forehead. "Douglas Kerchek?" said the doorman. "This way."

Douglas followed the doorman to an ancient Otis elevator, the hand-operated kind. "Top floor. Penthouse." The doorman ushered Douglas into the elevator, pulled a lever, and stepped out. *"Bonne chance."*

The elevator doors closed, and Douglas was alone, moving. The mahogany walls smelled like something Douglas couldn't place, a medieval monks' library, maybe, or the inside of a coffin. When he disembarked, the door to the Bonner penthouse was already open. Nicole stood leaning against the jamb.

"Good evening, Mr Kerchek."

Douglas made an effort not to widen his eyes. Nicole was wearing the most exquisite black silk evening gown he'd ever seen. It lay along the lines and curves of her body so perfectly that the material might have been woven around her as she stood there in the doorway. The gown was exactly as black as her hair, and, for a fantastic second, Douglas imagined that crushed black diamonds and the ink of several squid had gone into making the silk.

"Hello, Nicole," said Douglas. "You look . . . really nice."

"You have a question mark on your head," said Nicole.

Douglas sneezed, twice. Nicole blessed him. A man and a woman appeared behind her.

"My parents," said Nicole, not looking at them.

"Samson," announced the man.

"Paulette," said the woman, smiling.

Samson Bonner resembled a gigantic bass instrument. He was well over six feet tall, and although his torso sloped massively forward around the abdomen, it appeared to be formidably muscled. His voice was resoundingly deep, almost a shout, and his eyes were black. He was a renowned lawyer of unwavering conservative politics.

His wife, Paulette, was as skinny and straight as a flute.

"The teacher, the teacher," chirped Paulette. "Come in, come in."

They all moved inside. Samson Bonner shut the door. Paulette whisked Douglas's cake box off to another room.

"Cocktails," boomed Samson.

Douglas looked around. The Bonner penthouse was the kind of lair that nefarious urbanites like Lex Luthor occupied in films. The huge main room had a high ceiling and a marble floor. Lining one entire wall were shelves bearing leather-bound books that, for all Douglas knew, could be traced to the same monks' library he'd smelled in the elevator. Also in the room were two hunter-green couches, a hearth with a fire, a glass table laid for dinner, an oaken door that opened onto a study, and three tall windows. Through these, Manhattan could be seen, laid out like a map on which schemes were planned.

Paulette Bonner swept back into view, carrying a tray of glasses and a cocktail shaker. "Sidecars, Sidecars." She set the tray on an end table by the couches.

"We're a brandy family, Douglas," said Samson. "We have a gusto for brandy."

"Ho ho," said Douglas. He'd meant it to sound chipper and hale, but it didn't.

The women sat on one couch, the men on the other. Samson Bonner wore a fine, bone-colored suit. His wife, who had black hair like Nicole's, wore a gray dress. The fire crackled. Douglas sipped his drink, which tasted like limes. In his home town, Allentown, Pennsylvania, very few drinks contained limes.

"I'm so proud of Nicole," said Douglas. "Um, you must be, too."

"We are, we are," breathed Paulette.

"Well, hell." Samson Bonner punched Douglas on the shoulder. "Just because Princeton has a white-boy hoop club doesn't mean they can't compete. Am I wrong?"

"No," said Douglas, whose shoulder now hurt.

"So they're pick-and-roll," declared Samson. "So they're old-school backdoor. So what?"

"We're so pleased you've come," said Paulette.

Douglas glanced back and forth between the parents. Despite their bookshelves, he couldn't tell yet whether they were literary, like their daughter.

"How's your Sidecar, Mr Kerchek?" asked Nicole.

"It's brandy and Cointreau," explained Paulette.

"And limes!" shouted Samson.

Douglas smiled and nodded.

"Anyway," said Samson, "let's hear from the man." He patted Douglas's back.

A silence ensued. Douglas grinned foolishly until it hit him.

"What, you mean me?"

The Bonners sat waiting, looking at Douglas.

"Well." Douglas scratched his recently botched head. "What would you like to hear about?"

"Hell, we don't know." Samson har-hared.

"You want to hear about me? That I'm from Pennsylvania, that kind of thing?" Douglas looked at Nicole.

"Nah," said Samson. "Teach us something."

"Yes." Paulette's eyes flashed.

"Teach us something," said Samson, "or else no gnocchi for you."

Douglas laughed. No one joined him.

Nicole cleared her throat. "Father's serious, Mr Kerchek." She peered at her teacher over her glass. "He gets like this. You have to teach him and my mother something or the evening can't progress."

Douglas gazed at his student. He saw that she was in earnest, then he looked quickly away. Nicole's hair was pulled back taut against her head tonight, and Douglas feared that if he stared too long at the taper of her temples her father, the marine, would notice.

"Um. What would you like to learn?"

"Hell, we're easy." Samson punched Douglas again.

"Teach them a word," suggested Nicole. "Something quick. I'm hungry."

Douglas moved to the edge of the couch, out of Samson's range. He thought of things he knew well. He thought of books.

"I suppose," said Douglas, "I suppose I could tell you why I think Shakespeare named 'King Lear' 'King Lear.'"

Paulette looked anxious, as if Douglas were in peril.

"*Leer* is the German word for empty. And 'King Lear' is an existential play. The title character ends up mad, out in the wilderness, living in a hovel, like Job. He's a man stripped down, all alone with the truth of himself." Douglas raised his eyebrows. "An empty man."

"Bravo!" shouted Samson. He jabbed toward Douglas's shoulder, but Douglas stood up quickly. He poured himself a fresh Sidecar.

"Empty, empty." Paulette sounded delighted.

Nicole narrowed her eyes. "You never taught us that."

"What?" said Douglas.

"We read 'King Lear' last November. You never taught us about the German. About the name."

Douglas shrugged. He set down the cocktail shaker. "Well, it's just a theory I have. It's nothing proven."

"Wrong." Samson pointed at Douglas. "It's the truth. I know the truth when I hear it."

"Well," said Douglas.

"It's the truth and you found it." Samson gave Douglas the thumbs-up. "The evening can progress."

Nicole stood. "I think it's damn selfish, that's what I think." She glared at Douglas.

"What is?" said Douglas.

"You," snapped Nicole. "You, keeping your precious little theory all secret from your students."

"Now, wait a minute," said Douglas.

"No." Nicole crossed her arms under her breasts in a manner that Douglas could not ignore. "You're our teacher, Mr Kerchek. You're supposed to lay bare your thoughts on behalf of us girls."

"Looks like he kept some thoughts for himself." Samson winked at Douglas.

"Hmph." Nicole raised her chin, which made Douglas see her neck, the shadowy knife of her cleavage. "I am absolutely disappointed," she said icily, "and I will not speak again tonight until after the salad course."

Nicole left the couch and took her place at the table.

Samson rubbed his hands together. "Let's eat!" he cried.

During the shrimp cocktail, Douglas related much of his life to the Bonners. He was nervous because Nicole was moody and silent, and he ended up blurting out the stories of his postgraduate year in Japan, his bout with mononucleosis, his disastrous senior prom with Heather Angelona.

"You're feeling all right now, though?" said Samson.

Douglas looked up from his salad. "Sir?"

"You've recovered, I mean. From the mono."

"Oh. Yes, sir. I had it thirteen years ago."

"Bravo." Samson wolfed a chunk of cucumber. "Look, no more of this 'sir' business. I'm Samson, dammit."

"All right." Douglas tried to catch Nicole's eye. She sat across from him, while Samson and Paulette sat at the long ends of the table. When Nicole stared only into her salad, Douglas switched his gaze to the book wall behind her.

"So, Samson," said Douglas. "Paulette. Those are some wonderfully bound books there. Have you read most of them?"

Samson stared hard at Douglas. He let ten seconds pass.

"Douglas," said Samson. "I have read each and every one of them cover to cover."

"Really?" Douglas scanned the shelves again. "That's unbelievable."

Samson scowled. "Oh, is that what it is, Mr Harvard? Unbelievable?"

"I'm sorry," said Douglas quickly.

"You're a contentious bastard," declared Samson.

Douglas's stomach bottomed out, the way it had in high school before his boxing matches. "Samson, Mr Bonner. I certainly meant no insult."

"Ha!" shouted Samson. "Got you!"

Douglas looked at the Bonner women, who wore thin, knowing smirks.

"What?" said Douglas.

"I was giving you the business, Doug," chuckled Samson. "Had to test your mettle."

"Oh." Douglas took a gulp of his wine. "Ha-ha," he said weakly.

"I shall now rejoin the conversation," said Nicole.

"Hell." Samson pointed his fork at the books. "I've never read a single one of those things, Doug. They're a priceless collection."

"They're heirlooms," said Paulette.

"Right, heirlooms." Samson chewed and swallowed. "Nicole reads them. They belonged to my ancestor Vladimir Bonner. He was a prince from the Carpathian Mountains or some crazy bastard place." Samson waved his hand dismissively. "The point is, he was a prince, and these were his books."

"The point is, Bonners are royalty," said Nicole.

Samson slapped the table. "The gnocchi," he bellowed. "I made them myself." He glared around, as if expecting dissent.

Paulette served the main course, which Douglas had to admit was delicious. He sipped his wine, and the conversation mellowed. Samson spoke of common concerns—the mayor, the weather, the stock market. Douglas listened. He complimented Samson on the gnocchi. When Samson asked about his Allentown boyhood, Douglas mentioned the Eagle Scout he'd been, but did not mention the chipmunks he had killed with firecrackers. Paulette asked Douglas about his favorite films, and Douglas answered. Every time Douglas looked at Nicole, she looked right back at him. All in all, Douglas was enjoying himself. The Chardonnay settled lightly in his head, and he found himself wondering random things, like how the Yankees would do this season, how cold it was outside, how curvy Nicole had ever emerged from beanstalk Paulette. The gnocchi plates were cleared.

"Well, girls," said Samson, "let's cut to the chase."

Paulette placed a snifter of brandy before each person.

"Which chase is that?" said Douglas, smiling. He wiped his mouth with his napkin.

"We feel that you should marry Nicole," said Samson.

Douglas sneezed four times in a row. Everyone blessed him.

"Pardon?" said Douglas.

"Paulette and I would like to arrange a marriage between you and our daughter here. Our only child."

Douglas stared at the Bonners. They were all seated in their chairs, smiling politely. Nicole wore the look that she always wore just before she aced a test. Nobody laughed.

"You're kidding," said Douglas.

"Oh, no." Samson Bonner sipped his brandy. "I'm not giving you the business, Doug."

Douglas got the boxing feeling in his stomach again. When he was young, he'd participated in the Friday Night Smokers, weekly events at the Society of Gentlemen club. The Gentlemen were hardworking Allentowners who drank whiskey and played cards on Friday nights. Every weekend, they brought in a crew of boys from area high schools. To earn themselves rib-eye steak dinners, the boys donned gloves and duked it out in a lighted canvas ring in the center of the club while the men drank and cheered. To be picked to box a Smoker was the highest honor an Allentown boy could receive, and Douglas had been chosen to fight fourteen times. He'd won twelve of those fights, one by a knockout, and he'd never had his nose broken. Some nights even now, just before he fell asleep, Douglas remembered himself in the ring, fighting Heather Angelona's brother Carmine. Carmine had ten pounds on him, and he was beating Douglas on points till the third round, when Douglas delivered an uppercut that jacked Carmine right off the ground and dropped him unconscious. The men in the room roared like lions. The bell clanged. Douglas remembered the cigar smoke in his nose, blood on his face, and, strangely, no blood on Carmine's. Watching Mr Angelona revive his son with smelling salts, Douglas had wanted simultaneously to vomit and to shove his tongue into Heather Angelona's mouth.

Douglas shook his head, cleared it. He stood up. "Nicole," he said severely. "What's going on? Is this some joke, some bizarre family hoax?"

"No." Nicole rested her fingertips calmly on the table. "My parents would honestly like you to marry me. So would I."

"Please sit down, Douglas," said Paulette.

For once, her tone had no levity. Douglas sat. "This is nuts," he said. "We're just having dinner."

Samson Bonner rapped the table with his knuckles. "Hell, son,

Paulette and I have been happily married for twenty-five years, and guess what? My father set the whole thing up. He and Paulette's father were law partners."

"My maiden name is Depompis," explained Paulette.

"Right," said Samson. "Depompis. Anyway, our fathers saw that Paulette and I would stack up together. Well, we feel that you and Nicole stack up, too."

Douglas's head was swimming. "You've discuss this? As a family?"

"Sure," said Samson. "Every night for a week."

"Excuse me, Mr . . . Excuse me, Samson, but you don't even know me."

"Oh, hell." Samson swatted the air as if it held gnats. "Nicole knows you. She says you watch a movie every night just like she reads a book every night."

"It's adorable," said Paulette.

Douglas stared at his student. She smiled quickly.

"Nicole," he said. "You're nineteen."

"Twenty in September," said Nicole.

"We held her back," said Paulette. "In third grade."

"Well, twenty, then," said Douglas.

"She struggled with phonics," said Paulette.

"Excuse me." Douglas cleared his throat loudly. The Bonners hushed themselves.

"Listen," said Douglas, "you've— I've— This has been a lovely meal, but— Well, aren't you all being quite preposterous? As I was trying to point out—"

"Young man," said Samson, "do you not find Nicole attractive?"

Douglas shut his mouth. He kept expecting a game-show host to spring out from behind a curtain. Nicole sat opposite him in her impossibly black dress, watching him with her relentless blue eyes. For the first time, Douglas honestly considered what it would be like if she were his. He thought of Lillian Marx, the last woman he'd dated, who'd adored jazz. He imagined holding Nicole's hand, driving with her to Montauk in a convertible, the radio playing the punk bands he knew she liked. He blushed.

"Religion's not an issue," blustered Samson. "Nicole assures me that you're High Episcopal, same as we are. She admires your intellect, and you always give her an A. So what's your problem, Doug?"

"Douglas," said Paulette. "We're really very impressed with you. Especially now that we've met."

Douglas sat up very straight. "Yes. Well, As I was trying to say, Nicole's eleven years younger than I am. Doesn't that seem . . . problematic?"

"No," said Samson. "I've got twelve years on Paulette."

"Mr Kerchek," said Nicole. "Did you know, Mr Kerchek, that in centuries past a girl was often married and birthing offspring by fourteen?"

"Let's not rush into any birthing," chuckled Samson.

"This isn't the Middle Ages, Nicole." Douglas swallowed some brandy after all. "You haven't even been to college."

"Well, I'm going, aren't I?"

"Of course she is." Paulette sounded offended. "No daughter of mine will be denied an education because of her husband."

"Now, hold on," said Douglas.

"Hey," growled Samson. "You can have my daughter's hand, Doug, and we'll give you some starting-out money, but Princeton's nonnegotiable. Don't try to weasel her out of that."

"I wasn't."

"No weaseling," said Nicole.

Douglas sighed heavily. "I need to use the bathroom," he said.

"Well, hell," said Samson. "Who wouldn't?"

Paulette pointed to a hallway. "Third door on the right."

Douglas strode quickly out of the room. His mind was a blur. He thought of his unserved, uneaten German cake. He recalled a teaching class he'd once taken, where the instructor had told him to watch out for female students and their crushes.

Is that what this is? thought Douglas. A crush?

The door to the bathroom was slightly ajar. Douglas was about to push it fully open when he heard a toilet flush from within.

"Excuse me," he said automatically. He stepped back, surprised. Moments later, the door nudged open and a black cat stepped out of the bathroom. It stopped at Douglas's feet and looked directly up at him.

"John Stapleton," whispered Douglas.

"*Mrow,*" said John Stapleton.

The cat nibbled briefly at the toe of Douglas's left shoe, then proceeded down the hall, disappearing into the shadows.

This is insane, thought Douglas. This night, this family, this cat, all of them are certifiable. But the cat seemed like an omen, somehow, and as Douglas washed his face and hands in the bathroom sink, as he studied his goofy haircut and took deep, weight-lifting breaths to compose himself, he thought of Nicole. He thought of the simple silver-post earrings she always wore. He recalled the Melville she'd committed to memory, the respect she had for Graham Greene novels, the merciless grip she kept on her stick when she played field hockey. Her favorite film was "The Philadelphia Story," a tough favorite to argue against. He'd heard her rail passionately against the death penalty once during an ethics-class debate, and he'd seen her hold a faculty member's baby in her arms.

"I'd like to talk to Nicole alone," said Douglas, when he rejoined the Bonners.

"Of course you would," said Samson.

"Alone, alone." Paulette smiled wearily at Douglas.

"Use my study." Samson stood up, shook Douglas's hand.

They were alone. The study door was closed. Nicole sat on a daybed, her shoes off, her calves drawn together and to one side. Across the room, Douglas sat on the edge of a wooden chair, the top crossbar of which was embossed with a crest. Douglas thought that it might be the Bonner family crest, but he didn't ask.

Nicole cracked her knuckles. "In a minute, I'm going to start calling you Douglas instead of Mr Kerchek."

"Oh, really?"

Nicole sighed. "Mr Kerchek, please just listen. I'm going to say some things."

Douglas collected his thoughts. Outside the door was a married couple on a green couch, drinking brandy, perhaps petting John Stapleton. In the study with him was a headstrong young woman.

"Mr Kerchek," said Nicole, "you know that I'm smart. That I can think and read well, the way you could when you were nineteen. But I also know what the world is like, Mr Kerchek."

Douglas watched Nicole. She's serious, he thought. She's deadly serious.

"I know," said Nicole. "I know how long people go in this city without finding someone to love. I'm young, but I understand loneliness." Nicole rubbed her feet. "Listen, I know I can be irrational, Douglas."

Douglas caught his breath. He felt something in his spine—fear, maybe.

"Like tonight," said Nicole. "That 'King Lear' business. But here's something you probably don't know. I saw you at the Film Forum last week."

Douglas blushed again.

"They were showing 'The Gunfighter,' with Gregory Peck. It was last Tuesday, the 9 P.M. show. I saw it advertised in the paper, and I just knew you'd be there. So I went."

Douglas tried to remember what he'd worn that night, what candy he'd brought with him. A flannel shirt? Gummi Bears?

"I sat five rows behind you and watched your silhouette. I saw you admiring the guy who played the bartender. You know, the guy from 'On the Waterfront.'"

Douglas closed his eyes. She's right, he thought. She's nineteen and she's right.

"Anyway, whether you marry me or not, this is what I want to tell you." Nicole exhaled. "It's no good, Douglas."

Douglas kept his eyes closed. He was listening.

"It's no good the way you're living. All those weights you lift, all those miles you run, all those movies you see. It isn't right. It's lonely."

Douglas looked at her then. He saw her curves and her temples, but something else, too, something that lived behind her eyes.

"You're a good teacher and all, but you're just killing time, Douglas. I can tell."

Bullshit, thought Douglas. Then he thought, How? How am I killing it?

"I can tell from the books you assign, the ties you wear, everything." Nicole was not chewing her hair. "You're ready, Douglas. For *the* woman, the one you're supposed to marry." Nicole shrugged, just a little. "And I think she's me. I've dated some guys, and I know what's around, and— Well, I just know what I want."

"How?" blurted Douglas. His hands trembled on the snifter, so he put it down. He felt as if he might weep. "Are you in—" Douglas changed phrases. "Do you love me?"

Nicole petted her neck, sipped her brandy. "Look. I've got Princeton to go to. And I've got that huge heirloom library out there to read. I'm just saying that you should have a woman with you at the movies, and she should be me. I'm ready for her to be me."

Douglas couldn't sit still any longer. He stood up and paced. He wanted to shout or punch or be punched. He wanted something he knew the feeling of. He stalked over to Nicole, unsure of what to do.

"Easy, Douglas." Nicole moved back on the daybed.

"No." Douglas shook his head, went back to pacing. "No 'Easy, Douglas.' You have to tell me something here. I'm thirty-one, and I'm— I'm your *teacher*, for Christ's sake. I mean— Is this— Look, answer me, now, Nicole."

"O.K.," she whispered. "I will."

"Is this real? I mean, are you . . . in love with me?" He couldn't believe what he'd asked.

"I'm ready to be," said Nicole. "And I mean this as a compliment, but I've got nothing better to do."

Douglas stopped pacing. "I'm going crazy," he said softly. "I'm standing here, solidly, on my own two feet, and I'm going crazy.'"

Nicole smiled. She took his hand.

"Listen," she said. "I have the prom in a month, which my cousin Fred is escorting me to, and graduation's two weeks after that. It'll be hectic for a bit, but as of the first week of June I'm prepared to become completely infatuated with you."

Douglas laughed out loud, once, at the practicality in her voice. He thought of his mother, of Chiapas and the Mexicans, of the unbroken chain of essays that he'd corrected for the past six years. There might have been a thousand of those essays. And there might have been a time in history when all people spoke like Nicole Bonner.

"I can commute to Princeton," explained Nicole, "or else just come back to you on weekends. My family's a little eccentric, and I am, too, but, well, there it is. What do you think?"

Douglas pulled Nicole to her feet. He felt giddy, vicious. He didn't know what he felt. Like an animal, he set his teeth for one last stand.

"Nicole." His voice was low, almost mean. "If you're kidding about all this, and you tell me tomorrow that you're kidding, then I'll . . . I'll . . . " Douglas clenched and unclenched his fists.

"I'm not kidding," said Nicole.

Douglas looked out the window at New York City. He looked back at Nicole.

"You're sure?"

Nicole reached up, trailed one hand lightly over Douglas's haircut.

"Domestic shorthair," she whispered.

Douglas took both her hands in his. He was beaming. He felt slightly nauseous. "All right. All right, if you're serious, then I want you to do something for me."

Nicole frowned. "No sex till we're hitched. A kiss, maybe."

"Be quiet and listen." Douglas's voice quavered with pleasure. "I don't want you to kiss me. I want you to hit me."

"What?"

Douglas couldn't keep the grin, the old, triumphant sass, off his face. "I want you to punch me in the stomach as hard as you can."

Nicole stepped away. "You're insane."

"No." Douglas took her by the shoulders, squared her off facing him. "Trust me. If you do this, I'll know that *we're*— I'll just know."

Nicole laughed, just a little. "You're a freak."

"Hit me."

Nicole angled her head to one side. "You're serious."

"Give me your hand."

Nicole held out her right palm.

"Make a fist. No, like this, with your thumb outside. Good."

"How do you know how—"

"Shut up and hit me." Douglas sneered at her. "Come on. Let's see what you got."

A wicked joy stole over Nicole's face. "You better watch it."

"Hit me."

"I'll do it, Douglas," she warned.

"Go ahead."

Nicole drew her fist back to her hip. Her eyes checked the door that was hiding her parents. She looked to Douglas as if she would erupt with laughter, or something else, something he couldn't predict.

"Come on, punk." Douglas dared her, and that was it. Nicole shot her fist forward and showed him what he, what both of them, were in for.

Antonya Nelson

Female Trouble

From *Epoch*

McBride found himself at the Pima County Psychiatric Hospital in the middle of the day. "Don't visit me here," Daisy told him. She slid her palms over her frizzy white hair as if to keep it from flying off like dandelion fluff. "It embarrasses me, these crazy people make me ashamed."

"I thought you wanted to see me. I thought that was the point. Why else are you in Tucson?" Daisy, McBride's girlfriend of the year before, had been discovered on the highway near the Triple T truckstop carrying a portable typewriter, trying to hitch a ride. Native New Yorker, she'd never learned to drive; maybe that was why McBride had assumed she would stay in Salt Lake City, where he'd left her. He certainly preferred to think of that chapter as a closed one, a place he had chosen against.

Daisy said, "I want to see you when I'm normal again. I just feel like you're staring at me, at my flabby skin and everything." She began jerking her shoulders in some simulation of crying but her eyes remained dry. McBride did not wish to touch her. She'd taken on an institutional smell and her sweatsuit hid any physical charm. Her eyes had lost whatever snappish wit they'd once held, glazed with depression and the medication used to treat it. McBride reached to hold her and felt she was made of something more inert than her former substance, dull as clay, and pale as an albino, as if she'd been dipped in bleach. In the past, she'd been burnished, tanned twice weekly in a salon coffin, hair dyed golden and frowsily restrained with combs and barrettes, a Victoria's Secret kind of girl, pubic hair dyed to match.

Had his leaving her brought about such thorough transformation? He felt like asking her. He was sort of flattered, sort of appalled.

When she'd fallen in love with him she'd gone to his apartment and climbed into his bed and waited for him to come home. She was a free spirit with a crush, a mission, a taste for disaster. His roommate had greeted him in the kitchen that late night, wearing boxers and socks, whispering as he stepped daintily on tiptoes, "There's a *girl* in your bed" with such admiration and awe that McBride seemed stripped of very many options. A naked girl in your bed was not a thing to take lightly.

"Drunk?" he asked, pulling off his own clothes.

His roommate had given an elaborate impatient shrug and shiver: who cared? Or: of course drunk; you had to ask?

Was she desperate? No—devoted. Spontaneous. Outrageous. A girl on fire, burning so that you wanted to stand in the radiating glow, a girl on the verge, confident in not caring. The prospect of death did not deter her. She was up for whatever.

And this had led her here, McBride supposed, later and after, immolation imminent. The Arizona desert was forgiving in February, springlike by Eastern standards. They sat in the building's courtyard. A general wooden catatonia in the human population—patients and orderlies both—made the Adirondack chairs seem full of personality, resting at jaunty angles and in conversational clusters over the ever-green grass. Other visitors carried styrofoam cups of coffee to other patients, crossing the lawn quickly, trying to be spry in the face of lethargy. McBride felt trapped by his past, and kept sneaking covert glances at his watch. His tapping foot ached for an accelerator.

What he remembered about Daisy was sex. Even when he'd stopped loving her, he'd wanted to fuck her. They'd been strangers their first night together, Daisy waiting for him drunk on that crowded single mattress. His roommate's awe, "There's a *girl* in your bed." Like a gift, a girl between the sheets, a gift, this girl, like an animal in a gunnysack, and on fire, in heat.

Was there a word for the way you winced, recalling a former affection, that place in your ribcage that briefly collapsed, your glance that no longer lingered but skimmed over her face like a skipped stone over water?

Now Daisy said, "Look," and pointed toward the hospital entrance.

"Family theater." They watched a woman wrench herself free of the guiding hands of an older couple, her parents, McBride guessed, the three of them sharing a lankiness. Their daughter was easily in her forties, long-limbed and angry, crossing her arms defiantly and refusing to enter the front doors. McBride was sympathetic to the parents, who looked harried and doomed, as if they hadn't slept in days. Daisy said, "Old farts just want to get rid of her." McBride supposed that was true but he didn't blame them.

When the woman suddenly sprinted down the walk toward the street, the parents began shouting. The woman ran like a dancer, straight into the street without looking. Her mother screamed, putting her hands to her cheeks. Cars weaved around the daughter as she stood between lanes but nobody stopped driving. Nobody in Tucson ever stopped driving. The woman stood facing traffic like the oblivious prow of a ship. McBride looked to the orderlies, who'd jumped up yet made no move toward action.

"Help her," Daisy said to him, pushing his elbow from the chair arm. He rose and started reluctantly for the street, jogging in such a way that his teeth hurt. When he reached the woman she took his arm as if she'd been waiting for him, her partner on their dance stage. She stared at him with clear, unmedicated eyes, startled like a deer, pretty and skittish.

"What am I doing?" she asked.

McBride told her what he'd seen as he escorted her up the walk. They passed her parents, who simply watched as if at a wedding.

"*You'd* never do a thing like this," she informed McBride as they entered the building's foyer. She held his arm lightly, with long shaking fingers. A group had clustered at the commotion and now drifted away, disappointed at the tame outcome.

"A thing like what?"

"Like impulsive behavior. It's a feminine trait."

McBride recalled a similar complaint Daisy had made when he refused to try sushi or inhale an illicit powder. No, he wouldn't eat raw fish, or snort alien drug. Nor would he bolt, barefooted, into traffic.

"Party pooper," Daisy called him. "Wet blanket. Coward." What was so brave about taking risks, he'd asked her. What separated it from stepping off a cliff?

"You step off holding my hand," she'd said, popping a pill, removing a garment, switching off the headlights at high speed on a dark highway. But he'd wanted a bungee, a net, a loophole.

The woman's parents had followed them inside and now stood deferentially behind McBride. The woman let loose of his arm, surrendering to her parents. "This way," she said quietly, leading them toward the admissions desk.

Daisy had her eyes closed when McBride got back to their chairs. "I'm not asleep," she told him.

McBride sat on the arm of the chair, ready to leave.

"Fix everything?" she asked acidly; this was like her, to tell him to do something, then ridicule him for doing it.

"I should go," he said.

"You should," she agreed, starting to not-cry again.

"I'll come back."

"I'll be here."

At home that evening McBride's current girlfriend, Martha, sat on newspapers painting chairs. In her spare time she decorated secondhand furniture; her house was full of it, colorful as a toy store. Yellow snakes wound up the spindles of one chair, blue tulips drawn freehand popped along the arms of another. Sad music came from a bedroom, the mournful wailing of loons. Martha's gray head was tilted and her tongue was lodged beneath her upper lip in concentration. There was the odor of hearty food beneath the paint fumes, that and the burnt herby smell of marijuana, which she'd smoked earlier. The ordinariness of the evening, the simple and somehow unbelievable normalness of it—the way McBride could accept a healthy woman in the house where he lived doing something so utterly charming as painting furniture and cooking food—should have made him happy. Instead, he was irritated by the tableau. He felt domesticated, as if it had happened against his will. Time with Daisy, however brief, had left something under his skin.

"How was she?" Martha asked.

"Drugged. Nuts. I ended up dragging some other woman out of the street in front of the hospital."

"Alive?"

"More or less." He told her about the morning while she worked her brush around in her patient, stoned method. The room grew dim and she quit, leaning back on her hands, legs splayed open lazily. She was the first woman McBride had ever known who was not at war with her body: she liked it, it liked her. She walked around in the world unselfconscious inside of it, completely casual with its shortcomings as well as its gifts. Fond, as if of a beloved pet.

"Oh, Daisy," McBride said, trying to sound as if he could dismiss his old girlfriend, laboring to evoke that useful wince that meant he was over her, ashamed of former passion. "How was *your* day?"

Martha quoted some of her accident victims' depositions to cheer him up. She worked in the police court downtown taking statements from bad drivers. This was only one of her jobs. She also interviewed rape victims for a professor at the University of Arizona, having some talent at listening. She was thirty-six, six years older than McBride, prematurely gray, and had lived with a number of men so she knew how to do it. Calmly. With a great deal of forbearance and humor. Even her name: Martha. Not Muffy, not Mart, nothing cute or hip, an old-fashioned name designating a person with both feet on the ground. She said, "'Coming home I drove into the wrong house and collided with a tree I don't have.'"

McBride smiled. Martha smiled, too, and rose to extract whatever she had cooked from the oven, which had the bloody odor of red meat and mushrooms. Wine. He suspected she made up depositions but she swore they were authentic. Her favorite went: "I had been driving for forty years when I fell asleep at the wheel and hit a telephone pole." The rape victims she and McBride had agreed not to discuss.

They ate on the front porch in the breeze of an oscillating fan. Even in February, the birds went on and on, noisy as a coffee klatch. The next door neighbor, the transvestite, came out, as he always did, as the sun fell, lips a red bow, bosom an emphatic bolster. His era was the 50s: floral, with forgiving hemlines.

"Imagine going through all of that nonsense he must go through to look like that," McBride had once mistakenly said. The shaving, the plucking, the makeup, the heels: torture. Martha had thrown her head back to laugh. She could really laugh. "Just imagine," she'd said.

They waved, as usual. The pretense seemed to be that two people shared the little house next door, a man and a woman who were never seen together yet wore the same shoe size. "What*ever*," McBride muttered, also as usual. Martha liked her funky neighborhood. She liked the tree full of umbrellas as well as the lawn art on the corner, toasters and blenders and microwave ovens set out as ornaments among the plastic flowers and spinning pinwheels. She liked the car with toys glued to its chassis. She had told McBride, when he complained of the weirdness, that as he grew older he would treasure the odd, shun the ordinary, grow easy as she was with eccentricity. It would not threaten him so.

Personally, McBride thought that Martha lived among the bizarre in order not to feel so bizarre herself, normal by comparison. Plus, her neighbors' obvious dilemmas distracted her from her own, which was that she wanted a baby. Women were on timetables, cycles, deadlines. That ticking clock, bomb or alarm, irked McBride. His gender had forever, plenitude, a wealth of progeny waiting in the wings. Babies, like the rape interviews, was a topic best avoided.

Predictably, he dreamed about Daisy that night. He was in his old house, the one he'd grown up in in Oklahoma City. In the dream Daisy lived around the corner from his parents. She rented a small sunny room. McBride visited her there and she kissed him on the cheek. He woke feeling tender toward her. It had been such a sweet kiss, so innocent and discreet, like the kiss of a child, free of history or future, and it had such melancholy force that McBride woke in a state of pure desire, which impelled his waking Martha to make love with her, his fantasy life blurred by dream. Perhaps when he came, it was into the memory of his sleeping vision of Daisy. The memory—combined, Martha and Daisy, sanity and sickness—carried him through the day, their faces next to his, his sexual past shoved against his sexual present, an interesting friction.

He visited Daisy again a week later. The tenderness of his dream had faded. Her depression made him impatient. This aspect of Daisy seemed to him an enormous weakness and he did not tolerate weakness well, trying to get a handle on his own. She wore the same sweat suit, the same muzzy expression, the same drained pallor. Today it was cloudy but they sat in the same hopeful Adirondack chairs outside, staring at the front door as if the drama they'd witnessed last time might also replay itself, the middle-aged woman fleeing her parents, the need to run into traffic. McBride was annoyed to discover he had on the identical shirt he'd worn then, too.

Without apparent emotion, Daisy said, "I'm pregnant I think."

McBride looked hard at her, trying to figure where the sensible part of her went when the other part came out.

"Don't worry," she continued, "it's not yours."

"It *couldn't* be," he said.

"True." She said nothing for a while, then added, "I could have had your baby after you moved away. I could have left her in Salt Lake, given her up to the Mormons to raise. Don't men ever wonder what happens to their sperm? I'd worry, if I were a man, but men—it's all just hit and run."

What occurred to McBride was that all the nasty forces of nature had female pronouns, typhoons and tornadoes and those mythic creatures, the Furies and Sirens. They were powerful, and they sent you reeling, they trapped you.

"Daisy, what are you going to do?"

"I don't know." She shook her fluffy head. "I have to get off of these drugs if I'm pregnant, that's for sure. But what else? You got me." She picked at the chipped green paint on her chair arm for a few minutes in silence. Then added, "There were two men in Salt Lake. We all three lived together, very French-movie. Either one could be the dad, though they'd both suck at it."

McBride said, "You know, your life is kind of crisis-oriented, have you noticed that?"

She lifted her face to the brightest cloud, the one that hid the sun, and said, sullenly, "No," and then wouldn't say another word.

Two men. The image of Daisy at the fulcrum of a threesome wouldn't leave McBride. Somehow this wrinkle intrigued him, against his will. What kind of sleeping arrangements had prevailed? Was there an alpha male, stud one, stud two? Some homosexual stuff? How did the three of them behave at breakfast, sitting together over coffee in their underwear and ruffled hair?

At home Martha attempted to cheer him. "'To avoid hitting the bumper of the car in front, I struck the pedestrian.'"

McBride told her, "I'm starting to believe these reports of yours."

Martha feigned shock, sucking on a joint. "You mean you didn't before?"

"Not before Daisy."

"Daisy," Martha said, looking bemused, annoyed in the unthreatened way a strong woman does in the face of a puny one.

"She lived with two men at once, she says."

"She's done everything, that gal, all the things I always thought I would do. It's disappointing to realize how staid I've become." But she smiled. Her complacency didn't really trouble her—look at what surrounded her, arty furniture, queer neighbors, clacking birds.

The pregnancy part went unmentioned, but the next time he visited the hospital Martha wanted to come with him. She insisted. She drove. For someone who evaluated car accidents for a living, she handled an automobile very badly, swerving arrogantly through traffic, refusing to do head checks, one palm ever ready on the horn. She had lapses but mostly Martha was reliable, grown up. Now that he'd become one, it surprised McBride how few adults were grown ups. It still seemed all seventh grade, and you had to keep on your toes.

Daisy had dressed for McBride's visit this week. Someone—some anal retentive obsessive compulsive with a lot of time on her hands—had lassoed Daisy's wild hair into tiny braids which criss-crossed her shapely skull in a flattering style. The sweat suit had been traded for black jeans and a glossy button-down shirt, under which her breasts bobbed. She'd smeared makeup over the sores around her mouth and the dark circles beneath her eyes, and she looked like a country western singer ready to make a comeback. Next to her, Martha seemed far too robust, big and indestructible, like a Hereford beside an impala. McBride saw that the visit was going to go wrong in a way he hadn't anticipated.

Women intimidated Daisy; even in the sanest of moments she didn't like them, though she pretended otherwise. Without the possibility of an encounter ending in sex, Daisy was a bit at sea. McBride sat on the grass before the willing Adirondack chairs where the women sat leaning back, faces to the sun. He thought of triangles, the two women here together only because of him; the two men in Salt Lake maybe waiting to hear from Daisy, wandering around the house wondering what they were doing together, stuck with each other and a legally binding lease. Because he could come up with nothing to say in front of Martha, McBride understood he was not innocent in his current relationship with Daisy, a fact that made him tired of himself.

Martha said, "So how are you feeling?"

Daisy took the finger she was chewing from her mouth and said, "Sad. I'm having an abortion tomorrow and that makes me *really* sad, even though I don't think I'm ready for a child."

McBride felt Martha appraising him, compiling all the data, his not telling her about the baby, his phony forgetfulness on the matter. Then she nodded at Daisy. "That's understandable. I'm just now feeling ready for a child."

"You have time. You're not old."

"I *am* old, but it's nice of you to say. I've had three abortions and every time I think, I just saved another kid from being fucked up. It's one way not to feel bad."

"Well, tomorrow I'll save my second from being fucked up."

McBride was grateful he hadn't fathered any of these fetuses. Both women looked down at him, their expressions identical: what good was he, there on the grass? He didn't want to donate his sperm to Martha's desire, and though he was in the position of footstool, they couldn't even put their feet upon him.

"Coffee," he said, hopping to. And once he'd left them together he did not want to return and so roamed the hospital halls.

The place was poorly funded, understaffed, cheaply built and maintained. It was not old enough to seem Gothically romantic nor new enough to appear at least clean and modern. In all the popular spots, the carpet was worn through; the furniture was crooked, broken plastic from the 70s, and the windows were smudged with years' worth of fingerprints, people pressing against the glass, longing to escape the big box they seemed to find themselves trapped inside. Everywhere televisions, laughtracks and commercials fading in and out of every open doorway as McBride passed. Was there anything more representative of illness and confinement than daytime TV, anything more definitively the killing of time? This first floor was public; the upper ones required speaking with a station manager. To avoid returning to Martha and Daisy—he could see them from the second floor window near the elevator, still talking together in the sun, Daisy tilted back with her eyes closed, Martha watching her—he gave himself the challenge of lying his way past a station manager. The fourth was Daisy's floor; the higher one went, the crazier the occupants.

But it was no challenge at all. He merely mentioned Daisy's name and was pointed in the direction of her room. The woman at the desk didn't even have him sign in. He opened her dresser drawers and looked in her closet. Nothing but the portable typewriter she'd been found with on the highway. Also some odd articles of clothing, obviously stuff that had been donated, discards. Plain white underpants, high-waisted and modest, nothing like what she'd worn before. A picture of Jesus over her headboard, eyes pitched upward, just as exasperated as anyone else who had to deal with Daisy.

"I didn't know you were a patient here."

McBride whirled, caught. At the doorway stood the woman from the street, arms crossed as if chilly. She resembled Audrey Hepburn, he thought, willowy, frail and jittery as a stray. "I'm not," he said, recovering. "I'm waiting for Daisy."

"Daisy." She said it skeptically. "Well, I'm glad you're not a patient because I would feel bad about not struggling more if you were. Couldn't have let another inmate be my undoing."

McBride smiled because she seemed to be joking but she didn't return the smile. She simply walked away, as if he'd made the wrong answer, the bones of her ribs and hips visible beneath her gray dress. From the hallway, he looked back outside. The Adirondack chairs were abandoned, big yawning laps.

Somehow Daisy wound up at McBride's house. This was because it was officially, legally, Martha's house, and Martha had invited her. She didn't believe Daisy was crazy. Confused, yes. In trouble, yes. Maybe even more trouble than craziness but not crazy. The thing on the highway, with the typewriter? McBride whispered this in their bedroom after Daisy had fallen asleep on the study couch.

"She was pregnant," Martha said. "Overwrought."

"She still is pregnant."

"True. But that's only till tomorrow. Then we work on getting her off the heavy-duty meds."

"What makes you want to do this? You don't even know her."

"She's your friend," Martha said simply. She wore a large white night-gown with ruffles and lace, matronly on her though it would have seemed sexy and Victorian on someone else, someone skinny, anorexic or strung out like a junkie, like the woman at the hospital, like Daisy.

"She might still be in love with me," McBride warned Martha in the dark.

Martha laughed and wouldn't stop. It was lusty, gutsy laughter, and McBride didn't like that.

"What's funny? She might be."

"Oh you sound so serious, like you wouldn't be able to defend yourself." She held her hands above her head as if shielding herself from an oncoming train. "Stop, stop! Don't love me." She laughed again. "Gimme a break. You're a big strong man, capable of fending off a crazy woman's love."

"You said she wasn't crazy."

"She shows all the signs of molestation."

"Naturally. She's a tabloid story, waiting to happen."

"I'm pretty sure she's been sexually abused."

"Only with permission," McBride said. "Only because she wanted to be."

"You don't believe that." In fact he did believe it, but best to keep that to himself. Best to leave that can of worms in the cupboard. On this subject they could not have an agreeable conversation. Martha had interviewed over a hundred rape victims, her specific interest in their notions of dress and how they felt about their bodies, before and after. She and McBride lay with thoughts of rape between them, a few moments of respectful silence. She believed he was better than he was; often he did not feel like dispelling this.

Then she rolled on top of him and became heavy. She loved to start sex this way, covering him like a blanket, breathing into his neck, heat, comfort. Her bed she'd made herself, headboard a pilfered road sign from high school days. Her friends had wanted *Dip* or *Proceed with Caution* or *Men at Work* but what had Martha stolen? *Soft Shoulder.*

"The act of rape and the act of love are the same gesture," she'd told him once, explaining the messiness, the warring, scarring horror.

"Insert tab A into slot B," McBride said, deflecting, going for the joke.

"No, I mean that something twisted and confusing like that is called a paradox."

"A pair of ducks?" He didn't want to be educated; he knew he'd fail the final exam. He'd had it with complexity.

"A pair of fucked ducks."

There was something between McBride's girlfriends and it began to grow, like a romance, as if they had secrets. Daisy had only to say a word and the two of them would be uncontrollably amused, laughing so hard they couldn't speak. McBride vaguely remembered this about her, how she pulled into her private closet, made you feel that only you and she lived there, in the heady and ticklish dark. Her bratty sense of humor was surfacing, now that she'd stepped down from her meds. As well as her readiness to lie. "My brother was sexually ambivalent," she said, when the transvestite next door walked out one evening.

"Before or after the heroin overdose?" McBride said flatly. "Or maybe that was your cousin? She's always got a relative or ex-boyfriend to one-up with," he explained to Martha, who blinked at him, unmoved as a lizard.

"You're just jealous of my radar," Daisy claimed.

"Gaydar," Martha amended. And there they were, hysterical again.

There'd been no abortion, a decision made without McBride's input. One of those roommates in Utah had sent some little seed out innocent in the world, trapped and growing now inside crazy Daisy.

Meanwhile McBride continued to visit the county hospital. He went to see Claire. Claire: tall, and faintly British.

"Why are you here?" she asked him.

He shook his head. She never smiled, never let loose of a somehow reassuring seriousness. She was very somber. You could say anything. She never evaded. "Why are *you* here?" he asked.

"I can't keep house," she said. "I forget to eat. I take walks and get lost. I leave the doors unlocked. My parents' television and video camera and every single CD they owned were stolen last time they left me alone." Her parents were on an extended vacation in Greece. When they traveled, Claire stayed at the hospital.

"You're not sick," McBride told her, "you're just forgetful. If forgetfulness were an illness, the whole city would be in a strait jacket."

"I'm pathologically forgetful," Claire said. "I forget so I can hurt my parents."

"But not consciously?"

"Of course not consciously. They're retired, so this vacation they're taking is from me. Do you understand? They are sitting on a beach, a million miles away from their troubles. Meaning me. I am their troubles."

Then it was summer and McBride began sleeping with Claire. She put on her shoes and they signed her out and drove to a motel on the highway not far from the hospital. Coincidentally, it was across the street from the Triple T truckstop where Daisy had been found. $25, no questions asked. The cash exchange without receipt or bill, no evidence, no residue. What McBride liked about the Sands Motel was its air-conditioning—no swampy evaporative cooler here—which worked beautifully. Otherwise, the rooms were typically hideous and disturbing. They would not let you forget they'd accommodated hundreds of strangers before you, some sogginess in the carpet, lingering odor of cigarette, ripped sheet where someone else's toenail had pierced through. Claire in sex was the same as Claire in conversation: thoroughly confrontational, right there. "I've heard that this is the most sensitive spot on a man," she might say, pressing the pad of her thumb against his perineum.

"Yes," he would breathe, lifted as if upon a salty sea wave. "You heard right."

She had a thespian's voice, or a smoker's, and she hummed when she was up against McBride, melancholy and rousing as a distant train whistle. She alone called him by his first name, murmuring it. "Your name is like a kiss," she claimed, illustrating by placing it in the hollow of his throat. "Peter," she said, humming lungs, mouth releasing warm air. After sex she lay quietly on his chest and slept, a small smile on her lips. He nestled his palm against her scalp. She had a dainty head. Everywhere her bones were close to the surface, where her fair skin showed tiny blue veins, a network of hairline cracks, porcelain. When he pulled his hand away, her fine black hair shivered with static electricity. In sleep, she looked like what she must have looked like as a child, that smile like a dim memory, as if she were happy.

As he stroked her hair and the painfully knobby knuckles of her spinal column, he wondered why it was he had begun fucking older women. He thought he'd matured, but maybe younger women just didn't like him anymore. Was he more complicated, or more desperate? "We love each other's damage," Martha had once said, to explain their relationship. Apparently, Martha loved his, whatever it was. But only now did McBride actually follow her meaning. He couldn't have said that he loved Claire, but he felt ready to go to the mat for her. To protect this brief easy sleep. To defend her against her parents, for example, if need be, against her own self-loathing.

"You don't have to worry about suicide," she told him one day as he dropped her off after.

McBride had not, until that moment, given it a thought but from then on, of course, he thought of it frequently.

· · ·

"She hates me," McBride told Martha, referring to Daisy. What he meant was that he hated her.

He and Martha had met for lunch downtown near the courthouse where McBride was laying brick. The summer had become so hot that the workday began at five a.m., ending by one. Martha chewed her taco before answering. "She thinks you take me for granted."

"*I* take you for granted? The total stranger who's not even helping with bills, let along *house*keeping, thinks *I'm* taking you for granted?" He was outraged; then he remembered his affair with Claire and calmed down. The checks and balances of intimacy.

Martha smiled. "I have a feeling she's got a kind of crush on me, frankly. I think she thinks I saved her. She's had enough of men, for a while."

He didn't say that he didn't believe Daisy *could* capture a man, these days, so changed was her body, skin, appeal. She had an aura of illness, contagion, that only a maternal impulse could love. "How do I take you for granted?"

"I didn't say you did. Daisy said it."

"But why does she think so?"

Martha leaned forward over the paper wrappings of their lunch, looked at him with her healthy hazel eyes. "She says you used to be much more physical with her than you are with me."

"You listen to this stuff?" His voice was louder than he intended; the lawyers at the next table shifted. Daisy was right, and it made him want to go kill her.

Martha leaned back. "I'm not worried about us. I like you, I think you like me. We laugh enough, even though we don't fuck as often as we used to." She tilted her head, squinted; she could wait. "You asked me what Daisy thought and I told you, but it doesn't bother me. So don't fret."

McBride found Daisy in Martha's sewing room, asleep on the Hide-A-Bed. When he sat beside her she woke without alarm; nothing in human nature would surprise her.

She propped herself sleepily on an elbow, letting the sheet drop to reveal she wore a soiled spaghetti strap t-shirt, nipples large and brown through the sheer material, abdomen like a cantaloupe. "I was thinking you might come to me some day, Mac," she said, placing a warm hand on his thigh.

McBride stood abruptly. "I'm not seducing you," he told her. "I want you out of here, in fact. If you're well enough to think I'd sleep with you, you're well enough to get the fuck out."

"I know you're sleeping with someone else," Daisy said, her eyes leveraging the threat. She would tell. She would ruin his life. There was no correct response so he simply stared at her, hating her. Then she began crying, and it was all McBride could do to keep from throwing a tantrum himself. Her face before him—quivering chapped lips, fair eyebrows full of acne—seemed to want to be struck. What did she expect from him? It enraged him to see her sobbing; he felt like grabbing her by the shoulders and flinging her back against the couch. How dare she know his secret? She looked up from under her hair and suddenly smiled through her tears, as if she'd caught on to a trick. She was a slutty, easy girl, and McBride could not deny the appeal. He remembered her in bed: her pleasure came only in extremity, at the very moment that might mark pain. She liked to bite and be bitten, hair clutched and yanked. Now she laid a hand on his kneecap and spread her fingers slowly, as if she might insinuate herself just this way throughout his system. Infuriated, McBride lurched away, onto the floor. She followed, into his lap, and they were wrestling, Daisy sinking her teeth first into his arm and next his neck, hard enough for his nerves to trill. He put a knee between her legs and forced her arms apart. Below him, crucified, she breathed deeply, a strand of saliva across her cheek. The fact that her t-shirt and underwear did not cover her made McBride aware of her odor, which was powerful, unwashed and sexual. Rank, with a need to be hurt, and him not so far from obliging.

"Go away," he told her desperately. "Please. Go. Away." He felt his swelling erection as a betrayal—but of whom? What?

She rolled out from under him and curled toward the dark cavern beneath the bed like an animal. From the back she looked just like she always had, sinuous, nocturnal.

In the bathroom McBride tilted his head and checked the spot she'd bitten on his neck in the mirror. There were tiny broken capillaries but they looked enough like razor burn to reassure him his struggle with Daisy would go undiscovered. His heart, he noted, was beating so hard he could see it in his chest, in his reflection, pulsing there like a mouse in his pocket.

. . .

"If you want to make love with me, you can't do it with anyone else," Claire told him the next day as she ran her fingers over the bite marks on his arm. Leave it to the woman he didn't live with to sniff out his deception. "I know you live with Martha, but that doesn't necessarily mean you make love with her."

"We have sex," McBride told her, wondering why he found it necessary to convince her of this fact while obscuring others.

"Sex with someone you live with is more like masturbation," she said. "Just some warm object to rub on until you come. Do-it-yourself sex."

"I'm a do-it-yourselfer from way back," McBride said, wanting the punchline, wanting to stay out of the deep well, out of the tricky web. Women were so prone to abstraction, to pitching you into outer space. They were not afraid of the dark, the absence of gravity.

"Fucking her isn't necessarily making love," Claire said. "*We* make love." Then she fell into her post-coital nap, a little gift her body gave her, exhausted childish sleep.

He took home Claire's theory and tried it on the next time he and Martha had sex. In the living room, Daisy watched television, a habit she'd adopted at the psychiatric hospital and had not given up. She sat around the house indulging an adolescent appetite, Cheetos and Skittles, Count Chocula.

"Where are you?" Martha whispered in his face, holding it in her plump fingers, peering inside him, nose to nose. She was stoned, a state that made her want orgasm and honesty. McBride thought of Claire's words and Daisy's pregnant breasts while he worked his penis inside Martha. Where was he, indeed?

"You can go," she breathed into his ear, his mature girlfriend with her solid legs around his hips, feet locked behind him, "but you have to come back."

The next time he visited the hospital, Claire had been moved to a new ward. They were doing what an aide called a suicide watch. Claire had been caught sawing at her wrists, using a plastic knife but still. "Those things have serrated edges, man," the aide said. "Ser*rated*," he repeated.

McBride found her tranquilized, staring apathetically at a *New York Review of Books* tabloid. "I can't read this," she said. "The words are floating around like boats." Her wrists were wrapped with gauze, bright clean bracelets. "I feel poisoned," she declared, sailing the book review across the room like a Frisbee. "They're trying to kill me." Considering her behavior, McBride couldn't hold it against the hospital.

"Why?" he asked, hoping simplicity would be his strong suit.

"Why not, you big asshole? That's the real question." She drew a soppy breath, her fine features bruisey, as if she weren't getting enough oxygen. She cried in the slow, drugged way of hopeless sedation. "Asshole" was not really part of her vocabulary. That was the drugs talking.

"Baby," he said, embracing her, careful of her bandages.

"That's what I need," she said, "a term of endearment. *Muffin. Kitten.*"

"Maybe you should eat? You look kind of . . ."

"I hate fat," Claire said flatly. "I work hard to be thin. I *don't* eat, in order to be thin."

"That's kind of sick."

She simply stared at him, waiting for something she didn't know to emerge from his mouth. "Your girlfriend is fat," she added. It wasn't a good moment. McBride liked her better when she wasn't catty. Also, he was too tempted to respond in kind, to be catty with her. They could get nasty together, it turned out, eat each other's spleen. "She's a got a big *tush,* that girlfriend of yours."

"Where are Mom and Dad?"

"Flying home, wringing their . . ." She held out her own hands, illustrating by twisting her palms, wrists stiff in their wrapping. "They don't have a notion what to do."

"What should *I* do?" he asked.

"Save me," she said, collapsing against him. She wanted to take him with her, he thought. She was drowning, and if he did not escape this clutch, he would wind up washed ashore somewhere, bloated and blue.

"You can't save her," he told Martha that very night, referring to Daisy, hoping he was right. Daisy, seven months pregnant, had disappeared into South Tucson. The three of them had been eating Mexican food across from the greyhound track; they'd made money betting on those strange creatures, then celebrated with burritos and beer, Daisy on her best behavior, sipping a soda, consuming protein and calcium, like a good mother. But after the bathroom run, she was gone.

Their waiter gave an elaborate shrug, his mustache a wriggling caterpillar on his upper lip.

"Fucking Daisy," McBride said, vindicated. She could not be saved, see? "I guess we have to call the police." He got ahead of himself, saw himself standing around with a cop describing his lunatic ex-girlfriend, driving through dangerous South Tucson looking for a fuzzy-headed pregnant woman . . . But Martha was giving him such a glance full of disappointment and impatience that he returned to the present moment, Corona bottles, coagulated quesadilla.

"It scares me how much you hate her. You used to love her."

"Come on, Martha, she's manipulative and dishonest and so totally fucked up . . ." Wasn't the evidence capable of speaking for itself? Furthermore, he refused to believe he'd ever loved Daisy. No one could prove it.

"We have to find her," Martha said, rising from their booth. "You pay, I'll be out on 4th Ave., walking."

"You can't walk on 4th—" But she was through the door, and the waiter was handing McBride the ticket, shrugging again, apologetic.

They fought while they searched for Daisy. McBride considered how efficient the situation was—usually a fight required so much energy, such a commitment of time, the yelling part, the pulling-the-phone-out-of-the-wall part, the walk-around-the-block part, the silent thoughtful part, the making up part, the crying and fucking, headache and hangover, raked-over-the-coals, run-through-the-wringer, launched-into-space, deep-in-the-hole part. Hours could go by; a person could lose a day. So it was good, in his opinion, to be occupied with the quest for Daisy while they had their squabble. The problem was that Martha had more experience fighting, a more logical mindset, and made points like a lawyer. Like a public defender, the type doing pro bono business, the righteous path of the do-gooder. She took the moral high-road—Daisy in trouble, loyalty, humanity—which left McBride with the inevitable role of bastard. Add to this the affair with suicidal Claire, and you had the picture of a man in a futile argument, perhaps about to be dumped by a nice woman in whose nice house he was living, driving badly in a bad neighborhood, to boot.

He found himself hoping they would see Daisy out there in the dark.

But Daisy was gone for five days, and the fight with Martha wasn't resolved even after all that time. Somehow the stages had gotten messed up; they couldn't progress past sullen silence with each other. Martha was *disappointed* in him. He couldn't make himself fix it. She had every right to be *disappointed* in him. As much as he'd once lusted after Daisy, he now reviled her; that was what troubled Martha, the degree to which love could flip to hate. "Paradox," he wanted to tell her savagely. "That old saw."

He avoided Claire. He abandoned her by telling himself he was being true to Martha.

Daisy managed to phone them up from Phoenix, where a truck driver had left her after buying her a new wardrobe and giving her a stack of Watchtowers to contemplate. His name was Buck, and Daisy entered the house referring to his kindness constantly.

Martha hugged her wayward stray, patting Daisy's back maternally; McBride resisted the urge to punch her in the face.

"You're not a burden," Martha insisted when Daisy tried to explain her running away. "I want you to stay with me, even after the baby. I love babies." Embracing, the two women looked decidedly freakish, in McBride's opinion. "You're just bored," Martha insisted. "You need some meaningful activity during these last weeks. Maybe I could teach you how to drive?"

They settled on shopping. Neither of them was a mall type, which made the trip that much more thrilling. Daisy came home wearing her old perfume again, an expensive scent, describable in the way of fine wine: the amber plushness of pears, velvet, oak, wealth. McBride remembered it with equal parts revulsion and nostalgia.

"*Host*algia," he thought: sick desire.

That night, when he couldn't get into the spirit of a fashion show featuring maternity clothes and hair clips, Martha accused him of impersonating an adult. Abruptly she threw him a curve, direct from her stoned keenness. "Are you in love with someone else?"

"What?"

She waited.

"No," he croaked, wanting to ask if Daisy had told her something, knowing that would backfire. "No," he repeated, unconvincingly. Just a week ago it would have been a lie, but how could he explain now? The timing made him want to laugh like a madman.

"I'm sleeping in the sewing room tonight," Martha said, taking her pillow.

"Maybe you should fuck Daisy!" he blurted.

"Maybe I should," she agreed, calmly, leveling an unashamed glance in his direction.

Where did women get it, that composure, that open-minded fluid sense that not only might anything happen, but that it might be amazing? McBride could all too easily envision Daisy and Martha naked together, tongue to nape of neck, breast to breast, quivering haunch to ropy one, the homecoming embrace pushed to a climax. It was pretty, candlelit, its soundtrack full of saxophone.

Men with men: who could look upon it with anything but perplexity? Erections bobbing between them like those annoying trick snakes, coiled in a peanut can, unsealed and sent sproinging in your face. Ha ha. Meanwhile in the background, soundtrack a circus organ grinder, perhaps a kazoo.

He lay awake alone beneath the *Soft Shoulder* sign thinking of Martha. Was she trying to make him her little boy? Punish him? Improve him? "You know what your problem is?" she'd once told him, laughing yet serious, "You have gag reflex."

"Meaning?"

"Meaning, you can't deal." She did not suffer from this impediment. Why had she attached herself to *him?* Only lately had he wondered—was he a project, not unlike flaky Daisy, someone shellshocked and deemed for whatever reason worthy of Martha's concern? He didn't want to be her project. He preferred to think of himself as her willing plaything, the party boy, the one who could choose to leave the party. He paid rent, he stocked beer and toilet paper, he had volition.

"You're a coward," Martha told him in the morning. Overnight, she seemed to have chosen against him. She didn't even seem concerned enough to be hurt. Just that disappointed. "You won't commit to anything. The hard parts embarrass you. You feel like everything's a scene instead of just another opportunity to get close to someone. That's what's unforgivable. You're terrible in a crisis. You just want the easy parts, none of the work."

He could not think of Claire, but what he said was, "Is this about having a baby?"

"This is about *you,*" Martha said. "A topic with which you should be fairly familiar. This is about a woman you not only left behind like some dog on the highway, but about whom you won't say one kind word."

McBride had to marvel: even angry she wouldn't leave her prepositions dangling. "Not one," said Martha. "I can't get over what a jerk you seem to be. Actually, what I can't get over is that I'm in love with a jerk. I should know better."

"I love you, too," he said quickly.

Martha sighed. "That is *so* not the point."

Meanwhile, Claire's parents sprang her from the psych hospital, which meant that McBride had to sit in their living room drinking iced tea making small talk with them before taking Claire to the motel across from the Triple T. He was conducting an experiment, testing his maturity, trying to recapture what seemed to have scurried off. Were his intentions honorable? her parents' faces asked, forlorn, unsure how to behave if the answer were no. The scars on Claire's wrists were disconcerting, raised welts with tiny suture holes on either side.

"Will those go away?" he asked at the motel, putting his lips on her scars, working at not being disgusted.

"How should I know?" Claire was naked now, but what she'd removed were sea foam green scrubs, as if qualified to dress like a doctor, having hung around them for a while.

"Why so testy?" McBride asked, checking his watch. The iced tea and chat had seriously cut into their time. When Claire smacked him, he didn't know if it was for the question or the looking-at-the-watch. She was one unpredictable girl. They made love then, and following, went through the requisite small sleep. Everyone was different after sex; McBride preferred chatting, himself. Daisy, back when she'd been his girlfriend, smoked cigarettes afterward, like people in the 1940s movies, leaving little cinder burns in the bedsheets, soulful and alone, teary. Martha got talkative and affectionate, told jokes, tickled his ribs, wanted to eat sandwiches and leave crumbs. But Claire, she went into that wee coma.

Leaving McBride to think. Who did he love? Could he ask his women to put in bids for him, sell himself to the one who turned in the most impressive vita? Was he looking for a particular kind of woman and had to have these three to provide one whole? He considered the virtues of each—Martha's good humor and stability, Claire's startling honesty and tragic openness, Daisy's wild sexuality and obsessiveness—and understood their individual appeal as well as their limitations. But perhaps it was hav-

ing three of them that really excited him. His affection was maybe like a dropped watermelon, three rocking wet seedy parts. Or like a trident. He pictured his penis, three-pronged instead of one. Or maybe he needed the compounded guilt each relationship made him feel, especially as it related to the other two. High drama had its own charm, like living on a fault plane.

Claire's parents sat right where they'd been left, on plush Barca Loungers before the television. Their iced tea glasses still full of tea, diluted, sweating puddles. The strange stasis that had apparently prevailed here while McBride had been off in a rutting fever, ravishing their middle-aged daughter in a cheesy motel gave him pause. *This* gave him pause— her father looking sad, her mother looking sadder—not the preceding insanity.

He would not be back. His last look at Claire was like his first: she was with her parents, sullen, struggling.

He arrived home to find Daisy entertaining the transvestite. They sat in the chairs that McBride and Martha had used to sit in, in the breeze from the oscillating fan. The transvestite had left lipstick prints on a hand thrown coffee cup. In his large palms, the cup was dwarfed, silly. His nails, unpainted, were smooth, on the verge of being long, and his knuckles, McBride took a moment to notice, were shaved. Unbelievable. The man stayed seated as he extended one of these hands for a shake, like a lady.

"Alberta," he announced, "your neighbor."

"We've seen you around," McBride said, gripping a little too firmly, a little too masculinely.

"I love the furniture! Your wife is a*maz*ing with a paintbrush!"

"Not his wife," Daisy was quick to say. "How was *your* day, Mackle?" she asked coquettishly, grinning up at him, employing a long-ago pet name, reminding him of others: *Prozac,* because he'd pulled her out of a depression, way back when. *Moon Pie,* he'd called her. And meant it.

"I gotta pee," McBride said, exiting. Entering. Well, here was his house but where was his confidence about belonging in it? On the porch sat the man, the woman, the soon-to-be baby, a fundamental threesome unrelated and weird. "You're not strong enough to accept the limitations of others," insightful Martha had informed him. He wished she would quit knowing him so well, stop being so smart. Why *did* she love a jerk like him? Was that the weakness he would have to object to? He felt like a rung bell, jangling in a lonesome tower, village idiot down below yanking his chain.

"Did you know it was going to be black?" McBride asked Martha.

"I knew it was a fifty-fifty chance." Martha was flushed, wearing a set of green scrubs like the ones Claire owned. Six women had attended Daisy's labor and delivery, Daisy screaming like a tortured crow, the rest of them murmuring and assuring, room of pigeons. The baby, a perfectly healthy girl, was purple as a Nigerian. McBride could only gawk. No one else was fazed; their role was to adore, congratulate, rally. Martha cradled the baby in such a manner that McBride finally understood he would have to leave her. Already that baby meant more to her than he did, or could. Never had a decision been clearer. It made him feel oddly selfless, to see his responsibility.

"Isn't it amazing?" Martha positively glowed, face ruddy with the effort, good work, the species' only real priority. She could have been the mother herself, with her wide hips and open heart.

"Unbelievable," McBride said. He looked at the tiny bundle in her arms, dark and constricted. Hard to believe she'd grow up to wear cheap jewelry and eat junk food. Let boys put their hands between her thighs. "Reminds me of an eggplant," he told Martha.

She looked at him as if through the retracting lens of a spyglass: goodbye. "You're so cold," she said, turning back to the room of women.

The deal is, it always goes from bad to worse. The living trajectory, birth to death, going up means coming down. Like that.

McBride told himself these things as he drove to the hospital emergency room a week after Donatella's birth. Claire had jumped from one of Tucson's few overpasses into the traffic below. Everything was broken, head to toe; she would die. She lay now unconscious while a team of experts tried to put her back together. McBride was not innocent in this, as he had not seen her for more than a month, pretending he was tired, pretending he felt guilty about deceiving Martha, pretending he had problems as profound as hers. How was it that affection turned, tiny tender gears no longer meshing, gone suddenly, overnight, eroded with pity? Sour with scorn? When her mother called, three in the morning, Martha had handed him the phone with a single scathing word, that one that had been like a kiss: *"Peter."* They'd just failed to have sex, McBride pumping furiously, stiff as a stick of dynamite, unable to explode.

Now he screamed into the E.R. parking lot, horrified. One more portion of his life, another member of his tribe of female troubles, gone haywire. You build complication like a house of cards, geometrical, tricky, fragile. And like a child, you then like to step aside and stamp your feet, watch as it folds up on itself, flat one-dimensional deck. Dead.

Oh, those parents. Once again, sitting unmoving, identical drinks before them, same condensation. On the television: television. His intentions hadn't been honorable, apparently, after all. Had she wanted to die for his love, or its lack? She lay in the highly technical, highly temporary ICU, wrapped, strapped, tracheotomy tube in her neck, metal bolt in her skull, suction hose in her mouth, monitors around her like a recording studio, flashing numbers, graphs. Crust of rusty blood here and there, and her beautiful eyelashes, like folded fragile spider legs, wilted on those pale cheeks. Did this sleep replicate the one she fell into after sex? McBride swooned. Fainting wasn't what he had imagined. He was aware of himself crashing, vital fluids rushing from head, hands, feet to pool and churn in his stomach. His thought was that he would vomit, and be left empty as a pocket. And there was the nurse, the woman who, like a mother, materialized beside him at just the proper moment to smooth his brow, bring him round.

He held Claire's letter to him, unopened, missive from the grave, given over by the parents. Her heart, in his hands. On his porch sat four females, lover, ex-girlfriend, her black infant, and the neighbor who counted himself among the girls. Where did McBride fit? He could not be what they required. Nothing to do but squeeze out, he had already been squeezed out.

And he was glad, he told himself. Glad for his simple body, its fixtures out in the open, the expression on his face projecting exactly what was behind it in his head. What was it with women and all this hidden equipment? They dressed up, made-up, faked orgasms, cried when happy, laughed when bitter, stirred up protoplasmic stews of life and then pulled rabbits from hats, wreaked havoc all the wide world over, forever refusing to come clean.

That was how he wanted to feel, driving his car with his worldly pos-

sessions: clean. Free. Were those the same as being cold? Cowardly? He'd
left Salt Lake City and he could leave Tucson; the west was full of cities
where his slate would be blank, his plate would be empty. There was a girl
out there, he could almost see her, radiant, blond, a healthy hiker a few
years younger than he, straight teeth, muscular calves, sentimental taste in
music. He would find *her* . . . But how did that accident claim go, the one
that had amused him not so long ago? "I saw a slow moving, sad-faced old
gentleman as he bounded off the roof of my car . . . " Nothing to do but
plunge on. Set the cruise control, lower the windows, raise the radio, stay
between the broken yellow lines, and don't look back. No no no.

Elizabeth Graver

The Mourning Door

From *Ploughshares*

T HE FIRST thing she finds is a hand. In the beginning, she thinks it's a tangle of sheet or a wadded sock caught between the mattress cover and the mattress, a bump the size of a walnut but softer, more yielding. She feels it as she's lying, lazing, in bed. Often, lately, her body keeps her beached, though today the sun beckons, the dogwoods blooming white, the peonies' glossy buds specked black with ants. Tom has gone to work already, backing out of the driveway in his pickup truck. She has taken her temperature on the pink thermometer, noted it down on the graph—98.2, day eighteen, their thirteenth month of trying. She takes it again, to be sure, then settles back in, drifting, though she knows she should get up. The carpenters will be here soon; the air will ring with hammers. The men will find more expensive, unnerving problems with the house. She'll have to creep in her robe to the bathroom, so small and steady, like one of the pests they keep uncovering in this ancient, tilting farmhouse—powder post beetles, termites, carpenter ants.

She feels the bump in the bed the way she might encounter a new mole on her skin, or a scab that had somehow gone unnoticed, her hand traveling vaguely along her body until it stumbles, oh, what's this? With her shin, she feels it first, as she turns over, beginning to get up. She sends an arm under the covers, palpitates the bump. A pair of bunched panties, maybe, shed during sex and caught beneath the new sheet when she remade the bed? Tom's sock? A wad of tissue? Some unknown object (needle threader, sock darner, butter maker, chaff-separator?) left here by the generations of people who came before? The carpenters keep finding things in the walls and under the floor: the sole of an old shoe, a rusted nail, a bent horseshoe. A Depression-era glass bowl, unbroken, the green of key lime pie. Each time they announce another rotted sill, cracked joist, additional repair, they hand an object over, her consolation prize. The house looked so charming from the outside, so fine and perfectly itself. The inspector said go ahead, buy it. But you never know what's lurking underneath.

She gets out of the bed, stretches, yawns. Her gaze drops to her naked body, so familiar, the thin freckled limbs and flattish stomach. She has known it forever, lived with it forever. Mostly it has served her well, but lately it seems a foreign, uncooperative thing, at once insolent and lethargic, a taunt. Sometimes, though, she still finds in herself an energy that surprises her, reminding her of when she was a child and used to run—legs churning, pulse throbbing—down the long river path that led to her cousin's house.

Now, in a motion so concentrated it's fierce, she peels off the sheet and flips back the mattress pad. What she sees doesn't surprise her; she's been waiting so hard, these days, looking so hard. A hand, it is, a small, pink dimpled fist, the skin slightly mottled, the nails the smallest slivers, cut them or they'll scratch. Five fingers. Five nails. She picks it up; it flexes slightly, then curls back into a warm fist. Five fine fingers, none missing. She counts them again to be sure. *You have to begin somewhere,* the books say. *You have to relinquish control and let nature take its course.*

She hears the door open downstairs, the clomp of workboots, words, a barking laugh. Looking around, she spots on the bedroom floor, the burlap sack that held the dwarf liberty apple tree Tom planted over the weekend. She drops the hand into the bag, stuffs the bag under the bed. Still the air smells like burlap, thick and dusty. She pulls on some sweatpants, then thinks better of it and puts on a more flattering pair of jeans, and a T-shirt that shows off her breasts. She read somewhere that men are drawn to women with small waists and flaring hips. Evolution, the article said. A body built for birth. Her own hips are small and boyish; her waist does not cinch in. Her pubic hair grows thin and blond, grass in a drought. She doesn't want these workmen, exactly, but she would like them, for the briefest moment, to want her. As she goes barefoot down the stairs to make a cup of tea and smile at the men, she stops for a moment, struck by a memory of the perfect little hand; even the thought of it makes her gasp. The men won't find it. They're only working in the basement and the attic, structural repairs to keep the house from falling down.

In her kitchen, the three men: Rick and Tony and Joaquin. Their eyes flicker over her. She touches her hair, feels heavy with her secret, and looks down. More bad news, I'm afraid, Rick tells her. We found it yesterday, after you left—a whole section of the attic. What, she asks. *Charred,* he says dramatically. There must have been a fire; some major support beams are only three-quarter their original size. She shakes her head. Really? But the inspector never—I have my doubts, Rick says, about this so-called inspector of yours. Can you fix it, she asks. He looks at her glumly through heavy-lidded eyes. We can try, he answers. I'll draw up an estimate but we'll need to finish the basement before we get to this. Yes, she says vaguely, already bored. Fine, thanks.

Had she received such news the day before, it would have made her dizzy. A charred, unstable attic, a house whittled down by flames. She would have called Tom at work—You're not going to believe this—and checked how much money they had left in their savings account, and thought about suing the inspector and installing more smoke alarms, one in every room, blinking eyes. Today, though, she can't quite concentrate; her thoughts keep returning, as if of their own accord, to what she discovered in her bed. One walnut-sized hand, after thirteen months, after peeing into cups, tracking her temperature, making Tom lie still as a statue after he comes, no saliva, no new positions, her rump tilted high into the air afterward, an absurd position but she doesn't care.

After thirteen months of watching for the LH surge on the ovulation predictor kit—the deep indigo line of a good egg, the watery turquoise of a bad, and inside her own body, waves cresting and breaking, for she has become an ocean, or is it an oceanographer? *Study us hard enough,* the waves call out to her, *watch us closely enough and we shall do your will.* She has noted the discharge on her underpants—sticky, tacky, scant. Egg white, like she's a chef making meringues or a chicken trying to lay. *Get to know your body,* chant the books, the Web sites, her baby-bearing friends, and oh she has, she does, though it's beginning to feel like a cheap car she has leased for a while and is getting ready to return.

She still likes making love with Tom, the tremble of it, the slow, blue wash, the way they lie cupped together in their new, old house as it sits in the greening fields, on the turning earth. It's afterward that she hates. She can never fall asleep without picturing the spastic, thrashing tails, the egg's hard shell, the long, thin tubes stretched like IVs toward a pulsing womb. A speck, she imagines sometimes, the head of a pin, the dot of a period. The End—or maybe, if they're lucky, dot dot dot.

But the hand is so much bigger than that, substantial, real. Her own hands shake with relief as she puts on the tea water. Something is starting—a secret, a discovery, begun not in the narrow recesses of her body, but in the mysterious body of her house. The house has a door called the Mourning Door—the Realtor pointed it out the first time they walked through. It's a door off the front parlor and though it leads outside, it has no stoop or stairs, just a place for the cart to back up so the coffin can be carried away. Of course babies were born here, too, added the Realtor, her voice too bright. Probably right in this room! After she and Tom moved in, they decided only to use the door off the kitchen. Friendlier, she said, and after all, they're concentrating, these days, on making life.

When she goes back upstairs, she takes the burlap sack and a flashlight to the warm, musty attic, where Tom almost never goes. With the flashlight's beam, she finds, in one dark corner, the section where the fire left its mark. She touches the wood, and a smudge of ash comes off on her finger. She tastes it: dry powder, ancient fruit, people passing buckets, lives lost, found, lost. She leaves the sack in the other corner of the attic inside a box marked "Kitchen Stuff." Then she heads downstairs to wash her hands.

Three days later she is doing laundry when she comes across a shoulder, round and smooth. She knows it should be disconcerting to find such a thing separated from its owner, a shoulder disembodied, lying in a nest of dryer lint, tucked close to the wall. But why get upset? After all, the world is full of parts apart from wholes. A few months ago, she and Tom went to the salvage place—old radiator covers, round church windows, faucets and doorknobs, a spiral staircase leading nowhere. Then, they bought two doors and a useless unit of brass mailboxes, numbers fifteen through twenty-five. Now she wipes her hands on her jeans and picks the shoulder up. It is late afternoon, the contractors gone, Tom still at work. She brings the shoulder up to the attic and puts it in the sack with the hand. Then she goes to the bedroom, swallows a vitamin the size of a horse pill, climbs into bed, and falls asleep.

Whereas before she had been agitated, unable to turn her thoughts away, now she is peaceful, assembling something, proud. But tired, too—this is not unexpected; every day by four or five o'clock she has to sink into bed for a nap, let in dreams full of floaty shapes, closed fists, and open mouths. Still, most days, she gets a little something done. She lines a trunk with old wallpaper, goes for a walk in the woods with a friend, starts to plan a lesson sequence on how leaves change color in the fall. Her children are all away for the summer, shipped off to lakes and rivers and seas. Sometimes she gets a "Dear Teacher" postcard: *I found some mica. We went on a boat. I lost my ring in the lake.* The water in the postcards is always a vivid, chlorinated blue. She gets her hair cut, sees a matinee movie with her friend Hannah, starts to knit again. One night Tom remarks—perhaps with relief, perhaps with the slightest tinge of fear—that she seems back to her old self.

In the basement, the men put in lally columns, thick and red, to keep the first floor from falling in. They construct a vapor barrier, rewire the electricity. They sister the joists and patch the foundation. In her bedroom, she stuffs cotton in her ears to block the noise. She wears sweatpants or loose shorts now, and Tom's shirts. Each time she catches a glimpse of herself in the mirror, she is struck by how pretty she looks, her eyes so bright, almost feverish, her fingernails a flushed, excited pink.

She finds a foot with five perfect toes, and a second shoulder. She finds a leg, an arm. No eyes yet, no face. Everything in time, she tells herself, and at the Center for Reproductive Medicine they inject her womb with blue, and she sees her tubes, thin as violin strings, curled and ghostly on the screen. They have her drink water and lie on her back. They swab gel on her belly, and she neglects to tell them that her actual belly is at home, smelling like dust and apple wood, snoozing under the eaves. They say come in on day three, on day ten. They swab her with more gel and give her a rattle, loose pills in an amber jar. Tom goes to the clinic, and they shut him in a room with girlie magazines and take his fish. At home, while he is at the doctor's, she finds a tiny penis, sweet and curled. Tom comes home discouraged—rare for him. He lies down on the floor and sighs. She says don't worry, babe, and leans to kiss him on the arm. She would like to tell him about everything she has found, but she knows she must protect her secret. Things are so fragile, really. The earth settles, the house shifts. You put up a wall in the wrong place and so never find the hidden object in the eaves. You speak too soon and cause—with your hard, your hopeful words—a clot, a cramp. Things are so fragile, but then also not. Look at the ants, she tells herself, how they always find a place to make a nest. Look at the people of the earth, each one with a mother. At the supermarket, she stares at them—their hands, their faces, how neatly it all goes together, a completed puzzle.

She knows her own way is out of the ordinary, but then what is ordinary these days? She is living in a time of freezers and test tubes, of petri dishes and turkey basters, of trade and barter, test and track, mix and match. Women carry the eggs of other women, or have their own eggs injected back into them pumped with potential, four or six at a time. Sperm are washed and coddled, separated and sifted, like gold. Ovaries are inflated until they spill with treasures. The names sound like code words: GIFT, IUI, ZIFT. Though it upsets her to admit it, the other women at the Center disgust her a little. They seem so desperate, they look so swollen, but in all the wrong places—their eyes, their chins, their hearts. Not me, she thinks as the nurse calls her name and she rises with a friendly smile.

One day, she moves the burlap bag from the attic to the back of her bedroom closet. It's such a big house, and the attic is sweltering now, and soon the men will be working up there on the charred wood. Before, she and Tom lived in a tiny, rented bungalow and looked into each other's eyes a lot. She loves Tom; she really does, though lately he seems quite far away. Outside, here, is a swing set made of old, splintered cedar, not safe enough for use. But that same day, she finds an ear in it, tucked like a chestnut under a climbing pole. The tomatoes are ripe now. The sunflowers she planted in May are taller than she is, balancing their heads on swaying stalks. In the herb garden, the chives bear fat purple balls. The ear, oddly, is downed with dark hair, like the ear of a young primate. She holds it to her own ear as if she might hear something inside it—the sea, perhaps, a heartbeat or a yawn. It looks so tender that she wraps it in tissue paper before placing it in the bag.

One night on the evening news, she and Tom see a story about a girl who was in a car accident and went into a coma, and now the girl performs miracles and people think she's a saint. The news shows her lying in Worcester in her parents' garage, hitched to life support while pilgrims come from near and far: people on crutches, children with cancer, barren women, men dying of AIDS. Jesus, says Tom, shuddering. People will believe anything—how sick. But she doesn't think it's so sick, the way the vinyl-sided ranch house is transformed into a wall of flowers, the way people bring gifts—Barbie dolls, barrettes, Hawaiian Punch (the girl's favorite)—and a blind man sees again, and a baby blooms from a tired woman's torso, and the rest of the people, well, the rest sit briefly in the full lap of hope, then get in their cars and go home. The girl is pretty, even though she's almost dead. Her braid is black and shiny, her brow peaceful. Her mother, the reporter says, sponge-bathes her each morning and again at night. Her father is petitioning the Vatican for the girl to be made an official saint.

Days now, while the men work in the attic, she roams. She wanders the house looking for treasures, and on the days when she does not find them, she gets in her car and drives to town, or out along the country roads. Sometimes she finds barn sales and gets things for the house—a chair for Tom's desk, an old egg candler filled with holes. One day at a yard sale, she buys a sewing machine, though she's never used one. I'll give you the instruction book, the woman says. It's easy—you'll see. Also at this yard sale is a playpen, a high chair, a pile of infant clothes. The woman sees her staring at them. I thought you might be expecting, she says, smiling. But I didn't want to presume. As a bonus, she throws in a plump pincushion stabbed with silver pins and needles, and a blue and white sailor suit. It was my son's, she says, and from behind the house come—as if in proof—the shrieks of kids at play.

That night, with Tom in New York for an overnight meeting, she sets up the sewing machine and sits with the instruction manual in her lap. She slides out the trap door under the needle, examining the bobbin. Slowly, following the instructions, she winds the bobbin full of beige thread, then threads the needle. She gets the bag from the closet. She's not sure she's ready (the books say you're never sure), but at the same time her body is guiding, pushing, *urging* her. Breathe, she commands herself, and draws a deep breath. She has never done this before, never threaded the needle or assembled the pattern or put together the parts, but it doesn't seem to matter; she has a sense of how to approach it—first this, then this, then this. She takes a hand out of the bag and tries to stitch it to an arm, but the machine jams so she unwinds a length of thread from the bobbin, pulls a needle from the pincushion, and begins again, by hand.

Slowly, awkwardly, she stitches arm to shoulder, stops to catch her breath and wipe the sweat from her brow. She remembers back stitch, cross stitch; someone (her mother?) must have taught her long ago. She finds the other hand, the other arm. Does she have everything? It's been a long summer, and she's found so much; she might be losing track. If there aren't enough pieces, don't panic, she tells herself. He doesn't need to be perfect; she's not asking for that. He can be missing a part or two, he can need extra care. Her own body, after all, has its flaws, its stubborn limits. What, anyway, is perfect in this world? She'll take what she is given, what she has been able, bit by bit, to make.

She stitches feet to legs, carefully doing the seams on the inside so they won't show. She attaches leg to torso, sews on the little penis. The boy-child begins to stir, to struggle; perhaps he has to pee. Not yet, my love. Hold on. She works long and hard and late into the night, her body tight with effort, the room filled with animal noises that spring from her mouth as if she were someone else. She wishes, with a deep, aching pain, that Tom were here to guide her hands, to help her breathe and watch her work. Finally—it must be near dawn—she reaches into the bag and finds nothing. How tired she is, bone tired, skin tired. She must be finished, for she has used up all the parts.

Slowly, then, as if in sleep, she rises with the child in her arms. She has been working in the dark and so can't quite see him, though she feels his downy head, his foot and hand. He curls toward her for an instant as if to nurse, so she unbuttons her blouse and draws him near. He nuzzles toward her but does not drink, and she passes a hand over his face and realizes that he has no mouth. Carefully, in the dark, she inspects him with both her hands and mind: he has a nose but no mouth, wrists but no elbows. She spreads her palm over his torso, and her fingers tell her that he has kidneys and a liver but only six small ribs and half a heart. Oh, she tells him. Oh, I'm sorry. I tried so hard. I found and saved and stitched and tried so hard and yet—

She feels it first, before he goes: a spasm in her belly, a clot in her brain, a sorrow so thick and familiar that she knows she's felt it before, but not like this, so unyielding, so tangible. Six small ribs and only half a heart. While she holds him, he twitches twice and then is still.

Carrying him, she makes her way downstairs. It's lighter now, the purple-blue of dawn. She walks to the front parlor, past the TV, past the old honey extractor they found in the barn. She walks to the Mourning Door and tries to open it. It doesn't budge, wedged shut, and for a moment she panics—she has to get out now; the weight in her arms keeps getting heavier, a sack of stones. She needs to pass it through this door and set it down, or she will break. Trying to stay calm, she goes to the laundry room and finds a screwdriver, returns to the door, and wedges the tool in along the lock placket, balancing the baby on one arm. Finally the door gives, and she walks through it, forgetting that no steps meet it outside. Falling forward over the high ledge, she lands, stumbles, catches her balance (somehow, she hasn't dropped him) to stand stunned and breathless in the still morning air, her knees weak from landing hard.

Across the road, the sheep in the field have begun their bleating. A truck drives by, catching her briefly in its lights. She lowers her nose to the baby's head and breathes in the smell of him. He's lighter now, easier now. *Depart*, she thinks, the word an old prayer following her through the door. *Depart in peace*. With her hands, she memorizes the slope of his nose, the open architecture of his skull. She fingers the spirals of one ear. Then she turns and starts walking, out behind the house to the barn where a shovel hangs beside the hoe and rake. It's lighter now. A mosquito hovers close to her face. The day will be hot. Later, Tom will return. She buries the baby under a hawthorn tree on the backstretch of their land and leaves his grave unmarked. My boy, she says as she turns to go. Thank you, she says—to him or to the air—when she is halfway home. She sleeps all morning and gardens through the afternoon.

That night (day sixteen, except she's stopped charting), she and Tom make love, and afterward she thinks of nothing—no wagging fish, no hovering egg, no pathway, her thoughts as flat and clean as sheets. Tom smells like himself—it is a smell she loves and had nearly forgotten—and after their sex, they talk about his trip, and he runs a hand idly down her back. She is ready for something now—a child inside her or a child outside, come from another bed, another place. Or she is ready, perhaps, for no child at all, a trip with Tom to a different altitude or hemisphere, a rocky, twisting hike. They make love again, and after she comes, she cries, and he asks what, what is it, but it's nothing she can describe, it's where she's been, so far away and without him—in the charred attic, the tipped basement, where red columns try to shore up a house that will stand for as long as it wants to and fall when it wants to fall. Nothing, she says, and inside her something joins, or tries to join, forms or does not, and her dream, when she sleeps, is of the far horizon, a smooth, receding curve.

Pinckney Benedict

Zog-19: A Scientific Romance

From *Zoetrope: All-Story*

Z OG-19 IS learning to drive a stick shift. He backs up, judders to a stop, and stalls. It's a big Ford F-250 diesel that he is driving, and it's got a hinky clutch. The two shovel-headed dogs in the bed of the truck bark hysterically. On Zog-19's planet, there are no cars and trucks with manual transmissions. There are no motor vehicles at all. Zog-19 shakes his head, flaps his hands, stomps in on the hinky clutch, and twists the ignition key. The Ford rattles back into life. Zog-19 decides that he will sell the Ford at the first opportunity and replace it with a vehicle that has an automatic transmission. In his short time here on Earth, Zog-19 has had about all he can stand of stick shifts.

A woman watches Zog-19's struggles with the truck. She squints her eyes worriedly. She thinks she's watching Donny McGinty fighting the hinky clutch. She is Missus McGinty, she is Donny McGinty's wife. Zog-19 is not in fact young McGinty, but he resembles McGinty down to the most minute detail. Even McGinty's dogs believe that Zog-19 is McGinty. The problem is, Zog-19 does not know how to drive a stick shift, and McGinty does, McGinty *did.* McGinty knew how to do a blue million things that Zog-19 has never even so much as heard of on his own planet.

The Ford leaps forward several feet, stops, lurches forward again, dies. Missus McGinty shakes her head in disbelief. McGinty has never before, to her knowledge, had a bit of trouble with the truck, though that clutch often defies her. She is a small woman, and her legs aren't long enough or strong enough to manipulate the truck's pedals. Around her, around Missus McGinty and Zog-19, McGinty's little dairy operation—a hundred acres of decent land in the river bottom, inherited upon the death of McGinty's old man, and twenty-five complacent cows—is going to wrack and ruin. In the days when McGinty's old man ran the place, it gleamed, it glistened. No more, though. There are so many things that Zog-19 doesn't know how to accomplish.

Zog-19 waves to Missus McGinty from the truck. He wants badly to allay her apprehensions about him. "Toot toot," he says.

On Zog-19's planet, no one communicates by talking. All of Zog-19's people are equipped with powerful steam whistles. Well, not steam whistles exactly, because they sound using sentient gases rather than steam. The Zogs use their whistles to talk back and forth, using a system not unlike Morse code. On Zog-19's planet, "Toot toot" means "Don't worry." It also means "I love you" and "Everything is A-okay, everything is just peachy keen."

Zog-19 frets that McGinty's best friend, Angstrom, will notice the substitution. Zog-19 is not so good at imitating McGinty yet, but he is working hard to get better. Zog-19 is a diligent worker, even though he is not entirely sure what it is that he's supposed to accomplish here on Earth, in the guise of the farmer McGinty. He does know that he's supposed to act just the same as McGinty, and so for the moment he's working like heck at being McGinty.

"Goddamn it hurts," Angstrom says. He's got his arms wrapped around his middle, sways back and forth. He looks like a gargoyle, he looks like he should be a downspout on some French cathedral. Angstrom's belly hurts all the time. Maybe it's cancer, maybe it's an ulcer, maybe it's something else. Whatever it is, Angstrom can feel the blackness growing within him. At night, his hands and feet are cold as blocks of ice. The only thing that scares him more than whatever's going on inside him is how bad the cure for it might be.

Doctors killed Angstrom's old man. Angstrom's old man, strong as a bull, went to the doctors about a painful black dot on the skin of his back.

The doctors hollowed him out, and he died. So now Angstrom sits on a hard chair in his kitchen and rocks back and forth, looking like a gargoyle.

"Toot toot," says Zog-19. He likes Angstrom. He's glad McGinty had Angstrom for a friend, that Angstrom is by default Zog-19's friend now, but he wishes that Angstrom felt better. He worries that Angstrom will notice that he isn't McGinty. He wishes that he knew just a bit more clearly what his mission might be. He wishes that, whatever it is, someone else, someone more suitable, had been chosen for it.

Zog-19's planet is made of iron. From space, Zog-19's planet looks just like a giant steelie marble. The planet is called Zog. Zog-19's people are called the Zogs. Donny McGinty had a magnificent steelie marble when he was a little boy. He adored the slick, cool feel of the steelie in his hand, he loved the look of it, he loved the click it made when he flicked it against other marbles. He loved the rich tautness in the pit of his stomach when he sent his beloved steelie into battle, when he played marbles with other kids. When he was using that steelie as his striker, he simply could not be beaten. He was the marbles champion of his grammar school up in the highlands of Seneca County.

Those were good days for McGinty. McGinty's old man was alive, Angstrom's old man was alive, the little dairy farm shone like a jewel at a bend in the Seneca River and Angstrom's belly didn't hurt all the time. It seemed, when McGinty held that heavy, dully gleaming steelie in his hand, like they might all manage to live forever.

Zog-19's planet is a great hollow iron ball, filled with sentient gas. Zog-19's people are also made of iron, and they are also filled with sentient gas. When they walk, their iron feet strike the iron surface of the planet, and the whole thing rings just like a giant bell. With all the ringing, and all the tooting, Zog-19's planet can get very noisy.

Missus McGinty talks. She talks and talks. She keeps on talking about Angstrom, how she wishes that Angstrom would go to the doctor. He should go to the doctor, she says, or he should quit complaining. One or the other. She talks about Angstrom to avoid talking about McGinty. She has noticed all the changes in him lately—how could she not?—but she doesn't know that he's been replaced by Zog-19. She just thinks he's very, very sad about the death of his old man.

She has a great deal to say on the subject of Angstrom. He should wash more frequently, for one thing. It worries Zog-19 when she talks so much. On his planet, every time you talk through your whistle, you use up a little of your sentient gas. You've got a lot to start off with, so it doesn't seem to be a big deal at first; but little by little, you use it up, sure as shooting. When all the sentient gas is gone, that's it. Zog-19 watches Missus McGinty's mouth for telltale signs of the gas. He watches to see whether it's escaping. He thinks maybe it is. He does not want Missus McGinty to run out of sentient gas.

"You should wash more too," Missus McGinty tells him. "You're getting to be just like old dirty Angstrom." It's true, Zog-19 does not wash himself frequently. He is used to being made of iron. Washing frightens him. He has only recently been made into a creature of flesh, a creature that resembles McGinty down to the last detail, a creature that can pass muster with McGinty's dogs, and he has trouble recalling that he's no longer iron. Do you know what happens when you wash iron? It *corrodes*.

"You smell like a boar hog," says Missus McGinty. "I don't even like to be in the same bed with you anymore." Zog-19 knows that she's only saying these things because she loves him. On his planet, no one talks about anyone they don't love. They can't afford to waste the sentient gas. She loves him, and she loves Angstrom, too, she loves him like a brother. She and McGinty have known Angstrom all their lives. Zog-19 imagines that, once he is better able to imitate McGinty, once he forgets that he used to be made out of iron, he'll be able to love her as well.

But here's another thing that scares him: when people on Earth touch a piece of iron, he has noticed, they leave behind prints, they leave behind fingerprints. No two people on Earth, he has heard it said, have the same fingerprints. All those fingerprints, and every one different! No one on Zog-19's planet has any fingerprints at all. And these human fingerprints are composed of body oils, they are acid in their content. Unless they are swiftly scrubbed away, they oxidize the iron, they eat into it, they etch its surface with little ridges and valleys and hollows, they make smooth pristine iron into a rough red landscape of rust. Almost nothing could be worse for someone from the planet Zog than the touch of a human hand.

In the year 2347, space explorers from Earth will discover Zog-19's planet. The space explorers will leave their rusting fingerprints all over the iron surface of Zog. During their visit, the space explorers will discover that the sentient gas which fills the planet, and which coincidentally fills and animates the Zogs themselves, makes the space explorers' ships go very, very fast. Because they like to go very, very fast, they will ask the Zogs for the gas. They will ask politely at first.

Because the gas makes their planet ring so nicely under their iron feet, the Zogs will refuse it to them. The space explorers will ask again, less politely this time, more pointedly, and the Zogs will explain, with their thundering whistles, their immutable position on the matter.

War. At first, it looks as though the Zogs will easily win. They are numerous and powerful, and the space explorers are few and a long way from home. The Zogs are made of iron (to the space explorers, they look like great foundry boilers with arms and legs and heads), and the space explorers are made of water and soft meat. Their bones are brittle and break easily. "Toot toot," the Zogs will reassuringly say to one another as they prepare for battle. "Toot toot!"

But one of the space explorers will think of a thing: he will think of a way to magnetize the whole iron planet. He will think of a way to use vast dynamos to turn the entire planet into a gigantic electromagnet. He will get the idea from watching a TV show, one where a big electromagnet-equipped crane picks up a car, a huge old Hudson Terraplane, and drops it into a hydraulic crusher.

McGinty used to see this show in reruns every now and again, before he got replaced by Zog-19, and he was always amazed by what happened to that car. Every time the show played, the crusher mashed the car down into a manageable cube, not much larger than a coffee table. "Look at that," McGinty would say to Angstrom whenever the show was on. "That's my old man's car that's getting crushed."

McGinty's old man used to have a car just like that one when he was young, when he was McGinty's age, and he and McGinty's mother (though McGinty had not been born yet) would run around the county in that big old powerhouse of a car, blowing the horn in a friendly way and waving to everybody they knew, which was pretty much everybody they saw. McGinty does not know it, but he was conceived in the backseat of that Hudson Terraplane.

His old man wanted to sire a child, he wanted a son, and McGinty's mother was only too happy to oblige. While they were making love in the backseat of the Hudson, McGinty's mother's left heel caught the hornring on the steering wheel a pretty blow, and the horn sounded, just as McGinty's old man and his mother were making McGinty. And the sound it made? *Toot toot.*

"We don't make love anymore," says Missus McGinty, "not since your father died." Zog-19 has never made love to anyone.

On his planet, they do not have sex. They do not have babies. When a Zog runs out of sentient gas, it is simply replaced by another full-grown Zog more or less like it. Where do these new Zogs come from? No one knows. Perhaps the planet makes them. Once, the best thinkers on the planet Zog gathered together for a summit on the matter. They thought that they'd put their heads together and figure the thing out—where do new Zogs come from?—once and for all. But once they were all together, they got worried about losing all their sentient gas in the course of the palaver. They worried that they themselves would have to be replaced by the yet-unfathomed process of Zog regeneration. And so they figured, "What the heck?" and they went home again.

Missus McGinty leads Zog-19 into the cool bedroom of their farmhouse. She draws the shades. She does not ask him to speak. She undresses him and sponges him off with cool water. He does not corrode. She undresses herself. She is not built like a foundry boiler. Her pale, naked skin is luminous in the darkened room. She has a slender waist and a darling little dimple above each buttock. When he sees those dimples, Zog-19 says, "Toot toot."

Because she is only made of water and soft meat, Zog-19 is afraid that he will hurt her when he touches her. He is afraid that his dense, tremendous bulk will crush her, like the Hudson Terraplane on the TV show. He is afraid that his iron claws will puncture her skin. When she draws him to her, and when he enters her, he becomes momentarily convinced that he has injured her, and he tries to lift himself away. But she pulls him back again, with surprising strength, and he concedes, for a time, that he too is only made of water and meat.

So the space explorers will magnetize the planet, and the feet of the Zogs will stick to it like glue. Think of it! Poor Zogs. All they will be able to do is look up at the sky as the Earth ships descend. They will look up at the sky, and they will hoot at one another with their whistles. They will not say, "Toot toot," because things will not be A-okay, things will not be hunky-dory. Instead, as the space explorers land and rig up a great sharpened molybdenum straw that will penetrate the surface of Zog and siphon off the sentient gas, the Zogs will whistle, "Hoot hoot hoot," all over the planet.

To the Earthmen who are setting up the molybdenum straw, it will seem a very sad sound. It will also seem very loud, and every Earth space explorer will be issued a set of sturdy earmuffs to prevent damage to sensitive human eardrums. And the sound will mean this: it will mean "I'm sad" and "The end is near" and "We are most definitely screwed."

The loafers that hang out at the Modern Barbershop in Mount Nebo, where McGinty used to get his hair cut, and where Zog-19 goes now in imitation of McGinty, are convinced that the death of McGinty's old man has driven McGinty around the bend. They chuckle when McGinty says to them, "Toot toot." They try to jolly him out of the funk he is in.

They are by and large elderly fellows, the loafers, and they tell McGinty stories about his old man when his old man was young. They tell him stories about his old man roaring around the county in his big old Hudson Terraplane, a car so well made that, if McGinty's old man hadn't smashed it into a tree one drunken night, that car would still be out on the road today. All the loafers agree that nobody makes cars anymore that are anywhere near as good as that faithful Hudson.

They tell him other stories, too. They tell him how, when he was a little boy, he and his old man used to sing a song, to the delight of everybody in the barbershop. McGinty's old man would set young McGinty up in the barber's chair, and the barber would drape a sheet around young McGinty's neck and set to work with his comb and his flashing silver scissors and his long cutthroat razor, and McGinty's old man would stand before the chair, his arms spread like an orchestra conductor's, and he and young McGinty would sing. And the song they sang went like this: it went, "Well, McGinty is dead and McCarty don't know it, McCarty is dead and McGinty don't know it, and they're both of them dead, and they're in the same bed, and neither one knows that the other is dead."

There was a fellow named McCarty who always loafed at the Modern Barbershop, a tough old guy who had been a frogman in the Second World War, so it was like the McGintys were singing a song about themselves and about McCarty. The loafers at the barbershop loved the song when McGinty was a little boy, and remembering it now they love it all over again. They love it so much that they laugh, laugh really hard, laugh themselves breathless, and pretty soon it is hard to tell if it's a barbershop full of laughing old men or weeping old men.

Of course, when McGinty's old man sang the song, back in McGinty's childhood, both McGinty and McCarty were alive, even though the song said they were dead, and that made it all the funnier. But now McGinty really *is* dead, and McCarty really is dead, too, carried off by a wandering blood clot a decade before, and they are both buried out in the graveyard of the Evangelical Church of the New Remnant north of town, which is kind of like being in the same bed. None of the song was true before, and now a lot of it is true, and so it isn't all that funny.

"Poor McGinty," says one of the loafers, when they have all thought of how the song is true and not so funny anymore. And nobody knows whether he's talking about McGinty, or McGinty's old man.

Before long, the Earth spacemen, with their very, very fast spaceships, will manage to conquer the entire universe. Everywhere they go, the people who live there will ask them, "How in the heck do you make your spaceships go so darned fast?" The space explorers will be tempted to tell them, because they will want to boast about the clever way in which they defeated the Zogs, but they will play it cagey. They will keep their traps closed. They won't want anybody getting any ideas about using the sentient gas themselves.

Before long, also, the sentient gas that fills the planet of the Zogs will begin to run out. There will be that many Earth spaceships! And the space explorers will become very worried, because, even though they will have conquered the entire universe, they will nonetheless continue to think that there might be something beyond that which they might like to conquer as well.

McGinty and Angstrom also used to sing a song. They used to sing it when they got drunk. They used to sing it back in the days when McGinty's old man was alive, when Angstrom's old man was alive, back in the days when even McCarty, the tough old frogman, was alive. They would sing it while they played card games, Deuces and Beggar Your Neighbor.

They used to sing it to girls, too, because it was a slightly naughty song.

They used to love singing it to girls. And the song they sang went like this: it went, "Roll me over in the clover. Roll me over and do it again."

It was a simple, silly song, but it seemed to be about sex, and that was unusual in a place where almost nothing was about sex. So little was about sex in the Seneca Valley in the days when McGinty's old man and Angstrom's old man were alive that, weirdly, almost everything seemed to be about sex. Anything could make you think about sex in those days, even a silly little song, even a silly little song about clover. Clover is a kind of fodder that cows and sheep especially like. A clover with four leaves is said on Earth to be particularly lucky.

In addition to the hundred acres of decent bottomland, McGinty's old man also accumulated a little highland pasturage to the north of the valley, where he kept a few fat, lazy sheep. These mountain pastures were almost completely grown over in sweet clover. When McGinty and Angstrom sang the song, when they sang, "Roll me over in the clover," McGinty was always thinking about those pastures. He was thinking about rolling over a girl in the mountain pastures. He was thinking about rolling over a girl he knew who had sweet dimples above her buttocks. He was thinking about rolling her over in the cool mountain pastures.

And now Angstrom tries to teach the song to Zog-19. He cannot believe that McGinty has forgotten the song. Zog-19 understands that it's a song that he's supposed to know, supposed to like, and so he makes a diligent effort to learn it, for Angstrom's sake. Angstrom has been drinking, an activity that sometimes eases the pain in his belly and sometimes exacerbates it. For the moment, drinking seems to have eased the pain.

"Roll me over," sings Angstrom in his scratchy baritone voice.

"Over," sings Zog-19, in McGinty's pleasant, clear tenor.

"In the clover," sings Angstrom, waving a bottle.

"Clover," answers Zog-19. He does not know yet what clover is, but he likes the sound of it. He hopes that someone will teach him about clover, clover about which McGinty doubtless knew volumes, about which McGinty doubtless knew every little thing. He hopes that someone will teach him soon.

All this time, while they will have been out conquering the width and breadth of the universe, the space explorers will have kept the planet of

Zog magnetized, with the poor old Zogs stuck to its surface like flies stuck to a strip of flypaper.

The Zogs will still manage to talk back and forth between themselves. Mostly, what they will say is "Hoot hoot hoot." Sometimes one among them, a Zog optimist, will venture a "Toot toot," but he will inevitably be shouted down by a chorus of hooting.

Zog-19 wants the spinning radiator fan of the Ford F-250 to stop spinning, and so he simply reaches out a hand to stop it. On Zog, this would not have been a problem. The spinning steel fan blades might have struck a spark or two from his hard iron claws, and then the fan would have been stilled in his mighty grip.

On Earth, though, it is a big problem. On Earth Zog-19 is only made of water and soft meat. The radiator fan slices easily through the water and meat of his fingers. It sends the tips of two of the fingers cartwheeling off, sailing away to land God knows where, slashes tendons in the other fingers, cross-hatches his palm with bleeding gashes. Zog-19 holds his ruined hand up before his face, stares at it in horror. He knows that he has made a terrible mistake, a mistake of ignorance, and one that it won't be possible to remedy. He wants to shout for Missus McGinty, whose name he has only just mastered. He struggles to come up with her name, but the pain and terror of his hand have driven it from his memory. All that he can come up with is this: he calls out, "Hoot hoot hoot," in a pitiful voice, and then he collapses.

Probably by this point you have questions. How is it possible to know what will happen to the Zogs in the year 2347? That might be one of the questions. Easy. The Zogs have seen the future. They have seen the past, too. They watch it the way we watch television. Zog science makes it possible. They have seen what happened on the iron planet a million years ago, and what happened five minutes ago, and what will happen in the year 2347. They can watch the present, too, but they don't.

They have seen the space explorers from Earth. They have seen the depopulation of their planet, they have seen it emptied of its precious sentient gas. In fact, that episode of their history—a holocaust of such indescribable proportions that most Zogs can be brought to tears merely by the mention of it—is by far the most popular program on Zog. Every Zog watches it again and again, backward and forward. Every Zog knows by heart all its images—the Zogs stuck helplessly to the planet's iron surface, the molybdenum straw, the descent of the Earth ships on tongues of fire—and all its dialogue. They are obsessed with their own doom.

Another question: What is Zog-19 doing on Earth, in McGinty's exact form, with McGinty's wife and McGinty's dogs, and with McGinty's best friend, Angstrom? And: How was the switch accomplished? And what the heck happened to the real McGinty?

In a nutshell: Zog-19 was sent to Earth by a Zog scientist who was not enamored of the program, who hated what Fate held in store for Zog. His name was Zog-One-Billion, and he was a very important fellow. He was also brilliant. Being brilliant, he was able to invent a device that allowed him to send one of his own people to Earth in the guise of a human being. The device allowed him to examine Earth at his leisure, and to pick one of its citizens—the most likely of them, as he saw it, to be able to put a stop to the upcoming extermination of the Zogs—as a target for Zog replacement.

Zog-19 didn't go willingly. He had to do what Zog-One-Billion said because he had a lower number, a *much* lower number. The higher numbers tell the lower numbers what to do, and the lower numbers do it. It makes sense to the Zogs, and so that's how Zog society is arranged. Zog-19 couldn't even complain. Zog-One-Billion wanted him to be some unknown thing, a farmer named McGinty a galaxy away, and so Zog-19 had to be that thing that Zog-One-Billion wanted.

In all the excitement, the selection of McGinty and the sending of Zog-19 across the galaxy, Zog-One-Billion failed to explain to Zog-19 what precisely he was to undertake in order to avert the Zog apocalypse. It's possible that he didn't really have many firm ideas in that direction himself. There's no way of knowing because, as he sent Zog-19 on his long sojourn, he gave a last great toot of triumph and went still. His sentient gas was depleted.

What is known is this: it's known that, during his surveillance of Earth, Zog-One-Billion came particularly to like and admire human farmers. He saw them, for some reason, as the possible salvation of Zog. It is believed that he regarded farmers thus because many farmers own cows. Cows were particularly impressive to Zog-One-Billion, especially the big black-and-white ones that gave milk. These cows are called Holstein-Friesians, for a region in Europe, or just Holsteins for short.

There are no cows on Zog. There are no animals whatsoever. Cows burp and fart when they're relaxed. That's why it's a terrific compliment when a cow burps in your face, or if it farts when you're around. It means you don't make the cow nervous. You don't make all its innards tighten up.

McGinty didn't make his cows nervous. McGinty's cows were always terrifically relaxed around McGinty, as they always had been around McGinty's old man, and it's believed that this reaction in some way influenced the brilliant scientist Zog-One-Billion, that this lack of nerves on the part of the cows of McGinty attracted the attention of Zog-One-Billion from across the galaxy.

Perhaps the great Holstein-Friesians fascinated Zog-One-Billion because they reminded him of Zogs, because they reminded him of himself, with their great barrel bodies and their hard, blunt heads. Perhaps the burps and farts of the Holsteins reminded him of the sentient gas within himself, the sentient gas within every Zog, the sentient gas within the planet of Zog, the gas that made the iron planet ring in such an exotic and charming way. And yet—this would have been particularly impressive to Zog-One-Billion—cows never run out of gas, no matter how much of it they release. They manufacture the stuff! They are like gas factories made from water and soft meat.

And what happened to poor McGinty, the good-looking young dairy farmer with the beloved shovel-headed dogs and the beloved dimpled wife? Sad to say. Like the released sentient gas of Zog-One-Billion, McGinty simply . . . went away when Zog-19 replaced him. Drifted off. Dispersed. Vanished. Zog-One-Billion believed that McGinty's vanishment was the only way to save his beloved planet. If Zog-One-Billion, a very important Zog, was willing to make the ultimate sacrifice for the salvation of his planet and race, he must have reasoned, who was McGinty to object to making the same sacrifice? Of course, it wasn't McGinty's race or McGinty's planet, but there was no good way, given the enormous distances that separated them, for Zog-One-Billion to ask him.

Oh, McGinty is dead and McCarty don't know it. McCarty is dead and McGinty don't know it. They're both of them dead, and they're in the same bed, and neither one knows that the other is dead.

Just when it looks like the ships of the space explorers will run out of sentient gas, the planet of the Zogs having been utterly depleted in this respect; just when it looks like the space explorers will have to stop going very, very fast, one of their number (he was the same one who thought of magnetizing the iron planet of the Zogs) will remember a thing: he will remember that the Zogs themselves are filled with the self-same sentient gas. That gas is what makes the Zogs the Zogs, and each Zog is filled with quite a quantity of the stuff. He will remember it just in time!

Zog-19 cradles his wrecked hand against his chest. The hand is wrapped in a thick webbing of bandages. Zog-19 works hard to forget what the hand looked like after he stuck it into the blades of the radiator fan. He tries to think about what the hand looked like before that, the instant before, when the hand was reaching, and the hand was whole. Angstrom has just been by, and he brought the greetings of all the loafers down at the Modern Barbershop, who shook their heads sagely when they heard the news about the hand. Angstrom tried to interest Zog-19 in a rousing chorus of "Roll Me Over in the Clover," but Zog-19 couldn't forget about the hand long enough to sing. It did not take Angstrom long to leave.

Now Missus McGinty is with Zog-19. She holds his head cradled against her breasts. Zog-19's hand stings and throbs too much for him to take interest in the breasts, either. He does not know about healing. On Zog, no one heals. They are a hardy bunch, the Zogs, and usually last for thousands of years before all their gas is gone and they settle into de-animation. And all that time, all that time, the scars that life inflicts upon them gather on their great iron bodies, until, near the end, most Zogs come to look like rusted, pockmarked, ding-riddled caricatures of themselves. Zog-19 has no idea that his hand will not always hurt.

He is working very hard to listen to what Missus McGinty is telling him. She says it to him over and over, the same five words. And what she says is this: Missus McGinty, lovely dimpled Missus McGinty says, "Everything will be all right. Everything will be all right." Zog-19 knows what that phrase means. It means "Toot toot." He wants to believe it. He wants very badly to believe that everything will be all right.

Zog-19 is also working very hard to forget that he is Zog-19. He's not worried about the Zog extinction now. Right now he's worried about Zog-19, and about making Zog-19 believe that he is not made of iron, that he is made of water and soft meat. He is concerned with making Zog-19 believe that he is actually McGinty. He understands that, if he cannot forget that he is Zog-19, if he cannot come to believe that he is in fact what he seems to be, which is McGinty, he will—by accident, of course, by doing something that water and meat should never do—kill himself dead.

And so the intrepid space explorers will begin sticking sharpened molybdenum straws straight into the Zogs and drawing out their sentient gas. The Zogs will make a very good source of the gas, and the space explorers will be able to keep on going very, very fast. There is nothing beyond the universe they have conquered, they will discover that disheartening fact after a while, but they sure as heck won't waste any time getting there.

Drawing out the gas will de-animate the Zogs, of course. Magnetized as they are, the emptied iron Zogs won't seem to the space explorers much different from the full Zogs, except that they will be quiet, which won't be a problem. It will be, in fact, a decided benefit. Once they have de-animated many of the Zogs, the space explorers will find that they can take their earmuffs off. It will be more comfortable to work without the earmuffs, and so productivity and efficiency will both rise. They will go on sticking molybdenum straws into Zog after Zog and drawing out the sentient gas, until there will be only one unemptied Zog left.

This depletion will happen quickly, because once a space explorer hears about Zog and what the sentient gas can do, he will go there as quickly as possible (of course, he will leave much, much more quickly, thanks to the properties of the sentient gas when combined with Earth spaceships) in order to get his share. Most of the space explorers who come to Zog will never have seen the Zogs before they were magnetized, and so they won't be able to imagine why it might be a problem to empty a Zog of his gas. Except for the Zog's subsequent silence, it will seem the same afterward as it did before.

Everyone knows that the gas will run out—how could it not? And how could they not know?—but this knowledge will just make them swarm to Zog faster and faster, in ever-increasing numbers, because they won't want the gas to run out before they get there. What a dilemma.

Zog-19 rounds up his cows in the early morning for milking. It's still dark when he does so. Missus McGinty stays in bed while Zog-19 gathers the cows. Later, she will rise and make him breakfast, she will make him some pancakes. But now she is warm in bed, and dawn will brighten the sky soon, and she can hear Zog-19's voice out in the pasture, calling in the cows. He whoops and hollers, he sings out, and sometimes his voice sounds to her like a whistle, and sometimes it sounds like a regular voice.

The cows come trotting eagerly up to Zog-19. They follow him into the milking parlor. They are ready to be milked.

The cows are not nervous around Zog-19. Zog-19 is not nervous around the cows. The cows are large and black-and-white, they are noble Holstein-Friesians, and some of them weigh nearly a ton. If they wanted to, they could rampage and smash up the barn and smash up Zog-19 and smash up any of the water-and-meat people who got in their way, even though they themselves, the cows, are made only of water and meat, and not iron. Lucky for Zog-19—lucky for all of us!—that they never care to rampage.

Zog-19's favorite cow burps directly into his face. This is, as previously mentioned, high praise from a cow. A tag in the cow's ear reads 127. On Zog's planet, that number would make the cow the boss of Zog-19, since it is a higher number than nineteen. She would be able to tell him what to do, and he would have to do it, whether he wanted to or not. She would be able to tell him to go to some other planet for some half-understood reason, and replace some poor sap who lived there with his wife and his dogs, and Zog-19 would have to do just what she said.

Here, though, that number doesn't make the cow the boss of Zog-19. It doesn't make her the boss of anything, not even of the other cows with lower numbers. It's just a number. Cows never want to rampage, and they never want to be the boss.

When the cow burps in Zog-19's face, her breath is fragrant with the scent of masticated clover.

The last surviving Zog will be named Zog-1049. That is not a very impressive name for a Zog. Zog-1049 will only be more important than a thousand or so other Zogs, and he will be less important than many other Zogs. He will be much less important, for instance, than Zog-One-Billion, the Zog who sent Zog-19 to Earth to take McGinty's shape. Zog-One-Billion had a very impressive name, even though he didn't really know what he was doing. Zog-1049 will be, as you can see, more important than Zog-19, though not by much.

The space explorer's hand will rest on the big red button that will plunge the molybdenum straw into Zog-1049. He will wonder how much sentient gas the last Zog contains. He will wonder how far his ship will be able to go on that amount of gas, and how fast it will be able to get there.

Zog-1049 will say to the explorer, "Toot toot?" The space explorer will have heard it a million times, from a million Zogs, and still he won't know what it means. He won't know that it means "Don't you love me? I love you. Everything is hunky-dory."

When Zog-1049 realizes that the space explorer means to empty his sentient gas through the molybdenum straw no matter what he says, he will begin to hoot. "Hoot hoot hoot," he will say. He will hoot so long and so hard that he will expend a lot of his own gas this way. The space explorer will hate to hear Zog-1049 hoot so. He will know that it means the supply of sentient gas inside Zog-1049—and thus the supply of sentient gas in the entire universe—is dwindling ever faster. He will decide to stop contemplating Zog-1049 and go ahead and empty him.

The space explorer—whose name, by a vast coincidence that you have perhaps already intuited, will be Spaceman McGinty; he will be the great-great-great-however-many-greats-grandson of Missus McGinty and Zog-19—will take a final glance at this last of all the Zogs. He will take in the great iron foundry-boiler body, the sad, wagging head, the iron feet pinioned to the planet's surface by surging electromagnetic energy. He will take it all in, this pathetic, trapped creature, this iron being completely alien to him and useful to him only as fuel. And he will think he hears, as though they come to him from some realm far beyond his own, the lyrics of a silly song. They will ring in his head.

Roll me over in the clover.

Clover? Spaceman McGinty will never have seen clover. He will have heard of it, though, a family legend, passed down through the generations. Certainly there is no clover on Zog.

Roll me over and do it again.

The song will be a happy one. Looking at Zog-1049, and hearing the clover song in his head, Spaceman McGinty will feel unaccountably joyful. Looking at Zog-1049, Spaceman McGinty will think of cows, another family legend, great wide-bodied Holstein-Friesians, and he will think of clover, of a single lucky four-leaf clover, and of crickets hidden within the clover, and of sheep trit-trotting across mountain pastures, and of dogs at his heel. He will think of a little farm in a bend of the Seneca River, now lost forever. He will think—unreasonably, he will admit, but still he will think it—of McGinty his distant forebear, who for a time could say nothing but "toot toot" and "hoot hoot hoot," but who finally regained the power of human speech.

He will not know why he thinks of these things, but he will think of them. He will feel the joy of reunion, he will feel his family stretching out for hundreds of years behind him, and before him, too, a long line of honorable men and women, almost all farmers but for him, but for Spaceman McGinty. And his family, somehow, impossibly, will encompass poor old Zog-1049. What a peculiar family, these McGintys!

And remembering the cows, and the clover, and the farm, and the family, and the happy song, Spaceman McGinty will stay his hand.

Without the sentient gas that resides within Zog-1049, he will think, he will at last be able to settle down, this formerly peripatetic Spaceman McGinty, he will put down roots, perhaps he will find a planet somewhere that will accommodate him, where he can bust the sod like his ancestors and build a little house and even—dare he think it?—have a few cows, maybe some sheep, maybe some dogs. His blood will call him to it. And on his farm he will have the time he needs to think about the dark ringing hollowness at the core of him, the hollowness that has driven him out into the universe to discover and to conquer. And perhaps by its contemplation, he will be able to understand that hollowness, and even to fill it up, just a bit.

Zog-19 has discovered McGinty's sheep pastures, high up on the ridges at the northern end of the county. He has driven the Ford F-250 up there. He no longer wants to sell the Ford, because he has mastered the stick shift. He drives the truck as well as McGinty ever did, even though he is missing the tips of a couple of fingers from his right hand, his shifting hand. A lot of other things are coming along as well, but the farm still looks like hell, it still looks like an amateur's running it. McGinty's old man would have a fit if he were to rise up from the grave and have a look at it. Rust everywhere. Busted machinery. Still, progress is progress.

The hand is healing up all right, but at night the thick scar tissue across the palm itches like hell (it's a sign of healing, so Missus McGinty says, and she does not complain about the scar tissue or the missing tips of the fingers when Zog-19 comes to her in their bed), and he can sometimes feel the amputated finger joints tingling and aching. Sometimes, quite unexpectedly, he can feel McGinty in that same way, poor vanished McGinty, he can feel the pull of the man when he is performing some chore, when he's hooking Number 127 up to the milking machine, when McGinty's dogs come dashing up to him, when he runs the wrecked hand over Missus McGinty's dimples.

Sometimes Zog-19 feels as though McGinty is standing just behind him, as though McGinty is looking out through his eyes. Is there any way that McGinty could come back from the void? Zog-19 does not know. Zog-One-Billion didn't mention the possibility, but then of course there are a blue million things that Zog-One-Billion never mentioned, including stick shift automobiles and spinning radiator fan blades.

McGinty's dogs are with Zog-19 now, scrambling and scrabbling across the metal bed of the truck as it rumbles along the rutted mountain road, their nails scraping and scratching, in a fever of excitement as they recognize the way up to the sheep pastures, as they recognize the pastures themselves. It is lonely up here. It makes Zog-19 feel like he's the last creature on the planet when he comes up here.

He parks the truck, and the dogs are over the side of the truck bed and away; they are across the field before he can climb down from the cab. They swim through the clover like seals. Zog-19 shouts after them, he has learned their names, but they ignore him. Zog-19 doesn't mind. If he were having as much fun as they are, leaping out at each other in mock battle, rolling over and over in the lush, crisp grass, growling playfully, he would ignore him, too.

He strolls over to a sagging line of woven-wire fence, leans against it, breathes in, breathes out. He watches the sheep that drift across the field like small clouds heavy with snow. He has learned that he will have to shear them before long, that is part of his job, that is part of McGinty's job. He thinks that probably he can get one of the loafers down at the Modern Barbershop in Mount Nebo to tell him how to do such a thing. They seem to know pretty much everything that a man who wanted to imitate McGinty might care to know, and they're always happy to share. Needless to say, nothing on Zog ever needed shearing. Still, he imagines that he can handle it.

He whistles for the dogs, and they perk up their ears at the summons, then go back to playing. He smiles. He knows. After a while, they will tire. After a while, McGinty's dogs will run out of steam, and they will return to him on their own.

Spaceman McGinty—the only space explorer still on Zog—will shut down the great dynamos. It will be his final act before leaving the planet behind forever.

And the last Zog, unimportant Zog-1049, the final, last, and only Zog, will find himself his own master again. But how Zog has changed during his captivity! He knew something bad was happening, but trapped as he was, he could not imagine the scope of it, the impossible magnitude of the disaster. He will take up wandering the planet, he will pass through the rows upon rows of de-animated Zogs, empty, inert Zogs in their ranked silent billions. He will use his whistle, he will release his sentient gas, the last to be found anywhere, in copious, even reckless, amounts, calling out across the dead echoing iron planet for any compatriot, for any other Zog who is still living. "Toot toot," he will call. He will call, and he will call, and he will call.

Zog-19 enjoys a hearty breakfast. He's eating a tall stack of buckwheat pancakes just dripping with melted creamery butter and warm blackstrap molasses. He's never eaten anything that made him happier. He cleans his plate and offers it to Missus McGinty, who refills it with pleasure. McGinty always liked his pancakes and molasses, and to Missus McGinty this healthy appetite, this love for something from his past, a forgotten favorite, is a sure sign of McGinty's return.

He's been gone from her for a long time, someplace in his head, gone from her in a way that she can't imagine, and she's awfully happy to have him back. What brought him back? She does not know. She cannot venture a guess, and she does not care. She has wept many bitter tears over his absence, over his apparent madness, the amnesia, the peculiarity (small word for it), but she thinks that maybe she won't be crying quite so much in the days to come. Watching Zog-19 with his handsome young head low over his plate, tucking into the pancakes with vigor, his injured hand working the fork as of old, working it up and down and up again like the restless bucket of a steam shovel, she can believe this absolutely.

. . .

And what of the planet Zog? Depopulated, hollow Zog? Well, the space explorers, once they have finished with the sentient gas, the space explorers will feel just terrible about what they have done. They will be determined to make amends. And so they will do what Earth people can always be expected to do in a pinch: they will go to work with a great goodwill.

They will send all kinds of heavy moving equipment, bulldozers and end-loaders and cranes and trucks and forklifts, to Zog. They will work, and they will work, and they will work. They will raise up a great monument. They will move the bodies around, they will use the inanimate husks of the Zogs in building their monument (the materials being so close to hand, and free), they will pile them atop one another in great stacks that will stretch up and up into the Zog sky. They will use every de-animated Zog to make the memorial, every single one.

Zog-1049 will almost get swept up and used, too, but he will hoot desperately at the last minute, just as the blade of the snorting bulldozer is about to propel him into the mounting pile of the dead. The good-natured fellow who is driving the bulldozer will climb down, laughing with relief at the mistake he's nearly made, almost shoving the last living Zog into the memorial to the Zog dead, and he will brush Zog-1049 off, leaving some acid oil on Zog-1049's sleek iron body, and he will direct Zog-1049 to a safe spot from which to watch the goings-on without getting into any more trouble. The bulldozer operator will shake his head as Zog-1049 totters off across the empty landscape, hooting and tooting. Poor old thing, the bulldozer man will say to himself. He's gone out of his mind. And who can blame him!

Soon enough, the memorial will be finished. And it will be, all will agree, a magnificent testament to the remorse of mankind at their shocking treatment of the Zogs.

The memorial will be this: it will be a single word, a single two-syllable word, written in letters (and one mark of punctuation) tens of miles tall, the word itself hundreds of miles across. It will be a huge sign, the biggest sign ever made, a record-breaking sign in iron bodies, across the face of the iron planet, and, when the planet revolves on its axis so that the sign lies in daylight, so that the fierce sun of that system strikes lurid fire from the skins of the defunct Zogs, it will be visible from far out in space. It will be a word written across the sterile face of the steelie, the face occupied now only by eternally wandering Zog-1049, and the word will be this: the word will be *SORRY!*

Spaceman McGinty will, in the end, find himself on a sweet grass planet (plenty of clover there! and the breeze always blowing out of the east, blowing clover ripples across the face of the grass) far out at the raggedy edge of the universe. No one will live on the planet but McGinty and a primitive race of cricket people who communicate solely by rubbing their back legs together. The cricket people will live hidden in the tall grass, and McGinty will never so much as glimpse one of them, not in his whole life on their world. He will hear them though. He will hear them always. Their stridulation will make a soft, whispering, breezy music to which, at night, former spaceman McGinty will sometimes sing.

And what will he sing?

Sometimes he will sing, "McCarty is dead and McGinty don't know it. McGinty is dead and McCarty don't know it."

And other times he will sing, "Roll me over in the clover."

And still other times he won't sing at all, but will simply dance, naked and sweating and all alone; former Spaceman McGinty will dance along on the balls of his bare feet in the soft rustling waist-high grass of that lonely place.

All that, of course, is in the very far-off future.

Zog-19 is back in the sheep pastures. He feels relaxed, and he burps. A crisp breeze has sprung up, and he watches it play over the surface of the pastures; he enjoys the waves that the breeze sends shivering across the tops of the sweet clover. So much like water. Water used to frighten him, but he doesn't worry about it now.

McGinty is dead. McCarty is dead. Angstrom is dead.

The dogs are chivying the sheep over in the far part of the pasture. They are pretending that something, some fox or coyote or wolf or catamount, threatens the sheep, and they must keep the sheep tightly packed together, must keep them moving in a tightly knit body, in order to save their lives. The dogs love this game. The sheep aren't smart enough to know that there's no real danger, and they're bleating with worry.

"Hi," Zog-19 calls out to the dogs. More and more these days, he sounds like McGinty without even thinking about it. "Hi, you dogs! Get away from them woollies!" The dogs ignore him.

Let the dead bury their dead. That is what Missus McGinty tells him. There are so many dead. There is McGinty's old man, there is McCarty, there is Angstrom's old man, there is Angstrom, there is McGinty (though more and more these days, Zog-19 feels McGinty in the room with him, McGinty behind his eyes), there are the Zogs. What could Zog-19 do to prevent the tragedies that have unfolded, to prevent the tragedies that will continue to unfold in the world, across the galaxy? He's only a dairy farmer, he's a man who lives among the grasses. His cows like him. They are relaxed around him. They burp in his face to show their affection. What is there that a man can do?

"Toot toot," says Zog-19, experimentally, but it sounds like an expression from an unknown foreign language to him now.

Let the dead bury their dead.

Missus McGinty has come with him to the sheep pastures. Later in the day, they will shear the sheep together. It turns out that Missus McGinty is a champion sheep shearer, Seneca County 4-H, Heart Head Hands and Health, three years running. They'll have the sheep done in no time. Right now, though, they're in the act of finishing up a delicious picnic lunch. They're sitting together on a cheery red-and-white-checked picnic blanket, sitting in the wealth of the wind-rippled field of clover, Zog-19 and Missus McGinty. Around them are the remains of their meal: a thermos still half full of good cold raw milk, the gnawed bones of Missus McGinty's wonderful Southern-fried chicken, a couple of crisp Granny Smith apples. Yum.

McGinty would have given the dogs the chicken bones, but Zog-19 will not. He worries that they will crack the bones with their teeth, leaving razor-sharp ends exposed, and that they will then swallow the bones. He is afraid that the bones would lacerate their innards. That's one difference between Zog-19 and McGinty.

"Roll me over in the clover," Missus McGinty sings in her frothy alto voice. She's lying on the checked picnic blanket, and she plucks at Zog-19's sleeve. Her expression is cheerful but serious. She's fiddling with the buttons of her blouse. She takes Zog-19's hand and places it where her hand was, on the buttons. Zog-19 knows that it's now his turn to fiddle with the buttons.

The dogs are barking. The sheep are bleating. The buttons are beneath Zog-19's hand. Missus McGinty is beneath the buttons. The crickets are chirring loudly, hidden deep within the clover. McGinty is standing behind Zog-19 somewhere. The sun is hot on Zog-19's head. There is a four-leaf clover in this pasture, he knows. Somewhere, in amongst all the regular clover, there must be at least one. His head is swimming with the sun. He feels as though, if he does not move, if he does not speak, if he doesn't do something, something, something, and pretty damned quick, he is going to burst into flame.

Zog-19 can't know it, but it is time for him to resume the line that will lead to that far-off Spaceman McGinty, the one who will spare Zog-1049. It is time for him to sire a brand-new McGinty.

"Roll me over and do it again," Missus McGinty sings. The button comes off in Zog-19's hand. It is small in his scarred palm, like a hard, smooth little pill. He tosses it over his shoulder, laughing. He tosses it in McGinty's direction. He tugs at the next button down. He wants that one, too. He wants the one after that one. He wants them all. He wants them all.

The wind ripples the clover, the wind ripples Missus McGinty's chestnut hair.

Ron Carlson

At the Jim Bridger

From *Esquire*

H<small>E PARKED</small> his truck in the gravel in front of the Jim Bridger Lodge, and when he stepped out into the chilly dark, the dog in the back of the rig next to his was a dog that knew him. A lot of the roughnecks had dogs; you saw them standing in the beds of the four-wheel-drive Fords. It was kind of an outfit: the mud-spattered vehicle, the gear in back, a dog. This was a brown-and-white Australian shepherd who stood and tagged Donner on the arm with his nose, and when the man turned, the dog eyed him and nodded, or so it seemed. What he had done was step up on the wheel well and put his head out to be stroked.

"Scout," Donner said, and with a hand on the dog, he scanned the truck. Donner was four hundred miles from home. He knew the truck, too.

Donner had just come out of the mountains after a week fishing with a woman who was not his wife, and that woman now came around the front of Donner's vehicle. He stopped her. She smiled and came into his arms thinking this was another of his little moments. He'd been talking about a cocktail and a steak at the Jim Bridger for days, building it all up, playing the expert the way he did with everything. She was on his turf, and he tried to make each moment a ritual with all of his talking. He had more words than anyone she knew. Around the campfires at night, which he built with too much care, he'd make soup and fry fish and offer her a little of the special wine in a special glass, measured exactly, and he would talk about what night means and what this food before them would allow them to do and how odd it would be to sit in a chair in the Jim Bridger the night of their wacky end-of-season New Year's Eve party and order the big T-bone steak and eat it with a baked potato, which he would also describe in detail.

It was September and they'd gone in twelve miles, backpacking from the trailhead at Valentine Lake. A quarter mile from his truck, he'd stopped and put a burlap bag of Pacifico bottles in a stream. "We'll be glad to see those on Friday," he told her.

And that is what they had done today in the late afternoon, their legs sore. They'd walked through the sunny pines for two hours, not speaking, and then he'd stopped, and when she caught up with him, he knelt and pulled the dripping bag and its treasure into the sunlight. They sat on the bank and he opened the bottles with his knife. The cold brown bottles were slippery in their hands, the labels washed off, and they were like two people having their first beer on earth. She put her hand on the wet burlap. It was all as good as he'd said it would be.

They were both changed from the trip in ways they didn't understand. He was fighting a kind of terror that had grown, and now as he ran his hand under Scout's collar and scratched him, the feeling rose and tightened his throat.

"I know somebody in here," he said to her.

"I know you do," she said. "Happy New Year." She kissed him. She had given herself over to him sometime at midweek and was not even fighting the love that had taken her.

"No," he said, "really. I know this guy." He indicated the big truck. "I know this dog, Scout."

"Scout?" She'd heard about this dog.

"Right," he said. "The dog from the story."

She put both arms around him and asked, "Does this mean we don't get our steak?"

Inside, there were two little rooms, the small barroom with eight stools, a kind of narrow passage, and the dining room, which held a scattering of tables, each with a red checked tablecloth, just as he had told her. A dozen trophy heads protruded from the walls, twelve- and fourteen-point deer and over the fireplace a bull elk that would have gone a thousand pounds.

There was no one in the bar, though there were oilfield and hunting jackets on every stool and bottles and glasses standing all along the wooden surface, as if everyone had left suddenly mid-drink. Brenda Lee sang from the jukebox, "Fool #1." It was full of scratch friction, as if coming across the decades to find the room. The dining hall, too, was empty, though there were steak dinners on two of the tables and coats on some of the chairs. Donner sat the woman at a table, and then he saw something through the big back windows. They were flecked with white-and-gold spray and razored with a loopy script that read HAPPY NEW YEAR! Through the words, Donner could see a group of people out on the wooden deck, looking into Long Pond. "They're all out back," he said. "Some deal out back."

Donner had told the woman the second day of the trip that he had memorized her now, her back, the backs of her knees, the scar on her shoulder, her navel, her nipples, how her hair grew, the way she looked immediately after stepping out of her clothes, the way she looked an hour later. But as they opened the plastic menus in the dark little room and he looked across at her beneficent smile, he didn't even know who she was. This had all been accomplished on a rushing wave of what—adrenaline, lust, ego? Now that had collapsed and Donner felt ruined and hollow. He felt as if he'd used every gesture, every smile, and he knew that everything he did now was something borrowed.

"There it is," she said, pointing at the menu. She was euphoric. She'd been euphoric for days. "T-bone steak with a baked potato."

"There it is," he said.

The door opened and the conversation noise roared in like a draft and then people followed it in, one and two at a time. Donner saw Rusty right away, holding the door for a couple of his buddies, and Donner turned his back and faced the woman until he was sure they had passed through the room and back to the bar.

The waitress was the owner's wife, Kay. Donner knew her name, but she didn't know his. He was here once a year at most. She appeared in a big flannel shirt patterned red and black and a shiny tiara clipped on her head that in rhinestones read HAPPY NEW YEAR! and she kept the pencil, as he had described to the woman, behind her ear until she'd heard both their orders and then she wrote them down.

"What was that?" Donner asked her about the people coming in.

"Big Jesse our bull moose made an appearance across the pond," Kay told him. "He's still over there pulling tall grass off the bottom and eating like there's no tomorrow."

"A moose?" the woman said. "We saw a moose."

"We did," Donner said.

Early the second day, still hiking toward their lake, they had passed through a willow break, and in one of the beaver dams a cow moose was feeding. She was standing to her shoulders in the water and her huge head would descend and disappear and then emerge in a tremendous splash and her mouth would be full of dark-green reeds and she would chew and drip. It thrilled the woman, and she covered her face with her hands. She looked at Donner with a radical amazement, as if her understanding of the world had been reset, and she pulled him over a hillock and dropped her pack. They made love as he had never done with anyone, and not in a way he could easily describe, not voracious and not tender, but seriously perhaps, and it sobered him and offered the first caution as to the nature of what he was actually doing.

The waitress brought back a breadbasket and two plastic flutes of champagne. There was a little stone fireplace and Donner stoked the struggling fire with two fresh sections of split log. When he sat back down, she said, "So this is New Year's."

"It is."

She scanned the room. "And they'll close the shutters and all be gone tomorrow."

"Right, until May 1. But even that is early. The season here doesn't start until June."

Her eyes were on him, and she lifted her glass and held it until he touched it with his. She was waiting for him to say something, make a toast.

"Moose," he said. "God save the moose."

Now he saw her first confusion, and he worried she could read his face. He felt drained, but he smiled.

"Is that really Scout?" she said. "Isn't that amazing?"

"Yes it is, my dear," he said.

"So, is your friend in here?"

"Yes," he said. "He's sitting at the bar."

"Rusty?"

"That's his name," he said. "You remembered."

He didn't want to talk about this, but he would if she wanted, because he realized that he didn't want to talk about anything at all. From the moment the dog had touched him, everything was all gone. Donner was happy for the fire; if the grate had been dark, he feared he would have wept.

One year ago in September, on Donner's annual fishing trip, he'd gotten trapped by a surprise snowstorm in the Cascades, and he'd made a bad decision. It was now his favorite story, though he'd only told it twice, and when he told it, he told it carefully and honestly, owning all of his errors in the event. When he told it well, something in him knitted up taut and he felt centered and ready. He had told the woman who was not his wife the story over dinner at an Italian restaurant seven months ago, and it was the story that had kindled all of the rest.

The big mistake Donner made while fishing the year before was breaking camp late in the afternoon. He should have stayed put, as he had for three days while the snowfall continued without pause, steady and serious, as if trying to put the year out once and for all.

He had arrived in a thick dusk and set up camp, the tent, the little cook station and grill, the log bench, the clothesline, he always had a clothesline, and on the clothesline he always hung a thin cotton dish towel bordered by blue and green stripes. He woke the first day in the strange quiet and the even light and his tent half in on him. The snow was eight inches deep, and Donner had to dress carefully and search through the site for his gear. He broke dead limbs and made a small fire; he was a scrupulous fire maker, and he laid in wood for two days. He made a cup of coffee using the little press his wife had given him, and he brushed off a space on the log and sat down and let the snow gather on his shoulders.

He had the wrong shoes for such weather, but by being prudent and drying them each time he returned to the fire, he was still able to fish in Native Lake. He was mindful of the wet rocks and stood with his legs angled and cast a series of flies into the blizzard. It was mesmerizing watching the snow in its vast echelons disappear into the dark water, and he had the rich, high feeling that comes from being alone in real places.

He caught no fish on his flies. He did, however, take several cutthroat trout on his smallest Mepps spinners, something they could see. These fish he fried slowly in his old pan with olive oil and a little tarragon, and he ate them with his fingers right out of the pan as snow still fell. At night, he banked the fire with larger logs, and in the morning snow would cover them all, except for one small space where smoke would still be working its way into the cold new day.

He fished every year of his life, camping alone or with a partner, because, he said, it pinned everything else in his life in place. He came home tight with the regimen of sleeping on the ground and eating fish, and with a new effulgent appreciation for his house, the roof, the way the doors worked, chairs.

The year of the mistake he'd gone into the mountains under special pressure. Willem, his fourteen-year-old son, had run away that spring and then come back and then run off again with a group of eight or nine people, the oldest of whom was Donner's age. It had been a poisonous season of recrimination and fear. He had been a drummer in the school marching band, and then he was just gone and they did not know where.

In twelve years this had been the first snow, and it vexed Donner. He wished he had his gaiters. He ate cutthroat trout for three days, drank coffee, and on the fourth day he made his mistake. In the low, even snow light, he decided that he could no longer wait out the snow. He would hike down halfway to the highway, seven miles, camp there overnight, and then down the other seven to the highway, where the bus had let him off.

He should have waited for morning, but he could not. When he pulled the tent and packed it, the little rectangle under it was green as summer, the grass and wildflowers pressed and vivid there like a window onto another world.

He knew he'd made the mistake immediately because of the difficulty locating and keeping the trail. There were yellow blazes hacked into trees at the proper intervals, but the pack trail was impossible to see in the two-foot snow. The hidden rocks tripped him, and the game trails confused him. He was wet, but moving and warm. When dark took the sky, the snow persisted. He used his flashlight to find the marked trees.

As he had told the story to the woman in an Italian restaurant last February, it lived in him, each word, and he evoked the dark and the night and the snow. He told the next part scrupulously, how he'd followed the trail, breathing into the new night, and suddenly plunged into the huge open meadow. He had forgotten about it. The expanse glowed at him, offering no marker; the trail was lost. He walked into the snowfield, immediately regretting having left the trees, tramping through the powdered snow. A moment later he came to a rivulet he seemed to remember, the water amber and clear, and he walked right into it and watched the water flow over his boots. He was now somebody else, somebody he was curious about. It was a beautiful night, the snow tiny dots still wandering, floating all around the man. Habit, he supposed, not a decision, but habit, made the man walk on into the snow toward the distant trees. He was trying to take care. He looked at his watch, which he was trained to do when lost, but a moment later he couldn't remember what it had said. He looked again, wiping the crystal with his gloved first finger. He swore at the instrument and walked on, each step a kick into the deep drifts, listening to himself cursing. He fell frequently on the uneven ground and the falling filled his collar with snow and then his ear. Sometimes he'd stay down; he wasn't cold anymore.

He didn't remember getting up, but he was up and in the woods, his pack off, breaking dead limbs from trees, and he was on his knees with his fire kit, starting a fire with a little snarl of twigs, a fire that he nursed into the biggest fire he'd had all week.

As the fire grew in his story, the woman's expression, which was already serious in the restaurant candlelight, grew grave, her eyes on his face, glistening.

His fire worked its way down through the snow to the green forest floor and grew out in a dry circle. He pulled a downed limb over and hung his wet clothing on it piece by piece until he was standing on his towel before the vigorous fire naked, the dots of snow melting on his shoulders. He made some soup and set up his tent while his clothes dried. Hunkered down in the circle of warmth he had created, sipping the steaming tomato soup, he felt as alive as he ever had. One minute later a dog burst into the bright ring, splashing snow, before putting his iced muzzle onto his paws on the only patch of green grass in this whole world. The dog eyed the naked man. There had been no noise in the arrival, and Donner was sure at first that a coyote had made a mistake, but he stood his ground. Donner found the tags and collar frozen, and by the time he'd separated them and read, SCOUT, and a Wyoming phone number, he heard a deep voice call from the dark, "Hello, the camp!" When Rusty Patrick stamped into the light, he looked at Donner and pulled his snow-crusted glove off to shake hands. "Well, here's Adam. Is Eve in the tent?"

The steaks in the Jim Bridger were big, an end over each side of the huge paper plates, and the baked potatoes were monstrous. The only real silverware was the three-tined forks Kay brought them, and pocketknives. It was a trademark of the Bridger to give pocketknives for steaks. They were thick black Forest Master knives with three blades, but the nameplate on each read: BRIDGER CLUB. The woman loved this, and though she didn't look comfortable with the pocketknife, she went at the food with an energy and delectation that Donner envied.

All night long they'd shared the fun of the place. Diners getting up and throwing their plates into the fireplace and toasting, "Happy New Year!"

"They're not doing any dishes the last night of the year," Donner had told her.

When she talked now, her mouth was full, chewing, smiling, and Donner knew he had done it double. She was a woman who didn't talk with her mouth full, ever. She was in love, and it was his doing. When Kay passed with the bottle, the woman held out her glass for more wine, and Donner could see her beam. She was beaming.

A three-piece band was setting up in the corner, wiring the keyboard, as Donner and the woman finished their dinner.

"Are you going to speak to him?" she asked Donner. "Do I get to meet Rusty Patrick?"

The second thing Rusty Patrick had said to Donner a year ago in the snow camp was "I've had a pretty weird month all around." He worked a black revolver from his jacket pocket and showed it to Donner. There were frost starts in the bluing. Rusty hefted the gun and then lobbed it out over the fire into the snow. "I was dead for a while, but I guess I'm back. Do you know how fucking strange it was to see your fire? I came out of the trees and there's this fire."

His Levi's were frozen in stiff sheets, and his bootlaces were welded with ice. He kicked and beat at his clothing to peel it off, hanging it to dry. He'd been out to climb Mount Warren and had hit it way too light.

Both of his little toes were patched white with crystal frostbite, but he stood by the fire in his damp long underwear and toasted the falling snow with his coffee cup. "People in Sun Valley pay a thousand dollars a day for shit like this."

Donner did not mention the gun when he told the story, and he did not tell the woman or anyone else what happened the night he met Rusty Patrick in the snow camp. As the snow continued, they had another cup of coffee with a lick of whiskey in it, and they decided to walk out in the morning. With two of them, they reasoned, they could take turns breaking trail. They were above eleven thousand feet, and they were still ten miles from the road. Donner had set his tent on the snow, not bothering to kick a clearing for it, and none of the tree wells were large enough for the little two-man spring tent.

He felt odd, wired and wasted, and he understood somewhere deeper than he could reach that when he had seen the dog, he had let go of all the prudence he'd garnered all day. He was tired. Rusty Patrick wanted to talk and did talk for the hour they lay in the tent. Donner felt the snow hardening under them as they settled, and he worried faintly about the cold, but he just lay back and listened.

Rusty Patrick had a resonant voice, so he scraped a hard bass note once or twice in every sentence. He was a roughneck who'd been driving truck since the oil work had dried up. Now he hauled road gravel all over Wyoming. At thirty-three, he had never had a real girl until this last summer, when he fell in love with the new dispatcher, a woman named Darlene Youngman who had come west from Pennsylvania. It was the story of this girl that he told Donner.

Rusty Patrick talked in the icy tent, stopping every once in a while to pose a question. Donner was awake but not enough to answer, and after a pause, Rusty Patrick would continue. His heart was broken, he said. He thought that was all bullshit, a broken heart, before this deal. He fell in love with Darlene Youngman and she fell in love with him, and their dating closed in on them until they were spending weekends together at his place in Rawlins or hers in Rock Springs. "I mean, I see now that love is a kind of craziness, right? I was lit up like a refinery at night, blazing, nothing like it. It made everything make sense. My stupid life, the unending wind, the great state of Wyoming. You ever been in love?"

The dog came to the mouth of the tent and looked Donner in the eye.

Donner nodded his head and the dog stepped carefully in onto the sleeping bags, finally curling at their knees.

The cadence of Rusty Patrick's voice changed then, or so Donner thought from where he drifted, listening. He wanted to drop into sleep, and he could have, but there was something holding him back, some caution, some change in the air and the grip of the snowpack beneath him.

"My boss was a good guy, at least he had been good to me, keeping me on when a lot of men were laid off. His name was Bob Baxter. He took me aside years ago and told me privately to get my big-rig license, and I did what he said, and it saved me. But there was something else. He took an interest in Darlene." The company owner felt fatherly toward the young woman, and in all their hours together in the office, the man talked against Rusty Patrick, warning the woman about a man of his caliber. It was a steady lesson, an onslaught, and she didn't tell Rusty Patrick about it right away. Then, one weekend two weeks ago, he'd taken her over to the Western Wyoming campus at Rock Springs. He was excited. Their new life was diagrammed before them. He would move in with her and go to school; he had $9,000 in the bank, and he could work part-time in town during the two-year forestry program. Then they'd go together down to Utah State or Colorado State and their lives would really begin. He was way in, far gone. That's the way he had said it, "I was far gone. I mean, I'd brought up babies. I'd say anything and I meant it all." They were walking across the windy campus when she stopped and told him quietly that he would never come here. He was surprised by this and asked her why. This is not something you'll do, she told him. Her arms were folded and she went directly to his truck. When she didn't talk, he didn't talk, and he drove her home. When she walked to her door, he simply backed his rig and drove home. His ears were ringing. He hadn't talked to her since, but he'd gone in to see his boss. "I went to the office on that Saturday," Rusty whispered. "And Baxter was waiting for me."

Donner could feel Rusty's shoulder; he was crying, speaking sometimes through his teeth. "By then I was like a chunk of stone; it hurt so bad. There is nothing like it. It isn't your heart; it's your heart through every day of your goddamn life."

Now Rusty's voice was quieter and the words were spaced oddly, some run together and some repeated shakily and some falling at great intervals. "It took everything. I had. Not to kill the man," Rusty said. "I bought the gun. Fourhundredbucks. That was. Tuesday. We've been up above here. Since. Then. In this this this this snow."

The last word had been coughed out and immediately Rusty's breathing changed to shallow chuffing. It was late but the hard chill pressed in with a new edge; it had stopped snowing. Donner opened his eyes and listened, and he knew that after four days it had stopped snowing. The cold came down now with all the force of the hollow sky. He could feel the frigid air seizing his face, and his feet were aching again.

The story had made him sick. He imagined the big boyish figure of Rusty Patrick confronting an older man he thought of as a father and hearing such news. And the surprise of the surcease of falling snow was like terror, a blank, fearful void that came at Donner's heart. He tried to calm himself, but for the first time in the mountains he was afraid. It was very simple: He wanted to be home. The image of his son in his band uniform took the air from his lungs, the brass buttons of his red wool tunic, his high, proud face under the black beret, his seriousness with the snare drum. He wouldn't even accept any help loading the drums into the car, and when they arrived at school, he went wordlessly into the crowd. And then he disappeared. One night after practice, Donner waited with his wife and after 1:00 A.M., they called the police.

Donner was bumped from sleep by Rusty Patrick shaking beside him. At first, he thought the other man was sobbing, because he had heard it in his voice earlier, but it persisted, a rippling shudder. "Hey," Donner said, but even on an elbow, shaking the man, Donner couldn't wake Rusty Patrick. The dog held tight at the bottom of the sleeping bags, his eyes open. The cold was at Donner, blades of it against his exposed neck as he moved up and checked the other man. He ran a hand over Rusty's face and it came away wet, and then, cold or no, Donner sat up on his heels and shined the light on his tentmate. The face was gray and smeared with blood from a nosebleed. A delicate fringe of ice rimmed the hair, and Rusty Patrick was shivering in cramping spasms. His chest was wet. Donner was saying, "Come on, come on," as he unzipped their sleeping bags. The other man was damp, cold to the touch, dropping into hypothermia. Both of Donner's hands were bloody, and he was getting the blood everywhere as he cut away Rusty's underwear using his sheath knife. Both of the sleeping bags were superior grade, though the zippers wouldn't mesh.

Donner was talking the whole time now, saying simply, "Oh now, come on, now," and he slipped in with Rusty and wrapped the shell of his own bag over them as tightly as he could. It was what you did. There was no way to take the half hour to rekindle the fire and go that way. Rusty had gone to bed still wet and it had worked into him. Now Donner could feel the cold muscularity of the other man and he held him and moved slowly against him, his hands up and down, the tops of his feet up and down, his face against the side of Rusty Patrick's head. He'd need to bring him up five degrees.

Even dozing, he developed a rhythm, covering the naked body of Rusty Patrick in this embrace, this massage. It wore him down and he felt useless. He woke and renewed his movements. Donner rolled on top of Rusty and in slow degrees, as his strength left him, he let his weight descend. The dog moved up to them and Donner could feel the dog's breath against the side of his face. Rusty's shivering had subsided somewhat, but Donner could still feel the blood warm against his neck.

"Come on, now," he said, whispering, and when that litany lulled him to sleep, he started talking quietly to his son. "You can come home now," he started. "It's not a problem to cross through Indiana and then Nebraska . . ." and Donner listed the states one at a time in a prayer to his son. He spoke slowly, trying to lay out the fair terms of their rapprochement, so he might again be some part of his life, and in his recitation, he uttered their history, telling at length episodes they'd shared, especially the time they went onto the roof to retrieve the basketball. He'd gone up the ladder and his son had followed him onto the flat white surface the shape of Utah. It was littered with odd broken toys and an old volleyball as well as the ball he'd just heaved from the driveway. Each element of this scattered inventory brought a wave of revelation. The blue plastic elephant with three legs was five or six years old, sun-polished on one side, and Donner and Willem sat on the short rear wall of the roof, looking down at the neighbors' dog, who was swimming in the pool, and they talked about all the toys the elephant had been kindred to, and he asked him in real wonder how such a lost thing could get onto the roof.

Donner hugged the freezing man. He trapped Rusty's hands in the warmth between their legs. Their center was warm, and Donner moved against it until he felt himself stirred, a reflex he gave in to. Rusty Patrick's breathing had steadied into a rhythmic, easy stride cut from time to time with a short shudder. Donner was calling his name now, "Rusty, hey, Rusty." The man beneath him groaned in what might have been acknowledgment and moved, his eyes still shut, and then Donner knew that Rusty had taken him into his hands and they were together that way in the mountain tent.

In the morning Donner saw what he hadn't seen for five days: shadows on the tent, the shocking sunprint of tree limbs on the gray canvas. It warmed to 25 and then 30 degrees. They took a long time with their morning, boiling water for coffee and oatmeal and then another pan for washing. There was dried blood in their hair and faces and necks. The world was a blinding white, the sky blue in tiers to the horizon. They didn't speak, both men packing up carefully, wearing sunglasses against the crushing light. The muted concussions of snow bundles falling from the thawing limbs sounded all around them, and the dog Scout circled in the snow-packed camp space ready to go.

Donner told the woman the rest of the story: the warming, brilliant day in mid-September, and walking out of the mountains with Rusty Patrick and his dog. The dog disappeared right away and then five minutes later came along working two cows before him like an expert in snow herding. The men stopped to watch this display. Donner took off his jacket and tucked it into his pack. They would walk ten miles downhill on a snow-packed path behind an ever-increasing line of cows, which the dog urged and instructed, a kind of rare pleasure that comes once in a lifetime.

In that larger, well-lit world with a clear promise of tomorrow and home and hope, Donner thought it might be possible to speak to Rusty Patrick about what had happened, but at each juncture, as they stopped for water or granola bars or just to look the hundred miles east across the snow-patched plains, neither man spoke up except to say, "Some dog" or the like. When they shook hands that evening at the bus station in a town that Donner would never visit again, he thought: I'll never know any of this again, any of it, and I'll never see Rusty Patrick again.

Now in the Jim Bridger, Donner and the woman who was not his wife had thrown their paper plates and steak bones into the fireplace and moved their table to the periphery of the dining room, stacking it upside down on those already there. It was after eleven, and people, many wearing gold and silver paper party hats, danced. It was fun for the woman, and she held on to Donner's arm happily, pretending every so often to whisper something to him and kissing his neck instead. This was all better than he'd described it.

At one point, she bought an embroidered Jim Bridger cap from the little glass case, a turquoise cap with a moose underneath the name, and she announced it was for Willem, a present.

"I'm not sure that's a good idea," he said.

"He likes me; this is a good cap for him," the woman said. He didn't like her using his son's name. His wife's name had come up from time to time in the last few days, but it was just a fact, one he was steeled against. When she said his son's name, it just confused him. His son now had returned and gone off to a boarding school in California. It was true that the woman had given Willem things from time to time. She was young and knew what to get.

One of the band members had a full beard, and every third song he'd hoist his accordion and announce, "'The New Year's Polka,'" to which they'd danced already twice. Their waitress, Kay, danced every dance now in the warm wooden-floored room, each with a different young man. The employees were all going home and back to college, and she was dancing with them one by one. Donner had heard, through all the talking and the music and the dinner noise, the regular bass beat of Rusty Patrick's deep voice as he spoke to his mates in the other room. After a week of knowing what he was doing or pretending to know, Donner was dislocated and floating, his brave face paper-thin.

Donner saw Rusty Patrick turn and look into his face. Rusty's expression opened in strange surprise and he came immediately over to where Donner and the woman stood by the stone fireplace.

"No way!" he said, shaking Donner's hand. Then he said it again and clapped Donner in a hard embrace. He opened his mouth again to say something that would have been *What are you doing here?* or *Is it really you?* but with his mouth open, he just hugged Donner hard again.

They were spilling champagne, and Donner could sense the woman at his arm also against him, but he could not speak. The room seemed to be glowing. Donner could only put his arm around Rusty and hug him again, feeling the whiskers against the bones in his face. When they stood back, Rusty asked the woman, "So, you must be his wife?"

She took his arm in their close circle and said no, she was his friend.

"I'm Rusty," he said.

"I know," she said. "I've heard all about you." Now she had her hands on both of his forearms. "I've heard the wonderful story."

"One minute!" the bartender called. "Make amends or wait a year! Who needs champagne! Where's my sweetheart!" His wife, Kay, appeared at his back, and they kissed. The room was full, everyone shoulder to shoulder.

Rusty Patrick's face opened to Donner in a profound look, plaintive and deep. A basket full of noisemakers suddenly appeared between them, and the men took one each and started blowing the honking whistles until the accordion sounded the countdown: Ten. Nine. Eight. The men's look held. Donner felt a smooth hand on his face, and the woman pulled him down, and she kissed him tenderly, keeping her hand there as the minute and the hour and the year lapsed for the people in the Jim Bridger. A shotgun sounded from out on the highway, and paper dots fell into everyone's hair.

Immediately, the band fired up, and the room sorted itself out, alcoves of people widening until the dancers had some space. It was another version of "The New Year's Polka."

Rusty's buddies all slipped back into the bar, but Rusty Patrick came up to Donner, speaking in his ear. "How's your son?" the man said, his voice full of real concern. "Did he make it home? Did you talk to him?"

Donner could only nod at Rusty then and drop his eyes and step back. The young woman who was not his wife had snugged the turquoise cap onto her head and threaded her hair out the back in a ponytail. "Let's dance!" she called in the thrumming noise. "I haven't danced all year!"

Donner was watching what his body did, and what it did now was push Rusty and the woman together and smile at them. "Go to it!" he said. "This runs a thousand dollars a day in Sun Valley. I'm going to get some air."

Outside, the night was ripped, filled, up-ended with stars sizzling in the deep chill. Donner felt his scalp tighten against the gathering cold, and he blew great plumes into the air. He retrieved his binoculars from his car kit, and when he shut the door, the dog stood in Rusty's truck to be stroked.

"Come on, Scout," Donner said, patting his leg. "Let's go see the moose."

Scout stood two feet on the tailgate and Donner lifted the animal to the ground rather than have him jump. They walked around the side of the old Jim Bridger to the wooden deck over Long Pond. There were two people finishing an argument as he arrived and the woman said to the man, "That's four strikes, Artie, and you damn well know it." They went in, releasing a quick rush of noise.

The binoculars had belonged to Donner's father and they were the best set he'd ever seen. He sighted Jesse standing well into the trees on the far side. Donner breathed out and held so he could focus. The moose wasn't moving, and Donner couldn't tell if he was looking across at the party.

Certain decisions are made in daylight and certain decisions are made in darkness. Winter has its own decisions and summer has its own decisions as do spring and fall. Donner drew a chestful of the sharp air. He'd made a decision last February with the woman whom he could now see dancing inside the painted window. It was made in the frigid early twilight under low clouds while the car headlamps passing on the highway seemed useless little fires that wouldn't last the night, and that decision to use his story as he had, to show it to her, burn it like a match, had led to this new darkness and the longer night.

Louise Erdrich

Revival Road

From *The New Yorker*

F ROM THE air, our road must look like a length of rope flung down haphazardly, a thing of inscrutable loops and half-finished question marks. But there is a design to Revival Road. The beginning of the road is paved, though with a material inferior to that of the main highway, which snakes south from our college town into the villages and factory cities of New Hampshire. When the town has the money, the road is also coated with light gravel. Over the course of a summer, those bits of stone are pressed into the softened tar, making a smooth surface on which the cars pick up speed. By midwinter, though, the frost has crept beneath the road and flexed, creating heaves that force the cars to slow again. I'm glad when that happens, for children walk down this road to the bus stop below. They walk past our house with their dogs, wearing puffy jackets of saturated brilliance—hot pink, hot yellow, hot blue. They change shape and grow before my eyes, becoming the young drivers of fast cars that barely miss the smaller children, who, in their turn, grow up and drive away from here.

One day in the dead of winter, one of these young drivers appeared at our door, knocking so frantically that my mother called to me in alarm. I came rushing from the basement laundry room to see him standing behind the glass of the back storm door, jacketless and shivering. I saw that he was missing a finger from the hand he raised, and recognized him as the Eyke boy, now grown, years past fooling with his father's chainsaw.

But not his father's new credit-bought car. Davan Eyke had sneaked his father's automobile out for an illicit spin and lost control as he came down the hill beside our house. The car had slid toward a steep gully lined with birch and, by lucky chance, had come to rest pinned precisely between two trunks. The trees now held the expensive and unpaid-for white car in a perfect vise. Not one dent. Not one silvery scratch. Not yet. It was Davan's hope that if I hooked a chain to my Subaru and backed up the hill I would be able to pull his car gently free.

My chain snapped. So did many others over the course of the afternoon. At the bottom of the road, a collection of cars, trucks, equipment, and people gathered. As the car was unwedged, as it was rocked, yanked, pushed, and released, as other ideas were tried and discarded, and as the newness of the machine wore off, Davan saw that his plan had failed and he began to despair. With empty eyes, he watched a dump truck winch his father's vehicle half free, then slam it flat on its side and drag it shrieking up a lick of gravel that the town's road agent had laid down for traction.

Over the years our town, famous for the softness and drama of its natural light, has drawn artists from the large cities of the Eastern Seaboard. Most of them have had some success in the marketplace, and since New Hampshire does not tax income—preferring a thousand other less effective ways to raise revenue—they find themselves wealthier here, albeit slightly bored. For company, they are forced to rely on locals such as myself—a former schoolteacher, fired for insubordination, a semi-educated art lover. Down at the end of our road, in a large brick Cape attached to a white clapboard carriage house (now a studio), there lives such an artist.

Kurt Heissman is a striking man, formerly much celebrated for his assemblages of stone, but now mainly ignored. He hasn't produced a major piece in years. His works often incorporate massive pieces of native slate or granite, and he occasionally hires young local men to help with their execution. His assistants live on the grounds—there is a small cottage sheltered by an old white pine—and are required to be available for work at any time of the day or night. There is no telling when the inspiration to fit one stone in a certain position upon another may finally strike.

Heissman favors the heavy plaid woollens sold by mail, and his movements are ponderous and considered. His gray hair is cut in a brushy crewcut, the same do that Uncle Sam once gave him. Though he complains about his loss of energy, he is in remarkable health at fifty. His hands are oddly, surprisingly, delicate and small. His feet are almost girlish in their neatly tied boots, a contrast to the rest of him, so boldly cut and rugged. I have heard that the size of a man's hands and feet is an accurate predictor of the size of his sex, but with Kurt Heissman this does not prove to be the case. If this statement is crude, that is of no concern to me—I am citing a fact. I love the way this man is made.

The stones that he gathers for possible use intrigue me. I think I know, sometimes, what it is about them that draws him. He says that the Japanese have a word for the essence apparent in a rock, and I suppose that I love him for his ability to see that essence. I wish sometimes that I were stone. Then he would see me as I am: peach-colored granite with flecks of angry mica. My balance is slightly off. I am leaning toward him, farther, farther. Should I try to right myself? This is not an aesthetic choice.

When Davan Eyke was forced to leave home after the accident, he did not go far, just up to Kurt Heissman's little guest cottage beneath the boughs of the beautiful, enfolding pine. The tree has an unusually powerful shape, and Heissman and I have speculated often on its age. We are both quite certain that it was small, a mere sapling, too tender to bother with, when the agents of the English king first marked the tallest and straightest trees in the forests of New England as destined for the shipyards of the Royal Navy, where they would become masts from which to hang great sails. Any large pine growing now was a seedling when the pine canopy, so huge and dense that no light shone onto the centuries of bronze needles below, was axed down. This tree splits, halfway up its trunk, into three parts that form an enormous crown. In that crotch there is a raven's nest, which is unusual, since ravens are shy of Northeasterners, having a long collective memory for the guns, nets, and poisons with which they were once almost eradicated.

The ravens watched when Davan Eyke moved in, but they watch everything. They are humorous, highly intelligent birds, and knew immediately that Davan Eyke would be trouble. Therefore they disturbed his sleep by dropping twigs and pinecones on the painted tin roof of his cottage; they shat on the lintel, stole small things he left in the yard—pencils, coins, his watch—and hid them. They also laughed. The laughter of a raven is a sound unendurably human. You may know it, if you have heard it in your own throat, as the noise of that peculiarly German word *Schadenfreude*. Perhaps the raven's laughter, its low rasp, reminds us of the depth of our own human darkness. Of course, there is nothing human about it and its source is unknowable, as are the hearts of all things wild. Davan Eyke was bothered, though, enough so that he complained to Heissman about the birds.

"Get used to them" was all the artist said to Davan Eyke.

Heissman tells me this one day as I bring him the mail, a thing I do often when he feels close to tossing himself into the throes of some ambitious piece. At those times, he cannot or will not break the thread of his concentration by making a trip to the post office. There is too much at stake. This could be the day that his talent will resurrect itself painfully from the grief into which it has been plunged.

"I have in mind a perception of balance, although the whole thing must be brutally off the mark and highly dysphoric." He speaks like this— pompous, amused at his own pronouncements, his eyes brightening beneath their heavy white brows.

"Awkward," I say, to deflate him. "Maybe even ugly."

In his self-satisfaction there is more than a hint of the repressed Kansas farm boy he was when he first left home for New York City. That boy is buried under many layers now—there is a veneer of faked European ennui, an aggressive macho crackle, an edge of judgmental Lutheranism, and a stratum of terrible sadness over the not so recent loss of his second wife, who was killed in a car accident out West.

"Do you know," Heissman said once, "that a stone can be wedged just so into the undercarriage of a car that, when you press the gas pedal, it sticks and shoots the car forward at an amazing speed?" That was the gist of the fluke occurrence that had killed his wife. A high-school prank in Montana, near Flathead Lake. Stones on the highway. As she pressed on the brakes, Heissman says, her speed increased. Not a beautiful woman, in her pictures, but forceful, intelligent, athletic. She is resembled by their daughter, Freda, a girl who seems to have committed herself to dressing in nothing but black and purple since she entered Sarah Lawrence. When Heissman speaks of Freda's coming home for a weekend, his voice is tender, almost dreamy. At those times, it has a kind of yearning that I would do anything to hear directed toward me. I'm jealous. That is just the way it is. I tell myself that he sees Freda not as his actual self-absorbed and petulant daughter but as the incarnation of his lost wife. But I don't like Freda and she doesn't like me.

.   .   .

"He's not working out," Heissman says now, of Davan Eyke. "I shouldn't hire locals."

I shrug off his use of the word "local." After all, I am one, although I qualify in Heissman's mind as both local and of the larger world, since I spent several years in London, living in fearful solitude on the edge of Soho and failing my degree.

"You wouldn't have to hire anybody if you used smaller rocks," I answer, my voice falsely dismissive.

Our friendship is based, partly, on the pretense that I do not take his work, or his failure to work, seriously, and do not mind whether we are sexual or not, when in fact we both know that I value his work and am quietly, desperately, with no hope of satisfaction, in love with him. He believes that I am invulnerable. I protect myself with every trick I know.

"This guy's a brainless punk," Heissman continues.

"I thought you knew that when you hired him."

"I suppose I could have told by looking at him, but I didn't really look."

"The only job he's ever had was cutting grass, and half the time he broke the lawnmower. He broke so many on this road that people stopped hiring him. Still," I tell Heissman, "he's not a bad person, not even close to bad. He's just . . ." I try to get at the thing about Eyke. "He doesn't care about anything." My defense is lame, and my lover does not buy it.

"I was desperate. I was working on 'Construction No. 20.'"

"No. 20" is the working title of a piece commissioned many, many years ago by a large Minneapolis cereal company for its corporate grounds. It is still not finished.

Davan Eyke appears, and I stay and watch the two men wrestle steel and stone. Eyke looks slight next to his boss. Together, though, they haul stones from the woods, drag and lever blocks of pale marble delivered from the Rutland quarries. If Davan were artistic, this would be an ideal job, a chance to live close to and learn from a master. As it is, Davan's enthusiasm quickly gives way to the resentment he transfers from his father to his boss.

My mother sighs and makes a face when I tell her that Freda Heissman is visiting her father, and that he has invited us to dinner. Heissman often invites us to dinners that do not happen once Freda becomes involved. She rails against me; I suspect that she has prevailed upon her father more than once to break off our friendship. There is a low energy to Freda, a fantastic kind of drama, a way of doing ordinary things with immense conviction. When I first met her, it was hard to believe that the dots she splashed on paper, the C-plus science projects she displayed with such bravura were only adequate. Looking at her through the lens of her dead mother's image, however, Heissman is convinced that she is extraordinary.

I shouldn't be so hard on Freda, I suppose. But is it proper for the young to be so disappointing? And Heissman—why can't he see? I have dearly wished that she'd find a boyfriend for herself, and yet our sense of class distinction in this country is so ingrained that neither of us had considered Davan Eyke, either to dismiss or encourage such a match. There he was, sullenly enduring his surroundings, winging pebbles at the tormenting birds, but since he was not of the intelligentsia (such as we are) who live on Revival Road, he didn't occur to us.

This is the sort of family he is from: The Eykes. His father is a tinkering, sporadically employed mechanic. His mother drives the local gas truck. In their packed-earth yard, a dog was tied for many years, a lovely thing, part German shepherd and part husky, one eye brown and one blue. The dog was never taken off a short chain that bound it to the trunk of a tree. It lived in that tiny radius through all weathers, lived patiently, enduring each dull moment of its life, showing no hint of going mean.

I suppose I am no better than the Eykes. I called the Humane Society once, but when no one came and the dog still wound the chain one way and then the other, around and around the tree, I did nothing more. Rather than confronting the Eykes—which seemed unthinkable to me, since Mr. Eyke not only hauled away our trash but mowed our field and kept the trees in good condition by plucking away the tall grasses at their trunks—I was silent. From time to time, I brought the dog a bone when I passed, and felt a certain degree of contempt for the Eykes, as one does for people who mistreat an animal.

That is one failure I regret having to do with the Eykes. The other is my shortsightedness regarding Davan and Freda.

A turbulent flow of hormones runs up and down this road. On my walks, I've seen adolescence bolt each neighbor child upward like a sun-drunk plant. Most of the houses on the road are surrounded by dark trees and a tangle of undergrowth. No two are within shouting distance. Yet you *know,* merely by waving to the parents whose haunted eyes bore through the windshields of their cars. You hear, as new trail bikes and motorbikes rip the quiet, as boom boxes blare from their perches on newly muscled shoulders. The family cars, once so predictable in their routes, buck and raise dust as they race up and down the hill. This is a painful time, and you avert your eyes from the houses that contain it. The very foundations of those homes seem less secure. Love falters and blows. Steam rises from the ditches, and sensible neighbors ask no questions.

Davan hit like that, a compact freckled boy who suddenly grew long-jawed and reckless. Mother says that she knew it was the end when he started breaking lawnmowers, slamming them onto the grass and stones so savagely that the blades bent. She quietly had our mower fixed and did not hire him again. His brown hair grew until it reached his shoulders, and a new beard came in across his chin like streaks of dirt. Frighteningly, Davan walked the road from time to time, dressed in camouflage, hugging his father's crossbow and arrows, with which he transfixed woodchucks. That phase passed, and then he lapsed into a stupor of anger that lasted for years and culminated in the damage he did to his father's new car by driving it into the trees. It was the most expensive thing his family had ever bought, and since he left home soon after that, it was clear he was not forgiven.

Freda Heissman, on the other hand, had resolved her adolescence beautifully. After a few stormy junior-high-school years following her mother's death, she settled into a pattern of achieving small things with great flair, for, as I mentioned, she had no talents and was at most a mediocre student. She gave the impression that she was going places, though, and so she did go places. Still, her acceptance into a prestigious college was a mystery to all who knew her. Her teachers, including me, were stymied. Perhaps it was the interview, one woman told my mother.

Later, in the seething, watery spring darkness, Heissman enters our house via the back-porch screen door, to which he has the key. It is the only door of the house that unlocks with that key, and I keep things that way for the following reason: should I tire, should I have the enlightenment or the self-discipline or the good sense to stop Heissman from coming to me in the night, it will be a simple matter. One locksmith's fee. One tossed key. No explanation owed. Though my mother must sense, must conjecture, must know without ever saying so that Heissman's night visits occur, we do not speak of it and never have. Her room is at the other end of the house. We live privately, in many respects, and although this is how we prefer to live, there are times when I nearly spill over with the need to confide my feelings.

For when he steps into my room it is as though I am waking on some strange and unlikely margin. As though the ocean has been set suddenly before me. Landlocked, you forget. Then, suddenly, you are wading hip high into the surge of waves. There is so much meaning, so much hunger in our mouths and skin. This is happiness, I think every time. I've had lovers, several, and what I like best is the curious unfolding confessional quality of sex. I seek it, demand it of Heissman, and for a matter of hours he is bare to me, all candor and desire. He begs things of me. *Put your mouth here.* In nakedness we are the reverse of our day selves.

Ravens are the birds I'll miss most when I die. If only the darkness into which we must look were composed of the black light of their limber intelligence. If only we did not have to die at all and instead became ravens. I've watched these birds so hard that I feel their black feathers split out of my skin. To fly from one tree to another, the raven hangs itself, hawklike, on the air. I hang myself that same way in sleep, between one day and the next. When we're young, we think we are the only species worth knowing. But the more I come to know people, the better I like ravens. In this house, open to a wide back field and pond, I am living within their territory. A few years ago, there were eight or more of them in Heissman's white pine. Now just four live there, and six live somewhere in the heavy fringe of woods beyond my field. Two made their nest in the pine. Three hatchlings were reared. The other raven was killed by Davan Eyke.

You may wonder how on earth an undisciplined, highly unpleasant, not particularly coordinated youth could catch and kill a raven. They are infernally cautious birds. For instance, having long experience with poisoned carcasses, they will not take the first taste of dead food but let the opportunistic blue jays eat their fill. Only when they see that the bold, greedy jays have survived do the ravens drive them off and settle in to feed. Davan had to use his father's crossbow to kill a raven. One day when Heissman was gone, he sat on the front stoop of his little cottage and waited for the birds to gather in their usual circle of derision. As they laughed at him among themselves, stepping through the branches, he slowly raised the crossbow. They would have vanished at the sight of a gun. But they were unfamiliar with other instruments. They did not know the purpose or the range of the bow. One strayed down too far, and Davan's arrow pierced it completely. Heissman drove into the yard and saw Davan standing over the bird. Amazingly, it wasn't dead. With some fascination, Davan was watching it struggle on the shaft of the arrow, the point of which was driven into the earth. Heissman walked over, snapped the arrow off, and drew it tenderly, terribly, from the bird's body. For a moment the raven sprawled, limp, on the ground, and then it gathered itself, walked away, and entered the woods to die. Overhead and out of range, the other birds wheeled. For once, they were silent.

"Let me see the bow," Heissman said conversationally. Davan handed it to him, prepared to point out its marvellous and lethal features. "And the arrows." Davan handed those over, too. "I'll be right back," Heissman said.

Davan waited. Heissman walked across the yard to his woodpile, turned, and fitted an arrow into the groove. Then he raised the bow. Davan stepped aside, looked around for the target, looked uneasily back at Heissman, then touched his own breast as the sculptor lifted the shoulder piece. *Shot.* Davan leapt to the other side of the white pine and vaulted off into the brush. The arrow stuck in the tree, just behind his shoulder. Then Heissman laid the bow on the block he used to split his firewood. He axed the weapon neatly in half. He laid the arrows down next, like a bunch of scallions, and chopped them into short lengths. He walked into his house and phoned me. "If you see that boy running past your house," he said, "here's why."

"You shot at him?"

"Not to hit him."

"But still, my God."

Heissman, embarrassed, did not speak of this again.

Davan had saved enough money, from Heissman's pay (or so we thought), to buy himself an old Toyota, dusty red with a splash of dark rust on the door where a dent had raised metal through the paint. The car now spewed grit and smoke on the road as he drove it back and forth to town. He had returned to his room in his parents' house and he resumed his chore of feeding the dog every day, though he never untied it from the tree.

The dog's maple grew great patches of liver-colored moss and dropped dead limbs. Shit-poisoned, soaked with urine at the base, and nearly gir-dled by the continual sawing and wearing of the chain, the tree had, for years, yellowed and then blazed orange, unhealthily, the first of all the trees on the road. Then, one day that spring, it fell over, and the dog walked off calmly, like the raven, into the woods, dragging a three-foot length of chain. Only the dog didn't die. Perhaps it had been completely mad all along, or perhaps it was that moment after the tree went down when, unwrapping itself nervously, the dog took one step beyond the radius of packed dirt within which it had lived since it was a fat puppy. Perhaps that step, the paw meeting grass, rang along the spine of the dog, fed such new light into its brain that it could not contain the barrage of information. At any rate, the outcome of that moment wasn't to be seen for several weeks, by which time Davan had successfully raised dust near Freda on illicit vis-its, and had secretly taken her out with him to local parties, where at first she enjoyed her status as a college-goer and the small sensation caused by her New York clothing styles. Then, at some point, something awakened in her, some sense of pity or conscience. Before that, I'd seen nothing remarkable about Heissman's daughter, other than her clothes. Her unkindness, her laziness, her feeling of enormous self-worth—all were typical of women her age. Then, suddenly, she had this urge to care for and rescue Davan Eyke, an abrupt unblocking of compassion which made her come clean with her father, a humanity that thoroughly terrified Heissman.

I step out of the car with the mail and see Heissman standing, blocklike, in front of Davan, who slouches before the older man with obdurate weari-ness. Locked in their man-space, they do not acknowledge me. Heissman is, of course, telling Davan Eyke that he doesn't want him to see Freda. He probably calls Davan some name, or makes some threat, for Davan steps back and stares at him alertly, hands up, as though ready to block a punch, which never comes. Heissman kicks him over, instead, with a rageful ease that astonishes Davan Eyke. From the ground, he shakes his head in puz-zlement at Heissman's feet. When Heissman draws his leg back to kick again, I move forward. The kick stops midway. Davan rises. The two stare at each other with spinning hatred—I can almost see the black web between them. "Pay me," Davan says, backing away. "Say you won't see her first." Davan starts to laugh, raucous, crackling, a raven's laugh. I can still hear it through the car window when he revs and peels out. I don't understand why Heissman detests the boy so much; it is as though he has tapped some awful gusher in the artist and now, in a welter of frustrated energy, Heissman starts working. He finishes "No. 20." He produces, hardly sleeps. Hardly sees me.

It is difficult for a woman to admit that she gets along with her own mother. Somehow, it seems a form of betrayal. So few do. To join in the company of women, to be adults, we go through a period of proudly boasting of having survived our mothers' indifference, anger, overpowering love, the burden of their pain, their tendency to drink or teetotal, their warmth or coldness, praise or criticism, sexual confusion or embarrassing clarity. It isn't enough that our mothers sweated, labored, bore their daughters nobly or under total anesthesia or both. No. They must be responsible for our psychic weaknesses for the rest of their lives. It is all right to forgive our fathers. We all know that. But our mothers are held to a standard so exacting that it has no principles. They simply must be to blame.

I reject that, as my mother sits before me here. She has just had an operation to restore her vision. Her eyes are closed beneath small plastic cups and gauze bandages. When I change the gauze and put in the drops twice a day, it strikes me that there is something in the nakedness of her face and shut eyes that is like that of a newborn animal. Her skin has always been extremely clean and fine. Often, she has smelled to me of soap, but now she has added a light perfume, which enables her in her blindness to retrace her steps through the house with confidence, by smell.

That is how I know that she knows he has been here. Last night, he came down off the manic high in which he had hung between one uninspired month and the next. It is morning. Even to me, the house smells different after Heissman has made love to me in the night, more alive, alert with a fresh exquisite maleness. Still, for me to openly become Heissman's lover would upset the balance of our lives. My deadlocked secret love and unsecret contempt are the only hold I have over him, my only power. So things remain as they are. My mother and I maintain a calm life together. I do not dread, as others might, her increasing dependence. It is only that I have the strange, unadult wish that if she must pass into death, that rough mountain, she take me with her. Not leave me scratching at the shut seam of stone.

. . .

Spring on this road commences with a rush of dark rain, slick mud, and then dry warmth, which is bad for our wells and ponds but wonderful to see in the woods. New sounds, the rapturous trilling of peepers, that electric sexual whine, the caterwauling of the barred owls, startling us from sleep, raising bubbles of tension in my blood. I cannot imagine myself changing the lock. Without a word, without a sound, I circle Heissman, dragging my chain.

All of March, there is no sign of the dog that slipped free of the dead maple, and Mother and I can only assume that it has been taken in somewhere as a stray or, perhaps, shot from a farmer's back porch for running deer. That is how it probably survives—if it does—squeezing through a hole in the game-park fence, living on hand-raised pheasants and winter-killed carcasses.

The dog reappears in the full blush of April. During that week, leaves shoot from buds and the air films over with a bitter and intangible green that sweetens and darkens in so short a time. One balmy night, my neighbors up the road, the ones who clear-cut fifty acres of standing timber in four shocking days, have their cocker spaniel eaten. They leave the dog out all night on its wire run, and the next morning, from the back door, Ann Flaud in her nightgown pulls the dog's lead toward her. It rattles across the ground. At the end of it hangs an empty collar, half gnawed through.

There is little else to find. Just a patch of blood and the two long, mitteny brown ears. Coydogs are blamed—those mythical creatures invoked for every loss—then Satanists. I know it is the dog. I have seen her at the edge of our field, loping on long springy wolf legs. She does not look starved. She is alive—fat, glossy, huge.

She takes a veal calf for supper one night, pulled from its standup torture pen at the one working farm on the road that survived the eighties. She steals suet out of people's bird feeders, eats garbage, meadow voles, and frogs. A few cats disappear. She is now seen regularly, never caught. People build stout fences around their chicken pens. It is not until she meets the school bus, though, mouth open, the sad eye of liquid brown and the hungry eye of crystal blue trained on the doors as they swish open, that the state police become involved.

A dragnet of shotgun-armed volunteers and local police fans through the woods. Parked on this road, an officer with a vague memory of a car theft in Concord runs a check on Davan Eyke's red car as it flashes past. Eyke is on his way up to Heissman's, where Freda, less boldly attired than usual and biting black lacquer from her nails, waits to counsel him. They go for a walk in the woods, leaving the car in the driveway, in full view of Heissman's studio. They return, and then, despite Heissman's express, uncompromising, direct orders, Freda does exactly what young people sometimes do—the opposite. The human heart is every bit as tangled as our road. She gets into the car with Eyke.

On the police check, the car turns up stolen, and as it speeds back down from Heissman's an hour later the police officer puts on his siren and spins out in pursuit. There ensues a dangerous game of tag that the newspapers will call a high-speed chase. On our narrow roads, filled with hairpin turns, sudden drops, and abrupt hills, speed is a harrowing prospect. Davan Eyke tears down the highway, hangs a sharp left on Tapper Road, and jumps the car onto a narrow gravel path used mainly for walking horses. He winds up and down the hill like a slingshot, joins the wider road, then continues toward Windsor, over the country's longest covered bridge, into Vermont, where, at the first stoplight, he screeches between two cars in a sudden left-hand turn against the red. On blacktop now, the car is clocked at over a hundred miles per hour. There isn't much the police can do but follow as fast as they dare.

Another left, and it seems that Davan is intent on fleeing back toward Claremont, on the New Hampshire side. The police car radios ahead as he swings around a curve on two wheels and makes for the bridge that crosses the wide, calm Connecticut, which serves as a boundary between New Hampshire and Vermont. It is a cold, wet, late-spring afternoon, and, according to the sign that blurs before Davan's eyes, the bridge is liable to freeze before the road. It has. The car hits ice at perhaps a hundred and twenty and soars straight over the low guardrail. A woman in the oncoming lane says later that the red car was travelling at such a velocity that it seemed to gain purchase in the air and hang above the river. She also swears that she saw, before the car flew over, the white flower of a face pressing toward the window. No one sees a thing after that, although the fisherman pulling his boat onto shore below the bridge is suddenly aware of a great shadow behind him, as though a cloud has fallen out of the sky or a bird has touched his back lightly with its wing. He turns too slowly, even in his panic, to see anything but the river in its timeless run. The impact of the small car on the water is so tremendous that there is no ripple to mark its passage from a state of movement to complete arrest. It is as though the car and its passengers are simply atomized, reduced instantaneously to their elements.

Within fifteen minutes of the radio call, all the pickups and cars on our road gather their passengers and firearms and sweep away from the dog posse to the scene of greater drama at the bridge. Although the wreckage isn't found for days and requires four wetsuited divers to locate and gather, the police make a visit to Heissman's, on the strength of the woman witness's story. Believing that Freda has gone over the bridge as well, they take me along to break the news to my friend.

I wait on the edge of the field for Heissman, my hand on the stump of an old pine's first limb. I hear the ravens deep in the brush, the grating *haw-haw* of their announcement, and it occurs to me that he might just show up with Freda. But he doesn't, only shambles toward me alone at my call. I feel for the first time in our mutual life that I am invested with startling height, even power, perhaps more intelligence than I am used to admitting I possess. I feel a sickening omnipotence.

He starts at my naked expression, asks, "What?"

"Davan's car," I report, "went over the bridge."

I don't know what I expect, then, from Heissman. Anything but his offhand, strangely shuttered nonreaction. He apparently has no idea that Freda could be in the car. Unable to go on, I fall silent. For all his sullen gravity, Davan had experienced and expressed only a shy love for Heissman's daughter. It was an emotion he was capable of feeling, as was the fear that made him press the gas pedal. *The gas pedal,* I think. *The gas pedal and the wedged-in stone.*

I stare at Heissman. My heart creaks shut. I turn away from him and walk into the woods. At first, I think I'm going off to suffer like the raven, but as I walk on and on I know that I will be fine and I will be loyal, pathologically faithful. The realization grounds me. I feel more alive. The grass cracks beneath each step I take and the sweet dry dust of it stirs around my ankles. In a long, low swale of a field that runs into a dense pressure of trees, I stop and breathe carefully.

Whenever you leave cleared land, when you step from some place carved out, plowed, or traced by a human and pass into the woods, you must leave something of yourself behind. It is that sudden loss, I think, even more than the difficulty of walking through undergrowth, that keeps people firmly fixed to paths. In the woods, there is no right way to go, of course, no trail to follow but the law of growth. You must leave behind the notion that things are right. Just look around you. Here is the way things are. Twisted, fallen, split at the root. What grows best does so at the expense of what's beneath. A white birch feeds on the pulp of an old hemlock and supports the grapevine that will slowly throttle it. In the dead wood of another tree grows fungi black as devil's hooves. Overhead the canopy, tall pines that whistle and shudder and choke off light from their own lower branches.

The dog is not seen and never returns to Revival Road, never kills another spaniel or chicken, never appears again near the house where her nature devolved, never howls in the park, and never harms a child. Yet at night, in bed, my door unlocked, as I wait I imagine that she pauses at the edge of my field, suspicious of the open space, then lopes off with her length of chain striking sparks from the exposed ledge and boulders. I have the greatest wish to stare into her eyes, but if I should meet her face to face, breathless and heavy-muzzled, shining with blood, would the brown eye see me or the blue eye?

He has weakened, Heissman, he needs me these days. My mother says, out of nowhere, *He's not who you think he is.* I touch her shoulders, reassuringly. She shrugs me off because she senses with disappointment that I actually do know him, right down to the ground. Shame, pleasure, ugliness, loss: they are the heat in the night that tempers the links. And then there is forgiveness when a person is unforgivable, and a man weeping like a child, and the dark house soaking up the hollow cries.

William Gay

The Paperhanger

From *Harper's Magazine*

T HE VANISHING of the doctor's wife's child in broad daylight was an event so cataclysmic that it forever divided time into the then and the now, the before and the after. In later years, fortified with a pitcher of silica-dry vodka martinis, she had cause to replay the events preceding the disappearance. They were tawdry and banal but in retrospect freighted with menace, a foreshadowing of what was to come, like a footman or a fool preceding a king into a room.

She had been quarreling with the paperhanger. Her four-year-old daughter, Zeineb, was standing directly behind the paperhanger where he knelt smoothing air bubbles out with a wide plastic trowel. Zeineb had her fingers in the paperhanger's hair. The paperhanger's hair was shoulder-length and the color of flax and the child was delighted with it. The paperhanger was accustomed to her doing this and he did not even turn around. He just went on with his work. His arms were smooth and brown and corded with muscle and in the light that fell upon the paperhanger through stained-glass panels the doctor's wife could see that they were lightly downed with fine golden hair. She studied these arms bemusedly while she formulated her thoughts.

You tell me so much a roll, she said. The doctor's wife was from Pakistan and her speech was still heavily accented. I do not know single-bolt rolls and double-bolt rolls. You tell me double-bolt price but you are installing single-bolt rolls. My friend has told me. It is cost me perhaps twice as much.

The paperhanger, still on his knees, turned. He smiled up at her. He had pale blue eyes. I did tell you so much a roll, he said. You bought the rolls.

The child, not yet vanished, was watching the paperhanger's eyes. She was a scaled-down clone of the mother, the mother viewed through the wrong end of a telescope, and the paperhanger suspected that as she grew neither her features nor her expression would alter, she would just grow larger, like something being aired up with a hand pump.

And you are leave lumps, the doctor's wife said, gesturing at the wall.

I do not leave lumps, the paperhanger said. You've seen my work before. These are not lumps. The paper is wet. The paste is wet. Everything will shrink down and flatten out. He smiled again. He had clean even teeth. And besides, he said, I gave you my special cockteaser rate. I don't know what you're complaining about.

Her mouth worked convulsively. She looked for a moment as if he'd slapped her. When words did come they came in a fine spray of spit. You are trash, she said. You are scum.

Hands on knees, he was pushing erect, the girl's dark fingers trailing out of his hair. Don't call me trash, he said, as if it were perfectly all right to call him scum, but he was already talking to her back. She had whirled on her heels and went twisting her hips through an arched doorway into the cathedraled living room. The paperhanger looked down at the child. Her face glowed with a strange constrained glee, as if she and the paperhanger shared some secret the rest of the world hadn't caught on to yet.

In the living room the builder was supervising the installation of a chandelier that descended from the vaulted ceiling by a long golden chain. The builder was a short bearded man dancing about, showing her the features of the chandelier, smiling obsequiously. She gave him a flat angry look. She waved a dismissive hand toward the ceiling. Whatever, she said.

She went out the front door onto the porch and down a makeshift walkway of two-by-tens into the front yard where her car was parked. The car was a silver-gray Mercedes her husband had given her for their anniversary. When she cranked the engine its idle was scarcely perceptible.

She powered down the window. Zeineb, she called. Across the razed earth of the unlandscaped yard a man in a grease-stained T-shirt was booming down the chains securing a backhoe to a lowboy hooked to a gravel truck. The sun was low in the west and bloodred behind this tableau and man and tractor looked flat and dimensionless as something decorative stamped from tin. She blew the horn. The man turned, raised an arm as if she'd signaled him.

Zeineb, she called again.

She got out of the car and started impatiently up the walkway. Behind her the gravel truck started, and truck and backhoe pulled out of the drive and down toward the road.

The paperhanger was stowing away his T square and trowels in his wooden toolbox. Where is Zeineb? the doctor's wife asked. She followed you out, the paperhanger told her. He glanced about, as if the girl might be hiding somewhere. There was nowhere to hide.

Where is my child? she asked the builder. The electrician climbed down from the ladder. The paperhanger came out of the bathroom with his tools. The builder was looking all around. His elfin features were touched with chagrin, as if this missing child were just something else he was going to be held accountable for.

Likely she's hiding in a closet, the paperhanger said. Playing a trick on you.

Zeineb does not play tricks, the doctor's wife said. Her eyes kept darting about the huge room, the shadows that lurked in corners. There was already an undercurrent of panic in her voice and all her poise and self-confidence seemed to have vanished with the child.

The paperhanger set down his toolbox and went through the house, opening and closing doors. It was a huge house and there were a lot of closets. There was no child in any of them.

The electrician was searching upstairs. The builder had gone through the French doors that opened onto the unfinished veranda and was peering into the back yard. The back yard was a maze of convoluted ditch excavated for the septic tank field line and beyond that there was just woods. She's playing in that ditch, the builder said, going down the flag-stone steps.

She wasn't, though. She wasn't anywhere. They searched the house and grounds. They moved with jerky haste. They kept glancing toward the woods where the day was waning first. The builder kept shaking his head. She's got to be *somewhere,* he said.

Call someone, the doctor's wife said. Call the police.

It's a little early for the police, the builder said. She's got to be here.

You call them anyway. I have a phone in my car. I will call my husband.

While she called, the paperhanger and the electrician continued to search. They had looked everywhere and were forced to search places they'd already looked. If this ain't the goddamnedest thing I ever saw, the electrician said.

The doctor's wife got out of the Mercedes and slammed the door. Suddenly she stopped and clasped a hand to her forehead. She screamed. The man with the tractor, she cried. Somehow my child is gone with the tractor man.

Oh Jesus, the builder said. What have we got ourselves into here?

The high sheriff that year was a ruminative man named Bellwether. He stood beside the county cruiser talking to the paperhanger while deputies ranged the grounds. Other men were inside looking in places that had already been searched numberless times. Bellwether had been in the woods and he was picking cockleburs off his khakis and out of his socks. He was watching the woods, where dark was gathering and seeping across the field like a stain.

I've got to get men out here, Bellwether said. A lot of men and a lot of lights. We're going to have to search every inch of these woods.

You'll play hell doing it, the paperhanger said. These woods stretch all the way to Lawrence County. This is the edge of the Harrikan. Down in there's where all those old mines used to be. Allens Creek.

I don't give a shit if they stretch all the way to Fairbanks, Alaska, Bellwether said. They've got to be searched. It'll just take a lot of men.

The raw earth yard was full of cars. Doctor Jamahl had come in a sleek black Lexus. He berated his wife. Why weren't you watching her? he asked. Unlike his wife's, the doctor's speech was impeccable. She covered her face with her palms and wept. The doctor still wore his green surgeon's smock and it was flecked with bright dots of blood as a butcher's smock might be.

I need to feed a few cows, the paperhanger said. I'll feed my stock pretty quick and come back and help hunt.

You don't mind if I look in your truck, do you?

Do what?

I've got to cover my ass. If that little girl don't turn up damn quick this is going to be over my head. TBI, FBI, network news. I've got to eliminate everything.

Eliminate away, the paperhanger said.

The sheriff searched the floorboard of the paperhanger's pickup truck. He shined his huge flashlight under the seat and felt behind it with his hands.

I had to look, he said apologetically.

Of course you did, the paperhanger said.

Full dark had fallen before he returned. He had fed his cattle and stowed away his tools and picked up a six-pack of San Miguel beer and he sat in the back of the pickup truck drinking it. The paperhanger had been in the Navy and stationed in the Philippines and San Miguel was the only beer he could drink. He had to go out of town to buy it, but he figured it was worth it. He liked the exotic labels, the dark bitter taste on the back of his tongue, the way the chilled bottles felt held against his forehead.

A motley crowd of curiosity seekers and searchers thronged the yard. There was a vaguely festive air. He watched all this with a dispassionate eye, as if he were charged with grading the participants, comparing this with other spectacles he'd seen. Coffee urns had been brought in and set up on tables, sandwiches prepared and handed out to the weary searchers. A crane had been hauled in and the septic tank reclaimed from the ground. It swayed from a taut cable while men with lights searched the impacted earth beneath it for a child, for the very trace of a child. Through the far dark woods lights crossed and recrossed, darted to and fro like fireflies. The doctor and the doctor's wife sat in folding camp chairs looking drained, stunned, waiting for their child to be delivered into their arms.

The doctor was a short portly man with a benevolent expression. He had a moon-shaped face, with light and dark areas of skin that looked swirled, as if the pigment coloring him had not been properly mixed. He had been educated at Princeton. When he had established his practice he had returned to Pakistan to find a wife befitting his station. The woman he had selected had been chosen on the basis of her beauty. In retrospect, perhaps more consideration should have been given to other qualities. She was still beautiful but he was thinking that certain faults might outweigh this. She seemed to have trouble keeping up with her children. She could lose a four-year-old in a room no larger than six hundred square feet and she could not find it again.

The paperhanger drained his bottle and set it by his foot in the bed of the truck. He studied the doctor's wife's ravaged face through the deep blue light. The first time he had seen her she had hired him to paint a bedroom in the house they were living in while the doctor's mansion was being built. There was an arrogance about her that cried out to be taken down a notch or two. She flirted with him, backed away, flirted again. She would treat him as if he were a stain on the bathroom rug and then stand close by him while he worked until he was dizzy with the smell of her, with the heat that seemed to radiate off her body. She stood by him while he knelt painting baseboards and after an infinite moment leaned carefully the weight of a thigh against his shoulder. You'd better move it, he thought. She didn't. He laughed and turned his face into her groin. She gave a strangled cry and slapped him hard. The paintbrush flew away and speckled the dark rose walls with antique white. You filthy beast, she said. You are some kind of monster. She stormed out of the room and he could hear her slamming doors behind her.

Well, I was looking for a job when I found this one. He smiled philosophically to himself.

But he had not been fired. In fact now he had been hired again. Perhaps there was something here to ponder.

At midnight he gave up his vigil. Some souls more hardy than his kept up the watch. The earth here was worn smooth by the useless traffic of the searchers. Driving out, he met a line of pickup trucks with civil-defense tags. Grimfaced men sat aligned in their beds. Some clutched rifles loosely by their barrels, as if they would lay to waste whatever monster, man or beast, would snatch up a child in its slaverous jaws and vanish, prey and predator, in the space between two heartbeats.

Even more dubious reminders of civilization as these fell away. He drove into the Harrikan, where he lived. A world so dark and forlorn light itself seemed at a premium. Whippoorwills swept red-eyed up from the roadside. Old abandoned foundries and furnaces rolled past, grim and dark as forsaken prisons. Down a ridge here was an abandoned graveyard, if you knew where to look. The paperhanger did. He had dug up a few of the graves, examined with curiosity what remained, buttons, belt buckles, a cameo brooch. The bones he laid out like a child with a Tinkertoy, arranging them the way they went in juryrigged resurrection.

He braked hard on a curve, the truck slewing in the gravel. A bobcat had crossed the road, graceful as a wraith, fierce and lantern-eyed in the headlights, gone so swiftly it might have been a stage prop swung across the road on wires.

Bellwether and a deputy drove to the backhoe operator's house. He lived up a gravel road that wound through a great stand of cedars. He lived in a board-and-batten house with a tin roof rusted to a warm umber. They parked before it and got out, adjusting their gunbelts.

Bellwether had a search warrant with the ink scarcely dry. The operator was outraged.

Look at it this way, Bellwether explained patiently. I've got to cover my ass. Everything has got to be considered. You know how kids are. Never thinking. What if she run under the wheels of your truck when you was backing out? What if quicklike you put the body in your truck to get rid of somewhere?

What if quicklike you get the hell off my property, the operator said.

Everything has to be considered, the sheriff said again. Nobody's accusing anybody of anything just yet.

The operator's wife stood glowering at them. To have something to do with his hands, the operator began to construct a cigarette. He had huge red hands thickly sown with brown freckles. They trembled. I ain't got a thing in this round world to hide, he said.

Bellwether and his men searched everywhere they could think of to look. Finally they stood uncertainly in the operator's yard, out of place in their neat khakis, their polished leather.

Now get the hell off my land, the operator said. If all you think of me is that I could run over a little kid and then throw it off in the bushes like a dead cat or something then I don't even want to see your goddamn face. I want you gone and I want you by God gone now.

Everything had to be considered, the sheriff said.

Then maybe you need to consider that paperhanger.

What about him?

That paperhanger is one sick puppy.

He was still there when I got there, the sheriff said. Three witnesses swore nobody ever left, not even for a minute, and one of them was the child's mother. I searched his truck myself.

Then he's a sick puppy with a damn good alibi, the operator said.

That was all. There was no ransom note, no child that turned up two counties over with amnesia. She was a page turned, a door closed, a lost ball in the high weeds. She was a child no larger than a doll, but the void she left behind her was unreckonable. Yet there was no end to it. No finality. There was no moment when someone could say, turning from a mounded grave, Well, this has been unbearable, but you've got to go on with your life. Life did not go on.

At the doctor's wife's insistence an intensive investigation was focused on the backhoe operator. Forensic experts from the FBI examined every millimeter of the gravel truck, paying special attention to its wheels. They were examined with every modern crime-fighting device the government possessed, and there was not a microscopic particle of tissue or blood, no telltale chip of fingernail, no hair ribbon.

Work ceased on the mansion. Some subcontractors were discharged outright, while others simply drifted away. There was no one to care if the work was done, no one to pay them. The half-finished veranda's raw wood grayed in the fall, then winter, rains. The ditches were left fallow and uncovered and half-filled with water. Kudzu crept from the woods. The hollyhocks and oleanders the doctor's wife had planted grew entangled and rampant. The imported windows were stoned by double-dared boys who whirled and fled. Already this house where a child had vanished was acquiring an unhealthy, diseased reputation.

The doctor and his wife sat entombed in separate prisons replaying real and imagined grievances. The doctor felt that his wife's neglect had sent his child into the abstract. The doctor's wife drank vodka martinis and watched talk shows where passed an endless procession of vengeful people who had not had children vanish, and felt, perhaps rightly, that the fates had dealt her from the bottom of the deck, and she prayed with intensity for a miracle.

Then one day she was just gone. The Mercedes and part of her clothing and personal possessions were gone too. He idly wondered where she was, but he did not search for her.

Sitting in his armchair cradling a great marmalade cat and a bottle of

J&B and observing with bemused detachment the gradations of light at the window, the doctor remembered studying literature at Princeton. He had particular cause to reconsider the poetry of William Butler Yeats. For how surely things fell apart, how surely the center did not hold.

His practice fell into a ruin. His colleagues made sympathetic allowances for him at first, but there are limits to these things. He made erroneous diagnoses, prescribed the wrong medicines not once or twice but as a matter of course.

Just as there is a deepening progression to misfortune, so too there is a point beyond which things can only get worse. They did. A middle-aged woman he was operating on died.

He had made an incision to remove a ruptured appendix and the incised flesh was clamped aside while he made ready to slice it out. It was not there. He stared in drunken disbelief. He began to search under things, organs, intestines, a rising tide of blood. The appendix was not there. It had gone into the abstract, atrophied, been removed twenty-five years before, he had sliced through the selfsame scar. He was rummaging through her abdominal cavity like an irritated man fumbling through a drawer for a clean pair of socks, finally bellowing in rage and wringing his hands in bloody vexation while nurses began to cry out, another surgeon was brought on the run as a closer, and he was carried from the operating room.

Came then days of sitting in the armchair while he was besieged by contingency lawyers, action news teams, a long line of process servers. There was nothing he could do. It was out of his hands and into the hands of the people who are paid to do these things. He sat cradling the bottle of J&B with the marmalade cat snuggled against his portly midriff. He would study the window, where the light drained away in a process he no longer had an understanding of, and sip the scotch and every now and then stroke the cat's head gently. The cat purred against his breast as reassuringly as the hum of an air conditioner.

He left in the middle of the night. He began to load his possessions into the Lexus. At first he chose items with a great degree of consideration. The first thing he loaded was a set of custom-made monogrammed golf clubs. Then his stereo receiver, Denon AC3, $1,750. A copy of *This Side of Paradise* autographed by Fitzgerald that he had bought as an investment. By the time the Lexus was half full he was just grabbing things at random and stuffing them into the back seat, a half-eaten pizza, half a case of cat food, a single brocade house shoe.

He drove west past the hospital, the country club, the city-limit sign. He was thinking no thoughts at all, and all the destination he had was the amount of highway the headlights showed him.

In the slow rains of late fall the doctor's wife returned to the unfinished mansion. She used to sit in a camp chair on the ruined veranda and drink chilled martinis she poured from the pitcher she carried in a foam ice chest. Dark fell early these November days. Raincrows husbanding some far cornfield called through the smoky autumn air. The sound was fiercely evocative, reminding her of something but she could not have said what.

She went into the room where she had lost the child. The light was failing. The high corners of the room were in deepening shadow but she could see the nests of dirt daubers clustered on the rich flocked wallpaper, a spider swing from a chandelier on a strand of spun glass. Some animal's dried blackened stool curled like a slug against the baseboards. The silence in the room was enormous.

One day she arrived and was surprised to find the paperhanger there. He was sitting on a yellow four-wheeler drinking a bottle of beer. He made to go when he saw her but she waved him back. Stay and talk with me, she said.

The paperhanger was much changed. His pale locks had been shorn away in a makeshift haircut as if scissored in the dark or by a blind barber and his cheeks were covered with a soft curly beard.

You have grow a beard.

Yes.

You are strange with it.

The paperhanger sipped from his San Miguel. He smiled. I was strange without it, he said. He arose from the four-wheeler and came over and sat on the flagstone steps. He stared across the mutilated yard toward the tree-line. The yard was like a funhouse maze seen from above, its twistings and turnings bereft of mystery.

You are working somewhere now?

No. I don't take so many jobs anymore. There's only me, and I don't need much. What has become of the doctor?

She shrugged. Many things have change, she said. He has gone. The banks have foreclose. What is that you ride?

An ATV. A four-wheeler.

It goes well in the woods?

It was made for that.

You could take me in the woods. How much would you charge me? For what?

To go in the woods. You could drive me. I will pay you.

Why?

To search for my child's body.

I wouldn't charge anybody anything to search for a child's body, the paperhanger said. But she's not in these woods. Nothing could have stayed hidden, the way these woods were searched.

Sometimes I think she just kept walking. Perhaps just walking away from the men looking. Far into the woods.

Into the woods, the paperhanger thought. If she had just kept walking in a straight line with no time out for eating or sleeping, where would she be? Kentucky, Algiers, who knew.

I'll take you when the rains stop, he said. But we won't find a child.

The doctor's wife shook her head. It is a mystery, she said. She drank from her cocktail glass. Where could she have gone? How could she have gone?

There was a man named David Lang, the paperhanger said. Up in Galletin, back in the late 1800s. He was crossing a barn lot in full view of his wife and two children and he just vanished. Went into thin air. There was a judge in a wagon turning into the yard and he saw it too. It was just like he took a step in this world and his foot came down in another one. He was never seen again.

She gave him a sad smile, bitter and one-cornered. You make fun with me.

No. It's true. I have it in a book. I'll show you.

I have a book with dragons, fairies. A book where hobbits live in the Middle-Earth. They are lies. I think most books are lies. Perhaps all books. I have prayed for a miracle but I am not worthy of one. I have prayed for her to come from the dead, then just to find her body. That would be a miracle to me. There are no miracles.

She rose unsteadily, swayed slightly, leaning to take up the cooler. The paperhanger watched her. I have to go now, she said. When the rains stop we will search.

Can you drive?

Of course I can drive. I have drive out here.

I mean are you capable of driving now. You seem a little drunk.

I drink to forget but it is not enough, she said. I can drive.

After a while he heard her leave in the Mercedes, the tires spinning in the gravel drive. He lit a cigarette. He sat smoking it, watching the rain string off the roof. He seemed to be waiting for something. Dusk was falling like a shroud, the world going dark and formless the way it had begun. He drank the last of the beer, sat holding the bottle, the foam bitter in the back of his mouth. A chill touched him. He felt something watching him. He turned. From the corner of the ruined veranda a child was watching him. He stood up. He heard the beer bottle break on the flagstones. The child went sprinting past the hollyhocks toward the brush at the edge of the yard, tiny sepia child with an intent sloe-eyed face, real as she had ever been, translucent as winter light through dirty glass.

The doctor's wife's hands were laced loosely about his waist as they came down through a thin stand of sassafras, edging over the ridge where the ghost of a road was, a road more sensed than seen that faced into a half acre of tilting stones and fading granite tablets. Other graves marked only by their declivities in the earth, folk so far beyond the pale even the legibility of their identities had been leached away by the weathers.

Leaves drifted, huge poplar leaves veined with amber so golden they might have been coin of the realm for a finer world than this one. He cut the ignition of the four-wheeler and got off. Past the lowering trees the sky was a blue of an improbable intensity, a fierce cobalt blue shot through with dense golden light.

She slid off the rear and steadied herself a moment with a hand on his arm. Where are we? she asked. Why are we here?

The paperhanger had disengaged his arm and was strolling among the gravestones reading such inscriptions as were legible, as if he might find forebear or antecedent in this moldering earth. The doctor's wife was retrieving her martinis from the luggage carrier of the ATV. She stood looking about uncertainly. A graven angel with broken wings crouched on a truncated marble column like a gargoyle. Its stone eyes regarded her with a blind benignity. Some of these graves have been rob, she said.

You can't rob the dead, he said. They have nothing left to steal.

It is a sacrilege, she said. It is forbidden to disturb the dead. You have done this.

The paperhanger took a cigarette pack from his pocket and felt it, but it was empty, and he balled it up and threw it away. The line between graverobbing and archaeology has always looked a little blurry to me, he said. I was studying their culture, trying to get a fix on what their lives were like.

She was watching him with a kind of benumbed horror. Standing hip-slung and lost like a parody of her former self. Strange and anomalous in her fashionable but mismatched clothing, as if she'd put on the first garment that fell to hand. Someday, he thought, she might rise and wander out into the daylit world wearing nothing at all, the way she had come into it. With her diamond watch and the cocktail glass she carried like a used-up talisman.

You have break the law, she told him.

I got a government grant, the paperhanger said contemptuously.

Why are we here? We are supposed to be searching for my child.

If you're looking for a body the first place to look is the graveyard, he said. If you want a book don't you go to the library?

I am paying you, she said. You are in my employ. I do not want to be here. I want you to do as I say or carry me to my car if you will not.

Actually, the paperhanger said, I had a story to tell you. About my wife.

He paused, as if leaving a space for her comment, but when she made none he went on. I had a wife. My childhood sweetheart. She became a nurse, went to work in one of these drug rehab places. After she was there a while she got a faraway look in her eyes. Look at me without seeing me. She got in tight with her supervisor. They started having meetings to go to. Conferences. Sometimes just the two of them would confer, generally in a motel. The night I watched them walk into the Holiday Inn in Franklin I decided to kill her. No impetuous spur-of-the-moment thing. I thought it all out and it would be the perfect crime.

The doctor's wife didn't say anything. She just watched him.

A grave is the best place to dispose of a body, the paperhanger said. The grave is its normal destination anyway. I could dig up a grave and then just keep on digging. Save everything carefully. Put my body there and fill in part of the earth, and then restore everything the way it was. The coffin, if any of it was left. The bones and such. A good settling rain and the fall leaves and you're home free. Now that's eternity for you.

Did you kill someone, she breathed. Her voice was barely audible.

Did I or did I not, he said. You decide. You have the powers of a god. You can make me a murderer or just a heartbroke guy whose wife quit him. What do you think? Anyway, I don't have a wife. I expect she just walked off into the abstract like that Lang guy I told you about.

I want to go, she said. I want to go where my car is.

He was sitting on a gravestone watching her out of his pale eyes. He might not have heard.

I will walk.

Just whatever suits you, the paperhanger said. Abruptly, he was standing in front of her. She had not seen him arise from the headstone or stride across the graves, but like a jerky splice in a film he was before her, a hand cupping each of her breasts, staring down into her face.

Under the merciless weight of the sun her face was stunned and vacuous. He studied it intently, missing no detail. Fine wrinkles crept from the corners of her eyes and mouth like hairline cracks in porcelain. Grime was impacted in her pores, in the crepe flesh of her throat. How surely everything had fallen from her: beauty, wealth, social position, arrogance. Humanity itself, for by now she seemed scarcely human, beleaguered so by the fates that she suffered his hands on her breasts as just one more cross to bear, one more indignity to endure.

How far you've come, the paperhanger said in wonder. I believe you're about down to my level now, don't you?

It does not matter, the doctor's wife said. There is no longer one thing that matters.

Slowly and with enormous lassitude her body slumped toward him, and in his exultance it seemed not a motion in itself but simply the completion of one begun long ago with the fateful weight of a thigh, a motion that began in one world and completed itself in another one.

From what seemed a great distance he watched her fall toward him like an angel descending, wings spread, from an infinite height, striking the earth gently, tilting, then righting itself.

The weight of moonlight tracking across the paperhanger's face awoke him from where he took his rest. Filigrees of light through the gauzy curtains swept across him in stately silence like the translucent ghosts of insects. He stirred, lay still then for a moment getting his bearings, a fix on where he was.

He was in his bed, lying on his back. He could see a huge orange moon poised beyond the bedroom window, inksketch tree branches that raked its face like claws. He could see his feet bookending the San Miguel bottle that his hands clasped erect on his abdomen, the amber bottle hardedged and defined against the pale window, dark atavistic monolith reared against a harvest moon.

He could smell her. A musk compounded of stale sweat and alcohol, the rank smell of her sex. Dissolution, ruin, loss. He turned to study her where she lay asleep, her open mouth a dark cavity in her face. She was naked, legs outflung, pale breasts pooled like cooling wax. She stirred restively, groaned in her sleep. He could hear the rasp of her breathing. Her breath was fetid on his face, corrupt, a graveyard smell. He watched her in disgust, in a dull self-loathing.

He drank from the bottle, lowered it. Sometimes, he told her sleeping face, you do things you can't undo. You break things you just can't fix. Before you mean to, before you know you've done it. And you were right, there are things only a miracle can set to rights.

He sat clasping the bottle. He touched his miscut hair, the soft down of his beard. He had forgotten what he looked like, he hadn't seen his reflection in a mirror for so long. Unbidden, Zeineb's face swam into his memory. He remembered the look on the child's face when the doctor's wife had spun on her heel: spite had crossed it like a flicker of heat lightning. She stuck her tongue out at him. His hand snaked out like a serpent and closed on her throat and snapped her neck before he could call it back, sloe eyes wild and wide, pink tongue caught between tiny seed-pearl teeth like a bitten-off rosebud. Her hair swung sidewise, her head lolled onto his clasped hand. The tray of the toolbox was out before he knew it, he was stuffing her into the toolbox like a ragdoll. So small, so small, hardly there at all.

He arose. Silhouetted naked against the moon-drenched window, he drained the bottle. He looked about for a place to set it, leaned and wedged it between the heavy flesh of her upper thighs. He stood in silence, watching her. He seemed philosophical, possessed of some hard-won wisdom. The paperhanger knew so well that while few are deserving of a miracle, fewer still can make one come to pass.

He went out of the room. Doors opened, doors closed. Footsteps softly climbing a staircase, descending. She dreamed on. When he came back into the room he was cradling a plastic-wrapped bundle stiffly in his arms. He placed it gently beside the drunk woman. He folded the plastic sheeting back like a caul.

What had been a child. What the graveyard earth had spared the freezer had preserved. Ice crystals snared in the hair like windy snowflakes whirled there, in the lashes. A doll from a madhouse assembly line.

He took her arm, laid it across the child. She pulled away from the cold. He firmly brought the arm back, arranging them like mannequins, madonna and child. He studied this tableau, then went out of his house for the last time. The door closed gently behind him on its keeperspring.

The paperhanger left in the Mercedes, heading west into the open country, tracking into wide-open territories he could infect like a malignant spore. Without knowing it, he followed the selfsame route the doctor had taken some eight months earlier, and in a world of infinite possibilities where all journeys share a common end, perhaps they are together, taking the evening air on a ruined veranda among the hollyhocks and oleanders, the doctor sipping his scotch and the paperhanger his San Miguel, gentlemen of leisure discussing the vagaries of life and pondering deep into the night not just the possibility but the inevitability of miracles.

Dale Peck

Bliss

From *Zoetrope: All-Story*

M Y MOTHER'S killer was named Manson. The morning he was released from prison was sharp and hazy, a spring morning with a scattering of leftover clouds that dotted the sky like shredded bits of tissue paper floating in water. Everything seemed overdetermined that morning, all the details right out of that scene in the movie where The Killer Is Released. The shapeless clouds, the crisp diamond lattice of the chain-link fence through which I saw them, the fat gate guard, his uniform stretched so taut across the gelid curves of his body that it seemed to cry out for the pierce of bullet or knife. Black eye-shaped puddles reflected the limestone walls of the prison and rendered them hollow, insubstantial, penetrable, until a car traveling the length of the parking lot spat grit into them, causing the walls to disappear momentarily. Then the water stilled, revealing the image of Shenandoah Manson. He was dressed in stiff jeans and a chambray shirt faded nearly white, the sleeves rolled up over arms nearly as faded, and etched by pale blue veins and razor-blade-and-Bic-ink tattoos of Jesus, Mary, and a snarling Ford pickup. Over one shoulder hung the slack green lozenge of an army-issue duffel bag, and this bag slapped audibly against Shenandoah Manson's backside as he walked resolutely toward the open gate. Between the gate's pillars he paused, as the freed do. He took a deep breath. He smiled at the security guard. He squinted through the thick-lensed black-framed glasses that covered his eyes like a bandit's mask—a new pair since the last time I'd seen him—and then he started forward again, the *slap-a-dap* slap of the duffel bag coming at a slightly faster rhythm. As he reached my car I pressed a button which rolled down the passenger side window with a loud squeal. Shenandoah Manson started; nineteen years in prison hadn't made him any less jumpy. He leaned down and peered at me through his glasses, and the cut planes of his freshly shaven face filled the empty window. A thin line of light brown stubble traced the subcutaneous arc of his right jawbone. It was so close to my eyes that had I wanted to I could have counted the individual hairs.

I counted; there were sixteen, seven of which were gray. I smiled.

"Want a ride?"

On the morning after Shenandoah Manson killed my mother the sky was suitably gray, the clouds thick and portentous as a roll of toilet paper knocked in the bowl. They were just squeezing out their first drops as my father let me off at the edge of our yard, and I ran up the sidewalk and ducked into the house and even as I lifted my head to call her name I saw her on the floor at the foot of the stairs. The only blood on her body was a tiny spot below her left nostril. It was the size of the eraser on a new pencil, and it had bubbled up like yeasted bread before hardening into a brown scab. In the six or so hours since her death the rest of her body had stiffened too—not the skin, which had a Play-Dohy pliability, nor the bones, which seemed if anything to have softened, but something between the two. The first thing I tried to do was raise her head but her neck wouldn't bend. Then I tried to pull her hand to mine but it wouldn't come away from her body. It was only after I saw an unfamiliar pair of black glasses lying a few feet away that I ran outside to see if my father was still there, but he'd already gone back to his house. The rain seemed to have solidified in the air, and it fell without making any noise on the lawn.

Twenty years ago, Kansas: five-year-old boys weren't taught *911*. Five-year-olds were taught their names and addresses and phone numbers, they were taught *If I'm not here turn the TV on and wait for me to come home and only one pop before supper.* I went inside and shut the door. I didn't turn the television on but I did drink a can of pop even though it was only seven in the morning, and by the time the can was empty my mother's arm had softened up enough for me to pull her still-stiff fingers into my lap. The sleeve of her black plastic raincoat rustled when I moved her arm, and I didn't like the feel of it in my hands. I thought of taking it off but I only got as far as unzipping it. Underneath my mother wore her favorite pale pink dress, still belted at the waist with a thin gold buckle but ripped open at the throat where two buttons had popped off during her fall down the stairs, and atop her breastbone, twisted into a lazy figure eight, was a thin string of pearls. It was the pearls that stopped me. Their double loop—one curled around her neck, the other framing a patch of fading summer tan—seemed too delicate to disturb, and I forgot about removing the raincoat and reached instead for my pop. But it was empty save for a single tangy drop, and when it fell on my tongue I nearly gasped, and I held it there for a long time before swallowing—held it until I could shake the idea it was one of my mother's pearls I was swallowing.

The only thing that seemed to explain what I did after that was *wait for me to come home,* and I did, and it wasn't until late in the afternoon, when the school had called my father's house after calling my mother's several times, *and whatever you do don't pick up the phone,* that he came over and found us, her hand in mine, the empty can of pop, the eraserhead of dried blood—and the black glasses, which I still don't remember putting on, dangling off the end of my nose. It may seem horrific and who knows, maybe it was, but nearly fifteen years of passive recollection and another five of active retelling at Group have changed these memories into little more than scenic details, stock phrases I choose whether or not to voice. That's what they teach us in Group: we can choose to tell or not tell our stories, we can impose our own meanings on them rather than letting them have power over us. In Group they teach us to love what we hate. They teach us that the only way to stop hating is to turn it into love, blame has nothing to do with it they teach us, and, like you, the first time I heard such absurdities I laughed. I couldn't help myself, and I tried to hide it behind my hand, but still I laughed.

The woman before me had been talking about her husband, whom she'd found in a pool of his own blood. She didn't call it a *pool:* she called it a *gel.* She'd told this story so often she'd had time to replace the word *pool* with *gel* and *blood* with *essence,* and the knife which she called a *dagger* was stuck in the nineteenth of thirty-three stab wounds that had left her hsuband's skin *no more solid than the walls of Jericho come tumbling down.* Walter had told her that. Walter had told her it wasn't until the thirty-third thrust that he realized what he was doing, at which point he began reinserting the knife into each of the prior wounds *as if blood-hot metal could sear what had been so violently rendered,* and he was on what he thinks was the nineteenth hole when the police arrived. Nineteenth hole, someone said. Sounds like a golf course, and everyone laughed, Janyne Watson included, everyone laughed easily at Janyne Watson and what she had to say about Walter, the man who'd killed Janyne Watson's husband by stabbing him thirty-three, or, more accurately, forty-eight times. Janyne Watson said Walter told her this story during their most recent visit, *three years of weekly trips out to the penitentiary and finally!* and then Janyne Watson said Amen and a host of Amens came back at her. At the time I thought it strange that someone could laugh in the middle of a story like that and then wind it up with a word which means *so be it,* but even then I saw that the thing to do in Group is what everyone else does, so I said it too, or almost said it. I moved my lips but no sound passed them: *Amen.*

"So be it."

"Wha—?"

Shenandoah Manson jumped when I spoke, and I turned to him but didn't say anything. Behind his glasses his eyes were wide with confusion, but then he relaxed and chuckled and said, "Guess I'm a little jumpy, I guess," and I nodded but still didn't speak. My mouth was filled with an ancient flavor, that last drop of pop gone syrupy and metallic after hours lingering at the bottom of an open can, and even as Shenandoah Manson's window rolled down with a protesting squeal I remembered that one of the windows in the living room had been open that morning—the window which from the outside was hidden by a boxwood hedge—and the rain had come in steadily all day and rendered a patch of white carpeting a silvery gray the same color as the pearls on my mother's chest. Ahead of us a heat mirage wavered over the highway's arc of gray asphalt; next to me Shenandoah Manson exchanged a lungful of prison air for the windblown dust of his new condition, and then I remembered something else. I remembered touching my mother's belly. I'd just put my hand on it at first, but when nothing happened I pushed so hard a sigh was forced from her open mouth, and though what came out was, I do believe, invisible, still, I saw it, a cloud thick and pale green as a giant onion. It was nothing more than a blur, of course—everything seen through those glasses was no more frightening than a blur—but for a moment I caught a glimpse of that same cloud on the seat between me and Shenandoah Manson. When I turned I saw it was just his duffel bag. Nineteen years ago the mirage had also lasted only a moment: I'd reached a hand out to it and then, like my mother, like the apparition of water in the distance and like the hatred I'd once felt for Shenandoah Manson, it disappeared as soon as I got close.

Some men carry jail on their backs. They hunker down, hunched over under the weight of it, their shoulders drooping, their heads dropping into their chests. Shenandoah Manson was such a man. Oh, he talked a lot at first, but as we got closer to town his words slacked off, his back bowed even more, eventually he fell silent, his lowered eyes staring at his upturned hands, which rested a handcuff's width apart on the creases ironed into his jeans. The drive took nearly two hours, and during the ride his head sank lower and lower as his spine curved under his invisible burden. He didn't look up until we were a few blocks from my house, and then his head jerked up, he pushed his glasses up the bridge of his nose and looked out the windows, and then, with an almost audible gulp, he pushed his chin back into his chest. I thought about putting my hand on his knee then, telling him that I carried the same weight on my back: we all do. One of the things we learn in Group, one of the few things I have no trouble believing, is that no one's innocent after a crime. No one's free. And then I did put my hand on his knee, and Shenandoah Manson gulped again, and the muscles of his thighs were so taut it seemed I could feel his constricting throat under my fingers.

"My parents were never married," I said. "My grandma says my dad was a deadbeat, and she had plans. My mom had plans. She was working as a broker even before she got pregnant with me, and by the time—by that time she had a pretty good business, and she owned two houses in this neighborhood." Only then did I pat his knee and remove my hand. "So no."

Shenandoah Manson rubbed his knee as if checking for an injury. "No?"

"No, it's not the same house. My dad sold that one."

Shenandoah Manson looked again at the silvered wood of shingled roofs, at Bermuda grass and purple impatiens and the open-fan leaves of the spindly ginkgoes which had replaced the elms that had succumbed to blight a few years after he'd been convicted of murder, and then he said, "It was a nice house?"

"I guess. Kind of small I guess. A cottage really. My mom turned the attic into a second story, so we could have separate bedrooms." I tried to dam it, but the word poured out of me anyway. "Ironic, huh?"

"Ironic?"

"I mean, if she'd never put in the second story, there never would've been a staircase for her to fall down."

"Oh," Shenandoah Manson said. *"Ironic."*

When we got to my house Shenandoah Manson opened his car door well enough; he stood up, even managed to hoist his pack onto his shoulders. Then he just stood there in the afternoon sunlight, blinking, watching me through his glasses, and I was caught for a moment by the sight of the man who had killed my mother, standing on a mowed green square of suburban lawn. With his right hand, he fingered the spot over his heart where for nineteen years an ID number had been sewn into his shirts, but, finding nothing there, his fingers dug through the fabric into his skin. His foot scraped the dirt a little; other than that he didn't move. He blinked repeatedly, whether at me or the unbarred sun I couldn't tell.

I shook my head then, straightened my spine. "C'mon. You're a free man. Act like one."

For the first time his smile didn't seem forced. "Your front door locked?"

"Yeah. Why?"

"Well, seeing as my housebreaking days are behind me, there's not much for me to do till you unlock it."

He laughed a little, and I looked at him while he laughed, and when he was done I said, "Touché."

Inside, I said, "As you can see, it's way too big for one person. Too big for two really, that's why my mom rented this one out. There are four bedrooms upstairs, two bathrooms, down here there's a den, a screened-in porch, even a little maid's room off the kitchen."

"You sound like you got a bit of the broker in you too."

"Must run in the family."

We walked from room to room. The next thing Shenandoah Manson said was, "So, um, you got a girlfriend or anything?"

"I'm single," I said.

"Oh."

"And besides, I'm gay."

"Oh."

"That a problem?"

He shrugged. "Guess not. Guess I'd've thought you'd've mentioned it by now, is all."

"It never came up."

Shenandoah Manson cleared his throat. "Look," he said, "I don't wanna be a imposition."

"Shen," I said. "Can I call you Shen? Shen, this is the opposite of an imposition. This is a once-in-a-lifetime opportunity."

"That sounds like something you heard in Group."

"If it wasn't for Group we wouldn't know each other. You'd be sleeping on some cold sidewalk right now."

"It's noon," Shen said. "It's June."

"Things change. Especially the weather."

"I don't understand—" Shen began, but I spoke over him. "Listen to me, Shen. I don't understand either, but I know that this is something we need. Both of us need this, if we're ever going to move on."

But he just blinked his eyes. "I don't understand," he said again. "What do we need?"

We were in the kitchen when he said that. Shen had carried his bag from room to room, and now I said, "You wanna put that down? It looks heavy."

He laughed a little. Disjointed words dribbled from his lips, one at a time. "Oh . . . yeah . . . sure . . . I . . ." He caught sight of the maid's room through an open door, and he pantomined the fact that he was going to put his bag in there before he actually put it in there. When he came back, I had a bottle of whiskey in my hand, the glasses were already on the table, and Shen looked at the bottle and at me, and then his face broke into a grin.

"Welcome home," I said. "Welcome back."

I poured us each a shot and we touched glasses, but neither of us drank. Shen's hand slowly fell to the table, like a man losing an arm-wrestling match. He exchanged his drink for the car keys, which I'd tossed on the table when we came in.

"Seventy-six?"

I nodded.

For the first time he perked up. "No shit. I knew it, man. She's cherry." Then his smile faded again. "I went to jail in '76."

That seemed to me to be beside the point, but all I said was, "Last of the big Monte Carlos. Last, biggest, and best," and even before I finished Shen was shaking his head.

"Naw, man. Best was '72. Half Caddy, half tank, half wolverine. Climbing into that car was about as good as climbing into pussy."

Now I put my glass down. Behind his glasses, Shen's eyes closed.

"Aw man. Nineteen years. Aw *man.* The thought of pussy is like God, man. There was times I'd reach up outta my bunk and touch that shit like it was right there man, pussy like the size of a grizzly bear waiting to work me over. My cellie used to say, hey everybody, Shen's having the pussy dream again. I like to kill that nigger when he do that. I mean, I don't give a shit what nobody thinks about me but he woke me up, you know what I'm saying, and when that pussy was gone there was no getting it back until it *came* back. Nineteen years I been having that dream, and I swear to Christ that pussy got bigger every year. Big enough to open wide and swallow me whole, big enough to take me right back where I started from. Nineteen years. *Aw man.*"

When he was done I said, "She's yours if you want her."

"She?"

"The car, Shen. The car."

A new expression crossed his face, something that wasn't quite suspicion, and then Shen let go of the keys and picked up his glass and touched it to mine where it sat on the table. His eyes squinted shut as soon as the whiskey hit his throat, and he slipped the thumb and index finger of his free hand under his glasses to wipe a tear from beneath tightly squeezed lids; on the table, his hand pawed the formica, and I suddenly thought of a dog my father got me soon after I went to live with him. The dog had spent its life in a kennel, six or seven years, and when it was first set loose in the wide-open space of my father's yard the animal refused to run, to walk around even. It took just a few steps, wobbling like a newborn fawn, then turned and retraced its path, and then, eventually, turned again. It was months before the animal seemed to realize it was no longer in a cage, and as soon as it did it ran away and was never seen again.

I wondered if Shenandoah Manson would realize he was free. I wondered if—when—he'd run away from me, but when he spoke his voice was hoarse and dry. *"Aw man."*

. . .

That night I dreamed about Shenandoah Manson. I dreamed I measured every single part of his body with a tailor's tape, chest and waist, wrists and ankles, fingers and toes even, and then I sewed him a new suit of skin, this one fresh and white, clean of tattoos and history. He'd grinned sheepishly when I asked about the tattoos. They used to steal his glasses, he said, and they wouldn't give them back until he submitted one more time. Dumb asses could draw okay but they sure couldn't spell. He held out his arm: *Jezus.*

In the morning I knocked on the door to the maid's room before pushing it open. Shen slept through my knock, facedown on the little twin I'd bought a few weeks before he was paroled. He'd managed to undress before falling atop the sheets, and on his uncovered skin I could see more tattoos: a vine-wrapped cross on his calf, a snake's rattle-tail curled around his waist, and, on each shoulder blade, a little flightless wing. The rest of his skin was as pale and new as I'd dreamed it, save for a thin patch of hair above the label of his inside-out underwear (I could see him, glasses off, blurrily pulling them on at the sound of yesterday's reveille bell). The wings on Shen's shoulder blades flapped as he rubbed the hairs on the part of his back I was looking at, and then some prison sense must have told him he was being watched because his hand froze and his eyes sprang open. For a moment they were filled with fear and confusion, and even as he felt for his glasses on the floor I saw the two faded indentations high on his nose, and then his glasses were on his face and the confusion left his eyes, but not, immediately, the fear. He tried to smile, but it came off as a grimace, the grimace of a teenaged boy who looked incapable of killing a fly, let alone a woman.

"Aw man. What'd you put in my drink?"

"You're out of practice. You'll get used to it."

Shen grimaced again. "Maybe I should quit while I'm ahead."

"I'm going to work. I thought you might like to go."

"Go?"

"To work. With me. I talked to my supervisor, he said he could probably get you something in the warehouse. You don't have anything else lined up, do you?"

"Well, as a matter of fact, no."

"Good. You can drive me. Better get a move on, we'll be late."

In the car he was a kid again, a cocky seventeen-year-old whose rap sheet was filled with nothing more serious than a string of B-and-E's. He tilted the seat back, rolled up his sleeve before letting his tattooed arm hang out the open window; if he could have seen the front of the car without them, I'm sure he would have taken off his glasses. "Damn," he said. "Wish I still smoked. Car like this deserves a cigarette." He gunned it, and the speedometer's upward surge was matched by the gas gauge's downward spiral. "Fuck you, OPEC." He looked at me. "Goddamn camel jockeys took the fun outta everything." Ten hours later we were back at the kitchen table. Empty plates were pushed to one side, drinks sat between us, just pop this time, cold cans perspiring in the warm air. The workday had lasted two decades: Shen's five o'clock shadow was tinged with gray, and the hand he ran over his lined forehead revealed a receding hairline. His prison burden weighed heavy on his back tonight, and he slouched in his chair, occasionally stealing glances at me from the corner of his eye.

Finally I said, "Shoot."

Shen jumped. "Huh?"

"What's on your mind, Shen? You haven't said two words since we left work."

"Oh. It's just you said—" He pointed his finger at me, pulled the trigger, and then he looked a little shocked and he put his hand on his chair, under his leg. He was silent for another moment and then he said, "It's just—the house, the car, the job. It's a little much, especially on my first full day out. Don't get me wrong, man. It's not that I ain't grateful."

"One of the things they say in Group—"

I stopped because he was rolling his eyes.

"Hear me out, okay? One of the things they say in Group is that people spend their grief. They buy a bronze casket or a silver urn, they arrange to have roses put on the grave every month, every week even, every day. Okay? But other people invest it. My dad's one of those. He dropped the sixty-five grand he made off my mom's house into mutual funds. He made a couple of good guesses along the way, got lucky a few times, and here we are."

Shen just shrugged. "Whatever."

"What I'm trying to say, Shen, is that I can afford it. I'm saying it's worth it to me, whatever it costs."

"But what're you buying, man? Are you trying to buy me?"

I tried to laugh his fears away, but what could I say. The truth was I rec-

ognized his questions: I'd asked the same questions when I first went to
Group, until I realized there was no answer to them: you had to learn to
stop asking. I tried to explain it to him, told him I'd been doubtful too. I
told him how I'd sat there dumbfounded as Raylene Cummings recounted
the night Raymond Church had driven a knife into the meat of her right
shoulder and then, with the knife still lodged in place, had raped her.
Now, I told Shen, Raylene Cummings *paid visits out to the penitentiary*
once a week. She baked Raymond Church a cake on his birthday and he
knitted her loose cardigans with big wooden buttons which were easier for
her to fasten with just her left hand: nerve damage had left her right arm
numb and immobile, and it hung from her shoulder like a wet flag on a
windless day. I told Shen how Karl Grable had come home and found his
wife and son *like that.* Nearly twenty years afterward he still couldn't say
what *like that* meant, but every other Sunday *he took services out to the penitentiary* with Brian Dawes, the one who'd left Karl Grable's wife and son
like that, and he'd even bought Brian Dawes a white button-down shirt
and tie so he wouldn't have to sit in the Lord's cinder-block chapel in his
working clothes. And then I told Shen about Lucy Ames. Like me, Lucy
Ames had lost a parent. Unlike me, nine-year-old Lucy had sat in a chair
and watched as George Ferguson pistol-whipped her father in an attempt
to beat the location of his wife's jewelry box out of him. *Seven times he
popped him,* until on the seventh time the gun went off as it struck Mr.
Ames's face and the back of his head sprayed across the living room wall in
a wide arc *like a rainbow where all the colors are red.* Now Lucy Ames was
married to George Ferguson and *thanks to the grace of God and monthly
nuptial visits out to the penitentiary* she was expecting their second child.

And, I told Shen, it wasn't like these stories convinced me of anything,
but curiosity outweighed skepticism. At first I told myself I was going
back because I wanted to hear more of these fascinating tales, but eventually I realized I was curious about him. I realized I wanted to meet him.

I wanted to meet the man who killed my mother.

At some point while I spoke I'd picked up my empty pop can and used
my dinner knife to cut it in half, lengthwise. I didn't really register the
awful squeaking the dull blade made as it sawed through five inches of aluminum until the sound was gone, and then I looked up at Shen, who
stared at the cut-open can in my hands with the look of a rabbit transfixed
by a pair of oncoming headlights. I tried to grin, but even as my lips
curved I was bringing one half of the can to my mouth, my nostrils flared

at the long-ago scent, and then I stuck my tongue against the can's exposed inner surface. The taste was obscured by memory—rain, pearls, the fleeing genie of my mother's last, forced breath—and the only way I could share that with Shen was by holding the other half out to him. I waited to see what he would do, and after a long pause he pulled the twisted metal open like a halved fruit and raised it to his mouth. I watched his tongue flicker out and lick up the last few drops of pop. I think I was hoping he'd understand what I was trying to do because I needed him to explain it to me, but he was just as lost as I was, and just as caught up. Neither of us knew what we were working toward, but in the thin clink of metal against tabletop was the certainty that Shen would stick around until I'd done it.

The Circle was small, usually just six or seven people, sometimes as many as a dozen, every once in a while just two or three, and even with my sporadic attendance it wasn't long before I'd heard everyone's story, the pain, the loss, the grief, the inevitable victory signified by their presence in Group. Participation was voluntary, but members were strongly encouraged to testify, to relate their Incident and describe the aftermath and recovery. You might recognize some of the words from one of those survivor groups, but in Group we're taught not to think of survivors, or victims, or perpetrators: everyone's a person, before and after the Incident, and the only thing Group does is remind us of that fact. I managed to worm my way out of testifying for a long time but finally no one would listen to my excuses anymore and so I took my place in the center of the Circle and told them what I knew, which wasn't much. An apparent robbery, my mother's return home, a push down the stairs, a broken neck. Rigor mortis and the can of pop and then my father. I left out the glasses and the pearls and the cloud of green gas that I'd pushed out of my mother's belly because that didn't seem relevant, and when I'd finished telling the story Lucy Ferguson, gently rocking on her knee the eldest son of the man who had killed her father, said, *Well, what does he have to say about it?* I thought she meant my father, but she meant Shenandoah Manson, and when I told her I had no idea she said, *Well then I think it's high time you found out,* and Raylene Cummings said, *High time is better than no time,* and Janyne Watson led the chorus of Amens. The next day Lucy Ferguson picked me up when she went to visit her husband. *Out to the penitentiary.* I held George Jr. on my lap because Lucy Ferguson believed in God and she believed in Group but she didn't believe in child-safety seats. "Trap my baby boy in a hunk of burning metal?" she cooed. "How could I even think of such a thing?"

I don't know what I expected to happen when I confronted my mother's killer, but I certainly wasn't prepared for the sense of disappointment I felt when he shuffled into the room. The shuffling wasn't caused by leg irons or anything so dramatic: Shenandoah Manson was simply a man who shuffled, and stooped, and squinted behind silly Buddy Holly glasses held together at the bridge with a rolled-up Band-Aid. His skinny frame swam inside his orange jumpsuit. His hair was cut short, parted on the side, combed over neatly. He was thirty-two years old, but he looked and acted like a teenage refugee from some fifties sitcom, and I remember thinking that this wasn't the sort of man who could kill your mother. Shenandoah Manson's shuffling feet were loud on the concrete floor, the metal balls of his chair squeaked something awful when he pulled it away from the table to sit down, but after he'd slumped into his seat there was a long moment of silence between us, during which I heard Lucy Ferguson say, "Let's show Daddy our new tooth!" I considered opening lines: "I wish you were dead"; "You're a monster"; "I've dreamed of this day for years"; but none of these statements was true, not even the last, and in the end all I could come up with was "You're smaller than I expected." Shenandoah Manson blinked when I said that; I imagine he'd also expected something more dramatic. Behind his glasses his eyes flitted about, as if looking for something to say, and then he just said, "I, um, I'm five-foot-seven." He paused. "In my socks." Visiting sessions lasted an hour, and I had to wait another hour while Lucy Ferguson, after being thoroughly frisked, retired to a little tin trailer in the center of a chain-link cage in the prison yard. I held George Jr. in my lap and I silently repeated the words *my mother's killer is five-foot-seven* until Lucy Ferguson finally pushed open the trailer door and blew a kiss to her husband inside. *Five-foot-seven,* I told George Jr. *In his socks.*

After the first night I offered him an upstairs bedroom but Shen said maybe he was better where he was. A pattern developed: morning coffee, work, dinner, then story time. We talked for hours every night, sometimes while drinking, sometimes cold sober. I told Shen about Group and he told me about prison. Neither of us was telling the truth, really, by which I mean that neither of us was telling the other what he really wanted to know. Every night I started from the beginning, from my first appearance at a meeting, and worked forward; and every night Shen started at the end, from his long walk out those open gates, and worked backward, and both of our stories were bound by the same unmentioned endpoints: by my mother's death, and by our current cohabitation, and in some way these two things become conflated in my head, and, I think, in Shen's too, and our life together took on an inflection of punishment and pentinence. Unbidden, he drove me to and from work, signed his paychecks over to me for rent and food, cooked and cleaned and mowed the lawn, and he did it all with the same meek acquiescence with which he'd licked the inside of the pop can I'd given him on our second evening together. Sometimes when we'd been drinking he'd slouch in his chair and stare at me through his glasses, and sometimes, when we'd had too much, he'd take his glasses off and his eyes would glaze over and I knew I was little more than a pale blur to him, but even though I wanted to I never reached over and put his glasses on my own nose, even though I knew he wouldn't protest if I did. In fact the only thing that ever got a rise out of him was when I asked him to come to Group.

In my five years in Group only one member had ever brought in his Person. That's what we called them in Group: People. Not murderers or rapists or muggers or thugs. By calling them People we reminded ourselves that they were as human as we were. Clay Adams had run a pawnshop downtown for forty-five years, until the day Blake Moore came in and, in Blake's own words, *went a little crazy in the head I guess.* He hadn't brought a gun, he said, *'cause I was the kind of sonofabitch who'd've used it,* but relied instead on a cattle prod, which in an attempt to torture the existence of a safe out of Clay Adams he'd applied to the soles of the old man's feet again and again *till what they looked like,* Blake Moore said, *was Neapolitan ice cream, melted.* As it turned out there was no safe, and all Blake Moore got for his troubles was $5.47 from the till, a ceramic statue of two black panthers, and eight years in jail. Clay Adams had recovered the statue, and the money too, but, old and diabetic, he'd lost first his feet and eventually both legs up to the knee, *all told it took about a year and a half,* Clay Adams said. He was seventy-one years old when Blake Moore pushed him in his wheelchair into the center of the Circle and, eyes brimming with tears, presented Blake Moore with the statue he'd so coveted. He said, *I just want to thank you, Blake Moore, before God and Group for allowing me to forgive you and forgive myself for what happened.* Blake Moore had lost the tips of the fingers on his right hand beneath a metal press—*yes ma'am, license plates*—and with the smooth soft stumps he stroked the sleek black cats on his lap. After Blake Moore's trial the police had returned the statue to Clay Adams and he'd *dashed the damn thing to the ground,* but six years in Group and a lot of super glue had all but done the trick. One of the cats was missing an ear, *but an ear ain't much,* Clay Adams said, *or a foot. Or fingers,* Blake Moore added, *not when you get right down to it. Not compared to bliss.* And even at the time I knew there was something wrong with what they were saying, but the display was so compelling I was distracted. Not so long after that Clay Adams died of a stroke brought on by his diabetes, and about a year later Blake Moore went back to jail, this time for stealing cars, but the general consensus was that he'd been helped by his visit to us: at least he'd chosen a line of thievery which jeopardized no one's safety but his own.

But none of this impressed Shen. He shook his head and said:

"I don't like crowds."

"But that's the beauty of it. It's like the other people aren't there at all, and you can say the kinds of things you'd never say one on one, like this." I didn't look at Shen when I said that, because even though I knew what I was saying was true, I also knew that was the problem with Group. That feeling of superhuman isolation became all of you, obscuring everything else, and Shen seemed to sense this instinctively. In the end I struck a bargain with him: he could skip Group if he'd tell me something.

"Like what?"

My mouth watered, and I blushed and swallowed and said, "Why our house?"

Shen squirmed in his chair.

I said, "It was a small house, and this is a prosperous neighborhood. Why ours?"

"Your mom," Shen said, and stopped. "Your mom was on a date with this guy I knew. That's how I knew she wouldn't be home."

"My mother was on a date?"

Shen shrugged and refused to meet my gaze. "She was twenty-six years old. Just because she had a kid didn't mean she was—" He shrugged again.

We left it at that, and I went to the meeting on my own. Every week I'd ask him to join me, and every week he refused. Sometimes I demanded a piece of information in exchange for letting him off the hook, but eventually I gave up that practice because I didn't like the things he told me. I didn't like the fact that my mother had gone on a date with a man who was friendly with a housebreaker, and I didn't like the fact that my mother had been humming "Afternoon Delight" when she entered her house at one in the morning, and I didn't like the fact that Shenandoah Manson called our house a slim haul—*no silver, no cash, just a couple of rings and bracelets and shit, a pair of dinner-table candlesticks that were probably tin but just in case*—and I especially didn't like the fact that it was the candlesticks my mother had tripped over. When he heard my mother come in—humming "Afternoon Delight"—Shenandoah Manson had tried hiding in the linen closet at the top of the stairs, but my mother had apparently decided to take a shower, or maybe she just wanted to dry her hair. At any rate she went straight to the closet for a towel without even bothering to unzip her raincoat, and when she pulled open the door he screamed; she screamed; he dropped his near-empty bag of booty and ran and she ran after him, only to trip on the candlesticks and send them both sprawling down the stairs. Somewhere in the fall he lost his glasses and she lost her life, and when he figured out the latter fact he stumbled half blind out into the night.

I told him I didn't believe him.

"Neither did the court."

"Why should I believe you?"

"Look. The reason why I went to jail is 'cause if I hadn't of been in that house your mother wouldn't've died. Everything else is just kind of incidental. If it makes you feel better to think I pushed your mom down the stairs, fine: I pushed your mom down the stairs."

I suppose I liked that fact least of all.

Mead Pritchard was the one person nobody ever talked about in Group, Mead Pritchard and Howard Firth. Howard Firth had served seven years for shooting Mead Pritchard in the stomach during the course of a liquor store holdup, and when he was released Mead Pritchard had staked out Howard Firth's front porch for several weeks in an effort to befriend him, and then he'd disappeared, later to be found at the bottom of Pleasant Pond with an unopened sack of cement tied to his scarred belly. In the absence of Mead Pritchard, Howard Firth's name never came up, but when Mead's did people tended to say *he did what he had to do,* and I wondered if they would say that about me, but I doubted it.

I sensed my interest in Group waning after Shen finally told me how my mother died, but for some reason my interest in him seemed to grow; though I continued to go to meetings, I'd sometimes sneak out during a coffee break. I'd drive home and park down the block, and then I'd stand outside the windows spying on Shen as he watched TV with the lights off or slept with the lights on, until the night I came home and saw neither lamplight nor the TV's flickering glow. And I admit: the first emotion I felt was relief, but it was almost immediately blotted out by loss. I thought Shen had finally left me, but something, either nineteen years in prison or the few months we'd spent together, had skewed his sense of priorities. Shenandoah Manson could have gotten away if he'd wanted, but he chose to get laid first.

My first thought was that the woman in Shen's bed looked like the kind of woman who might sleep with a man even if she knew he was a paroled murderer: too tan, too plump, too thirty-nine. When I snapped on the light she reacted calmly, lazily pulling the sheet over her body, but it took me a moment to realize Shen was calm too. He hadn't jumped when I came into the room, only lain on his back with his uncovered eyes pointed at the ceiling. I told myself it was the woman who angered me, her lack of shame, and it was her I lashed at first.

"Don't you know what he did?" I said to her. "He killed my mother." And then I added, *"Not yours."*

I clocked her reaction on her face: oh-my-God, oh-you're-joking, oh-my-God-you're-not-joking. Before I left the room I picked up Shen's glasses from the floor. I waited in the hallway, and after I heard the front door close I went back to the maid's room. Shen was still on the bed, his face still pointed at the ceiling, and I went over and sat on the edge of the little twin mattress. They'd hadn't gotten very far. At any rate Shen's underwear was still on, right side out this time, and the bed was so narrow my hip pressed against the thin fabric.

"Can I have my glasses back."

Shen's voice was not quite flat when he spoke. There was an edge of steel to his words, and I wondered if I should be afraid of him. But the truth is I wasn't afraid. The truth is it was hard for me to believe Shenandoah Manson had killed my mother, let alone that he could kill me.

Aloud, I said: "I used to wonder if you'd saved me. If she would've married some jerk who'd've beat the shit out of me. Who knows, maybe you even saved her. He could've beat her, taken everything she worked so hard for. But that was before I met you."

"Can I have my glasses back."

"It was only after I met you that I realized I'd been deprived of something. I'm sure I felt it before, that's why I went to Group, but it was only as I got to know you and realized you were a real person that I began to realize my mother had been a person too, although what kind of person I'll never know."

"I want my glasses back."

"You probably never saw her, did you? With your glasses, I mean. She was pretty. A lot prettier than that woman you just had in here."

He rolled over then. I don't know if he did it out of disgust or shame or if he simply didn't want to be touching me anymore, but he rolled over onto his stomach and as soon as he had he froze. The little wing on his left shoulder blade fluttered as a muscle underneath it twitched, but it became nothing more than a shadow after I put on his glasses, and my hand became a pale triangle at the end of my arm as it reached toward the shadow on his back. It seemed to me that the tattoo was colder than the rest of his skin, but that was probably just my imagination. I could feel my heart pounding in my chest as my hand slipped down the length of Shen's spine, until it came to rest on the rattlesnake's tail poking toward the thin nest of hair in the small of his back. I wondered if this is what Shen had felt when he pried open our window that night, this inexorable pull into the near future. It was then that I understood that ignorance really is bliss, not knowledge, because once you start learning you can't stop until you know everything.

"Shen," I said now, but he didn't answer me. He didn't move either, and I squeezed onto the bed until my lips were right next to his ear. "I'll trade you," I said. "For your glasses."

Murad Kalam

Bow Down

From *Harper's Magazine*

OTHERS CAME to claim the house the first year after the widow passed, young men in small would-be gangs from the adjoining wards, brandishing sticks and bats and knives, none older than fourteen, and for stretches of time the house was lost to Turtle until he could gather enough young South Phoenix delinquents to reclaim it. Small street scuffles, rocks hurled from fists, young men sniped at from the almond trees with BB guns, and drunken battles and raids of screaming boys, the smashing of beer bottles against little skulls, chains whipped against fleeing backs, and once Turtle's own Huffy dirt bike stolen from his back yard in revenge, the front window of his grandmother's house—it sat a block from the dead woman's house—smashed with a brick. Then followed night rumbles, standoffs, and one great and final bloody melee in the house itself, each room filled with the high shouts of pubescent boys, the slapping and beating of little fists, until the police station dispatched three cars and policemen came rushing through the front door, through the red parlor, up the carpeted stairs, the South Phoenix boys dragged out of the condemned house, lined up before the bushes, the great white columns of the porch, for all the neighbors watching from their stoops to behold. The boy made truces, treaties, negotiations in the moonlit cotton fields, south, beneath the jagged black mountaintops where opposing lines of bastards stood on the dirt: Turtle and some adversary face-to-face, shouts and shoves. The boy would not give up the house, and none of them, none of his enemies, could hold the house for any length of time, because Turtle had always the advantage of blood desire.

He'd found her facedown dead, his neighbor (the woman who'd loaned his mama sugar), her arms and legs splayed out like scissors across the ruddy red carpet of the parlor. He'd let himself in to find the obese body laid out at the bottom of the stairs in the hot room, the woman in full rigor, her walking cane slanting against her wide back, glowing in the light of the ceiling lamp. He'd knocked twice and used his key, and now he stood, a twelve-year-old boy, before the corpse, the dead woman's groceries in his hands, five minutes silent, gazing at the waxen brown flesh, dead calves slanted against the bottom stairs, the back of her mauve patterned dress flung back, the wooden cane glowing in the parlor light. The ceiling fan shook. Turtle dropped the grocery bags on the parlor floor and walked backward, like a child retracing his own footprints in a thick tuft of snow, to the door, down the stoop, then turned and ran home. Ran right into his grandmother's room, and he hugged her hips until the old woman pushed him away, and then he told her, each word forming slowly on his pale lips. The old woman had been relieved to know that it was only the death of the widow. She embraced the boy, babied him the whole day. His mother, when she returned from work, thought it sweet that the boy had been so affected by the death of the old widow, and so the death became one of her warmest memories of Turtle.

In three long months he'd won the house. The Maryvale boys did not come back. The dead woman's sons came from Texas, upright Christian types in collared shirts, wide-eyed, surveying the street, as if they could not recognize their boyhood house. The street had become a slum, the house nearly worthless. Turtle gaped at them from the shade of his grandmother's stoop, the two sons climbing the stoop, taking their mother's most precious belongings, those things that seemed in an instant to represent her, leaving the house to rot.

Now it was Turtle's house. He spent each night in the house with a half-breed Mexican boy from Washington Street named Adolpho. They slept on the floors of each tepid room, on the red velvet carpet of the parlor. They discovered in the house secret hiding places, cubbyholes, with the same ease, the same inevitability, with which they'd found each other on the outlays of South Side Middle School, spending their truant mornings together, sipping Mad Dog, picking fights in the b-ball court. The house seemed for Turtle a literal blessing; he confessed to Adolpho that this was the only good thing that had ever happened to him since his daddy left.

They searched the attic, waved a flashlight in the cubbyholes, searched the top-floor bedroom, the balcony. You could even hide in the four-foot weeds out back. You could sleep in the very dirt, embedded, could watch the Southern Pacific trains cutting past Grand Avenue. You could lie in the back yard on cold dirt and watch the airplanes ascending from the airport, could hear the barks of hustlers and the prostitutes from the motel a block down.

Adolpho knew the house was damned, cursed, haunted, and so refused to stay in the house alone at night, but Turtle did not care. He needed only a flashlight, his Walkman radio, a pillow. He would lie on a mere blanket, listening to the radio, the sound of the descending and ascending planes, rubbing his fingers through the thick and ubiquitous red carpet—it covered all the floors, the stairs; it matched the sofa, the drapes—would fall asleep not five feet from where the old woman had tripped down the stairs and died.

The two sons had taken very little from the house. Pictures and portraits still hung on the dusty walls, the two boys in Afros, yellowed Kodaks from the Seventies. High school diplomas, certificates of achievement, acceptance letters for each to Southern Methodist University. The dead woman, Mrs. Walker, the woman who'd loaned his mama sugar, and her husband in a ghastly oil painting. Some family patriarch in a sepia-toned daguerreotype discovered in the second-floor bedroom.

So much had been left behind. Adolpho searched upstairs and in the kitchen as Turtle ran through the dead woman's closet. Adolpho was wild, a fool, wrecking the house, but Turtle was careful, meticulous. Utensils, china, plastic cups, foodstuffs, cookware, remained in the kitchen. Pots and pans under the stove. Spices and nutmeg in the cupboards. One drawer absolutely empty except for crumbs. Another contained odd bills, a Christmas bow, four thumbtacks, twist ties, a flyswatter, and three 20-cent stamps. Sixty dollars in an envelope, old crumpled bills of which Turtle pocketed $20, splitting the purported $40 with Adolpho. He was the sovereign of the house, and the house held endless surprises, offerings.

Adolpho called from upstairs as Turtle removed a bottle of Bayer from a drawer, a tube of Preparation H, Ben-Gay, a tube of Vagisil, a pink comb with hairs, a coupon for Depend undergarments. On the top of the dresser (standing on his tiptoes) Turtle fingered the dog-eared pages of a *Reader's Digest,* a *People* magazine, a biography of the Reverend Billy Graham. Adolpho came running down the stairs and into the bedroom in a pink nightgown, swishing his hips like a woman, calling Turtle's name in a lilted voice. He was wearing the dead woman's wig. Turtle removed from the dresser drawer a gilded scrapbook: PICTURES & MEMORIES.

The next year there were small weekend gatherings with adolescent girls, would-be sex parties, midnight games of spin the bottle, truth or dare, where once Turtle's little brother, Eddie, was forced to kiss a fat mulatto girl named Beatrice (whom Turtle called "Beastrice"). Eddie had no memory of the dead woman, only the shock on Turtle's face the year before when he came running home, and for this reason associated the house with the death. Turtle would blow out the candle and whisper ghost stories, his square face floating above the flashlight, to the young men and women coupled, or lying alone, in sleeping bags on the carpet: it was then that Eddie and the others would stare up from the floor at the pictures and portraits and certificates on the walls and imagine the woman's life. Some part of Eddie was always thrilled and frightened at this, on the brink of fleeing home and sleeping next to his mother as Turtle described the look on the woman's face, how he could hear the blood thickening in her veins, everyone at this moment secretly watching the staircase, its upper half pitch-black, as if at any moment a specter might come hurrying down those stairs. If the shame of a fast break remained equal to his fear, Eddie would shut his eyes and focus on the sound of the constant passing cars slowing and turning down Van Buren, would imagine the street, the dark and sinful street, Van Buren, beyond the little park and its tree, which sat before his grandmother's house, his bedroom, would imagine his mother sleeping in her bed, and the comfort of her hip, the warmth and security of her presence, as the girls (two or three to every boy) began to scream at the sight of Adolpho shrieking down the stairs in the dead woman's nightgown and wig.

Later, slow jams blasting from the boom box, new couples messed around in the various rooms, in corners of the parlor. Advanced lovers, the young harlots who even at thirteen possessed reputations, would leave with Turtle or Adolpho to the separate bedrooms as others, Eddie and the neglected sisters, the perpetual third wheels, those too fat or too ugly or too plain or too virtuous to be taken into one of the functional bedrooms, lay on the parlor carpet, everyone smoking menthol cigarettes and listening to the boom box. In an hour or two one or both of the two beds, the bed upstairs or Mrs. Walker's own bed on the same floor, would be heard through the music to creak, Eddie imagining the soft violence of the act, his brother and Adolpho naked with naked girls, an act that seemed so poisonous, forever out of reach and impossible even when simultaneously a john's car would park right then outside the great house and Eddie would be reminded of the sound of sex heard at night when the prostitutes of Van Buren and their johns would, against all complaints of his mother and the other neighbors, park their cars and commit the act before Eddie's very window, and Eddie from his bed could hear through the car windows of the johns the sound of the black voices of the prostitutes commanding and directing the act hurriedly, calling out, "Shoot that hot cum out, shoot that hot juicy cum out, shoot that hot juicy cum out, baby," their voices tinged with such fear that Eddie would forever associate sex with a kind of hurry, a desperation, a transaction, the shaking of expensive leased cars, the taxis, the arrogance of condoms strewn out on their sidewalk the next morning. Toothless prostitutes with tracks in their arms had made Turtle impatient with girls; as often as not his impatience brought him spectacular failure in the heat and the darkness, the silence, the pressing of clothed groins together when he pushed too far, too fast. Beyond petting and necking he was at a loss as to what to whisper to any girl (and this was a fair number) who held over him any reasonable degree of morality, pedigree, or looks to cajole her into making the bed creak. It was these thirteen-year-old girls who came rushing out of the dead woman's bedroom (even as Adolpho's bed could be heard to creak upstairs) and out into the parlor of chatting and smoking others, to the front porch, to be joined in seconds by their neglected third-wheel girlfriends, who were secretly enthralled with Turtle's failure. Adolpho scored better because he knew to be patient and because he was not so profoundly and singularly bad-looking as Turtle.

By the time Tessa came from Oakland Turtle claimed not only the house but blocks of Van Buren Street as well, streetwalkers twice his age. He found her climbing off a Greyhound bus from Los Angeles in a gray sweat suit, hair pulled back, he sitting with Adolpho and Eddie at the end of the bus stop in the open terminal courtyard on a concrete bench beneath the station clock. He resonated a sense of purpose, and he could spot the girls coming off the bus, always lost looking, carting a beat-up Samsonite or a laundry bag.

That such a young boy would approach her like this, Tessa thought. "Somebody pay you to talk to me?" Turtle shook his head. A vacant house, his house, he told her, sat only a few blocks away, and it was safe. She panned the street for a lurking pimp. She saw Eddie, a little boy, standing with them. Why not? She shouldered her bag and followed Turtle back to the house, and they shared a bucket of Kentucky Fried Chicken above a Coleman lamp in the cleared-out living room.

"You like the first black people I seen since I got off this bus," she said, folding a napkin across her lap. She lowered her eyes and waited for Turtle to eat before she took a small bite of her drumstick.

"Lots of black people in Oakland? 'Cause I gots people in Cali, East L.A., parts," Adolpho said.

"Oakland gots mad black people," she said. "A whole bunch of black folk."

"I'm gonna tell you this right now," Turtle said above the lamp, wiping his chin. "Niggers in Phoenix is weak, but you with some real niggers right now."

Tessa smiled, as if a realization of her good fortune had swept across her face. She laughed. The boy was so young, so cocky. She watched darkness settle on the abandoned furniture, the floor. It was a house. She bowed her head, gave a nervous laugh. She thanked them for the chicken. She went to the window and looked at the street beyond the park.

"I will take you to the street," said Turtle.

"I know about which street. My one friend told me. Van William."

"Van Buren. I best take you."

"You is very pretty, mad pretty," said Adolpho.

"Don't tell nobody, but I think I'm scared."

"For the reason of you ain't done it before, for the reason of you don't know the area."

"I done it before. For two months. In Cali and New Mexico. How I heard of this." She rubbed her cheek with her fingers and studied the mascara on her fingertips. "Can you watch my things here tomorrow, till I get a room?"

Turtle nodded. "That's my word."

A car passed, reflected lights yawing across the walls.

She glared at them. "If y'all little motherfuckers try and vic my shit."

"Come on now," said Turtle.

Eddie had fallen asleep on the couch in darkness. Tessa sat next to him, set his head upon her lap, rubbed his neck, applied to his ear, his forehead, the same absent strokes of fingers used to check the condition of her mascara. They fell silent. The room smelled of Tessa's perfume, dust. Turtle sensed her worrying. Adolpho spoke. "Turtle will show you the street, and we will watch your things. This is our house. It's all good. You is very pretty, girl. You'll be like the prettiest one out there. Phoenix is tight."

She did not remove her makeup. It was thick, coating her face, unneeded, like her fear of the boys. She stroked the little boy's hair as he slept on her thighs. "This boy," she said. "He is so good. He does not shout. He does not cause trouble, talk back." She turned to Turtle. "This your little brother? You best take him home."

"Sleep over here all the time."

"It's like a feeling you get." She turned, looking behind her, through the den window again, at the empty street beyond the little park. "Like bad things."

"Bad things will happen."

"Like something bad will happen. Like you made a bad decision." She coughed. The room was so hot even in darkness.

"You just scared for the reason of you ain't know nobody. You know us."

"People who lived here got evicted?"

Adolpho turned.

"Yeah," Turtle said.

Out front a woman and her daughter were shouting, their voices slapping against the black windows of the row houses along the street. The 11:18 Southern Pacific shoved across Grand Avenue.

Tessa slept on the sofa, her arms wrapped around the boy, Adolpho and Turtle beside her on blankets on the floor. In the morning the roar of the garbage trucks, the shouts of workers, boots on the sidewalk, woke them and then lulled them back to sleep.

.   .   .

Eddie woke first. The storm doors smacked three times against the door-jamb until there were voices, the voices of boys. Eddie thought it was the police come to check up on the condition of the house as they sometimes did. The front door burst open and Maryvale boys swept into the parlor from the porch, numberless, wild, boys in loose-fitting shirts, some nine, twelve, fifteen of them, shouting at Turtle and Adolpho, beating Turtle with fists, smacking wooden baseball bats against his skinny thighs. They ranged through the house from room to room, in twos and threes, with-out order or reason, without explanation, a barking confusion, breaking the windows, pissing in the corners. They beat Eddie with their fists until they realized he was too young and sent him running home. Others cor-nered Adolpho in the kitchen and beat him until he escaped and ran after Eddie without a seeming thought for Turtle. A nameless acned boy, the oldest of them, took Tessa by the hair and dragged her up the stairs where others, knowing, followed. Four encircled Turtle and beat and kicked him where he lay and spat on his face and cursed him. This continued, bedlam in the dead woman's house, until Adolpho appeared at the back door with his brother's .38 and ran up the stairs and three times shot it. Tessa went silent. Boys came flushing down the red velvet stairs, two trailing blood from thighs and arms, leaving streaks and swabs of blood across the wall-paper and doorknobs. The next hour the house was empty; the three of them, Adolpho, Tessa, and Turtle, sat in the sweltering darkness of the sec-ond floor, waiting for the cops to leave the yard, silent excepting Tessa, who shook, sobbing beneath her fingers. How they would not stop knock-ing at the front door, the cops, knocking, peeking through first-floor win-dows, looking about and shouting at the house from the grass below, whispering into radios.

Tessa did not move from the upstairs bedroom for three days. In com-pensation for the ordeal, the valuables yanked from her suitcase, all in her reliance on his promise that the house was safe, Turtle fed her and, at Tessa's request, furnished her with enough liquor to maintain a numbing three-day drunkenness, enough to blunt the pain, sent his little brother into the second-floor room to lie with her on the naked mattress, so that she might squeeze him like a baby doll, so that she might stop sobbing. On the fourth day she could walk, maintain composure, and journeyed over to Van Buren Street, swearing to the boys that never again would she sleep in the house, returning the very same night to sleep. Turtle watched her wander out of the house to the street in the sweat suit she'd worn on the Greyhound, and each night visited her after the completion of her rounds, at the Coral Reef Motel on 19th Avenue. He brought her Snickers and M&M's, brought her leftovers Adolpho's mother had cooked, sometimes sleeping next to her in the bed, if only so that she might have something to hold, stroke his cheek, might take solace, drifting to sleep to the sound of the trucks thundering up the I-17.

Someone always had to watch the house. Someone had to keep vigil over it; someone had to keep the voices down at night when the police made their sweeps, shoved their cruisers down the narrow street. Someone had to check the condition of the wooden boards, to maintain the facade of its abandonment. Someone must always defend condemned property against transients.

Turtle owned a .25, which fit snugly into the back pocket of his jeans and which he was not afraid to brandish. After months of waving off the Van Buren traffic he turned the nuisance to his advantage and began to rent floor space to vagrants at $2 per day, $4 per day for the bedrooms. The condemned house seemed to beckon newcomers from California—a steady stream of crackheads and slum lunatics, runaway teens who discovered the house while whoring their way back east from Hollywood. None of them stayed for more than a week, and all of them, as if part of Turtle's secret criterion, his forming criminal genius, were inevitably too drunken, too Sherm-, smack-, or crack-addicted, too desperate, too rootless, too burned-out, to challenge the very serious thirteen-year-old boy with the .25. On the last day of March of that year Turtle decided to hire seven- and eight-year-old boys to watch the house from the project playground across the street and from the high tower windows of the subsidized Section 8 apartments—at $3 a day per watcher—for any sudden influx of suspicious or seemingly unregistered occupants, great bursts of activity, clandestine migrations of street bums through the back door. By the end of September he was losing money on the cost of lookouts. The fleabag motel down the street charged $17.50 per night per person; the flophouses of Madison Street, $7 per night. Turtle would charge $4 for floor space and $6 for use of one of the bedrooms. He would buy simple locks for the bedrooms, might even clean up the other rooms and put locks on them too. He could make as much as $29, even $70 per night, more.

Could hire one boy to scope the streets and hype the secret flophouse to the bums and beggars. Hire another two kids to watch the place. Strap them with a couple .22s. Lysol to subdue the stench. Buy cheap field blankets from the Army-Navy.

For a period this arrangement netted Turtle $40 per day, minus overhead, until the house became a headache, and the increased traffic, the shouts, meant constant worry. Turtle could hear them from his bed at night: a burst of drunken revelry, a bottle of Night Train smashed against the kitchen floor, a thudding, and always the phantom hissing of the long forbidden crack pipe sounding down the black street. He could somehow distinguish those sounds that emanated from the dead woman's house from the shouts of young girls in the project towers, their children shouting back from the gravel below, the hookers and johns bouncing and breathing in the cars along the street . . . They were mocking him, the transients, the drunks, the slum lunatics, the hookers, daring him to come out of his bed, out of the corner house, to come hurrying down the dark street, past the park, the limbs of the leafless trees like black wires snapping at his head, to walk beneath the curling blanched palmettos, to walk among the roving bands of angry black youths, scowling boys older than he, to take refuge from them behind the trees, in the shrubs that lined the sidewalk, the project towers of looking eyes, down the dark, knowing, watching street itself, and then to sneak through the back door into the dead woman's house (which he did with perfect discipline) and stand before them, beneath them, a mere boy, waving the .25, kicking their shins, throwing stones and snatches of dirt in the faces of the bearded lunatics, as the prostitutes folded over in laughter at the little boy, the fair-skinned boy from down the street, their landlord, the boy, the boy!

Soon the house could not be contained. Turtle's efforts had proven futile. He'd moved on to better hustles, and he'd long ago learned to maintain in all ventures a good effort/profit ratio. He did, however, almost for the sake of posterity, of memory, make his weekly stomps through the house at fourteen, accompanied by small crews: Adolpho at his side with a baseball bat, some ghetto boys, the very boys, now grown, who had once watched the house from the project windows, Turtle waving now a .38 or a .45, collecting small and insubstantial monies, crumpled bills, from the half-sleeping streetwalkers, the meth addicts, the muttering crack fiends, all the gypsies of the house. They had ruined the house, had deposited bunches of burnt aluminum foil, spent pipes, filters, needles, cigarette butts, beer glass, rubbers, coffee filters, dried semen, spit, feces, snot, piss, bubble gum, vomit, trash, mud, blood, on every floor, on every wall. They had cut up the ruddy red carpets, torn down the ceiling fan in the parlor, smashed, for no reason at all, the dead woman's portraits, burned her nightgowns, shat and bled menses in the bathtub, had ruined the house. In a petty rage some dirty vagrant had ripped the woman's scrapbook to shreds, had tossed her torn pictures, her memories, the memories of a woman who in her lifetime had loaned Turtle's mama sugar, tossed her memories into every corner of the house; and the doors of the bedrooms for which Turtle had charged, in a kind of charity, just $6 a night for privacy, for the dignity of a room that locked, had been long since jimmied and now hung off the doorjambs. These bedrooms had long ago been discovered by the prostitutes and their johns. The mattresses were naked. The smell of fornication was as palpable as the odor of sulfur when it is burned. Only the mirror and the dresser remained in Mrs. Walker's old bedroom, behind which Turtle kept his stash. Even the brilliant red wallpaper had been scraped off the walls.

For this, for the collective abuse of two years' transients, druggies, slackjawed hustlers, teen hookers, queers, deadbeats, narcos, plunger pushers, Turtle found himself doling out beatings to the prostitutes, raping them sometimes, beating the street beggars with baseball bats, thinking, I could have charged twice as much, I could have made you pay, but I didn't, and you ruined the house, you dirty bitches, you pie-backs, you phonies!

George Saunders

Pastoralia

From *The New Yorker*

1.

I HAVE TO admit I'm not feeling my best. Not that I'm doing so bad. Not that I really have anything to complain about. Not that I would actually verbally complain if I did have something to complain about. No. Because I'm Thinking Positive/Saying Positive. I'm sitting back on my haunches, waiting for people to poke in their heads. Although it's been thirteen days since anyone poked in their head and Janet's speaking English to me more and more, which is partly why I feel so, you know, crummy.

"Jeez," she says first thing this morning. "I'm so tired of roast goat I could scream."

What am I supposed to say to that? It puts me in a bad spot. She thinks I'm a goody-goody and that her speaking English makes me uncomfortable. And she's right. It does. Because we've got it good. Every morning, a new goat, just killed, sits in our Big Slot. In our Little Slot, a book of matches. That's better than some. Some are required to catch wild hares in snares. Some are required to wear pioneer garb while cutting the heads off chickens. But not us. I just have to haul the dead goat out of the Big Slot and skin it with a sharp flint. Janet just has to make the fire. So things are pretty good. Not as good as in the old days, but then again, not so bad.

In the old days, when heads were constantly poking in, we liked what we did. Really hammed it up. Had little grunting fights. Whenever I was about to toss a handful of dirt in her face I'd pound a rock against a rock in rage. That way she knew to close her eyes. Sometimes she did this kind of crude weaving. It was like: Roots of Weaving. Sometimes we'd go down to Russian Peasant Farm for a barbecue, I remember there was Murray and Leon, Leon was dating Eileen, Eileen was the one with all the cats, but now, with the big decline in heads poking in, the Russian Peasants are all elsewhere, some to Administration but most not, Eileen's cats have gone wild, and honest to God sometimes I worry I'll go to the Big Slot and find it goatless.

2.

This morning I go to the Big Slot and find it goatless. Instead of a goat there's a note:

Hold on, hold on, it says. *The goat's coming, for crissake. Don't get all snooty.*

The problem is, what am I supposed to do during the time when I'm supposed to be skinning the goat with the flint? I decide to pretend to be desperately ill. I rock in a corner and moan. This gets old. Skinning the goat with the flint takes the better part of an hour. No way am I rocking and moaning for an hour.

Janet comes in from her Separate Area and her eyebrows go up.

"No freaking goat?" she says.

I make some guttural sounds and some motions meaning: Big rain come down, and boom, make goats run, goats now away, away in high hills, and as my fear was great, I did not follow.

Janet scratches under her armpit and makes a sound like a monkey, then lights a cigarette.

"What a bunch of shit," she says. "Why you insist, I'll never know. Who's here? Do you see anyone here but us?"

I gesture to her to put out the cigarette and make the fire. She gestures to me to kiss her butt.

"Why am I making a fire?" she says. "A fire in advance of a goat. Is this like a wishful fire? Like a hopeful fire? No, sorry, I've had it. What would I do in the real world if there was thunder and so on and our goats actually ran away? Maybe I'd mourn, like cut myself with that flint, or maybe I'd kick your ass for being so stupid as to leave the goats out in the rain. What, they didn't put it in the Big Slot?"

I scowl at her and shake my head.

"Well, did you at least check the Little Slot?" she says. "Maybe it was a small goat and they really crammed it in. Maybe for once they gave us a nice quail or something."

I give her a look, then walk off in a rolling gait to check the Little Slot. Nothing.

"Well, freak this," she says. "I'm going to walk right out of here and see what the hell is up."

But she won't. She knows it and I know it. She sits on her log and smokes and together we wait to hear a clunk in the Big Slot.

About lunch we hit the Reserve Crackers. About dinner we again hit the Reserve Crackers.

No heads poke in and there's no clunk in either the Big or Little Slot.

Then the quality of light changes and she stands at the door of her Separate Area.

"No goat tomorrow, I'm out of here and down the hill," she says. "I swear to God. You watch."

I go into my Separate Area and put on my footies. I have some cocoa and take out a Daily Partner Performance Evaluation Form.

Do I note any attitudinal difficulties? I do not. How do I rate my Partner overall? Very good. Are there any Situations which require Mediation?

There are not.

I fax it in.

3.

Next morning, no goat. Also no note. Janet sits on her log and smokes and together we wait to hear a clunk in the Big Slot.

No heads poke in and there's no clunk in either the Big or Little Slot.

About lunch we hit the Reserve Crackers. About dinner we again hit the Reserve Crackers.

Then the quality of light changes and she stands at the door of her Separate Area.

"Crackers, crackers, crackers!" she says pitifully. "Jesus, I wish you'd talk to me. I don't see why you won't. I'm about to go bonkers. We could at least talk. At least have some fun. Maybe play some Scrabble."

Scrabble.

I wave good night and give her a grunt.

"Bastard," she says, and hits me with the flint. She's a good thrower and I almost say ow. Instead I make a horselike sound of fury and consider pinning her to the floor in an effort to make her submit to my superior power etc. etc. Then I go into my Separate Area. I put on my footies and tidy up. I have some cocoa. I take out a Daily Partner Performance Evaluation Form.

Do I note any attitudinal difficulties? I do not. How do I rate my Partner overall? Very good. Are there any Situations which require Mediation?

There are not.

I fax it in.

4.

In the morning in the Big Slot there's a nice fat goat. Also a note:

Ha ha! it says. *Sorry about the no goat and all. A little mix-up. In the future, when you look in here for a goat, what you will find on every occasion is a goat, and not a note. Or maybe both. Ha ha! Happy eating! Everything's fine!*

I skin the goat briskly with the flint. Janet comes in, smiles when she sees the goat, and makes, very quickly, a nice little fire, and does not say one English word all morning and even traces a few of our pictographs with a wettened finger, as if awestruck at their splendid beauty and so on.

Around noon she comes over and looks at the cut on my arm, from where she threw the flint.

"You gonna live?" she says. "Sorry, man, really sorry, I just like lost it."

I give her a look. She cans the English, then starts wailing in grief and sort of hunkers down in apology.

The goat tastes super after two days of crackers.

I have a nap by the fire and for once she doesn't walk around singing pop hits in English, only mumbles unintelligibly and pretends to be catching and eating small bugs.

Her way of saying sorry.

No one pokes their head in.

5.

Once, back in the days when people still poked their heads in, this guy poked his head in.

"Whoa," he said. "These are some very cramped living quarters. This really makes you appreciate the way we live now. Do you have call-waiting? Do you know how to make a nice mushroom cream sauce? Ha ha! I pity you guys. And also, and yet, I thank you guys, who were my precursors, right? Is that the spirit? Is that your point? You weren't ignorant on purpose? You were doing the best you could? Just like I am? Probably someday some guy representing me will be in there, and some punk who I'm precursor of will be hooting at me, asking why my shoes were made out of dead cows and so forth? Because in that future time, wearing dead skin on your feet, no, they won't do that. That will seem to them like barbarity, just like you dragging that broad around by her hair seems to us like barbarity, although to me, not that much, after living with my wife fifteen years. Ha ha! Have a good one!"

I never drag Janet around by the hair.

Too cliché.

Just then his wife poked in her head.

"Stinks in there," she said, and yanked her head out.

"That's the roasting goat," her husband said. "Everything wasn't all prettied up. When you ate meat, it was like you were eating actual meat, the flesh of a dead animal, an animal that maybe had been licking your hand just a few hours before."

"I would never do that," said the wife.

"You do it now, bozo!" said the man. "You just pay someone to do the dirty work. The slaughtering? The skinning?"

"I do not either," said the wife.

We couldn't see them, only hear them through the place where the heads poke in.

"Ever heard of a slaughterhouse?" the husband said. "Ha ha! Gotcha! What do you think goes on in there? Some guy you never met kills and flays a cow with what you might term big old cow eyes, so you can have your shoes and I can have my steak and my shoes!"

"That's different," she said. "Those animals were raised for slaughter. That's what they were made for. Plus I cook them in an oven, I don't squat there in my underwear with smelly smoke blowing all over me."

"Thank heaven for small favors," he said. "Joking! I'm joking. You squatting in your underwear is not such a bad mental picture, believe me."

"Plus where do they poop," she said.

"Ask them," said the husband. "Ask them where they poop, if you so choose. You paid your dime. That is certainly your prerogative."

"I don't believe I will," said the wife.

"Well, I'm not shy," he said.

Then there was no sound from the head-hole for quite some time. Possibly they were quietly discussing it.

"Okay, so where do you poop?" asked the husband, poking his head in.

"We have disposable bags that mount on a sort of rack," said Janet. "The septic doesn't come up this far."

"Ah," he said. "They poop in bags that mount on racks."

"Wonderful," said his wife. "I'm the richer for that information."

"But hold on," the husband said. "In the old times, like when the cave was real and all, where then did they go? I take it there were no disposal bags in those times, if I'm right."

"In those times they just went out in the woods," said Janet.

"Ah," he said. "That makes sense."

You see what I mean about Janet? When addressed directly we're supposed to cower shrieking in the corner but instead she answers twice in English?

I gave her a look.

"Oh, he's okay," she whispered. "He's no narc. I can tell."

In a minute in came a paper airplane: our Client Vignette Evaluation.

Under *Overall Impression* he'd written: *A-okay! Very nice.*

Under *Learning Value* he'd written: *We learned where they pooped. Both old days and now.*

I added it to our pile, then went into my Separate Area and put on my footies. I filled out my Daily Partner Performance Evaluation form. Did I note any attitudinal difficulties? I did not. How did I rate my Partner overall? Very good. Were there any Situations which required Mediation?

There were not.

I faxed it in.

6.

This morning is the morning I empty our Human Refuse bags and the trash bags and the bag from the bottom of the sleek metal hole where Janet puts her used feminine items.

For this I get an extra sixty a month. Plus it's always nice to get out of the cave.

I knock on the door of her Separate Area.

"Who is it?" she asks, playing dumb.

She knows very well who it is. I stick in my arm and wave around a trash bag.

"Go for it," she says.

She's in there washing her armpits with a washcloth. The room smells like her, only more so. I add the trash from her wicker basket to my big white bag. I add her bag of used feminine items to my big white bag. I take three bags labeled Caution Human Refuse from the corner and add them to my big pink bag labeled Caution Human Refuse.

I mime to her that I dreamed of a herd that covered the plain like the grass of the earth, they were as numerous as grasshoppers and yet the meat of their humps resembled each a tiny mountain etc. etc., and sharpen my spear and try to look like I'm going into a sort of prehunt trance.

"Are you going?" she shouts. "Are you going now? Is that what you're saying?"

I nod.

"Christ, so go already," she says. "Have fun. Bring back some mints."

She has worked very hard these many months to hollow out a rock in which to hide her mints and her smokes. Mints mints mints. Smokes smokes smokes. No matter how long we're in here together I will never get the hots for her. She's fifty and has large feet and sloping shoulders and a pinched little face and chews with her mouth open. Sometimes she puts on big ugly glasses in the cave and does a crossword: very verboten.

Out I go, with the white regular trash bag in one hand and our mutual big pink Human Refuse bag in the other.

7.

Down in the blue-green valley is a herd of robotic something-or-others, bent over the blue-green grass, feeding I guess? Midway between our mountain and the opposing mountains is a wide green river with periodic interrupting boulders. I walk along a white cliff, then down a path marked by a yellow dot on a pine. Few know this way. It is a non-Guest path. No Attractions are down it, only Disposal Area 8 and a little Employees Only shop in a doublewide, a real blessing for us, we're so close and all.

Inside the doublewide are Marty and a lady we think is maybe Marty's wife but then again maybe not.

Marty's shrieking at the lady, who's writing down whatever he shrieks.

"Just do as they ask!" he shrieks, and she writes it down. "And not only that, do more than that, son, more than they ask! Excel! Why not excel? Be excellent! Is it bad to be good? Now son, I know you don't think that, because that is not what you were taught, you were taught that it is good to be good, I very clearly remember teaching you that. When we went fishing, and you caught a fish, I always said good, good fishing, son, and when you caught no fish, I frowned, I said, bad catching of fish, although I don't believe I was ever cruel about it. Are you getting this?"

"Every word," the lady says. "To me they're like nuggets of gold."

"Ha ha," says Marty, and gives her a long loving scratch on the back, and takes a drink of Squirt and starts shrieking again.

"So anyways, do what they ask!" he shrieks. "Don't you know how much we love you here at home, and want you to succeed? As for them, the big-wigs you wrote me about, freak them big-wigs! Just do what they ask though. In your own private mind, think what you like, only do what they ask, so they like you. And in this way, you will succeed. As for the little-wigs you mentioned, just how little are they? You didn't mention that. Are they a lot littler wig than you? In that case, freak them, ignore them if they talk to you, and if they don't talk to you, go up and start talking to them, sort of bossing them around, you know, so they don't start thinking they're the boss of you. But if they're the same wig as you, be careful, son! Don't piss them off, don't act like you're the boss of them, but also don't bend over for some little shit who's merely the same wig as you, or else he'll assume you're a smaller wig than you really actually are. As for friends, sure, friends are great, go ahead and make friends, they're a real blessing, only try to avoid making friends with boys who are the same or lesser wig than you. Only make friends with boys who are bigger wigs than you, assuming they'll have you, which probably they won't. Because why should they? Who are you? You're a smaller wig than them. Although then again, they might be slumming, which would be good for you, you could sneak right in there."

Marty gives me a little wave, then resumes shrieking.

"I don't want to put the pressure on, son," he says. "I know you got enough pressure, with school being so hard and all, and you even having to make your own book covers because of our money crunch, so I don't want to put on extra pressure by saying that the family honor is at stake, but guess what pal, it is! You're it, kid! You're as good as we got. Think of it, me and your mother, and Paw-Paw and Mee-Maw, and Great Paw-Paw, who came over here from wherever he was before, in some kind of boat, and fixed shoes all his life in a shack or whatever? Remember that? Why'd he do that? So you could eventually be born! Think of that! All those years of laundry and stuffing their faces and plodding to the market and making love and pushing out the babies and so on, and what's the upshot? You, pal, you're the freaking upshot. And now there you are, in boarding school, what a privilege, the first one of us to do it, so all's I'm saying is, do your best and don't take no shit from nobody, unless taking shit from them is part of your master plan to get the best of them by tricking them into being your friend. Just always remember who you are, son, you're a Kusacki, my only son, and I love you. Ack, I'm getting mushy here."

"You're doing great," says the lady.

"So much to say," he says.

"And Jeannine sends her love too," says the lady.

"And Jeannine sends her love too," he says. "For crissake's sake, Jeannine, write it down if you want to say it. I don't have to say it for you to write it. Just write it. You're my wife."

"I'm not your wife," says Jeannine.

"You are to me," says Marty, and she sort of leans into him and he takes another slug of the Squirt.

I buy Janet some smokes and mints and me a Kayo.

I really like Kayo.

"Hey, you hear about Dave Wolley?" Marty says to me. "Dave Wolley from Wise Mountain Hermit? You know him? You know Dave?"

I know Dave very well. Dave was part of the group that used to meet for the barbecues at Russian Peasant Farm.

"Well, wave bye-bye to Dave," Marty says. "Wise Mountain Hermit is kaput. Dave is kaput."

"I've never seen Dave so upset," says Jeannine.

"He was very freaking upset," says Marty. "Who wouldn't be? He was superdedicated."

Dave was superdedicated. He grew his own beard long instead of wearing a fake and even when on vacation went around barefoot to make his feet look more like the feet of an actual mountain ascetic.

"The problem is, Wise Mountain Hermit was too far off the beaten path," Marty says. "Like all you Remotes. All you Remotes, you're too far off the beaten path. Think about it. These days we got very few Guests to begin with, which means we got even fewer guests willing to walk way the hell up here to see you Remotes. Right? Am I right?"

"You are absolutely right," says Jeannine.

"I am absolutely right," says Marty. "Although I am not happy about being absolutely right, because if you think of it, if you Remotes go kaput, where am I? It's you Remotes I'm servicing. See? Right? Give him his mints. Make change for the poor guy. He's got to get back to work."

"Have a good one," says Jeannine, and makes my change.

It's sad about Dave. Also it's worrisome. Because Wise Mountain Hermit was no more Remote than we are, plus it was much more popular, because Dave was so good at dispensing ad-libbed sage advice.

I walk down the path to the Refuse Center and weigh our Human Refuse. I put the paperwork and the fee in the box labeled Paperwork and Fees. I toss the trash in the dumpster labeled Trash, and the Human Refuse in the dumpster labeled Caution Human Refuse, then sit against a tree and drink my Kayo.

8.

Next morning in the Big Slot is a goat and in the Little Slot a rabbit and a note addressed to Distribution:

Please accept this extra food as a token of what our esteem is like, the note says. *Please know that each one of you is very special to us, and are never for-*

gotten about. Please know that if each one of you could be kept, you would be, if that would benefit everyone. But it wouldn't, or we would do it, wouldn't we, we would keep every one of you. But as we meld into our sleeker new organization, what an excellent opportunity to adjust our Staff Mix. And so, although in this time of scarcity and challenge, some must perhaps go, the upside of this is, some must stay, and perhaps it will be you. Let us hope it will be you, each and every one of you, but no, as stated previously, it won't, that is impossible. So just enjoy the treats provided, and don't worry, and wait for your supervisor to contact you, and if he or she doesn't, know with relief that the Staff Remixing has passed by your door. Although it is only honest to inform you that some who make the first pass may indeed be removed in the second, or maybe even a third, depending on how the Remixing goes, although if anyone is removed in both the first and second pass, that will be a redundant screw-up, please ignore. We will only remove each of you once. If that many times! Some of you will be removed never, the better ones of you. But we find ourselves in a too-many-Indians situation and so must first cut some Indians and then, later, possibly, some chiefs. But not yet, because that is harder, because that is us. Soon, but not yet, we have to decide which of us to remove, and that is so very hard, because we are so very useful. Not that we are saying we chiefs are more useful than you Indians, but certainly we do make some very difficult decisions that perhaps you Indians would find hard to make, keeping you up nights, such as which of you to remove. But don't worry about us, we've been doing this for years, only first and foremost remember that what we are doing, all of us, chiefs and Indians both, is a fun privilege, how many would like to do what we do, in the entertainment field.

Which I guess explains about Dave Wolley.

"Jeez," says Janet. "Let the freaking canning begin."

I give her a look.

"Oh all right all right," she says. "Ooga mooga. Ooga ooga mooga. Is that better?"

She can be as snotty as she likes but a Remixing is nothing to sneeze at.

I skin and roast the goat and rabbit. After breakfast she puts on her Walkman and starts a letter to her sister: very verboten. I work on the pictographs. I mean I kneel while pretending to paint them by dipping my crude dry brush into the splotches of hard colorful plastic meant to look like paint made from squashed berries.

Around noon the fax in my Separate Area makes the sound it makes when a fax is coming in.

Getting it would require leaving the cave and entering my Separate Area during working hours.

"Christ, go get it," Janet says. "Are you nuts? It might be from Louise."

I go get it.

It's from Louise.

Nelson doing better today, it says. *Not much new swelling. Played trucks and ate 3 pcs bologna. Asked about you. No temperature, good range of motion in both legs and arms. Visa is up to $6800, should I transfer to new card w/lower interest rate?*

Sounds good, I fax back. *How are other kids?*

Kids are kids are kids, she faxes back. *Driving me nuts. Always talking.*

Miss you, I fax, and she faxes back the necessary Signature Card.

I sign the card. I fax the card.

Nelson's three. Three months ago his muscles stiffened up. The medicine they put him on to loosen his muscles did somewhat loosen them, but also it caused his muscles to swell. Otherwise he's fine, only he's stiff and swollen and it hurts when he moves. They have a name for what they originally thought he had, but when the medication made him swell up, Dr. Evans had to admit that whatever he had, it wasn't what they'd originally thought it was.

So we're watching him closely.

I return to the cave.

"How are things?" Janet says.

I grimace.

"Well, shit," she says. "You know I'm freaking rooting for you guys."

Sometimes she can be pretty nice.

9.

First thing next morning Greg Nordstrom pokes his head in and asks me to brunch.

Which is a first.

"How about me?" says Janet.

"Ha ha!" says Nordstrom. "Not you. Not today. Maybe soon, however!"

I follow him out.

Very bright sun.

About fifty feet from the cave there's a red paper screen that says Patience! Under Construction, and we go behind it.

"You'll be getting your proxy forms in your Slot soon," he says, spreading out some bagels on a blanket. "Fill out the proxy as you see fit, everything's fine, just vote, do it boldly, exert your choice, it has to do with your stock option. Are you vested? Great to be vested. Just wait until you are. It really feels like a Benefit. You'll see why they call Benefits Benefits, when every month, ka-ching, that option money kicks up a notch. Man, we're lucky."

"Yes," I say.

"I am and you are," he says. "Not everyone is. Some aren't. Those being removed in the Staff Remixing, no. But you're not being removed. At least I don't think so. Now Janet, I have some concerns about Janet, I don't know what they're going to do about Janet. It's not me, it's them, but what can I do? How is she? Is she okay? How have you found her? I want you to speak frankly. Are there problems? Problems we can maybe help correct? How is she? Nice? Reliable? It's not negative to point out a defect. Actually, it's positive, because then the defect can be fixed. What's negative is to withhold valuable info. Are you? Withholding valuable info? I hope not. Are you being negative? Is she a bit of a pain? Please tell me. I want you to. If you admit she's a bit of a pain, I'll write down how positive you were. Look, you know and I know she's got some performance issues, so what an exciting opportunity, for you to admit it and me to hear it loud and clear. Super!"

For six years she's been telling me about her Pap smears and her kid in rehab and her mother in Fort Wayne who has a bad valve and can't stand up or her lungs fill with blood etc. etc.

"I haven't really noticed any problems," I say.

"Blah blah blah," he says. "What kind of praise is that? Empty praise? Is it empty praise? I'd caution against empty praise. Because empty praise is what? Is like what? Is a lie. And a lie is what? Is negative. You're like the opposite of that little boy who cried Wolf. You're like that little boy who cried No Wolf, when a wolf was in fact chewing on his leg, by the name of Janet. Because what have I recently seen? Having seen your Daily Partner Performance Evaluation Forms, I haven't seen on them a single discouraging word. Not one. Did you ever note a single attitudinal difficulty? You did not. How did you rate your Partner overall? Very good, always, every single day. Were there ever any Situations which required Mediation? There were not, even when, in one instance, she told a guy where you folks pooped. In English. In the cave. I have documentation, because I read that guy's Client Vignette Evaluation."

It gets very quiet. The wind blows and the paper screen tips up a bit. The bagels look good but we're not eating them.

"Look," he says. "I know it's hard to be objective about people we come to daily know, but in the big picture, who benefits when the truth is not told? Does Janet? How can Janet know she's not being her best self if someone doesn't tell her, then right away afterwards harshly discipline her? And with Janet not being her best self, is the organization healthier? And with the organization not being healthier, and the organization being that thing that ultimately puts the food in your face, you can easily see that, by lying about Janet's behavior, you are taking the food out of your own face. Who puts the cash in your hand to buy that food in your face? We do. What do we want of you? We want you to tell the truth. That's it. That is all."

We sit awhile in silence.

"Very simple," he says. "A nonbrainer."

A white fuzzy thing lands in my arm hair. I pick it out.

Down it falls.

"Sad," he said. "Sad is all it is. We live in a beautiful world, full of beautiful challenges and flowers and birds and super people, but also a few regrettable bad apples, such as that questionable Janet. Do I hate her? Do I want her killed? Gosh no, I think she's super, I want her to be praised while getting a hot oil massage, she has some very nice traits. But guess what, I'm not paying her to have nice traits, I'm paying her to do consistently good work. Is she? Doing consistently good work? She is not. And here you are, saddled with a subpar colleague. Poor you. She's stopping your rise and growth. People are talking about you in our lounge. Look, I know you feel Janet's not so great. She's a lump to you. I see it in your eye. And that must chafe. Because you are good. Very good. One of our best. And she's bad, very bad, one of our worst, sometimes I could just slap her for what she's doing to you."

"She's a friend," I say.

"You know what it's like, to me?" he says. "The Bible. Remember that part in the Bible when Christ or God says that any group or organization of two or more of us is a body? I think that is so true. Our body has a rotten toe by the name of Janet, who is turning black and stinking up the joint, and next to that bad stinking toe lives her friend the good non-stinker toe, who for some reason insists on holding its tongue, if a toe can be said to have a tongue. Speak up, little toe, let the brain know the state of the rot, so we can rush down what is necessary to stop Janet from stinking. What will be needed? We do not yet know. Maybe some antiseptic, maybe a nice sharp saw with which to lop off Janet. For us to know, what must you do? Tell the truth. Start generating frank and nonbiased assessments of this subpar colleague. That's it. That is all. Did you or did you not in your Employment Agreement agree to complete, every day, an accurate Daily Partner Performance Evaluation Form? You did. You signed in triplicate. I have a copy in my dossier. But enough mean and sad talk, I know my point has been gotten. Gotten by you. Now for the fun. The eating. Eating the good food I have broughten. That's fun, isn't it? I think that's fun."

We start to eat. It's fun.

"Broughten," he says. "The good food I have broughten. Is it brought or broughten?"

"Brought," I say.

"The good food I have brought," he says. "Broughten."

10.

Back in the cave Janet's made a nice fire.

"So what did numbnuts want?" she says. "Are you fired?"

I shake my head no.

"Is he in love with you?" she says. "Does he want to go out with you?"

I shake my head no.

"Is he in love with me?" she says. "Does he want to go out with me? Am I fired?"

I do not shake my head no.

"Wait a minute, wait a minute, go back," she says. "I'm fired?"

I shake my head no.

"But I'm in the shit?" she says. "I'm somewhat in the shit?"

I shrug.

"Will you freaking talk to me?" she says. "This is important. Don't be a dick for once."

I do not consider myself a dick and I do not appreciate being called a dick, in the cave, in English, and the truth is, if she would try a little harder not to talk in the cave, she would not be so much in the shit.

I hold up one finger, like: Wait a sec. Then I go into my Separate Area and write her a note:

Nordstrom is unhappy with you, it says. *And unhappy with me because I have been lying for you on my DPPEFs. So I am going to start telling the truth. And as you know, if I tell the truth about you, you will be a goner, unless you start acting better. Therefore, please start acting better. Sorry I couldn't say this in the cave, but as you know, we are not supposed to speak English in the cave. I enjoy working with you. We just have to get this thing straightened out.*

Sitting on her log she reads my note.

"Time to pull head out of ass, I guess," she says.

I give her a thumbs-up.

11.

Next morning I go to the Big Slot and find it goatless. Also there is no note.

Janet comes out and hands me a note and makes, very quickly, a nice little fire.

I really appreciate what you did, her note says. *That you tole me the truth. Your a real pal and are going to see how good I can be.*

For breakfast I count out twenty Reserve Crackers each. Afterward I work on the pictographs and she pretends to catch and eat small bugs. For lunch I count out twenty Reserve Crackers each. After lunch I pretend to sharpen my spear and she sits at my feet speaking long strings of unintelligible sounds.

No one pokes their head in.

When the quality of light changes she stands at the door of her Separate Area and sort of wiggles her eyebrows, like: Pretty good, eh?

I go into my Separate Area. I take out a Daily Partner Performance Evaluation Form.

For once it's easy.

Do I note any attitudinal difficulties? I do not. How do I rate my Partner overall? Very good. Are there any Situations which require Mediation?

There are not.

I fax it in.

12.

Next morning I go to the Big Slot and again find it goatless. Again no note.

Janet comes out and again makes, very quickly, a nice little fire.

I count out twenty Reserve Crackers each. After breakfast we work on the pictographs. After lunch she goes to the doorway and starts barking out sounds meant to indicate that a very impressive herd of feeding things is thundering past etc. etc., which of course it is not, the feeding things, being robotic, are right where they always are, across the river. When she barks I grab my spear and come racing up and join her in barking at the imaginary feeding things.

All day no one pokes their head in.

Then the quality of light changes and she stands at the door of her Separate Area giving me a smile, like: It's actually sort of fun doing it right, isn't it?

I take out a Daily Partner Performance Evaluation Form.

Again: Easy.

Do I note any attitudinal difficulties? I do not. How do I rate my Partner overall? Very good. Are there any Situations which require Mediation?

There are not.

I fax it in.

Also I write Nordstrom a note:

Per our conversation, it says, *I took the liberty of bringing Janet up to speed. Since that time she has been doing wonderful work, as reflected in my (now truthful!!) Daily Partner Performance Evaluation Forms. Thank you for your frankness. Also, I apologize for that period during which I was less than truthful on my DPPEFs. I can see now just how negative that was.*

A bit of ass-kissing, yes.

But I've got some making up to do.

I fax it in.

13.

Late in the night my fax makes the sound it makes when a fax is coming in.

From Nordstrom:

What? What? it says. *You told her? Did I tell you to tell her? And now you have the nerve to say she is doing good? Why should I believe you when you say she is doing good, when all that time she was doing so bad you always said she was doing so good? Oh you have hacked me off. Do you know what I hate? Due to my childhood? Which is maybe why I'm so driven? A liar. Dad lied by cheating on Mom, Mom lied by cheating on Dad, with Kenneth, who was himself a liar, and promised, at his wedding to Mom, to buy me three ponies with golden saddles, and then later, upon divorcing Mom, promised to at least get me one pony with a regular saddle, but needless to say, no ponies were ever gotten by me. Which is maybe why I hate a liar. SO DON'T LIE ANYMORE. Don't lie even one more time about that hideous Janet. I can't believe you told her! Do you really think I care about how she is? I KNOW how she is. She is BAD. But what I need is for you to SAY IT. For reasons of documentation. Do you have any idea how hard it is to fire a gal, not to mention an old gal, not to mention an old gal with so many years of service under her ancient withered belt? There is so much you don't know, about the Remixing, about our plans! Do not even answer me, I am too mad to read it.*

Which is not at all what I had in mind.

No doubt my status with Nordstrom has been somewhat damaged.

But okay.

Janet is now doing better and I am now telling the truth. So things are as they should be.

And I'm sure that, in the long run, Nordstrom will come to appreciate what I've accomplished.

14.

Next morning I go to the Big Slot and again find it goatless. Again no note.

Janet comes out and makes, very quickly, a nice little fire.

We squat and eat our Reserve Crackers while occasionally swatting each other with our hands. We get in kind of a mock squabble and scurry around the cave bent over and shrieking. She is really doing very well. I pound a rock against a rock in rage, indicating that I intend to toss some dirt in her face. She barks back very sharply.

Someone pokes their head in.

Young guy, kind of goofy-looking.

"Bradley?" Janet says. "Holy shit."

"Hey, nice greeting, Ma," the guy says, and walks in. He's not supposed to walk in. No one's supposed to walk in. I can't remember a time when anyone has ever just walked in.

"Fucking stinks in here," he says.

"Don't you *even* come into my workplace and start swearing," Janet says.

"Yeah right, Ma," he says. "Like you never came into my workplace and started swearing."

"Like you ever had a workplace," she says. "Like you ever worked."

"Like jewelry making wasn't work," he says.

"Oh Bradley you are so full of it," she says. "You didn't have none of the equipment and no freaking jewels. And no customers. You never made a single piece of jewelry. You just sat moping in the basement."

Just our luck: Our first Guest in two weeks and it's a relative.

I clear my throat. I give her a look.

"Give us five freaking minutes, will you, Mr. Tightass?" she says. "This is my kid here."

"I was conceptualizing my designs, Ma," he says. "Which is an important part of it. And you definitely swore at my workplace. I remember very clearly one time you came down into the basement and said I was a fucking asshole for wasting my time trying to make my dream come true of being a jewelry maker."

"Oh bullshit," she says. "I never once called you a asshole. And I definitely did not say fucking. I never say fuck. I quit that a long time ago. You ever hear me say fuck?"

She looks at me. I shake my head no. She never says fuck. When she means fuck she says freak. She is very very consistent about this.

"What?" says Bradley. "He don't talk?"

"He plays by the rules," she says. "Maybe you should try it sometime."

"I was trying," he says. "But still they kicked me out."

"Kicked you out of what?" she says. "Wait a minute, wait a minute, go back. They kicked you out of what? Of rehab?"

"It's nothing bad, Ma!" he shouts. "You don't have to make me feel ashamed about it. I feel bad enough, being called a thief by Mr. Doe in front of the whole group."

"Jesus, Bradley," she says. "How are you supposed to get better if you get kicked out of rehab? What did you steal this time? Did you steal a stereo again? Who's Mr. Doe?"

"I didn't steal nothing, Ma," he says. "Doe's my counselor. I borrowed something. A TV. The TV from the lounge. I just felt like I could get better a lot faster if I had a TV in my room. So I took control of my recovery. Is that so bad? I thought that's what I was there for, you know? I'm not saying I did everything perfect. Like I probably shouldn't of sold it."

"You sold it?" she says.

"There was nothing good ever on!" he says. "If they showed good programs I just know I would've gotten better. But no. It was so boring. So I decided to throw everybody a party, because they were all supporting me so well, by letting me keep the TV in my room? And so, you know, I sold the TV, for the party, and was taking the bucks over to the Party Place, to get some things for the party, some hats and tooters and stuff like that, but then I've got this problem, with substances, and so I sort of all of a sudden wanted some substances. And then I ran into this guy with some substances. That guy totally fucked me! By being there with those substances right when I had some money? He didn't care one bit about my recovery."

"You sold the rehab TV to buy drugs," she says.

"To buy substances, Ma, why can't you get it right?" he says. "The way we name things is important, Ma, Doe taught me that in counseling. Look, maybe you wouldn't have sold the TV, but you're not an inadvertent substance misuser, and guess what, I am, that's why I was in there. Do you hear me? I know you wish you had a perfect son, but you don't, you have an inadvertent substance misuser who sometimes makes bad judgments, like borrowing and selling a TV to buy substances."

"Or rings and jewels," says Janet. "My rings and jewels."

"Fuck, Ma, that was a long time ago!" he says. "Why do you have to keep bringing that old shit up? Doe was so right. For you to win, I have to lose. Like when I was a kid and in front of the whole neighborhood you called me an animal torturer? That really hurt. That caused a lot of my problems. We were working on that in group right before I left."

"You were torturing a cat," she says. "With a freaking prod."

"A prod I built myself in metal shop," he says. "But of course you never mention that."

"A prod you were heating with a Sterno cup," she says.

"Go ahead, build your case," he says. "Beat up on me as much as you want, I don't have a choice. I have to be here."

"What do you mean, you have to be here?" she says.

"Ma, haven't you been listening?" he shouts. "I got kicked out of rehab!"

"Well you can't stay here," she says.

"I have to stay here!" he says. "Where am I supposed to go?"

"Go home," she says. "Go home with Grammy."

"With Grammy?" he says. "Are you kidding me? Oh God, the group would love this. You're telling a very troubled inadvertent substance mis-user to go live with his terminally ill grandmother? You have any idea how stressful that would be for me? I'd be inadvertently misusing again in a heartbeat. Grammy's always like: Get me this, get me that, sit with me, I'm scared, talk with me, it hurts when I breathe. I'm twenty-four, Ma, baby-sitting brings me down. Plus she's kind of deranged? She sort of like hallucinates? I think it's all that blood in her lungs. The other night she woke up at midnight and said I was trying to steal something from her. Can you believe it? She's like all kooky! I wasn't stealing. Her necklaces got tangled up and I was trying to untangle them. And Keough was trying to help me."

"Keough was at the house?" she says. "I thought I told you no Keough."

"Ma, Jesus Christ, Keough's my friend," he says. "Like my only friend. How am I supposed to get better without friends? At least I have one. You don't have any."

"I have plenty of friends," she says.

"Name one," he says.

She looks at me.

Which I guess is sort of sweet.

Although I don't see why she had to call me Mr. Tightass.

"Fine, Ma," he says. "You don't want me staying here, I won't stay here.

You want me to inadvertently misuse substances, I'll inadvertently misuse substances. I'll turn tricks and go live in a ditch. Is that what you want?"

"Turn tricks?" she says. "Who said anything about turning tricks?"

"Keough's done it," he says. "It's what we eventually come to, our need for substances is so great. We can't help it."

"Well, I don't want you turning tricks," she says. "That I don't go for."

"But living in a ditch is okay," he says.

"If you want to live in a ditch, live in a ditch," she says.

"I don't want to live in a ditch," he says. "I want to turn my life around. But it would help me turn my life around if I had a little money. Like twenty bucks. So I can go back and get those party supplies. The tooters and all? I want to make it up to my friends."

"Is that what this is about?" she says. "You want money? Well I don't have twenty bucks. And you don't need tooters to have a party."

"But I want tooters," he says. "Tooters make it more fun."

"I don't have twenty bucks," she says.

"Ma, please," he says. "You've always been there for me. And I've got a bad feeling about this. Like this might be my last chance."

She pulls me off to one side.

"I'll pay you back on payday," she says.

I give her a look.

"Come on, man," she says. "He's my *son*. You know how it is. You got a sick kid, I got a sick kid."

My feeling is, yes and no. My sick kid is three. My sick kid isn't a con man.

Although at this point it's worth twenty bucks to get this guy out of the cave.

I go to my Separate Area and get the twenty bucks. I give it to her and she gives it to him.

"Excellent!" he says, and goes bounding out the door. "A guy can always count on his ma."

Janet goes straight to her Separate Area. The rest of the afternoon I hear sobbing.

Sobbing or laughing.

Probably sobbing.

When the quality of light changes I go to my Separate Area. I make cocoa. I tidy up. I take out a Daily Partner Performance Evaluation Form.

This is really pushing it. Her kid comes into the cave in street clothes, speaks English in the cave, she speaks English back, they both swear many many times, she spends the whole afternoon weeping in her Separate Area.

Then again, what am I supposed to do, rat out a friend with a dying mom on the day she finds out her screwed-up son is even more screwed up than she originally thought?

Do I note any attitudinal difficulties? I do not. How do I rate my Partner overall? Very good. Are there any Situations which require Mediation?

There are not.

I fax it in.

15.

Late that night my fax makes the sound it makes when a fax is coming in.

From Louise:

Bad day, she says. *He had a fever then suddenly got very cold. And his legs are so swollen. In places the skin looks ready to split. Ate like two handfuls dry Chex all day. And whiny, oh my God the poor thing. Stood on the heat grate all day in his underwear staring out the window. Kept saying where is Daddy, why is he never here? Plus the Evemplorine went up to $70 for 120 count. God, it's all drudge drudge drudge, you should see me, I look about ninety. Also a big strip of trim or siding came floating down as we were getting in the car and nearly killed the twins. Insurance said they won't pay. What do I do, do I forget about it? Will something bad happen to the wood underneath if we don't get it nailed back up? Ugh. Don't fax back, I'm going to sleep.*

Love, Me.

I get into bed and lie there counting and recounting the acoustic tiles on the ceiling of my darkened Separate Area.

One hundred forty-four.

Plus I am so hungry. I could kill for some goat.

Although certainly, dwelling on problems doesn't solve them. Although on the other hand, thinking positively about problems also doesn't solve them. But at least then you feel positive, which is, or should be, you know, empowering. And power is good. Power is necessary at this point. It is necessary at this point for me to be, you know, a rock. What I need to remember now is that I don't have to solve the problems of the world. It is not within my power to cure Nelson, it is only necessary for me to do what I can do, which is keep the money coming in, and in order for me to keep the money coming in, it is necessary for me to keep my chin up, so I can continue to do a good job. That is, it is necessary for me to avoid dwelling negatively on problems in the dark of night in my Separate Area, because if I do, I will be tired in the morning, and might then do a poor job, which could jeopardize my ability to keep the money coming in, especially if, for example, there is a Spot Check.

I continue to count the tiles but as I do it try to smile. I smile in the dark and sort of nod confidently. I try to positively and creatively imagine surprising and innovative solutions to my problems, like winning the Lotto, like the Remixing being discontinued, like Nelson suddenly one morning waking up completely cured.

16.

Next morning is once again the morning I empty our Human Refuse bags and the trash bags and the bag from the bottom of the sleek metal hole.

I knock on the door of her Separate Area.

"Enter," she says.

I step in and mime to her that I dreamed of a herd that covered the plain like the grass of the earth, they were as numerous as grasshoppers and yet the meat of their humps resembled each a tiny mountain etc. etc.

"Hey, sorry about yesterday," she says. "Really sorry. I never dreamed that little shit would have the nerve to come here. And you think he paid to get in? I very much doubt it. My guess is, he hopped the freaking fence."

I add the trash from her wicker basket to my big white bag. I add her bag of used feminine items to my big white bag.

"But he's a good-looking kid, isn't he?" she says.

I sort of curtly nod. I take three bags labeled Caution Human Refuse from the corner and add them to my big pink bag labeled Caution Human Refuse.

"Hey, look," she says. "Am I okay? Did you narc me out? About him being here?"

I give her a look, like: I should've but I didn't.

"Thank you *so* much," she says. "Damn, you're nice. From now on, no more screw-ups. I swear to God."

Out I go, with the white regular trash bag in one hand and our mutual big pink Human Refuse bag in the other.

17.

Nobody's on the path, although from the direction of Pioneer Encampment I hear the sound of rushing water, possibly the Big Durn Flood? Twice a month they open up the Reserve Tanks and the river widens and pretty soon some detachable house parts and Pioneer wagons equipped with special inflatable bladders float by, while from their P.A. we dimly hear the sound of prerecorded screaming Settlers.

I walk along the white cliff, turn down the non-Guest path marked by the little yellow dot, etc. etc.

Marty's out front of the doublewide playing catch with a little kid.

I sit against a tree and start my paperwork.

"Great catch, son!" Marty says to the kid. "You can really catch. I would imagine you're one of the very best catchers in that school."

"Not exactly, Dad," the kid says. "Those kids can really catch. Most of them catch even better than me."

"You know, in a way I'm glad you might quit that school," says Marty. "Those rich kids. I'm very unsure about them."

"I don't want to quit," says the kid. "I like it there."

"Well, you might have to quit," says Marty. "We might make the decision that it's best for you to quit."

"Because we're running out of money," says the kid.

"Yes and no," says Marty. "We are and we aren't. Daddy's job is just a little, ah, problematical. Good catch! That is an excellent catch. Pick it up. Put your glove back on. That was too hard a throw. I knocked your glove off."

"I guess I have a pretty weak hand," the kid says.

"Your hand is perfect," says Marty. "My throw was too hard."

"It's kind of weird, Dad," the kid says. "Those kids at school are better than me at a lot of things. I mean, like everything? Those kids can really catch. Plus some of them went to camp for baseball and camp for math.

Plus you should see their clothes. One kid won a trophy in golf. Plus they're nice. When I missed a catch they were really really nice. They always said, like, Nice try. And they tried to teach me? When I missed at long division they were nice. When I ate with my fingers they were nice. When my shoes split in gym they were nice. This one kid gave me his shoes."

"He gave you his shoes?" says Marty.

"He was really nice," explains the kid.

"What were your shoes doing splitting?" says Marty. "Where did they split? Why did they split? Those were perfectly good shoes."

"In gym," says the kid. "They split in gym and my foot fell out. Then that kid who switched shoes with me wore them with his foot sticking out. He said he didn't mind. And even with his foot sticking out he beat me at running. He was really nice."

"I heard you the first time," says Marty. "He was really nice. Maybe he went to being-nice camp. Maybe he went to giving-away-shoes camp."

"Well, I don't know if they have that kind of camp," says the kid.

"Look, you don't need to go to a camp to know how to be nice," says Marty. "And you don't have to be rich to be nice. You just have to be nice. Do you think you have to be rich to be nice?"

"I guess so," says the kid.

"No, no, no," says Marty. "You don't. That's my point. You don't have to be rich to be nice."

"But it helps?" says the kid.

"No," says Marty. "It makes no difference. It has nothing to do with it."

"I think it helps," says the kid. "Because then you don't have to worry about your shoes splitting."

"Ah bullshit," says Marty. "You're not rich but you're nice. See? You were nice, weren't you? When someone else's shoes split, you were nice, right?"

"No one else's shoes ever split," says the kid.

"Are you trying to tell me you were the only kid in that whole school whose shoes ever split?" says Marty.

"Yes," says the kid.

"I find that hard to believe," says Marty.

"Once this kid Simon?" says the kid. "His pants ripped."

"Well, there you go," says Marty. "That's worse. Because your underwear shows. Your pants never ripped. Because I bought you good pants.

Not that I'm saying the shoes I bought you weren't good. They were very good. Among the best. So what did this Simon kid do? When his pants ripped? Was he upset? Did the other kids make fun of him? Did he start crying? Did you rush to his defense? Did you sort of like console him? Do you know what console means? It means like say something nice. Did you say something nice when his pants ripped?"

"Not exactly," the kid says.

"What did you say?" says Marty.

"Well, that boy, Simon, was a kind of smelly boy?" says the kid. "He had this kind of smell to him?"

"Did the other kids make fun of his smell?" says Marty.

"Sometimes," says the kid.

"But they didn't make fun of your smell," says Marty.

"No," says the kid. "They made fun of my shoes splitting."

"Too bad about that smelly kid though," says Marty. "You gotta feel bad about a kid like that. What were his parents thinking? Didn't they teach him how to wash? But you at least didn't make fun of his smell. Even though the other kids did."

"Well, I sort of did," the kid says.

"When?" says Marty. "On the day his pants ripped?"

"No," the kid says. "On the day my shoe split."

"Probably he was making fun of you on that day," suggests Marty.

"No," the kid says. "He was just kind of standing there. But a few kids were looking at my shoe funny. Because my foot was poking out? So I asked Simon why he smelled so bad."

"And the other kids laughed?" says Marty. "They thought that was pretty good? What did he say? Did he stop making fun of your shoes?"

"Well, he hadn't really started yet," the kid says. "But he was about to."

"I bet he was," says Marty. "But you stopped him dead in his tracks. What did he say? After you made that crack about his smell?"

"He said maybe he did smell but at least his shoes weren't cheap," says the kid.

"So he turned it around on you," says Marty. "Very clever. The little shit. But listen, those shoes weren't cheap. I paid good money for those shoes."

"Okay," says the kid, and throws the ball into the woods.

"Nice throw," says Marty. "Very powerful."

"Kind of crooked though," says the kid, and runs off into the woods to get the ball.

"My kid," Marty says to me. "Home on break from school. We got him in boarding school. Only the best for my kid! Until they close us down, that is. You heard anything? Anything bad? I heard they might be axing Sheep May Safely Graze. So that's like fifteen shepherds. Which would kill me. I get a lot of biz off those shepherds. Needless to say, I am shitting bricks. Because if they close me, what do you think happens to that kid out there in the woods right now? Boarding school? You think boarding school happens? In a pig's ass. Boarding school does not happen, the opposite of boarding school happens, and he will be very freaking upset."

The kid comes jogging out of the woods with the ball in his hand.

"What are you talking about?" he says.

"About you," Marty says, and puts the kid in a headlock. "About how great you are. How lovable you are."

"Oh that," the kid says, and smiles big.

18.

That night around nine I hear a sort of shriek from Janet's Separate Area.

A shriek, and then what sounds like maybe sobbing.

Then some louder sobbing and maybe something breaking, possibly her fax?

I go to her door and ask is she okay and she tells me go away.

I can't get back to sleep. So I fax Louise.

Everything okay? I write.

In about ten minutes a fax comes back.

Did Dr. Evans ever say anything about complete loss of mobility? it says. *I mean complete. Today I took the kids to the park and let Ace off the leash and he saw a cat and ran off. When I came back from getting Ace, Nelson was like stuck inside this crawling tube. Like he couldn't stand up? Had no power in his legs. I mean none. That fucking Ace. If you could've seen Nelson's face. God. When I picked him up he said he thought I'd gone home without him. The poor thing. Plus he had to pee. And so he'd sort of peed himself. Not much, just a little. Other than that all is well, please don't worry. Well worry a little. We are at the end of our rope or however you say it, I'm already deep into the overdraft account and it's only the 5th. Plus I'm so tired at night I can't get to the bills and the last time I paid late fees on both Visas and the MasterCard, thirty bucks a pop, those bastards, am thinking about just sawing off my arm and mailing it in. Ha ha, not really, I need that arm to sign checks.*

Love, Me

From Janet's Separate Area come additional sobbing and some angry shouting.

I fax back:

Did you take him to Dr. Evans? I say.

Duh, she faxes back. *Have appt for Weds, will let you know. Don't worry, just do your job and also Nelson says hi and you're the best dad ever.*

Tell him hi and he's the best kid, I fax back.

What about the other kids? she faxes back.

Tell them they're also the best kids, I fax back.

From Janet's Separate Area comes the sound of Janet pounding on something repeatedly, probably her desk, presumably with her fist.

19.

Next morning in the Big Slot is no goat. Just a note.

From Janet:

Not coming in, it says. *Bradley lied about the tooters and bought some you-know-what. Big suprise right? Is in jail. Stupid dumbass. Got a fax last night. Plus my Ma's worse. Before she couldnt get up or her lungs filled with blood? Well now they fill with blood unless she switchs from side to side and who's there to switch her? Before Mrs Finn was but now Mrs Finn got a day-job so no more. So now I have to find someone and pay someone. Ha ha very funny, like I can aford that. Plus Bradley's bail which beleve me I have defnitely considered not paying. With all this going on no way am I caving it up today. I'm sorry but I just cant, don't narc me out, okay? Just this one last time. I'm taking a Sick Day.*

She can't do that. She can't take a Sick Day if she's not sick. She can't take a Sick Day because she's sad about someone she loves being sick. And she certainly can't take a Sick Day because she's sad about someone she loves being in jail.

I count out ten Reserve Crackers and work all morning on the pictographs.

Around noon the door to her Separate Area flies open. She looks weird. Her hair is sticking up and she's wearing an I'm With Stupid sweatshirt over her cavewoman robe and her breath smells like whiskey.

Janet is wasted? Wasted in the cave?

"What I have here in this album?" she says. "Baby pictures of that fucking rat Bradley. Back when I loved him so much. Back before he was a druggie. See how cute? See how smart he looked?"

She shows me the album. He actually does not look cute or smart. He looks the same as he looked the other day, only smaller. In one picture he's sitting on a tricycle looking like he's planning a heist. In another he's got a sour look on his face and his hand down some smaller kid's diaper.

"God, you just love the little shits no matter what, don't you?" she says. "You know what I'm saying? If Bradley's dad woulda stuck around it might've been better. Bradley never knew him. I always used to say he took one look at Bradley and ran off. Maybe I shouldn't of said that. At least not in front of Bradley. Wow. I've had a few snorts. You want a snort? Come on, live a little! Take a Sick Day like me. I had three BallBusters and half a bottle of wine. This is the best Sick Day I ever took."

I guide her back to her Separate Area and push her sternly in.

"Come on in!" she says. "Have a BallBuster. You want one? I'm lonely in here. You want a BallBuster, Señor Tightass?"

I do not want a BallBuster.

What I want is for her to stay in her Separate Area keeping very quiet until she sobers up.

All day I sit alone in the cave. When the quality of light changes I go into my Separate Area and take out a Daily Partner Performance Evaluation Form.

When I was a kid, Dad worked at Kenner Beef. Loins would drop from his belt and he'd cut through this purple tendon and use a sort of vise to squeeze some blood into a graduated beaker for testing, then wrap the loin in a sling and swing it down to Finishing. Dad's partner was Fred Lank. Lank had a metal plate in his skull and went into these funks where he'd forget to cut the purple tendon and fail to squeeze out the blood and instead of placing the loin in the sling would just sort of drop the loin down on Finishing. When Lank went into a funk, Dad would cover for him by doing double loins. Sometimes Dad would do double loins for days at a time. When Dad died, Lank sent Mom a check for a thousand dollars, with a note:

Please keep, it said. *The man did so much for me.*

Which is I think part of the reason I'm having trouble ratting Janet out.

Do I note any attitudinal difficulties? I do not. How do I rate my Partner overall? Very good. Are there any Situations which require Mediation?

There are not.

I fax it in.

20.

Next morning in the Big Slot is no goat, just a note:

A question has arisen, it says. *Hence this note about a touchy issue that is somewhat grotesque and personal, but we must address it, because one of you raised it, the issue of which was why do we require that you Remote Attractions pay the money which we call, and ask that you call, the Disposal Debit, but which you people insist on wrongly calling the Shit Fee. Well, this is to tell you why, although isn't it obvious to most? We hope. But maybe not. Because what we have found, no offense, is that sometimes you people don't get things that seem pretty obvious to us, such as why you have to pay for your Cokes in your fridge if you drink them. Who should then? Did we drink your Cokes you drank? We doubt it. You did it. Likewise with what you so wrongly call the Shit Fee, because why do you expect us to pay to throw away your poop when after all you made it? Do you think your poop is a legitimate business expense? Does it provide benefit to us when you defecate? No, on the contrary, it would provide benefit if you didn't, because then you would be working more. Ha ha! That is a joke. We know very well that all must poop. We grant you that. But also, as we all know, it takes time to poop, some more than others. As we get older, we notice this, don't you? Not that we're advocating some sort of biological plug or chemical constipator. Not yet, anyway! No, that would be wrong, we know that, and unhealthy, and no doubt some of you would complain about having to pay for the constipators, expecting us to provide them gratis.*

That is another funny thing with some of you, we notice it, namely that, not ever having been up here, in our shoes, you always want something for nothing. You just don't get it! When you poop and it takes a long time and you are on the clock, do you ever see us outside looking mad with a stopwatch? So therefore please stop saying to us: I have defecated while on the clock, dispose of it for free, kindly absorb my expense. We find that loopy. Because, as you know, you Remote Locations are far away, and have no pipes, and hence we must pay for the trucks. The trucks that drive your poop. Your poop to the pipes. Why are you so silly? It is as if you expect us to provide those Cokes for free, just because you thirst. Do Cokes grow on trees? Well, the other thing that does not grow on a tree is a poop truck. Perhaps someone should explain to you the idea of how we do things, which is to make money. And why? Is it greed? Don't make us laugh. It is not. If we make money, we can grow, if we can grow, we can expand, if we can expand, we can continue to employ you, but if we shrink, if we shrink or stay the same, woe to you, we would not be vital. And so help us help you, by not whining about your Disposal Debit, and if you don't like how much it costs, try eating less.

And by the way, we are going to be helping you in this, by henceforth sending less food. We're not joking, this is austerity. We think you will see a substantial savings in terms of your Disposal Debits, as you eat less and your Human Refuse bags get smaller and smaller. And that, our friends, is a substantial savings that we, we up here, will not see, and do you know why not? I mean, even if we were eating less, which we already have decided we will not be? In order to keep our strength up? So we can continue making sound decisions? But do you know why we will not see the substantial savings you lucky ducks will? Because, as some of you have already grumbled about, we pay no Shit Fee, those of us up here. So that even if we shat less, we would realize no actual savings. And why do we pay no Shit Fee? Because that was negotiated into our contracts at Time-of-Hire. What would you have had us do? Negotiate inferior contracts? Act against our own healthy self-interest? Don't talk crazy. Please talk sense. Many of us have Student Loans to repay. Times are hard, entire Units are being eliminated, the Staff Remixing continues, so no more talk of defecation flaring up, please, only let's remember that we are a family, and you are the children, not that we're saying you're immature, only that you do most of the chores while we do all the thinking, and also that we, in our own way, love you.

For several hours Janet does not come out.

Probably she is too hungover.

Around eleven she comes out, holding her copy of the memo.

"So what are they saying?" she says. "Less food? Even less food than now?"

I nod.

"Jesus Christ," she says. "I'm starving as it is."

I give her a look.

"I know, I know, I fucked up," she says. "I was a little buzzed. A little buzzed in the cave. Boo-hoo. Don't tell me, you narced me out, right? Did you? Of course you did."

I give her a look.

"You didn't?" she says. "Wow. You're even nicer than I thought. You're the best, man. And starting right now, no more screw-ups. I know I said that before. But this time, for real. You watch."

Just then there's a huge clunk in the Big Slot.

"Excellent!" she says. "I hope it's a big thing of Motrin."

But it's not a big thing of Motrin. It's a goat. A weird-looking goat. Actually a plastic goat. With a predrilled hole for the spit to go through. In the mouth is a Baggie and in the Baggie is a note:

In terms of austerity, it says. *No goat today. In terms of verisimilitude, mount this fake goat and tend as if real. Mount well above fire to avoid burning. In event of melting, squelch fire. In event of burning, leave area, burning plastic may release harmful fumes.*

I mount the fake goat on the spit and Janet sits on the boulder with her head in her hands.

21.

Next morning is once again the morning I empty our Human Refuse bags and the trash bags and the bag from the bottom of the sleek metal hole where Janet puts her used feminine items.

I knock on the door of her Separate Area.

Janet slides the bags out, all sealed and labeled and ready to go.

"Check it out," she says. "I'm a new woman."

Out I go, with the white regular trash bag in one hand and our mutual big pink Human Refuse bag in the other.

I walk along the white cliff, then down the path marked by the small yellow dot on the pine etc. etc.

On the door of Marty's doublewide is a note:

Due to circumstances beyond our control we are no longer here, it says. *But please know how much we appreciated your patronage. As to why we are not here, we will not comment on that, because we are bigger than that. Bigger than some people. Some people are snakes. To some people, fifteen years of good loyal service means squat. All's we can say is, watch your damn backs.*

All the best and thanks for the memories,

Marty and Jeannine and little Eddie.

Then the door flies open.

Marty and Jeannine and little Eddie are standing there holding suitcases.

"Hello and good-bye," says Marty. "Feel free to empty your shit bag inside the store."

"Now, Marty," says Jeannine. "Let's try and be positive about this, okay? We're going to do fine. You're too good for this dump anyway. I've always said you were too good for this dump."

"Actually, Jeannine," Marty says. "When I first got this job you said I was lucky to even get a job, because of my dyslexia."

"Well, honey, you are dyslexic," says Jeannine.

"I never denied being dyslexic," says Marty.

"He writes his letters and numbers backwards," Jeannine says to me.

"What are you, turning on me, Jeannine?" Marty says. "I lose my job and you turn on me?"

"Oh Marty, I'm not turning on you," Jeannine says. "I'm not going to stop loving you just because you've got troubles. Just like you've never stopped loving me, even though I've got troubles."

"She gets too much spit in her mouth," Marty says to me.

"Marty!" says Jeannine.

"What?" Marty says. "You can say I'm dyslexic, but I can't say you get too much spit in your mouth?"

"Marty, please," she says. "You're acting crazy."

"I'm not acting crazy," he says. "It's just that you're turning on me."

"Don't worry about me, Dad," the kid says. "I won't turn on you. And I don't mind going back to my old school. Really I don't."

"He had a little trouble with mean kids in his old school," Marty says to me. "Which is why we switched him. Although nothing you couldn't handle, right, kid? Actually, I think it was good for him. Taught him toughness."

"As long as nobody padlocks me to the boiler again," the kid says. "That part I really didn't like. Wow, those rats or whatever."

"I doubt those were actual rats," says Marty. "More than likely they were cats. The janitor's cats. My guess is, it was dark in that boiler room and you couldn't tell a cat from a rat."

"The janitor didn't have any cats," the kid says. "And he said I was lucky those rats didn't start biting my pants. Because of the pudding smell. From when those kids pinned me down and poured pudding down my pants."

"Was that the same day?" Marty says. "The rats and the pudding? I guess I didn't realize them two things were on the same day. Wow, I guess you learned a lot of toughness on that day."

"I guess so," the kid says.

"But nothing you couldn't handle," Marty says.

"Nothing I couldn't handle," the kid says, and blinks, and his eyes water up.

"Well, Christ," Marty says, and his eyes also water up. "Time to hit the road, family. I guess this it. Let's say our good-byes. Our good-byes to Home Sweet Home."

They take a little tour around the doublewide and do a family hug, then drag their suitcases down the path.

I go to the Refuse Center and weigh our Human Refuse. I put the paperwork and the fee in the box labeled Paperwork and Fees. I toss the trash in the dumpster labeled Trash, and the Human Refuse in the dumpster labeled Caution Human Refuse.

I feel bad for Marty and Jeannine, and especially I feel bad for the kid.

I try to imagine Nelson padlocked to a boiler in a dark room full of rats.

Plus now where are us Remotes supposed to go for our smokes and mints and Kayos?

22.

Back at the cave Janet is working very industriously on the pictographs.

As I come in she points to my Separate Area while mouthing the word: Fax.

I look at her. She looks at me.

She mouths the words: Christ, go. Then she holds one hand at knee level, to indicate Nelson.

I go.

But it's not for me, it's for her.

Ms. Foley's fax appears to be inoperative? the cover letter says. *Kindly forward the attached.*

Please be informed, the attached fax says, *I did my very best in terms of your son, and this appeared, in my judgment, to be an excellent plea bargain, which, although to some might appear disadvantageous, ten years is not all that long when you consider all the bad things that he has done. But he was happy enough about it, after some initial emotions such as limited weeping, and thanked me for my hard work, although not in those exact words, as he was fairly, you know, upset. On a personal note, may I say how sorry I am, but also that in the grand scheme of things such as geology ten years is not so very long really.*

Sincerely,

Evan Joeller, Esq.

I take the fax out to Janet, who reads it while sitting on her log.

She's sort of a slow reader.

When she's finally done she looks crazy and for a minute I think she's going to tear the cave apart but instead she scoots into the corner and starts frantically pretending to catch and eat small bugs.

I go over and put my hand on her shoulder, like: Are you okay?

She pushes my hand away roughly and continues to pretend to catch and eat small bugs.

Just then someone pokes their head in.

Young guy, round head, expensive-looking glasses.

"Bibby, hand me up Cole," he says. "So he can see. Cole-Cole, can you see? Here. Daddy will hold you up."

A little kid's head appears alongside the dad's head.

"Isn't this cool, Cole?" says the dad. "Aren't you glad Mommy and Daddy brought you? Remember Daddy told you? How people used to live in caves?"

"They did not," the little boy says. "You're wrong."

"Bibby, did you hear that?" the dad says. "He just said I'm wrong. About people living in caves."

"I heard it," says a woman from outside. "Cole, people really did use to live in caves. Daddy's not wrong."

"Daddy's always wrong," says the little boy.

"He just said I'm always wrong," the dad says. "Did you hear that? Did you write that down? In the memory book? Talk about assertive! I should be so assertive. Wouldn't Norm and Larry croak if I was suddenly so assertive?"

"Well, it couldn't hurt you," the mom says.

"Believe me, I know," the dad says. "That's why I said it. I know very well I could afford to be more assertive. I was making a joke. Like an ironic joke at my own expense."

"I want to stab you, Dad," says the little boy. "With a sharp sword, you're so dumb."

"Ha ha!" says the dad. "But don't forget, Cole-Cole, the pen is mightier than the sword! Remember that? Remember I taught you that? Wouldn't it be better to compose an insulting poem, if you have something negative about me you want to convey? Now that's real power! Bibby, did you hear what he said? And then what I said? Did you write all that down? Also did you save that Popsicle wrapper? Did you stick it in the pocket in the back cover of the memory book and write down how cute he looked eating it?"

"What your name?" the little boy yells at me.

I cower and shriek in the corner etc. etc.

"What your name I said!" the little boy shouts at me. "I hate you!"

"Now, Cole-Cole," says the dad. "Let's not use the word hate, okay, buddy? Remember what I told you? About hate being the nasty dark crayon and love being the pink? And remember what I told you about the clanging gong? And remember I told you about the bad people in the old days, who used to burn witches, and how scary that must've been for the witches, who were really just frightened old ladies who'd made the mistake of being too intelligent for the era they were living in?"

"You are not acceptable!" the kid shouts at me.

"Ha ha, oh my God!" says the dad. "Bibby, did you get that? Did you write that down? He's imitating us. Because we say that to him? Write down how mad he is. Look how red his face is! Look at him kick his feet. Wow, he is really pissed. Cole, good persistence! Remember how Daddy told you about the little train that could? How everyone kept trying to like screw it and not give it its due, and how finally it got really mad and stomped its foot and got its way? Remember I told you about Chief Joseph, who never stopped walking? You're like him. My brave little warrior. Bibby, give him a juice box. Also he's got some goo-goo coming out of his nosehole."

"Jesus Christ," Janet mumbles.

I give her my sternest look.

"What was that?" said the dad. "I'm sorry, I didn't hear you. What did you say?"

"Nothing," Janet says. "I didn't say nothing."

"I heard you very clearly," says the dad. "You said Jesus Christ. You said Jesus Christ because of what I said about the goo-goo in my son's nosehole. Well, first of all, I'm sorry if you find a little boy's nosehole goo-goo sickening, it's perfectly normal, if you had a kid of your own you'd know that, and second of all, since when do cavepeople speak English and know who Jesus Christ is? Didn't the cavepeople predate Christ, if I'm not mistaken?"

"Of course they did," the mom says from outside. "We just came from Christ. Days of Christ. And we're going backwards. Towards the exit."

"Look, pal, I got a kid," says Janet. "I seen plenty of snot. I just never called it goo-goo. That's all I'm saying."

"Bibby, get this," the dad says. "Parenting advice from the cavelady. The cavelady apparently has some strong opinions on booger nomenclature. For this I paid eighty bucks? If I want somebody badly dressed to give me a bunch of lip I can go to your mother's house."

"Very funny," says the mom.

"I meant it funny," says the dad.

"I was a good mom," Janet says. "My kid is as good as anybody's kid."

"Hey, share it with us," says the dad.

"Even if he is in jail," says Janet.

"Bibby, get this," says the dad. "The cavelady's kid is in jail."

"Don't you *even* make fun of my kid, you little suckass," says Janet.

"The cavelady just called you a suckass," says the mom.

"A little suckass," says the dad. "And don't think I'm going to forget it."

Soon flying in through the hole where the heads poke in is our wadded-up Client Vignette Evaluation.

Under *Learning Value* he's written: *Disastrous. We learned that some*

*caveladies had potty mouths. I certainly felt like I was in the actual Nean-
derthal days. Not!*

Under *Overall Impression* he's written: *The cavelady called me a suckass
in front of my child. Thanks so much! A tremendous and offensive waste of
time. LOSE THE CAVELADY, SHE IS THE WORST.*

"Know what I'm doing now?" the guy says. "I'm walking my copy
down to the main office. Your ass is grass, lady."

"Oh shit," Janet says, and sits on the log. "Shit shit shit. I really totally
blew it, didn't I?"

My God, did she ever. She really totally blew it.

"What are you going to do, man?" Janet says. "Are you going to narc
me out?"

I give her a look, like: Will you just please shut up?

The rest of the day we sit on our respective logs.

When the quality of light changes I go to my Separate Area and take
out a Daily Partner Performance Evaluation Form.

A note comes sliding under my door.

I have a idea, it says. *Maybe you could say that ashole made it all up? Like
he came in and tried to get fresh with me and when I wouldnt let him he
made it up? That could work. I think it could work. Please please don't narc
me out, if I get fired I'm dead, you know all the shit that's going on with me,
plus you have to admit I was doing pretty good before this.*

She was doing pretty good before this.

I think of Nelson. His wispy hair and crooked nose. When I thank him
for bravely taking all his medications he always rests his head on my shoulder and says, No problem. Only he can't say his *r*'s. So it's like: No
pwoblem. And then he pats my belly, as if I'm the one who bravely took all
my medications.

Do I note any attitudinal difficulties?

I write: *Yes.*

How do I rate my Partner overall?

I write: *Poor.*

Are there any Situations which require Mediation?

I write: *Today Janet unfortunately interacted negatively with a Guest.
Today Janet swore at a Guest in the cave. Today Janet unfortunately called a
Guest a "suckass," in English, in the cave.*

I look it over.

It's all true.

I fax it in.

23.

A few minutes later my fax makes the sound it makes when a fax is coming in.

From Nordstrom:

This should be sufficient! it says. *Super! More than sufficient. Good for you. Feel no guilt. Are you Janet? Is Janet you? I think not. I think that you are you and she is she. You guys are not the same entity. You are distinct. Is her kid your kid? Is your kid her kid? No, her kid is her kid and your kid is your kid. Have you guilt? About what you have done? Please do not. Please have pride. What I suggest? Think of you and Janet as branches on a tree. While it's true that a branch sometimes needs to be hacked off and come floating down, so what, that is only one branch, it does not kill the tree, and sometimes one branch must die so that the others may live. And anyway, it only looks like death, because you are falsely looking at this through the lens of an individual limb or branch, when in fact you should be thinking in terms of the lens of what is the maximum good for the overall organism, our tree. When we chop one branch, we all become stronger! And that branch on the ground, looking up, has the pleasure of knowing that he or she made the tree better, which I hope Janet will do. Although knowing her? With her crappy attitude? Probably she will lie on the ground wailing and gnashing her leaves while saying swear words up at us. But who cares! She is gone. She is a goner. And we have you to thank. So thanks! This is the way organizations grow and thrive, via small courageous contributions by cooperative selfless helpers, who are able to do that hardest of things, put aside the purely personal aspect in order to see the big picture. Oh and also, you might want to be out of the cave around ten, as that is when the deed will be done.*

Thanks so much!

Greg N.

I lie there counting and recounting the acoustic tiles on the ceiling of my darkened Separate Area.

One hundred forty-four.

24.

Next morning is not the morning I empty our Human Refuse bags and the trash bags and the bag from the bottom of the sleek metal hole, but I get up extremely early, in fact it is still dark, and leave Janet a note saying I've gone to empty our Human Refuse bags and our trash bags and the bag from the bottom of her sleek metal hole etc. etc., then very quietly sneak out of the cave and cross the river via wading and sit among the feeding things, facing away from the cave.

I sit there a long time.

When I get back, Janet's gone and the door to her Separate Area is hanging open and her Separate Area is completely empty.

Except for a note taped to the wall:

You freak you break my heart, it says. *Thanks a million. What the fuck am I supposed to do now? I guess I will go home and flip Ma from side to side until she dies from starving to death because we got no money. And then maybe I will hore myself with a jail gard to get Bradley out. I cant beleve after all this time you tern on me. And here I thought you were my frend but you were only interested in your own self. Not that I blame you. I mean, I do and I dont. Actually I do.*

You bastard,

Janet.

There are several big clunks in the Big Slot.

A goat, some steaks, four boxes of hash browns, caramel corn in a metal tub, several pies, bottles of Coke and Sprite, many many small containers of Kayo.

I look at that food a long time.

Then I stash it in my Separate Area, for later use.

For lunch I have a steak and hash browns and some pie and a Kayo.

Eating hash browns and pie and drinking Kayo in the cave is probably verboten but I feel I've somewhat earned it.

I clean up the mess. I sit on the log.

Around two there is a little tiny click in the Little Slot.

25.

A memo, to Distribution:

Regarding the rumors you may have lately been hearing, it says. *Please be advised that they are false. They are so false that we considered not even bothering to deny them. Because denying them would imply that we have actually heard them. Which we haven't. We don't waste our time on such nonsense. And yet we know that if we don't deny the rumors we haven't heard, you will assume they are true. And they are so false! So let us just categorically state that all the rumors you've been hearing are false. Not only the rumors you've heard, but also those you haven't heard, and even those that haven't yet been spread, are false. However, there is one exception to this, and that is if the rumor is good. That is, if the rumor presents us, us up here, in a positive light, and our mission, and our accomplishments, in that case, and in that case only, we will have to admit that the rumor you've been hearing is right on target, and congratulate you on your fantastic powers of snooping, to have found out that secret super thing! In summary, we simply ask you to ask yourself, upon hearing a rumor: Does this rumor cast the organization in a negative light? If so, that rumor is false, please disregard. If positive, super, thank you very much for caring so deeply about your organization that you knelt with your ear to the track, and also, please spread the truth far and wide, that is, get down on all fours and put your own lips to the tracks. Tell your friends. Tell friends who are thinking of buying stock. Do you have friends who are journalists? Put your lips to their tracks.*

Because what is truth? Truth is that thing which makes what we want to happen happen. Truth is that thing which, when told, makes those on our team look good, and inspires them to greater efforts, and causes people not on our team to see things our way and feel sort of jealous. Truth is that thing which empowers us to do even better than we are already doing, which by the way is fine, we are doing fine, truth is the wind in our sails that blows only for us. So when a rumor makes you doubt us, us up here, it is therefore not true, since we have already defined truth as that thing which helps us win. Therefore, if you want to know what is true, simply ask what is best. Best for us, all of us. Do you get our drift? Contrary to rumor, the next phase of the Staff Remixing is not about to begin. The slightest excuse, the slightest negligence, will not be used as the basis for firing the half of you we would be firing over the next few weeks if the rumor you have all probably heard by now about the mass firings were true. Which it is not. See? See how we just did that? Transformed that trashy negative rumor into truth? Go forth and do that, you'll see it's pretty fun. And in terms of mass firings, relax, none are forthcoming, truly, and furthermore, if they were, what you'd want to ask yourself is: Am I Thinking Positive/Saying Positive? Am I giving it all I've got? Am I doing even the slightest thing wrong? But not to worry. Those of you who have no need to be worried should not in the least be worried. As for those who should be worried, it's a little late to start worrying now, you should have started months ago, when it could've done you some good, because at this point, what's decided is decided, or would have been decided, if those false rumors we are denying, the rumors about the firings which would be starting this week if they were slated to begin, were true, which we have just told you, they aren't.

More firings?

God.

I return to the log.

Sort of weird without Janet.

Someone pokes their head in.

A young woman in a cavewoman robe.

26.

She walks right in and hands me a sealed note.

From Nordstrom:

Please meet Linda, it says. Your total new Partner. Sort of cute, yes? Under that robe is quite a bod, believe me, I saw her in slacks. See why I was trying to get rid of Janet? But also you will find she is serious. Just like you. See that brow? It is permanent, she had it sort of installed. Like once every six months she goes in for a touch-up where they spray it from a can to harden it. You can give it a little goose with your thumb, it feels like real skin. But don't try it, as I said, she is very serious, she only let me try it because I am who I am, in the interview, but if you try it, my guess is? She will write you up. Or flatten you! Because it is not authentic that one caveperson would goose another caveperson in the brow with his thumb in the cave. I want us now, post-Janet, to really strive for some very strict verisimilitude. You may, for example, wish to consider having such a perma-brow installed on yourself. To save you the trouble of every day redoing that brow, which I know is a pain. Anyway,

I think you and Linda will get along super. So here is your new mate! Not that I'm saying mate with her, I would not try that, she is, as I said, very serious, but if you were going to mate with her, don't you think she looks more appropriate, I means she is at least younger than Janet and not so hard on the eyes.

I put out my hand and smile.

She frowns at my hand, like: Since when do cavepeople shake hands?

She squats and pretends to be catching and eating small bugs.

How she knows how to do that, I do not know.

I squat beside her and also pretend to be catching and eating small bugs.

We do this for quite some time. It gets old but she doesn't stop, and all the time she's grunting, and once or twice I could swear she actually catches and eats an actual small bug.

Around noon my fax makes the sound it makes when a fax is coming in.

From Louise? Probably. Almost definitely. The only other person who ever faxes me is Nordstrom, and he just faxed me last night, plus he just sent me a note.

I stand up.

Linda gives me a look. Her brow is amazing. It has real actual pores on it.

I squat down.

I pretend to catch and eat a small bug.

The fax stops making the sound it makes when a fax is coming in. Presumably the fax from Louise is in the tray, waiting for me to read it. Is something wrong? Has something changed? What did Dr. Evans say about Nelson's complete loss of mobility?

Five more hours and I can enter my Separate Area and find out.

Which is fine. Really not a problem.

Because I'm Thinking Positive/Saying Positive.

Maybe if I explained to Linda about Nelson it would be okay, but I feel a little funny trying to explain about Nelson so early in our working relationship.

All afternoon we pretend to catch and eat small bugs. We pretend to catch and eat more pretend bugs than could ever actually live in one cave. The number of pretend bugs we pretend to catch and eat would in reality basically fill a cave the size of our cave. It feels like we're racing. At one point she gives me a look, like: Slow down, going so fast is inauthentic. I slow down. I slow down, monitoring my rate so that I am pretending to catch and eat small bugs at exactly the same rate at which she is pretending to catch and eat small bugs, which seems to be prudent, I mean, there is no way she could have a problem with the way I'm pretending to catch and eat small bugs if I'm doing it exactly the way she's doing it.

No one pokes their head in.

Andrea Barrett

Servants of the Map

From *Salmagundi*

1.

H E DOES not write to his wife about the body found on a mountain that is numbered but still to be named: not about the bones, the shreds of the tent, the fragile, browning skull. He says nothing about the diary wedged beneath the rock, or about how it felt to turn the rippled pages. Unlike himself, the surveyor thinks, the lost man traveled alone. Not attached to a branch, however small and insignificant, of the Great Trigonometrical Survey of India. On this twig charged to complete the Kashmir Series, he is nothing. A leaf, an apricot, easily replaced; a Civil Junior Sub-Assistant in the Himalayan Service.

The surveyor, whose name is Max Vigne, reads through the diary before relinquishing it to his superiors. The handwriting trembled in the final pages, the entries growing shorter and more confused. Hail storms, lightning storms, the loss of a little shaving mirror meant to send a glinting signal from the summit to the admiring crowds below—after noting these, the lost man wrote:

"I have been fasting. Several weeks—the soul detaches from the flesh. The ills of spirit and body are washed away and here on the roof of the world, in the abode of snow, one becomes greatly strengthened yet as fresh as a child."

Although Max pauses in wonder over these lines, he still doesn't share them with his wife. Instead he writes:

April 13, 1863

Dear Clara—

I can hardly understand where I am myself; how shall I explain it to you? Try to imagine the whole chain of the Himalaya, as wide as England and four times its length. Then imagine our speck of a surveying party tucked in the northwest corner, where the Great Himalaya tangles into the Karakoram—or not quite there, but almost there. We are at the edge of the land called Baltistan, or Little Tibet: Ladakh and Greater Tibet lie to the east. And it is so much more astonishing than we imagined. The mountains I wrote you about earlier, which we crossed to enter the Vale of Kashmir— everything I said about them was true, they dwarf the highest peaks I saw at home. But the land I am headed toward dwarfs in turn the range that lies behind me. Last Wednesday, after breakfast, the low clouds lifted and the sun came out. To the north a huge white mass remained, stretching clear across the horizon. I was worried about an approaching storm. Then I realized those improbable masses were mountains, shimmering and seeming to float over the plains below.

How I wish you could see this for yourself. I have had no mail from you since Srinagar, but messengers do reach us despite our frequent moves and I am hopeful. This morning I opened an envelope from the little trunk you sent with me. Have any of my letters reached you yet? If they have, you will know how much your messages have cheered me. No one but you, my love, would have thought to do this. On the ship, then during our tedious journey across the plains to the Pir Panjal; and even more throughout the weeks of preparation and training in Srinagar, your words have been my great consolation. I wait like a child on Christmas Eve for the dates you have marked on each envelope to arrive: I obey you, you see; I have not cheated. Now that the surveying season has finally begun and we're on the move, I treasure these even more. I wish I had thought to leave behind a similar gift for you. The letters I wrote you from Srinagar—I know the details about my work could not have been of much interest to you. But I mean to do better, now that we're entering this astonishing range. If I share with you what I see, what I feel: will that be a kind of gift?

Yours marked to be opened today, the anniversary of that wonderful walk along the Ouse when I asked you to marry me and, against a background of spinning windmills and little boys searching for eels, you stood so sleek and beautiful and you said "yes"—it made me remember the feel of your hand in mine, it was like holding you. I am glad you plan to continue with your German. By now you must have opened the birthday gifts I left for you. Did you like the dictionary? And the necklace?

I should try to catch you up on our journeys of these last few weeks. From Srinagar we labored over the Gurais pass, still knee-deep in snow: my four fellow plane-tablers, the six Indian chainmen, a crowd of Kashmiri and Balti porters, and Michaels, who has charge of us for the summer. Captain Montgomerie of the Bengal Engineers, head of the entire Kashmir Series, we have not seen since leaving Srinagar. I am told it is his habit to tour the mountains from April until October, inspecting the many small parties of triangulators and plane-tablers, of which we are only one. The complexities of the Survey's organization are beyond explaining: a confusion of military men and civilians, Scots and Irish and English; and then the assistants and porters, all races and castes. All I can tell you is that, although we civilians may rise in the ranks of the Survey, even the most senior of us may never have charge of the military officers. And I am the most junior of all.

From the top of the pass I saw the mountain called Nanga Parbat, monstrous and beautiful, forty miles away. Then we were in the village of Gurais, where we gathered more provisions and porters to replace those returning to Srinagar. Over the Burzil pass and across the Deosai plateau—it is from here that I write to you, a grassy land populated by chattering rodents called marmots. The air is clear beyond clearness today and to the north rises that wall of snowy summits I first mistook for a cloud: the Karakoram range, which we are to map. Even this far away I can see the massive glaciers explored by Godfrey Vigne, to whom I am so tangentially related.

I wonder what he would have thought of me ending up here?

Often people ask if I'm related to that famous man but I deny it; it would be wrong of me, even now that he's dead, to claim such a distant connection. My eccentric, sometimes malicious supervisor, Michaels (an Irishman and former soldier of the Indian Army), persists in calling me "Mr. Vaahn-ya," in an atrocious French accent. This although I have reminded him repeatedly that ours is a good East Anglian family, even if we do have Huguenot ancestors, and that we say the name "Vine."

All the men who've explored these mountains—what a secret, isolated world this is! A kind of archipelago, sparsely populated, visited now and again by passing strangers; each hidden valley an island unto itself, inhabited by small groups of people wildly distinct from each other—it is as if, at home, a day's journey in one direction brought us to Germany, another's to Africa. As if, in the distance between the fens and the moors, there were twenty separate kingdoms. I have more to tell you, so much more, but it is late and I must sleep.

What doesn't he tell Clara? So much, so much. The constant discomforts of the body, the hardships of the daily climbs, the exhaustion, the loneliness: he won't reveal the things that would worry her. He restrains himself, a constant battle; the battle itself another thing he doesn't write about. He hasn't said a word about the way his fellow surveyors tease him. His youth, his chunky, short-legged frame and terribly white skin; the mop of bright yellow hair on his head and the paucity of it elsewhere: although he keeps up with the best of them, and is often the last to tire, he is ashamed each time they strip their clothes to bathe in a freezing stream or a glacial tarn. His British companions are tall and hairy, browning in the sun; the Indians and Kashmiris and Baltis smoother and slighter but dark; he alone looks like a figure made from snow. The skin peels off his nose until he bleeds. When he extends his hat brim with strips of bark, in an effort to fend off the burning rays, Michaels asks him why he doesn't simply use a parasol.

Michaels himself is thickly pelted, fleshy and sweaty, strong-smelling and apparently impervious to the sun. They have all grown beards, shaving is impossible; only Max's is blonde and sparse. He gets teased for this, for the ease with which he burns, and sometimes, more cruelly, for the golden curls around his genitals. Not since he was fourteen, when he first left school and began his apprenticeship on the railway survey, has he been so mocked. Then he had his older brother, Laurence, to protect him. But here he is on his own.

The men are amused not only by his looks, but by his box of books and by the pretty, brass-bound trunk that holds Clara's precious gift to him: a long series of letters, some written by her and others begged from their family and friends. The first is dated the week after he left home, the last more than a year hence; all are marked to be opened on certain dates and anniversaries. Who but Clara would have thought of such a gift? Who else would have had the imagination to project herself into the future, sensing what he might feel like a week, a month, a year from leaving home and writing what might comfort him then?

His companions have not been so lucky. Some are single; others married but to wives they seem not to miss or perhaps are even relieved to have left behind. A Yorkshireman named Wyatt stole one of Clara's missives from Max's campstool, where he'd left it while fetching a cup of tea. "Listen to this," Wyatt said: laughing, holding the letter above Max's head and reading aloud to the entire party. "Max, you must wear your woolly vest, you know how cold you get." Now the men ask tauntingly, every day, what he's read from the trunk. He comforts himself by believing that they're jealous.

A more reliable comfort is his box of books. In it, beyond the mathematical and cartographical texts he needs for his work, are three other gifts. With money she'd saved from the household accounts, Clara bought him a copy of Joseph Hooker's *Himalayan Journals.* This Max cherishes for the thought behind it, never correcting her misapprehension that Sikkim, where Hooker traveled in 1848, is only a stone's throw from where Max is traveling now. At home, with a map, he might have put his left thumb on the Karakoram range and his right, many inches away to the east, on the lands that Hooker explored: both almost equally far from England, yet still far apart themselves. Clara might have smiled—despite her interest in Max's work, geography sometimes eludes her—but that last evening passed in such a flurry that all he managed to do was to thank her. For his brother Laurence, who gave him a copy of Charles Darwin's *Origin of Species,* he'd had only the same hurried thanks. On the fly-leaf, Laurence had written: "New ideas, for your new life. Think of me as you read this; I will be reading my own copy in your absence and we can write to each other about what we learn."

Repeatedly Max has tried to keep up his end of this joint endeavor, only to be frustrated by the book's difficulty. For now he has set it aside in favor of a more unexpectedly useful gift. Clara's brother, far away in the city of New York, works as an assistant librarian and sometimes sends extra copies of the books he receives to catalog. "Not of much interest to me," he wrote to Max, forwarding Asa Gray's *Lessons in Botany and Vegetable Physiology.* "But I know you and Clara like to garden, and to look at flowers in the woods—and I thought perhaps you would enjoy this."

At first, finding his companions uncongenial, Max read out of boredom and loneliness. Later he fell under the spell of the books themselves. The drawings at the back of Gray's book, the ferns and grasses and seedpods and spore capsules: how lovely these are! As familiar as his mother's eyes; as distant as the fossilized ferns found by a British explorer on the shores of Melville Island. As a boy he'd had a passion for botany: a charmed few years of learning plants and their names before the shock of his mother's death, his father's long decline, the necessity of going out, so young, to earn a living and help care for his family. Now he has a family of his own. Work of his own, as well, which he is proud of. But the illustrations draw him back to a time when the differences between a hawkweed and a dandelion could fascinate him for hours.

Charmed by the grasses of the Deosai plateau, he begins to dip into Dr. Hooker's book as well. Here, too, he finds much of interest. When he feels lost, when all he's forgotten or never knew about simple botany impedes his understanding, he marks his place with a leaf or a stem and turns back to Gray's manual. At home, he thinks, after he's safely returned, he and Clara can wander the fields as they did in the days of their courtship, this time understanding more clearly what they see and teaching these pleasures to their children. He copies passages into his notebook, meaning to share them with her:

LESSON I. BOTANY AS A BRANCH OF NATURAL HISTORY

The Organic World is the world of organized beings. These consist of *organs;* of parts which go to make up an *individual,* a *being.*

And each individual owes its existence to a preceding one like itself, that is, to a parent. It was not merely formed, but *produced.* At first small and imperfect, it grows and develops by powers of its own; it attains maturity, becomes old, and finally dies. It was formed of inorganic or mineral matter, that is, of earth and air, indeed; but only of this matter under the influence of life; and after life departs, sooner or later, it is decomposed into earth and air again.

He reads, and makes notes, and reads some more. The *Himalayan Journals,* he has noticed, are "Dedicated to Charles Darwin by his affectionate friend, Joseph Dalton Hooker." What lives those men lead: far-flung, yet always writing to each other and discussing their ideas. Something else he hasn't told Clara is this: Before leaving Srinagar, in a shop he entered meaning only to buy a new spirit level, he made an uncharacteristically impulsive purchase. A botanical collecting outfit, charming and neat; he could not resist it although he wasn't sure, then, what use he'd make of it. But on the Deosai plateau he found, after a windstorm, an unusual primrose flowering next to a field of snow. He pressed it, mounted it—not very well, he's still getting the hang of this—and drew it; then, in a fit of boldness, wrote about it to Dr. Hooker, care of his publisher in England. "The willows and stonecrops are remarkable," he added. "And I am headed higher still; might the lichens and mosses here be of some interest to you?" He doesn't expect that Dr. Hooker will write him back.

In his tent made from blankets, with a candle casting yellow light on the pages, Max pauses over a drawing of a mallow. About his mother, who died when he was nine, he remembers little. In a coffin she lay, hands folded over her black bombazine dress, face swollen and unrecognizable. When he was five or six, still in petticoats, she guided him through the marshes. Her pale hands, so soon to be stilled, plucked reeds and weeds and flowers. *You must remember these,* she said. *You must learn the names of the wonderful things surrounding us.* Horsetails in her hands, and then in his; the ribbed walls and the satisfying way the segments popped apart at the swollen joints. Pickerel rush and mallow and cattail and reed; then she got sick, and then she died. After that, for so many years, there was never time for anything but work.

2.

May 1, 1863

Dearest Clara—

A great day: as I was coming down an almost vertical cliff, on my way back to camp, a Balti coming up from the river met me and handed me a greasy, dirty packet. Letters from you, Laurence, and Zoe—yours were marked "Packet #12," which I had thought lost after receiving #13 and #14 back in Srinagar. From those earlier letters I knew you had been delivered safely of our beloved Joanna, and that Elizabeth had welcomed her new sister and all three of you were well: but I had no details, and to have missed not only this great event but your account of it made me melancholy. How wonderful then, after five long months, to have your description of the birth. All our family around you, the dawn just breaking as Joanna arrived and Elizabeth toddling in, later, to peer at the infant in your arms: how I wish I had been with you, my love.

And how I wish I knew what that long night and its aftermath had really been like; you spare my feelings, I know. You say not a word about your pains and trials. In #13 you mentioned recovering completely from the milk fever, but in #12 you did not tell me you had it, though you must have been suffering even then. Did we understand, when I took this position, how hard it would be? So many months elapse between one of us speaking, the other hearing; so many more before a response arrives. Our emotions tag so far behind the events. For me, it was as if Joanna had been born today. Yet she is five months old, and I have no idea of what those months have brought. Zoe says Elizabeth is growing like a cabbage, and Laurence says he heard from your brother in New York and that the family is thriving; how fortunate that the wound to his foot, which we once so regretted, has saved him from conscription.

I am well too, though terribly busy. But what I want, even more than sleep, is to talk to you. Everything I am seeing and doing is so new—it is nothing, really, like the work I did in England—so much is rushing into me all at once—I get confused. When I lie down to sleep everything spins in my brain. I can only make sense of my new life the way I have made sense of everything, since we first met: by describing it to you. That great gift you have always had of *listening*, asking such excellent questions—when I tell you enough to let you imagine me clearly, then I can imagine myself.

So, my dearest: imagine this. If this were an army (it almost is; three of Montgomerie's assistants are military officers, while others, like Michaels and his friends, served in the military forces of the East India Company until the Mutiny, then took their discharge rather than accept transfer to the British Army), I'd be a foot-soldier, far behind the dashing scouts of the triangulating parties who precede us up the summits. It is they who measure, with the utmost accuracy, the baseline between two vantage points, which becomes the first side of a triangle. They who with their theodolites measure the angles between each end of that line and a third high point in the distance: and they who calculate by trigonometry the two other sides of the triangle, thus fixing the distance to the far point and the point's exact position. One of the sides of that triangle then becomes the base for a new triangle—and so the chain slowly grows, easy enough to see on paper but dearly won in life. In the plains these triangles are small and neat. Out here the sides of a tri-angle may be a hundred miles or more.

Is this hard to follow? Try to imagine how many peaks must be climbed. And how high they are: 15,000 and 17,000 and 19,000 feet. My companions and I see the results of the triangulators' hard work when we follow them to the level platforms they've exposed by digging through feet of snow, and the supporting pillars they've constructed from rocks. Imagine a cold, weary man on the top of a mountain, bent over his theodolite and waiting for a splash of light. Far from him, on another peak, a signal squad manipulates a heliotrope (which is a circular mirror, my dear, mounted on a staff so it may be turned in any direction). On a clear day it flashes bright with reflected sunlight. At night it beams back the rays of a blue-burning lamp.

The triangulators leap from peak to peak; if they are the grasshoppers, we plane-tablers are the ants. At their abandoned sta-tions we camp for days, collecting topographical details and filling in their sketchy outline maps. You might imagine us as putting muscle and sinew on the bare bones they have made. Up through the snow we go, a little file of men; and then at the station I draw and draw until I've replicated all I see. I have a new plane-table, handsome and strong. The drawing-board swivels on its tripod, the spirit level guides my position; I set the table directly over the point corresponding to the plotted site of my rough map. Then I rotate the board with the sheet of paper pinned to it until the other main landscape features I can see—those the triangulators have already plotted—are positioned correctly relative to the map.

As I fill in the blank spaces with the bends and curves of a river valley, the dips and rises of a range, the drawing begins to resemble a map of home. For company I have the handful of porters who've carried the equipment, and one or two of the Indian chainmen who assist us—intelligent men, trained at Dehra Dun in the basics of mapping and observation. Some know almost as much as I do, and have the additional advantage of speaking the local languages as well as some English. When we meet to exchange results with those who work on the nearby peaks and form the rest of our group, the chainmen gather on one side of the fire, sharing food and stories. In their conversations a great idea called "The Survey" looms like a disembodied god to whom they—we—are all devoted. Proudly, they refer to both themselves and us as "Servants of the Map."

I will tell you what your very own Servant of the Map saw a few days ago. On the edge of the Deosai plateau, overlooking Skardu, I saw two far-away peaks towering above the rest of the Karakoram, the higher gleaming brilliant blue and the lower yellow. These are the mountains which Montgomerie, seven years ago, designated K1 and K2. K2 the triangulators have calculated at over 28,000 feet: imagine, the second highest mountain in the world, and I have seen it! The sky was the deepest blue, indescribable, sparkling with signals the heliotropes of the triangulating parties twinkled at one another. Do you remember our visit to Ely Cathedral? The way the stone rose up so sharply from the flat plain, an explosion of height—it was like our first glimpse of that, magnified beyond reason and lit all about by fireflies.

We have thunderstorms almost every day, they are always terrifying; the one that shook us the afternoon I saw K2 brought hail, and lightning so close that sparks leapt about the rocks at my feet and my hair bristled and crackled. The wind tore my map from the drawing board and sent it spinning over the edge of the plain, a white bird flying into the Indus valley below. But I do not mean to frighten you. I take care of myself, I am as safe as it is possible to be in such a place, I think of you constantly. Even the things I read remind me of you.

In Asa Gray's book, I read this today, from "Lesson VII: Morphology of Leaves"—

We may call foliage the natural form of leaves, and look upon the other sorts as special forms,—as transformed leaves . . . the Great Author of Nature, having designed plants upon one simple plan, just adapts this plan to all cases. So, whenever any special purpose is to be accomplished, no new instruments or organs are created for it, but one of the three general organs of the vegetable, root, stem, or leaf, is made to serve the purpose, and is adapted by taking some peculiar form.

Have I told you I have been working my way through this manual, lesson by lesson? I forget sometimes what I have written to you and what I have not. But I study whenever I can and use what I learn to help make sense both of my surroundings and of what I read in the *Himalayan Journals:* which I treasure, because it's from you. As the book Laurence gave me requires more concentration than I can summon I've set it aside for now (my guilty secret; don't tell him this): but Dr. Hooker I think even more highly of since my arrival here. The rhododendron that Zoe, my thoughtful sister, gave us as a wedding present—do you remember how, when it first flowered, we marveled at the fragrant, snowy blossoms with their secret gold insides? It was raised in a greenhouse in St. John's Wood, from seeds sent back by Dr. Hooker. I wish I could have been with you this spring to watch it bloom.

I am drifting from my point, I see. Forgive me. The *point,* the reason I copy this passage, is not to teach you about leaves but to say these words brought tears to my eyes; they made me think of our marriage. When we were together our lives were shaped like our neighbors', as simple as the open leaves of the maple. Now we are apart, trying to maintain our connection over this immense distance. Trying to stay in touch without touch; which effort changes us deeply, perhaps even deforms us.

To an outsider we might now look like the thick seed leaves of the almond or the bean, or the scales of buds or bulbs; like spines or tendrils, sepals or petals, which are also altered leaves. Do you know that, in certain willows, pistils and stamens can sometimes change into each other? Or that pistils often turn into petals in cultivated flowers? Only now do I begin to grasp the principles of growth and change in the plants I learned to name in the woods, those we have grown at home—there is a science to this. Something that transcends mere identification.

I wander, I know. Try to follow me. The point, dear heart, is that through all these transformations one can still discern the original morphology; the original character is altered yet not lost. In our separation our lives are changing, our bond to each other is changing. Yet still we are essentially the same.

I love you. So much. Do you know this?

It is raining again, we are damp and cold. I miss you. All the time.

Max regards the last page of his letter doubtfully. That business about the alteration of leaves; before he sends it, he scratches out the line about the effects of his and Clara's separation. *Deform:* such a frightening word.

His days pass in promiscuous chatter, men eating and drinking and working and snoring, men sick and wounded and snow-blind and wheezing; always worries about supplies and medicines and deadlines. He is never alone. He has never felt lonelier. There are quarrels everywhere: among the Indian chainmen, between the chainmen and the porters, the porters and his fellow plane-tablers; between the plane-tablers and the triangulators; even, within his own group, among the parties squatting on the separate peaks. Michaels, their leader, appears to enjoy setting one team against another. Michaels takes the youngest of the porters into his tent at night; Michaels has made advances toward Max and, since Max rebuffed him, startled and furious, has ceased speaking with him directly and communicates by sarcastic notes.

Wyatt has approached Max as well; and a man from another party—

the only one as young as Max—with a shock of red hair as obtrusive as a kingfisher's crest. Now all three are aligned against him. When the whole group meets he has seen, in the shadows just beyond the ring of light sent out by the campfire, men kneeling across from each other, britches unbuttoned, hands on each other. . . . He closed his eyes and turned his back and blocked his ears to the roar of laughter following his hasty departure. Yet who is he to judge them? So starved for love and touch is he that he has, at different times, found himself attracted to the middle-aged, stiff-necked wife of an English official in Srinagar, a Kashmiri flower-seller, a Tibetan herdsman, the herdsman's dog. He has felt such lust that his teeth throb, and the roots of his hair; the skin of his whole body itching as if about to explode in a giant sneeze.

In the act of writing to Clara, Max makes for himself the solitude he so desperately needs. He holds two strands of her life: one the set of letters she writes to him now—or not *now*, but as close to now as they can get, four months earlier, five, six—and the other the set of letters she wrote secretly in the months before he left, trying to imagine what he might need to hear. Occasionally he has allowed himself the strange pleasure of opening one letter from each set on the same day. A rounded image of Clara appears when he reads them side by side: she is with him. And this fills him with a desire to offer back to her, in his letters, his truest self. He wants to give her everything: what he is seeing, thinking, feeling; who he truly is. Yet these days he scarcely recognizes himself. How can he offer these aberrant knots of his character to Clara?

He tries to imagine himself into the last days of her pregnancy, into the events of Joanna's birth, the fever after that. He tries to imagine his family's daily life, moving on without him. Clara is nursing Joanna, teaching Elizabeth how to talk, tending the garden, watching the flowers unfold; at night, if she is not too weary, she is bending over her dictionary and her German texts, and then . . . He wonders what would happen if he wrote, *Tell me what it feels like to lie in our bed, in the early morning light, naked and without me. Tell me what you do when you think of me. What your hands do, what you imagine me doing.*

He doesn't write that; he doesn't write about what he does to himself on a narrow cot, in a tent made from a blanket strung over a tree-limb, the wind whistling as he stifles his groans with a handkerchief. Even then he doesn't feel alone. Close by, so near, his companions stifle noises of their own. His only truly private moments are these: bent over a blank page, dreaming with his pen.

3.

June 11, 1863

Dearest, dearest Clara—

The packet containing this letter will follow a very zigzag course on its way to you; a miracle that my words reach you at all. Or that yours reach me—how long it has been since the last! A ship that sailed from Bordeaux in March is rumored to have arrived at Bombay and will, I hope, have letters from you. Others from England have reached me—yet none from you—which is why I worry so. But already I hear your voice, reminding me that the fate of mail consigned to one ship may differ so from that consigned to another. I know you and the girls are well.

I am well too, although worried about you. I do what I can to keep busy. Did I tell you that I received, in response to some modest botanical observations I had sent to Dr. Hooker, a brief reply? He corrected my amateur mistakes, suggested I gather some specimens for him, and told me his great love of mosses dated from the time he was five or six. His mother claims that when he was very tiny he was found grubbing in a wall, and that when she asked what he was doing, he cried that he had found *Bryam argenteum* (not true, he notes now), a pretty moss he'd admired in his father's collection. At any age, he says—even mine—the passion for botany may manifest itself.

I found this touching and thought you would too. And I'm honored that he would answer me at all. In the hope of being of further use to him, I plan to continue my observations. Where I am now—deep in the heart of the Karakoram—nothing grows but the tiny lichens and mosses that are Dr. Hooker's greatest love. I can do little with them yet, they're extremely difficult. Except for them the landscape is barren. No one lives here: how would they live? Yet people do pass through from the neighboring valleys, the glaciers serving as highways through the mountains: I have met Hunzakuts, Baltis, Ladakhis and Nagiris and Turkis. But so far no travelers from home, although I hear rumors of solitary wanderers, English and German and French. One elderly adventurer has apparently haunted these mountains for decades, staying at times in Askole and Skardu; traveling even on the Baltoro Glacier and its branches—can this be true? If he exists, no one will tell me his name.

Around me is a confused mass of rock and glacier and mist, peaks appearing then disappearing beyond the curtains of clouds. The glaciers, covered with rocks and striated like frozen rivers, you would never mistake for snowfields or for anything else; the porters fear them and have their own names for them, while the chainmen claim that, deep within them, are the bodies of men who died in the mountains and are now being slowly carried down the stream of ice. Some decades from now, at the foot of the glacier, a glove or a couple of bones may be spit out.

I have seen wild sheep the size of ponies. I have slept ten nights at a stretch above 15,000 feet; I have woken buried in snow, lost in clouds; days have passed when I could make no sightings and sketch no maps, when we have nothing to eat and huddle together forlornly, watching avalanches peel down the side of the peaks. The weather here is beastly. At the snout of the Baltoro we were nearly swept away by a river leaping from an ice cave. There are no vistas when one travels the glaciers, more a sense of walking along a deep corridor, framed by perpendicular walls. I have a headache nearly all the time, and my neck aches from always gazing upward. The mornings are quiet, everything frozen in place by the frosts of the night. By afternoon the landscape has come alive, moving and shifting as rocks fall, walls of mud slide down, hidden streams dammed by the ice break free with a shout. No place for men.

I travel now in a party of six. Me in charge, the sole Englishman (the others lead similar parties, on other glaciers, on their way to other peaks); two Indian assistants who aid me with the measurements and mapping; three porters. We are on the Baltoro itself as I write. So frequent are the crevasses, and so deceitfully covered with snow, that we tie ourselves together with ropes and move like a single long caterpillar. Yesterday we stopped by the edge of a huge open fissure and, while the other men rested, I tied all our ropes together and sounded the depth; 170 feet of rope failed to reach bottom. Framing us, on both sides of the glacier, are some of the world's highest peaks.

My task has been to map where Montgomerie's K2 lies in relation to the Karakoram watershed. And this I have done, though there is no clear sight of it from the glacier itself. With my men I climbed the flank of an enormous mountain called Masherbrum. My men—I ought to try and tell you what it's like to live in such enforced companionship. They . . . I will save this for another letter. You know how awkward I have always been. With my own family, with you, I can be myself but here, with strangers—it is terrible, the old shyness seizes me. Without you by my side, to start the conversation and set everyone at ease, I am so clumsy. I do try, but it does no good. Especially with the porters and the chainmen I am at a loss. The barriers of language and our very different circumstances and habits and religions—I ought to be able to break through these, given the bonds of our shared work. Somewhere they too have wives and children, families and homes but I can't imagine them, I can't see these men in any other setting and I think they can't see me any more clearly. For them, I am simply the person who gives orders. In my early days surveying seemed like a perfect career for such a solitary creature as myself. I didn't understand that, out here, I would be accompanied ceaselessly by strangers.

Yet one does not need to talk all the time. And some things are beyond conversation—several thousand feet up the flank of Masherbrum, as we were perched on a sharp bleak shoulder, there it suddenly rose: K2, sixteen or seventeen miles away, separating one system of glaciers from another. We believe the reason it has no local name is that it isn't visible from any inhabited place; the nearest village is six days' march away and the peak is hidden by others, almost as large. I cannot tell you how it felt to see it clearly. I have spent two days here, mapping all the visible peaks and their relationships to each other and the glaciers.

I will entrust this to the herdsman I met, who is on his way to Skardu; may it find its way to you. One of our porters speaks a language somewhat familiar to this herdsman. The pair had a discussion involving much pointing at Masherbrum, an insistent tone on the part of the porter, violent head-shakings from the herdsman. Later I asked the porter what they'd been talking about. The herdsman had asked where we'd been; the porter had shown him the shoulder from which we saw K2. "You have never been there," the herdsman apparently said. "No one can go there. It is not for men."

He does not write to Clara about his glacial misadventures. Walking along on a hazy day with his party strung out behind him, he had seen what resembled a small round rock perched on the ice in the distance. Fresh snow had fallen the night before and the glare was terrible; over his eyes he'd drawn a piece of white muslin, like a beekeeper's veil, which cut the worst of the blinding light but dimmed the outlines of everything. One of his companions had bound a sheet of slit paper over his eyes, while others had woven shades from the hair of yaks' tails or had unbound their own hair and combed it forward until it screened their eyes. Max was nearly upon the round rock before he recognized it as a head.

A narrow crevasse, its opening covered by drifted snow; a wedge-shaped crack the width of a man at the top, tapering swiftly to a crease: inspecting it, with his veil raised, Max could imagine what had happened. The testing step forward, the confident placement of the second foot; and then one last second of everyday life before the deceitful bridge crumbled and the man plunged down, leaving his head and neck above the surface. The slit would have fit as intimately as a shroud, trapping the man's feet with his toes pointed down. No room to flex his knees or elbows and gain some purchase—but his head was free, he was breathing, he wasn't that cold and surely—surely?—he could pull himself out.

The man had a name, although it would take a while to determine it: Bancroft, whom Max had met only once, a member of one of the triangulating parties, disappeared three days before Max arrived. The ice inside the crevasse, warmed by the heat it stole from Bancroft's body, would have melted and pulled him inch by inch farther down, chilling him and slowing his blood, stealing his breath as fluid pooled in his feet and legs and his heart struggled to push it back up. By nightfall, with the cold pouring down from the stars, the cold wind pouring down from the peaks, the slit which had parted and shaped itself to Bancroft's body would have frozen solid around him. After hours of fruitless work, Max and his companions had reluctantly left Bancroft in a grave that would move until someone, a lifetime away, would puzzle over the boots and bones deposited in a moraine.

Max had not told Clara any of this: it would have frightened her. It frightened him. And yet despite that he went walking alone, ten days later. The sun was out, the sky was clear; the men had stopped in the middle of the afternoon, refused to go farther without a rest, and set up camp against his wishes. Irritated, he'd refused to waste the day. He'd mapped this section already, but wanted more detail for his sketches: how the ice curved and cracked as it ground past the embracing wall of the mountain. In Wales, when he was being trained, he and Laurence had seen erratic boulders and mountains with deeply scored flanks which were caused, said the bookish young man who led them, by a glacial period that covered all Europe with ice. Now it was as if he'd walked backward into that earlier time.

He fell into a fissure, forty feet deep. A leaf of ice, like the recalcitrant piece of heartwood bridging two halves of a split log, stretched between the uphill and downhill walls of the crevasse and broke his fall. He landed face down, embracing a narrow slab, calling himself back to life and aware of his arms and legs dangling into space. Above him was a ceiling of snow, with a narrow slit of blue sky where his body had broken through. He could move his feet, his hands, his shoulders; apparently nothing was broken. Slowly, hugging the ice with his thighs, he sat upright. Before him the uphill wall of the crevasse glimmered smooth in the blue shadows. Slim ribs of ice, bulges and swellings reminiscent of Clara's back and belly. Behind him the downhill wall was jagged and white and torn. To his right the crevasse stretched without end, parallel faces disappearing into darkness. But to his left the walls appeared to taper together.

He might make of himself a bridge, he thought. A bridge of flesh, like the bridge of ice. With his back pressed against the wet uphill wall, his legs extended and his boots pressed into the crunching, jagged downhill wall, he suspended himself. He moved his right foot a few inches, then his left; sent all his strength into the soles of his feet and then slid his back a few inches, ignoring the icy stream that chattered so far below. Again and again, right foot, left foot, heave. Time stopped, thinking stopped, everything stopped but these small painful motions. The walls drew closer together and he folded with them, his legs bending at the knees, then doubled, until finally he was hung in a sideways crouch.

He reached the corner without knowing what he'd do when he got there. The crevasse was shaped like a smile; where the two lips met, the bottom also curved up. He released his right leg and let it slide down, touching some rubble on which he might balance. He stood, he straightened partway. Soaked, scared, exhausted, and so cold. Above him was not the sky, but a roof of snow. Like a mole he scratched at the bottom surface. He tore his fingernails and ripped his hands. When he realized what was happening he stopped digging with his right hand and dug only with his left.

He dug himself out. He hauled himself up. How many hours did this take? His left hand was bloody and blue, his right torn but still working; how lucky he had been. On the surface of the glacier, under the setting sun, he closed his eyes and fixed in his mind the dim, shadowed, silent grave he'd known for a few hours. Among the things he would not write Clara—he would never write a word of this—was how seductive he'd found the cold and quiet. How easy he would have found it to sleep on the leaf of ice, his head pillowed on his arm while snow drifted over the broken roof, sealing him in silent darkness. Nothing would have been left of him but his books and maps, and the trunk with Clara's letters. So many still unopened, dated months in the future, a year in the future. It was the thought of not getting to read them that made him wake up.

4.

July 21, 1863

Dear heart—

This week I received your Packet #15, from March; you cannot know what a relief it is to hear from you. But why do I say that when I know you suffer the same torments? It is very upsetting to hear that none of my letters have reached you, and that you have as yet no news of my travels across the country to Kashmir, never mind news of my journeys in the mountains. Although perhaps by now you do: it was still *March*, I remind myself, when you hadn't heard from me. It may be September or December before you receive this, and you will be in possession of all my other letters by then, smiling to see me worry in this.

We heard a ship leaving Calcutta was burnt down to the water-line just after it embarked; all the passengers were saved but every-thing else on board was lost and I wonder if some of my letters were on it, now bits of ash on the sea. When I think about the hands through which these must pass, to find their way to you: a passing herdsmen to another party of the Survey, to another messenger, to some official in Srinagar; perhaps to Calcutta, perhaps to Bombay; through a merchant's hands, or a branch of the military: hand to hand to hand, to a ship, or several ships: and the hazards of weather and human carelessness every inch of the way. . . . My dear, you must keep these accidents in mind, when you worry about me. It grieves me to think of your suffering. Remember the promise we made to each other, to consider not just the accidents that might happen to us, but to our correspondence. Remember how tough I am. How prudent.

Thank you for the story about Elizabeth and the garden. I love to think about the three of you, bundled up and watching the birds as they flick within the branches on the hedgerow. Joanna in your arms, Elizabeth darting along the hawthorns, pursuing the spar-rows: these glimpses of your life together keep me going. If you knew how much I miss you . . . but I have promised myself I will write *sensibly*. I want you to think of me as I am, as you have always known me, and not as a stranger perpetually complaining. I'm glad Mrs. Moore's nephew—Gideon?—has been so helpful during his stay with his aunt and has been able to solve the problem with the drains. When next you see him, please tell him I am grateful. Do you see him often?

I received with the letters from you and our family two more let-ters from Dr. Hooker. He *has* received mail from me, from as late as April; how is it my letters are reaching him but not you? When I get home I will let you read what he writes, you will find it fascinating. He is in touch with botanists and collectors all over the world; involved with so many projects and yet still he takes the time to encourage an amateur such as myself. On his own journey, he said, as he climbed from the terai to the snowline he traversed virtually the entire spectrum of the world's flora, from the leech-infested, dripping jungle to the tiny lichens of the Tibetan plateau. I have a similar opportunity, he says. If I am wise enough to take it. I copy for you here a little paragraph, which he included with questions about what is growing where, and requests for a series of measurements of temperature and altitude.

"When still a child," he writes, "my father used to take me on excursions in the Highlands, where I fished a good deal, but also botanized; and well I remember on one occasion, that, after returning home, I built up by a heap of stones a representation of one of the mountains I had ascended, and stuck upon it specimens of the mosses I had collected, at heights relative to those at which I had gathered them. This was the dawn of my love for geographical botany. It pleases me greatly that, though you have started your botanizing as a grown man, you may come to share a similar passion."

Is that not a lovely tale? The mountain was a little one, by our standards here, less than 4,000 feet. He has been very encouraging of my efforts and with his help I have set myself a study plan, as if I'm at university. I would like to make myself *worthy*; worthy to write to such a man as Dr. Hooker, and receive a response. Worthy of seeking an answer to the question that now occupies everyone: how the different forms of life have reached their present habitats. When else will I have a chance like this?

What draws me to these men and their writings is not simply their ideas but the way they defend each other so vigorously and are so firmly bound. Hooker, standing up for Darwin at Oxford and defending his dear friend passionately. Gray, in America, championing Darwin in a series of public debates and converting the world of American science one resistant mind at a time. Our group here is very different. Although the work gets done—the work always gets done, the maps accumulate—I have found little but division and quarrels and bad behavior.

You may find my handwriting difficult to decipher; I have suffered much from snowblindness. And a kind of generalized mountain sickness as well. We are so high, almost all the time; the smallest effort brings on fatigue and nausea and the most piercing of headaches. I sleep only with difficulty; it is cold at night, and damp. Our fires will not stay lit. But every day brings new additions to our map, and new sketches of the topography: you will be proud of me, I am becoming quite the draughtsman. And I manage to continue with my other work as well. I keep in mind Hooker's travails in Nepal and Sikkim: how, in the most difficult of circumstances, he made excellent and detailed observations of his surroundings. I keep in mind Godfrey Vigne, and all he managed to note. Also a man I did not tell you about before, whose diary passed through my hands: how clearly he described his travels, despite his difficulties! By this discipline, and by my work, I hold myself together.

This week my party climbed a peak some 21,000 feet high. We were not the first ones here: awaiting us was the station the strongest and most brilliant of the triangulators built last season. I have not met him, he remains an almost mythical creature. But I occupied his heap of stones with pride. He triangulated all the high peaks visible from here and the map I have made from this outline, the curves of the glaciers and the jagged valleys, the passes and the glacial lakes—Clara, how I wish you could see it! It is the best thing I have ever done and the pains of my body are nothing.

I have learned something, these past few months. Something important. On the descent from such a peak, I have learned, I can see almost nothing: by then I am so worn and battered that my eyes and mind no longer work correctly; often I have a fever, I can maintain no useful train of thought, I might as well be blind.

On my first ascents, before I grasped this, I would make some notes on the way up but often I would skip things, thinking I would observe more closely on the way down. Now I note *everything* on the way up. As we climbed this giant peak I kept a notebook and pencil tied to my jacket pocket and most of the time had them right in my hand: I made note of every geological feature, every bit of vegetation or sign of a passing animal; I noted the weather as it changed over the climb, the depth of the snow, the movements of the clouds. This record—these records, I do this now with every ascent—will I think be invaluable to subsequent travelers. When I return I plan to share them with Dr. Hooker and whoever else is interested.

It's an odd thing, though, that there is not much pleasure in the actual recording. Although I am aware, distantly, that I often move through scenes of great beauty, I can't *feel* that as I climb; all is lost in giddiness and headache and the pain of moving my limbs and drawing breath. But a few days after I descend to a lower altitude, when my body has begun to repair itself—then I look at the notes I made during my hours of misery and find great pleasure in *them*. It is odd, isn't it? That all one's pleasures here are retrospective; in the moment itself, there is only the moment, and the pain.

I must go. A messenger from Michaels came by the camp this morning with new instructions and leaves soon to contact three other parties; if I put this into his hands it will find its way down the glacier, out of the mountains, over the passes. To you.

After relinquishing the letter to Michaels' messenger, he thinks: What use was that? For all those words about his work, he has said little of what he really meant. How will Clara know who he is these days, if he hides both his worries, and his guilty pleasures? He still hasn't told her about the gift he bought for himself. A collecting box, like a candle-box only flatter, in which to place fresh specimens. A botanical press, with a heap of soft dry-ing-paper, to prepare the best of his specimens for an herbarium; and a portfolio in which to lay them out, twenty inches by twelve, closed with a sturdy leather strap and filled with sheets of thin, smooth, unsized paper. Always he has been a man of endless small economies, saving every penny of his pay, after the barest necessities, for Clara in England. He has denied himself warm clothes, extra blankets, the little treats of food and drink on which the other surveyors squandered their money in Srinagar, and before. But this one extravagance he couldn't resist: not a dancing-girl, not a drunken evening's carouse, but still he is ashamed.

A different kind of shame has kept him from writing about the doubts that plague his sleepless nights. He knows so little, really—why does he think his observations might be useful? He ought to be content with the knowledge that the work he does each day is solid, practical, strong; these maps will stand for years. In Dehra Dun, and in Calcutta and back in England, copyists and engravers will render from his soiled rough maps clean and permanent versions. In a year the Series will be complete: Jammu and Kashmir, Khagan, Ladakh and Baltistan, caught in a net of lines; a topographical triumph. Still he longs to make some contribution more purely his.

He dreams of a different kind of map, in shades of misty green. Where the heads of the Survey see the boundaries of states and tribes, here the watershed between India and China, there a plausible boundary for Kashmir, he sees plants, each kind in a range bounded by soil and rainfall and altitude and temperature. And it is this—the careful delineation of the boundaries of those ranges, the subtle links between them—that has begun to interest him more than anything else. *Geographical botany*, Dr. Hooker said. What grows where. Primulas up to this level, no higher; deodar here, stonecrops and rock jasmines giving way to lichens. . . . Why do rhododendrons grow in Sikkim, and not here? He might spend his life in the search for an answer.

Part of the reason he's formed no close ties to either the men with whom he daily climbs and maps, nor those who lead the other small parties, is that when they gather at night they argue about the ebb and flow not of plant life, but of politics. The Sikh Wars and the annexation of the Punjab, the administration of Lord Dalhousie, the transfer of power from the East India Company to the Crown, the decisions of the regional revenue officers—it is embarrassing, how little all this interests him. Among the surveyors are military men who have served in the Burmese War, or in Peshawar; who survived the Mutiny or, in various mountains, that stormy year when supplies to the Survey were interrupted and bands of rebels entered Kashmir. He ought to find their stories fascinating. Germans and Russians and Turks and Chinese, empires clashing; Dogras and Sikhs, spies and informants—currents no one understands, secrets it might take a lifetime to unravel. Yet of all this, two stories only have stayed with him.

The first he heard on a snow bench carved in a drift on a ridge, from an Indian chainman who'd served for a while in the Bengal Army, and who worked as Max's assistant for two weeks, and then disappeared. They were resting. The chainman was brewing tea. At Lahore, he said, his regiment had been on the verge of mutiny. On a June night in 1857, one of the spies the suspicious British officers had planted within the regiment reported to the Brigadier that the sepoys planned an uprising the following day. That night, when the officers ordered a regimental inspection, they found two sepoys with loaded muskets.

There was a court-martial, the chainman said. He told the story quietly, as if he'd played no part in it; he had been loyal, he said. He had been simply an observer. Indian officers had convicted the two sepoys and sentenced them to death. "There was a parade," the chainman said. His English was very good, the light lilting accent at odds with the tale he told. "A formal parade. We stood lined up on three sides of a square. On the fourth side were two cannon. The sepoys—"

"Did you know them?" Max had asked.

"I knew both of them, I had tried to talk them out of their plan. They were . . . the officers lashed those two men over the muzzles of the cannons. Then they fired."

Below them the mountains shone jagged and white, clean and untenanted. Nearby were other Englishmen, and other Indians, working in apparent harmony in this landscape belonging to neither. Yet all this had happened only six years ago.

"There was nothing left of them," the chainman said. He rose and kicked snow into the fire; the kettle he emptied and packed tidily away. "Parts of them came down like rain, bits of bone and flesh, shreds of uniforms. Some of us were sprinkled with their blood."

"I . . . ," Max had murmured. What could he say? "A terrible thing," he said. The chainman returned to work, leaving Max haunted and uneasy.

The other story was this, which Michaels encouraged a triangulator to tell one night when three different surveying teams gathered in a valley to plan their tasks for the next few weeks. An Indian atrocity to match the British one: Cawnpore, a month after the incident reported by the chainman. Of course Max had heard of the massacre of women and children there. No one in England had escaped that news, nor the public frenzy that followed. But Michaels' gruff, hard-drinking companion, who in 1857 had been with a unit of the Highlanders, told with relish certain details the newspaper hadn't printed.

"If you had seen the huts," said Michaels' friend: Archdale, Max thought his name was. Or maybe Archvale. "A hundred and twenty women and children escaped the first massacre on the river boats—the mutineers rounded them up and kept them in huts. We arrived not long after they were butchered. I saw those huts, they looked like cages where a pack of wild animals had been set loose among their prey."

"Tell about the shoes," Michaels had called from the other side of the fire. All the men were drinking; Michaels had had a case of brandy carried in from Srinagar. His face was dark red, sweating, fierce. That night, as always, he ignored Max almost completely.

"The shoes," Archdale said. He emptied his glass and leaned forward, face shining in the firelight. "Picture this," he said. "I go into one hut and the walls are dripping with blood, the floor smeared, the smell unthinkable. Flies buzzing so loudly I thought I'd go mad. Against one wall is a row of women's shoes, running with blood, draped with bits of clothing." The Indian chainmen and the Balti porters were gathered around their separate fires, not far away: could they hear Archdale? Max wondered. Was it possible Archdale would say these things within earshot of them? "Against the other wall, a row of children's shoes, so small, just like those our children wear at home. And"—he leaned farther forward here—"do you know what was in them?"

No one answered. Was Joanna wearing shoes yet? Max wondered. "What?" he'd said, unable to stop himself.

"Feet!" Archdale roared. "*Feet!* Those filthy animals, those swine, they had lopped off the children's feet. We found the bodies in the well."

That terrible story had set off others; the night had been like a night in hell; Max had fled the campfire soon after Archdale's tirade and rolled himself in a blanket in a hollow, far from everyone, carved into the rocky cliffs. When he woke he'd been surprised not to find the campground littered with bodies.

Since hearing those tales he has wondered how there could be so much violence on both sides; and how, after that, Englishmen and Indians could be up in these mountains, working so calmly together. How can he make sense of an empire founded on such things? *Nothing,* he thought after hearing those stories. And still thinks. *I understand nothing.*

Dr. Hooker wrote at great length, in a letter Max didn't mention to Clara, about the problems of packing botanical collections for the journey home: the weight, the costs; the necessity of using Ward's cases; the crating of tree-ferns and the boats to be hired. How kind he was, to take such trouble in writing Max, and to warn him of these potential hazards! And yet how little Dr. Hooker understands Max's own situation. There is no possibility of paying for such things, without depriving Clara and his daughters. His collections are limited to the scraps he can dry and preserve in his small press—bad enough he spent money on that—the herbarium sheets he can carry; the sketches and observations in his notebook. He can offer Dr. Hooker only these, but they are not nothing and he hopes his gifts will be received without disappointment.

The lost man whose skull he found, when he first entered these mountains: at least that solitary explorer left behind a record of the movements of his soul. What is he doing, himself? Supporting his family, advancing his career; when he returns to England, he'll have no trouble finding a good position. But he would like also to feel that he has *broadened* himself. Hunched over his plane-table, his temples pounding as he draws the lateral moraines of the glacier below him, he hears his mother's voice.

Look. Remember this. The ribbon of ice below him turns into a snow-covered path that curves through the reeds along the river and vanishes at the horizon; across it a rabbit is moving and his mother stands, her hand in his, quietly keeping him company. They watch, and watch, until the path seems not to be moving away from them, but toward them; the stillness of the afternoon pouring into their clasped hands. *There is something special in you,* she said. *In the way you see.*

A few days ago, on his twenty-eighth birthday, he opened the birthday greeting Clara had tucked in his trunk. She had written about the earlier birthdays they'd shared. And about this one, as she imagined it: *Your companions, I know, will have made you a special birthday meal. Perhaps you'll all share a bottle of brandy, or whatever you drink there. I am thinking of you, and of the birthdays in the future we will once more spend together.*

Reading this, he'd felt for the first time that Clara's project might fail. He is no longer the person she wrote to, almost a year ago now. She may have turned into someone else as well. That Gideon she mentions, that nice young man who prunes the trees and brings her wood and does the tasks Max ought to be doing himself: what other parts of Max's life is he usurping? Max conjures up someone broad-shouldered, very tall—Max and Clara are almost the same height—unbuttoning his shirt and reaching out for Clara . . . impossible, it makes him want to howl. Surely she wouldn't have mentioned him if their friendship were anything but innocent. Yet even if it is, it will have changed her.

He himself has changed so much, he grows farther daily from her picture of him. There was no birthday celebration; he told no one of this occasion. If he had, there would have been no response. It is his mother, dead so many years, who seems to speak most truly to the new person he is becoming. As if the years between her death and now were only a detour, his childhood self emerging from a long uneasy sleep. Beyond his work, beyond the mapping and recording, he is *seeing;* and this—it is terrifying—is becoming more important to him than anything.

5.

October 1, 1863

Dearest Clara—

Forgive me for not writing in so long. Until I received your Packets #17, 18, and 19, all in a wonderful clump last week (#16, though, has gone astray), I had almost given up hope of us being in touch before winter. I should have realized your letters couldn't find me while we were among the glaciers. We are in the valley of the Shighar now, and from here will make our way back to Srinagar. I don't yet know what my winter assignment will be. The triangulating parties will winter at the headquarters in Dehra Dun, recalibrating the instruments and checking their calculations and training new assistants. There is talk of leaving a small group of plane-tablers in Srinagar, to complete topographical maps of the city and the outlying areas and lakes. I will let you know my orders as soon as I get them.

At least you know I am alive now. Though how can you make sense of my life here on the evidence of one letter from when I first arrived in Kashmir, and one from deep in the mountains? The others—I must have faith they will find their way to you. Your description of your journey to London, trudging through those government offices as you tried to get some word of me—this filled me with sadness, and with shame. You are generous to say it is not my fault that you went so long without word of me, that you blame a careless ship's captain, clumsy clerks, and accidents: but it is my fault, still. I am the one who left home. And that I have not written these last weeks—can you forgive me? I console myself with the thought that, since my earlier letters were so delayed, perhaps a trickle of them will continue to reach you during the gap between then and now. But really my only excuse is the hardships of these last weeks. I am so weary; the cold and the altitude make it hard to sleep. And when I do catch a few brief hours I am plagued by nightmares. The men I work with tell me stories, things I would never repeat to you; and though I try not to think about them they haunt me at night.

The season in the mountains is already over; we stayed too long. We crossed one high pass after another during our retreat. And Clara, you can't imagine the weather. I couldn't work on my maps, or keep up my notes, or even—my most cherished task—write to you; when I heated the inkpot, the ink still froze on its short journey to the paper. My hands were frozen, my beard a mass of icicles. I wore everything you packed for me, all at once, and still couldn't stay warm. Lambs' wool vest and drawers, heavy flannel shirt and lined chamois vest, wool trousers and shirt, three pairs of stockings and my fur-lined boots, thick woolen hat, flannel-lined kidskin jacket, over that my big sheepskin coat and then a Kashmir shawl wrapped twice about me, binding the whole mass together—I sweated under the weight of all this, yet grew chilled the instant we stopped moving. Nights were the worst, there is no firewood in the mountains and we had already used up all we'd carried. Food was short as well.

I shouldn't tell you these things; never mind. Now that we are down in the valleys things are easier. And I am fine. Soon enough we'll reach Srinagar, and whether I stay there or move on to Dehra Dun I am looking forward to the winter. Long quiet months of cleaning up my sketch maps, improving my drawings, fitting together the sections into the larger picture of the Himalayan system. From either place I may write to you often, knowing the chances of you getting my letters in just a few months are good: and I may look forward to receiving yours with some regularity. Still I have some of the letters in your trunk to look forward to, as well: I ration these now, I open one only every few weeks, sometimes ignoring the dates with which you marked them. Forgive me, I save them for when I most need them. This evening, before I began to write to you, I opened one intended for Elizabeth's birthday. How lovely to be reminded of that happy time when you leaned on my arm, plump and happy as we walked in the garden and waited for her birth. The lock of Elizabeth's hair you enclosed I have sewn into a pouch, which I wear under my vest.

What else do I have to tell you? So much has happened these last weeks that I don't know how to describe it all; and perhaps it wouldn't interest you, it is just my daily work. Yesterday I had a strange encounter, though. Camped by the edge of a river, trying to restore some order to my papers while my companions were off in search of fuel, I looked up to see a stranger approaching; clearly a European although he wore clothes of Kashmiri cut. When I invited him to take tea with me he made himself comfortable and told me about himself. A doctor and an explorer, elderly; he calls himself Dr. Chouteau and says he is of French birth, though his English is indistinguishable from mine. This he explains by claiming to have left home as a boy of fourteen; claiming also to have been exploring in these mountains for over forty years. We did not meet in Srinagar, he told me, because he lives in a native quarter there. I think he may be the solitary traveler of whom I heard such odd rumors earlier in the season, though when I asked him this he shrugged and said, "There are a few of us."

We passed together the most interesting afternoon I've had in weeks. My own companions and I have grown weary of each other, we seldom speak at all; but Dr. Chouteau talked without stopping for several hours. A great liar, I would have to say. Even within those hours he began to contradict himself. But how intriguing he was. He is very tall, thin and hawk-nosed, with a skin burnt dark brown by years in the sun and deeply lined. His rag-tag outfit he tops with a large turban, from which sprout the plumes of some unidentifiable bird. He showed me his scars: a round one, like a coin, on the back of one hand, and another to match on the front—here a bullet passed through, he said, when he was fighting in Afghanistan. A hollow in his right calf, where, in Kabul, a bandit hacked at him with a sword as he escaped by horse. For some time he lived among a Kafir tribe, with a beautiful black-eyed mistress; the seam running from eyebrow to cheekbone to chin he earned, he says, in a fight to win her. He has been in Jalalabad and the Kabul river basin; in the Pamirs among the Kirghiz nomads; in Yarkand and Leh, Chitral and Gilgit.

Or so he says. Myself, I cannot quite credit this; he is elusive regarding his travel routes, and about dates and seasons and companions. But perhaps he truly did all these things, at one time or another, and erases the details and connections out of necessity: I think perhaps he has been a spy. For whom?

I try to forget what you have said about the way you gather with our families and friends and pass these letters around, or read them out loud; if I thought of that I would grow too self-conscious to write to you at all. But I will tell you one peculiar thing about Dr. Chouteau if you promise to keep this to yourself. He has lived to such a robust old age, he swears, by the most meticulous attention to personal hygiene. And how has he avoided the gastric complaints that afflict almost all of us when we eat the local foods? A daily clyster, he says. The cleansing enema he administers to himself, with a special syringe. I have seen this object with my own eyes, he carries it with him and showed it to me. It looked rather like a hookah. Far better this, he said, looking at my bewildered countenance, than the calomel and other purgatives on which less wise travelers rely.

Some of the other things he told me I can't repeat, even to you: they have to do with princes and dancing-girls, seraglios and such-like: when I am home again I will share these with you, in the privacy of our own bed.

Clara, I am so confused. Meeting this stranger made me realize with more than usual sharpness how lonely I am, how cut off I feel from all that is important to me. My past life seems to be disappearing, my memories grow jumbled. Who was the Max Vigne who went here or there, did this or that? It's as if I am dissolving and reforming; I am turning into someone I don't recognize. If I believed in the doctrine of the transmigration of souls, I might suspect that the wind is blowing someone else's soul in through my nostrils, while my old soul flies out my ears. In the mountains I lay awake in the cold, frozen despite my blankets, and my life in England—my boyhood, even my life with you—passed by my eyes as if it had been lived by someone else. Forgive these wanderings. The household details of which you wrote, the problems with the roof, the chimney, the apple trees—I know I should offer some answers in response to your questions but it feels pointless. You will have long since had to resolve these things before you receive my advice. I trust your judgment completely.

Good night; the wind is blowing hard. What a fine thing a house is. In my tent I think of you and the girls, snug inside the walls.

After that, he does not write to Clara for a while.

The river valleys, the high plains, the dirt and crowds and smells and noise of Srinagar, where the surveying parties are reshuffled and he finds himself, with three other plane-tablers, left behind in makeshift quarters, with preliminary maps of the city and the valley and vague instructions to fill in the details while everyone else (Michaels too; at least he is finally free of Michaels!) moves on to Dehra Dun, not to return until spring: and still, he does not write Clara. He does not write to anyone, he does not keep up his botanical notes, he makes no sketches other than those required for the maps. He does his work, because he must. But he does no more. He cannot remember ever feeling like this.

6.

If he could make himself write, he might say this:

Dearest Clara—

Who am I? Who am I meant to be? I imagine a different life for myself, but how can I know, how can anyone know, if this is a foolish dream, or a sensible goal? Have I any scientific talent at all? Dr. Hooker says I do, he has been most encouraging. If he is right, then my separation from you means something, and the isolation I've imposed on myself, and the long hours of extra work. But if I have no real gift, if I am only deluding myself . . . then I am wasting everything.

There is something noble, surely, in following the path of one's gifts; don't we have a duty to use our talents to the utmost? Isn't any sacrifice, in the pursuit of that, worthwhile? In these past months I have often felt that the current which is most truly me, laid aside when I was still a boy and had to face the responsibilities of family life, has all this time continued to flow the way water moves unseen beneath the glaciers. When I am alone, with my notes and plants and the correlations of weather and geology and flora springing clear before me, I feel: This is who I am. This is what I was born to do. But if in fact I have no real capacity for this work, if it is only my vanity leading me down this path—what then?

He has grown morose, he knows. Worse than morose. Maudlin, self-pitying. And self-deluding: not just about his possible talents, but in the very language with which he now contemplates writing Clara. Nobility, duty, sacrifice—whose words are those? Not his. He is using them to screen himself from the knowledge of whatever is shifting in him.

On the journey back to Srinagar, among the triangulators and plane-tablers led by Michaels and eventually joined by Captain Montgomerie himself, he was silent, sullen, distant. If he could, he would have talked to no one. In Srinagar, once the crowd of officers and triangulators left for Dehra Dun, he felt still worse. Investigating the streets and alleys, the outlying villages and the limestone springs, he was charmed by what he saw and wished it would stay the same. But meanwhile he couldn't help hearing talk of his government annexing Kashmir and turning the valley into another Simla: a retreat for soldiers and government officials, people he would prefer to avoid.

When he returns at night to the room he shares with three other plane-tablers, he flops on his cot and can't understand why he feels so trapped. The walls that shelter him from the cold and the wind—didn't he miss these? Perhaps it isn't the dark planks and the stingy windows that make him grind his teeth, but his companions' self-important chatter about measurements and calculations, possibilities for promotion. He shuts his ears to them and imagines, instead, talking with the vainglorious old explorer whose tales left him feeling lost, and full of questions.

The stories he wrote to Clara were the least of what happened that afternoon. Dr. Chouteau had been everywhere, Max learned. Without a map; maps meant nothing to him. Max's work he'd regarded with detached interest, almost amusement. Looking down at the sheets of paper, the carefully drawn cliffs and rivers and glaciers, Dr. Chouteau had said, *I have been here. And here. Here. And so many other places.* He spoke of the gravestone, seen in Kabul, that marked the resting place of an Englishman who'd passed through there a century and a half ago. Of wandering Russians, Austrians, Chinese, Turks, the twists and turns of the Great Game, the nasty little wars. Godfrey Vigne, he'd said—*Isn't it odd, that you share that last name?*—had been no simple traveler, but a British spy. Those forays into Baltistan a way of gathering information; and his attempts to reach Central Asia a way of determining that the only routes by which the Russians might enter India lay west of the Karakoram. *I knew him,* Dr. Chouteau said. *We were in Afghanistan together. He was the one who determined that Baltistan has no strategic importance to the British plans for India.*

More than anyone else, Dr. Chouteau made Max understand the purpose of his work. *I never make maps,* Dr. Chouteau said. *Or not maps anyone else could read. They might fall into the wrong hands.* Max's maps, he pointed out, would be printed, distributed to governments, passed on to armies and merchants and travelers. Someone, someday, would study them as they planned an invasion, or planned to stop one. What can Max's insignificant hardships matter, when compared to the adventures of such solitary travelers as Dr. Chouteau, or the lost man he saw when he first arrived in the mountains; of Godfrey Vigne or of Dr. Hooker? In Srinagar, Max understands that his journeys have been only the palest imitations of theirs.

He hasn't heard from Dr. Hooker in months. And although he knows he ought to understand, from Clara's trials, that accident may have been at work, he interprets this as pure rejection. The observations he sent weren't worthy; Hooker has ceased to reply because Max's work is of no interest. All he will leave behind are maps, which will be merged with all the other maps, on which he will be nameless: small contributions to the great Atlas of India, which has been growing for almost forty years. In London a faceless man collates the results of the triangulations into huge unwieldy sheets, engraved on copper or lithographed: two miles to an inch, four miles to an inch—what will become of them? He knows, or thinks he knows, though his imagination is colored by despair: They will burn, or be eaten by rats and cockroaches, or obliterated by fungus. Frayed and dust-stained, uncatalogued, they'll be sold as waste paper, or burned. Those that survive will be shared with allies, or hidden from enemies.

Max might write to Dr. Hooker about this; in Sikkim, he knows, Dr. Hooker and a companion had been seized while botanizing and held as political hostages. That event had served as excuse for an invasion by the British Army and the annexation of southern Sikkim. Although Dr. Hooker refused to accompany the troops, he gave the general in charge of the invasion the topographical map he'd drawn. That map was copied at the Surveyor General's office; another map, of the Khasia Hills, made its way into the Atlas of India, complimented by all for its geological, botanical, and meteorological notes. Max has seen this one himself, though its import escaped him at the time. Dr. Hooker did it in his spare time, tossing off what cost Max so much labor.

But what is the point of tormenting himself? In the increasing cold he reads over Dr. Hooker's letters to him, looking for the first signs of disfavor. The letters are imperturbably kind, he can find no hint of where he failed. For comfort he turns, not to the remaining letters in Clara's trunk—those forward-casting, hopeful exercises make him feel too sad—but instead to the first of her letters to reach him. From those, still brave and cheerful, he works his way into the later ones. A line about Joanna's colic, and how it lingered; a line about the bugs in the rhubarb: unsaid, all the difficulties that must have surrounded each event. *The roof is leaking, the sink is broken, Elizabeth has chicken pox,* Clara wrote. *Zoe is bearing bravely her broken engagement, but we are all worried about her.* What she means is: *Where are you, where are you? Why have you left me to face this all alone?*

Her packet #16, which failed to reach him in October with the rest of that batch, has finally arrived along with other, more recent letters. In early April she described the gardens, the plague of slugs, the foundling sparrow Elizabeth had adopted and Joanna's avid, crawling explorations; the death of a neighbor and the funeral, which she attended with Gideon. Gideon, again. Then something broke through and she wrote what she'd never permitted herself before:

"Terrible scenes rise up before my eyes and they are as real as the rest of my life. I look out the window and I see a carriage pull up to the door, a man steps out, he is bearing a black-bordered envelope; I know what is in it, I know. He walks up to the door and I am already crying. He looks down at his shoes. I take the letter from him, I open it; it is come from the government offices in London and I skip over the sentences which attempt to prepare me for the news. I skip to the part in which it says you have died. In the mountains, of an accident. In the plains, of some terrible fever. On a ship which has sunk—I read the sentences again and again—they confirm my worst fears and I grow faint—hope expires in me and yet I will not believe. In the envelope too, another sheet: The words of someone I have never met, who witnessed your last days. *Though I am a stranger to you, it is my sad duty to inform you of a most terrible event.* And then a description of whatever befell you; and one more sheet, which is your last letter to me.

You see how I torment myself. I imagine all the things you might write. I imagine, on some days, that you tell me the truth; on others that you lie, to spare my feelings. I imagine you writing, *Do not grieve too long, dearest Clara. The cruelest thing, when we think of our loved ones dying in distant lands, is the thought of them dying alone and abandoned, uncared for—but throughout my illness I have had the attentions of kind men.* I imagine, I imagine . . . how can I imagine you alive and well, when I have not heard from you for so long?

I am ashamed of myself for writing this. All over Britain other women wait, patiently, for soldiers and sailors and explorers and merchants—why can't I? I will try to be stronger. When you read this page, know that it was written by Clara who loves you, in a moment of weakness and despair."

At least that is past now, for her; from her other letters he knows she was finally reassured. But that she suffered like this; that he is only hearing about it now . . . to whom is she turning for consolation?

Winter drags on. Meetings and work; official appearances and work; squabbles and work. Work. He does what he can, what he must. Part of him wants to rush home to Clara. To give up this job, this place, these ambitions; to sail home at the earliest opportunity and never to travel again. It has all been too much: the complexities and politics, the secrets underlying everything. Until he left England, he thinks now, he had lived in a state of remarkable innocence. Never, not even as a boy, had he been able to fit himself into the world. But he had thought, until recently, that he might turn his back on what he didn't understand and make his own solitary path. Have his own heroes, pursue his own goals. But if his heroes are spies; if his work is in service of men whose goals led to blood-stained rooms and raining flesh—nothing is left of the world as he once envisioned it.

He wanders the city and its outskirts, keeping an eye out, as he walks, for Dr. Chouteau. He must be here; where else would he spend the winter? Stories of that irascible old man, or of someone like him, surface now and then; often Max has a sense that Dr. Chouteau hides down the next alley, across the next bridge. He hears tales of other travelers as well—Jacquemont and Moorcroft, the Schlagintweit brothers, Thomas Thomson and the Baron von Hugel. The tales contradict each other, as do those about Dr. Chouteau himself. In one story he is said to be an Irish mercenary, in another an American businessman. Through these distorted lenses Max sees himself as if for the first time, and something happens to him.

That lost man, whose skull he found when he first arrived in the mountains—is this what befell him? As an experiment, Max stops eating. He fasts for three days and confirms what the lost man wrote in his diary: his spirit soars free, everything looks different. His mother is with him often, during that airy, delirious time. Dr. Chouteau strolls through his imagination as well. In a brief break in the flow of Dr. Chouteau's endless, self-regarding narrative, Max had offered an account of his own experiences up on the glacier. His cold entombment, his lucky escape; he'd been humiliated when Dr. Chouteau laughed and patted his shoulder. *A few hours,* he said. *You barely tasted the truth. I was caught for a week on the Siachen Glacier, in a giant blizzard. There is no harsher place on this earth; it belongs to no one. Which won't keep people from squabbling over it someday. The men I traveled with died.*

When Max hallucinates Dr. Chouteau's voice emerging from the mouth of a boatwoman arguing with her neighbor, he starts eating again, moving again. The old maps he's been asked to revise are astonishingly inaccurate. He wanders through narrow lanes overhung by balconies, in and out of a maze of courtyards. The air smells of stale cooking oil, burning charcoal, human excrement. He makes his way back and forth across the seven bridges of Srinagar so often he might be weaving a web. Temples, mosques, the churches of the missionaries; women carrying earthenware pots on their heads; barges and bakeshops and markets piled with rock salt and lentils, bottles of ghee—his wanderings he justifies as being in service to the map, although he also understands that part of what drives him into the biting air is a search for Dr. Chouteau. If Max could find him, if he could ask him some questions, perhaps this unease that has settled over him might lift.

As winter turns into early spring, as he does what he can with his map of the valley and, in response to letters from Dehra Dun, begins preparations for another season up in the mountains, his life spirals within him like the tendril of a climbing plant. One day he sits down, finally, with Laurence's gift to him and begins working slowly through the lines of Mr. Darwin's argument. The ideas aren't unfamiliar to him; as with the news of Cawnpore and the Mutiny, he has heard them summarized, read accounts in the newspapers, discussed the outlines of the theory of descent with modification with Laurence and others. But when he confronts the details and grasps all the strands of the theory, it hits him like the knowledge of the use made of Dr. Hooker's maps, or the uses that will be made of his own. He scribbles all over the margins. At first he writes Laurence simply to say: *I am reading it. Have you read it? It is marvelous. The world is other than we thought.* But a different, more complicated letter begins to unfurl in his mind.

A mountain, he reads, *is an island on the land. The identity of many plants and animals, on mountain-summits, separated from each other by hundreds of miles of lowlands, where the alpine species could not possibly exist, is one of the most striking cases known of the same species living at distant points, without the apparent possibility of their having migrated from one to another . . . the glacial period affords a simple explanation of these facts.*

He closes his eyes and sees the cold sweeping south and covering the land with snow and ice, arctic plants and animals migrating into the temperate regions. Then, centuries later, the warmth returning and the arctic forms retreating northward with the glaciers, leaving isolated representatives stranded on the icy summits. *Along the Himalaya,* Mr. Darwin writes, *at points 900 miles apart, glaciers have left the marks of their former low descent; and in Sikkim, Dr. Hooker saw maize on gigantic ancient moraines.* The point of Dr. Hooker's work, Max sees, is not just to map the geographical distribution of plants but to use that map in service of a broader theory. Not just, *The same genus of lichen appears in Baltistan and in Sikkim.* But, *The lichens of the far ends of the Himalaya are related, descending from a common ancestor.*

It is while his head is spinning with these notions that, on the far side of the great lake called the Dal, near a place where, if it was summer, the lotus flowers would be nodding their heads above their enormous circular leaves, by a chenar tree in which herons have nested for generations, he meets at last not Dr. Chouteau, but a woman. Dark-haired, dark-eyed: Dima. At first he speaks to her simply to be polite, and to conceal his surprise that she'd address him without being introduced. Then he notices, in her capable hands, a sheaf of reeds someone else might not consider handsome, but which she praises for the symmetry of their softly drooping heads. Although she wears no wedding ring, she is here by the lake without a chaperone.

The afternoon passes swiftly as they examine other reeds, the withered remains of ferns, lichens clustered on the rocks. Her education has come, Max learns, from a series of tutors and travelers and missionaries; botanizing is her favorite diversion. He eyes her dress, which is well-cut although not elaborate; her boots, which are sturdy and look expensive. From what is she seeking diversion? She speaks of plants and trees and gardens, a stream of conversation that feels intimate yet reveals nothing personal. In return he tells her a bit about his work. When they part, and she invites him to call on her a few days later, he accepts. Such a long time, since he has spoken with anyone congenial.

Within the week, she lets him know that he'd be welcome in her bed; and, gently, that he'd be a fool to refuse her. Max doesn't hide from her the fact that he's married, nor that he must leave this place soon. But the relief he finds with her—not just her body, the comforts of her bed, but her intelligence, her hands on his neck, the sympathy with which she listens to his hopes and longings—the relief is so great that sometimes, after she falls asleep, he weeps.

"I have been lonely," she tells him. "I have been without company for a while." She strokes his thighs and his sturdy smooth chest and slips down the sheets until their hipbones are aligned. Compactly built, she is several inches shorter than him but points out that their legs are the same length; his extra height is in his torso. Swiftly he pushes away a memory of his wedding night with long-waisted Clara. The silvery filaments etched across Dima's stomach he tries not to recognize as being like those that appeared on Clara, after Elizabeth's birth.

He doesn't insult her by paying her for their time together; she isn't a prostitute, simply a woman grown used, of necessity, to being kept by men. Each time he arrives at her bungalow he brings gifts: little carved boxes and bangles and lengths of cloth; for her daughter, who is nearly Elizabeth's age, toy elephants and camels. Otherwise he tries to ignore the little girl. Who is her father, what is her name? He can't think about that, he can't look at her. Dima, seeming somehow to understand, sends her daughter off to play with the children of her servants when he arrives. Through the open window over her bed he sometimes hears them laughing.

Dima has lived with her father in Leh and Gilgit and here, in a quarter of Srinagar seldom visited by Europeans; she claims to be the daughter of a Russian explorer and a woman, now dead, from Skardu. For some years she was the mistress of a Scotsman who fled his job with the East India Company, explored in Ladakh, and ended up in Kashmir; later she lived with a German geologist. Or so she says. In bed she tells Max tales of her lovers, their friends, her father's friends—a secret band of wanderers, each with a story as complicated as Dr. Chouteau's. Which one taught her botany? In those stories, and the way that she appears to omit at least as much as she reveals, she resembles Dr. Chouteau himself, whom she claims to know. A friend of her father's, she says. A cartographer (but didn't he tell Max he never made maps?) and advisor to obscure princes; a spendthrift and an amateur geologist. Bad with his servants but excellent with animals; once he kept falcons. She knows a good deal about him but not, she claims, where he is now.

One night, walking back from her bungalow, a shadowy figure resembling Dr. Chouteau appears on the street before Max and then disappears into an alley. Although the night is dark, Max follows. The men crouched around charcoal braziers and leaning in doorways regard him quietly. Not just Kashmiris: Tibetans and Ladakhis, Yarkandis, Gujars, Dards—are those Dards?—and Baltis and fair-haired men who might be Kafirs. During this last year, he has learned to recognize such men by their size and coloring and the shape of their eyes, their dress and weapons and bearing. As they have no doubt learned to recognize Englishmen. If Dr. Chouteau is among them, he hides himself. For a moment, as Max backs away with his hands held open and empty before him, he realizes that anything might happen to him. He is no one here. No one knows where he is. In the Yasin valley, Dr. Chouteau said, he once stumbled across a pile of stones crowned by a pair of hands. The hands were white, dessicated, bound together at the wrists. Below the stones was the remainder of the body.

When he leaves the alley, all Max can see for a while are the stars and the looming blackness of the mountains. How clear the sky is! His mind feels equally clear, washed out by that moment of darkness.

During his next weeks with Dima, Clara recedes—a voice in his ear, words on paper; mysterious, as she was when he first knew her. Only when Dima catches a cold and he has to tend her, bringing basins and handkerchiefs and cups of tea, does he recollect what living with Clara was really like. Not the ardent, long-distance exchange of words, on which they've survived for more than a year, but the grit and weariness of everyday life. Household chores and worries over money, a crying child, a smoking stove; relatives coming and going, all needing things, and both of them stretched so thin; none of it Clara's fault, it is only life. Now it is Dima who is sick, and who can no longer maintain her enchanting deceits. The carefully placed candles, the painted screen behind which she undoes her ribbons and laces to emerge in a state of artful undress, the daughter disposed of so she may listen with utmost attention to him, concentrate on him completely—all that breaks down. One day there is a problem with her well, which he must tend to. On another her daughter—her name is Kate—comes into Dima's bedroom in tears, her dress torn by some children who've been teasing her. He has to take Kate's hand. He has to find the other children and scold them and convince them all to play nicely together, then report back to Dima how this has been settled. He is falling, he thinks. Headfirst, into another crevasse.

During Dima's illness it is with some relief—he knows it is shameful—that he returns at night to his spartan quarters. Through the gossip that flies so swiftly among the British community, the three other surveyors have heard about Dima. Twice Max was spotted with her, and this was all it took; shunned alike by Hindus and Moslems, Christians and Sikhs, she has a reputation. That it is Max she's taken up with, Max she's chosen: to Max's amazement and chagrin, his companions find this glamorous. They themselves have found solace in the brothels; Srinagar is filled with women and they no longer turn to each other for physical relief. But to them, unaware of Dima's illness and her precarious household, Max's situation seems exotic. The knowledge that he shares their weaknesses, despite the way he has kept to himself—this, finally, is what makes Max's companions accept him.

They stop teasing him. They ask him to drink with them, to dine with them; which, on occasion, he does. They ask for details, which he refuses. But despite his reticence, his connection to Dima has made his own reputation. When the rest of the surveyors return from Dehra Dun and they all head back to the mountains, Max knows he will occupy a different position among them. Because of her, everything will be different, and easier, than during the last season. It is this knowledge that breaks the last piece of his heart.

April arrives; the deep snow mantling the Pir Panjal begins to shrink back from the black rock. Max writes long letters to Laurence, saying nothing about Dima but musing about what he reads. Into Srinagar march triangulators in fresh tidy clothes, newly trained Indian assistants, new crowds of porters bearing glittering instruments, and the officers: Michaels among them. But Michaels can no longer do Max any harm. Max and his three companions present their revised map of Srinagar, and are praised. Then it is time to leave. Still Max has no answers. Dr. Chouteau has continued to elude him; Dima, fully recovered now, thanks him for all his help, gives him some warm socks, and wishes him well with his work.

Which work? Even to her he has not admitted what he is thinking about doing these next months. He holds her right hand in both of his and nods numbly when she says she will write him, often, and hopes that he'll write her. Hopes that they'll see each other again, when the surveying party returns to Srinagar.

More letters. Another person waiting for him. "Don't write," he says, aware the instant he does so of his cruelty. The look on her face—but she has had other lovers (how many lovers?) and she doesn't make a scene. Perhaps this is why he chose her. When they part, he knows he will become simply a story she tells to the next stranger she welcomes into her life.

And still he does not write Clara. Other letters from her have arrived, which he hasn't answered: six months, what is he thinking? Not about her, the life she is leading in his absence, the way her days unfold; not what she and their children are doing, their dreams and daily duties and aspirations and disappointments. Neither is he thinking about Dima; it is not as if his feelings for her have driven out those he has for Clara. He isn't thinking about either of them. This is his story, his life unfolding. The women will tell the tale of these months another way.

7.

April 21, 1864

My dearest, my beloved Clara—
Forgive me for not writing in so long. I have been sick—nothing serious, nothing you need worry about, although it did linger. But I am fully recovered now, in time to join the rest of the party on our march back into the mountains. This season, I expect, will be much like the last. Different mountains, similar work; in October I will be done with the services I contracted for and the Survey will be completed. From my letters of last season you will have a good idea of what I'll be doing. But Clara—

Max pauses, then crosses out the last two words. What he should say is what he knows she wants to hear: that when October comes he'll be on his way back to her, as they agreed. But he doesn't want to lie to her. Not yet.

His party is camped by a frozen stream. The porters are butchering a goat. Michaels, in a nearby tent, has just explained to the men their assignments for the coming week; soon it will be time to eat; Max has half an hour to finish this letter and no way to say what he really means: that after the season is finished, he wants to stay on.

Everything has changed for me, he wants to say. *I am changed, I know now who I am and what I want and I can only hope you accept this, and continue to wait for me. I want to stay a year longer. When the Survey ends, in October, I want to wait out the winter in Srinagar, writing up all I have learned and seen so far; and then I want to spend next spring and summer traveling by myself. If I had this time to explore, to test myself, discover the secrets of these mountains—it would be enough, I could be happy with this, it would last me the rest of my life. When I come home, I mean to try to establish myself as a botanist. I have no hope of doing so without taking this time and working solely on my studies.*

But he can't write any of that. Behind him men are laughing, a fire is burning, he can smell the first fragrance of roasting meat. He is off again to the cold bare brilliance of a place like the moon, and what he can't explain, yet, to Clara is that he needs other time, during the growing season, to study the plants in the space between the timberline and the line of permanent snow. How do the species that have arisen here differ from those in other places? How do they make a life for themselves, in such difficult circumstances?

But how could Clara possibly understand this? He will break it to her gently, he thinks. A hint, at first; a few more suggestions in letters over the coming months; in September he'll raise the subject. Perhaps by then he'll have more encouragement from Dr. Hooker, which he can offer to Clara as evidence that his work is worthwhile. Perhaps by then he'll understand how he might justify his plans to her. For now—what else can he say in this letter? He has kept too much from her, these last months. If his letters were meant to be a map of his mind, a way for her to follow his trail, then he has failed her. Somehow, as summer comes to these peaks and he does his job for the last time, he must find a way to let her share in his journey. But for now all he can do is triangulate the first few points.

—I have so much to tell you, Clara. And no more time today; what will you think, after all these months, when you receive such a brief letter? Know that I am thinking of you and the girls, no matter what I do. I promise we'll do whatever you want when I return: I know how much you miss your brother, perhaps we will join him in New York. I would like that, I think. I would like to start over, all of us, someplace new. Somewhere I can be my new self, live my new life, in your company.

Next to my heart, in an oilskin pouch, I keep the lock of Elizabeth's hair and your last unopened letter to me, with your solemn instruction on the envelope: *To Be Opened if You Know You Will Not Return to Me.* If the time comes, I will open it. But the time won't come; I will make it back, I will be with you again.

This comes to you with all my love, from your dearest

Max

Contributors' Notes

Jurors

Short-Listed Stories

2001 Magazine Award

Magazines Consulted

Permissions Acknowledgments

Contributors' Notes

ANDREA BARRETT is the author of five novels, most recently *The Voyage of the Narwhal,* and a collection of short fiction, *Ship Fever,* which received the 1996 National Book Award. Her new collection, *Servants of the Map,* will be published by W.W. Norton in 2002. She and her husband live in Rochester, New York.

"I wrote so many drafts of 'Servants of the Map,' over such a long time, that even I can't quite understand where the story came from. Reading about surveyors and mountaineers and explorers in the Himalaya, of course; I've long been fascinated by that area. Thinking about letters, which play such a large role in my life, and how they can both bind and separate people. But my experiences of winter camping and climbing in the Adirondacks also fed into this; as did a sunny day on a snowfield in the Pyrenees, when I turned at the sound of my husband's shout to see him, roped some feet behind me, disappearing into a small crevasse; and also the delights, a few years later, of dangling deep inside a large crevasse on the Athabasca Glacier, safely tied onto a climbing rope in the hands of a very good guide."

PINCKNEY BENEDICT grew up on his family's dairy farm in the mountains of southern West Virginia. He has published two collections of short fiction and a novel. His stories have appeared, among other places, in

Esquire, Prize Stories 1999: The O. Henry Awards, The Pushcart Prize XXI: Best of the Small Presses, Zoetrope: All-Story, Ontario Review, Story, and *The Oxford Book of American Short Stories.* He is an associate professor in the Creative Writing Program at Hollins University in Roanoke, Virginia.

"This is the first love story I've ever written, and (even though the protagonist is an iron alien filled with sentient gas) the most autobiographical of my stories. I feel like McGinty/Zog—that sense that I'm out of place and out of time, that I'm intended for some task that I don't clearly understand and that probably has little importance—pretty much constantly. I loved writing this story. I often wish that I could just go on writing it for all time, which is probably one of the reasons it's so darn long."

T. CORAGHESSAN BOYLE is the author of fourteen books of fiction, including, most recently, *After the Plague* (2001), *A Friend of the Earth* (2000), *T. C. Boyle Stories* (1998), and *Riven Rock* (1998), as well as *The Road to Wellville, The Tortilla Curtain, World's End,* and *Water Music.* He is the grateful recipient of a number of honors and awards, including the PEN/Faulkner Award for the best American novel of the year and the PEN/Malamud Award in the short story. He earned his M.F.A. and Ph.D. degrees from the University of Iowa and is a member of the English Department at the University of Southern California in Los Angeles.

"The world in which we live is open to the minutest scrutiny, from the tracking of invisible planets to the unmasking of quarks and the mapping of the human genome, but at its essence it remains a dark and mysterious place. I write fiction in order to address and measure my response to that darkness and that mystery. I don't know how to feel, actually, unless I can sort things out in a story or novel.

" 'The Love of My Life' is my response to a disturbing news item of a few years back, a story reported more widely on the east coast than the west. It came to me in its rawest form, and then I did a little digging—just enough to assess the facts—and invented a scenario to explain how such a thing could have happened. In the process, I've written a meditation on first love and its urges and how it often conflicts with established norms and mores. But of course, I say this clinically, and in hindsight. The story should break your heart. I know it broke mine."

RON CARLSON lives in Arizona. He is the author of five books of fiction, most recently the story collection *The Hotel Eden.* His stories have appeared in *Esquire, Harper's, GQ, Playboy, Epoch,* and other periodicals as well dozens of anthologies, including *The Best American Short Stories, The Pushcart Prize* anthology, and *The Norton Anthology of Contemporary Fiction.* His young adult novel *The Speed of Light* will be published next year by HarperCollins.

"I've always loved stories about radical moments in the wilderness. This is my little tribute to 'To Build a Fire.' My fiction depends many times on place, and here at the center I wanted real snow and plenty of it, enough to believe, enough to have changed Donner, enough to allow the rest. There were many surprises in the draft, none larger for me than when the young woman says to Rusty, 'I've heard about you.' I didn't know I was writing a story about stories. I stayed with the name Donner, even after I saw what the story contained."

DAN CHAON is the author of two collections of stories: *Fitting Ends* (Triquarterly Books/Northwestern University Press, 1996) and *Among the Missing* (Ballantine, 2001), in which the story "Big Me" appears. His work has been featured in a number of journals and anthologies, including *The Best American Short Stories 1996* and *The Pushcart Prize XXIV.* He lives in the Cleveland area with his wife, Sheila Schwartz (herself a 1999 O. Henry Award winner), and their two sons. He teaches at Oberlin College, and is at work on a novel titled *You Remind Me of Me.*

"You know how sometimes writers will say that they wrote their prizewinning story in one feverish all-night sitting and then watched the sunrise feeling refreshed and glad to be alive? I hate those kind of writers very much, because that never happens to me.

"What's worse, I have to admit that this particular piece was one of the evilest, stubbornest stories I've ever dealt with. Oh, yes, in the beginning it was all an innocent lark, and there was a lot of stuff in it that was fun to write and think about—the imaginary city, the blackouts, the fake girlfriend, the cat torture—but soon things turned nasty. The story absolutely refused to cohere or develop any plotlike forward movement. It was very uncompromising and selfish, and I probably wrote twenty drafts of this story over a period of several years, developing a fairly ugly love-hate relationship with it. At one point my long-suffering wife absolutely refused to look at yet another version of the creature, and I took to sending it to unaware friends and asking their opinions. I don't quite know how it happened, but at some point my various readers started saying, 'This seems pretty close to being finished,' instead of 'Um, Dan, this makes absolutely no sense.'

"In any case, the original impetus behind the story is probably lost in the long hallway of drafts that led up to the final version. I guess I can autobiographically reveal that when I was a preteen, I actually did write a very officious letter to the Future Me, which I later found among some old childhood stuff when I was cleaning out my parents' house after they died, and I did feel a twinge of enmity toward the self-important and conde-scending little person I'd once been. I'll also tell that the hardest part of the story for me—the final confrontation between Andy and Mickleson—was ultimately written as I actually acted out the scene late one night. Imagine our poor neighbor lady glancing over and seeing me prancing around my study, gesticulating and saying things like 'Hold still, I'll whisper,' and then writing wildly on a legal pad. My neighbor closed her curtain dis-creetly, as I suppose I should have as well.

"My thanks to Peter Stitt of *The Gettysburg Review,* who liked the story enough to publish it, to all the friends who waded through drafts, and most especially to my wife, Sheila Schwartz, who is both a wise and patient reader and the writer whose work most inspires me."

LOUISE ERDRICH is the author of *Love Medicine, The Beet Queen, The Antelope Wife,* and other novels. She lives in Minnesota. Her most recent novel is *The Last Report on the Miracles at Little Horse.*

"'Revival Road' grew little by little, over the course of thirteen years. I revised it endlessly, sometimes adding just a sentence every few months, then leaving it alone for another few months. It is not part of a novel or collection, so far."

WILLIAM GAY is the author of two novels, *The Long Home* and *Provinces of Night.* His work has appeared in various magazines including *Harper's Magazine, The Oxford American,* and *The Atlantic Monthly,* and in *New Stories from the South* (1999 and 2000). He lives in Hohenwald, Ten-nessee, and in Oxford, Mississippi, where he is at work on a novel and a collection of short stories.

"Certain people, upon reading 'The Paperhanger,' have looked at me in a speculative way, and a few have asked, 'How much of you is there in the paperhanger or of the paperhanger in you?' I'm fond of this story because it is purely the work of imagination. I am not the paperhanger, and luckily I have never met him."

ELIZABETH GRAVER is the author of a story collection, *Have You Seen Me?*, and two novels, *Unravelling* and *The Honey Thief*. Her work has appeared in two previous editions of *Prize Stories: The O. Henry Awards* (1994 and 1996), as well as in *Best American Short Stories* and *Best American Essays*. She teaches at Boston College.

"I was making the bed one day and passed my hand over a bump that felt like a small fist. The story grew from there. I was trying to get pregnant at the time, and while we ended up not having to enter the maze of reproductive technology, I had friends who were deep inside that maze. The story came, I suppose, from watching them navigate a world that seemed as surreal as my story, as well as from my own anticipatory anxiety. I'm used, as a writer, to being able to *make* things, to spin them out of thin air—with enough hard work, enough deep attention. Trying to have a baby demands a kind of surrender to the body that I found at once difficult and moving. Our daughter, Chloe, was born right before 'The Mourning Door' appeared in *Ploughshares*."

MURAD KALAM is a third-year law student at Harvard Law School. He was born in Seattle, Washington, and grew up in Arizona, outside of Phoenix. "Bow Down" is his first published short story and represents the beginning of his novel *Night Journey*. He is at work on a second novel.

"Woodland Avenue is a very real South Phoenix street and resembles the Woodland Avenue of my imagination excepting that the park stretches out, and there are more trees. I had no sense of the setting while scratching out the novel in college back East. I simply picked the street off a Phoenix map. It was not until I came back to Phoenix to work that I went to the street and got a sense of it. Woodland Avenue sits at the back side of the state capitol and equidistant to both the red light district and the Madison Street Jail.

"I can still remember the day that the story came alive for me, the last epiphany. I was putting it through an old IBM Selectric, literally retyping what had been a dry scene when the story revealed itself—the absurdity of a young boy ruling over grown transients and prostitutes, a boy running a flophouse with the discernment of an M.B.A., a burgeoning predator, who is evil and industrious and sometimes benevolent. I always took this sudden explosion to be evidence of the staying power of a good clacking electric typewriter as a writing/revising tool. I never find revision monotonous. If you think revising fiction can be monotonous, try Civil Procedure."

FRED G. LEEBRON's novels include *Out West, Six Figures,* and the forthcoming *At the End of the Day.* His stories have appeared in *TriQuarterly, DoubleTake, Tin House, The Threepenny Review, The Pushcart Prize XXV,* and elsewhere. He lives in Gettysburg, Pennsylvania, with his wife and two children.

"This story was like many others for me: in it I tried to write from a present personal dilemma into an unknowable future. In one sense, then, the writing was cathartic; in another sense it was exploratory. But it was not supposed to be predictive, and it ultimately wasn't factual. Mostly, when I was writing it, I was thinking about the limits of one person's empathy in the face of another person's mortality. Then I was thinking about empathy in general. Then I was using words that I would never use, like 'mercy' or 'denial,' and then I tried to find a way out."

ALICE MUNRO lives in Huron County, Ontario, Canada. She has published several books of short stories.

"I was thinking about a sick wife, a husband infatuated with a responsive but strangely innocent young woman. Then I got two gifts—the joke, which gave me the family in the trailer, the dogs, etc., and then the road, a real road just like the one described, which could have led to the bridge but actually didn't, and that road gave me the drive, the boy, the stars, the kiss. Oh, yes, there was a real porcupine, surprised at night. It all worked together."

ANTONYA NELSON is the author of three novels and four short story collections, including the forthcoming *Female Trouble* (Scribner, 2002). She teaches creative writing at New Mexico State University and in the Warren Wilson M.F.A. Program. She lives in Telluride, Colorado, and Las Cruces, New Mexico, with her husband, Robert Boswell, and their two children.

"'Female Trouble' was begun when I was once nostalgic for my graduate school days at the University of Arizona. I tossed together images from that time and place: a fellow student writer driven to wandering with a typewriter roadside; umbrellas and appliances used as lawn art; accident depositions found in the *Arizona Daily Star;* and the insane transience of objects of affection. I think I wrote the story with the hope that I would learn to resemble steady, openhearted Martha rather than fickle and unbrave McBride."

JOYCE CAROL OATES is the author most recently of the novel *Blonde* and the story collection *Faithless: Tales of Transgression.* Recent stories of hers have appeared in *Salmagundi, Boulevard, Harper's Magazine, Playboy, The Paris Review,* and *The Best American Short Stories of the 20th Century,* edited by John Updike. She is a coeditor of *Ontario Review* and professor of humanities at Princeton.

"Since the death of my father, Frederic Oates, in May 2000, I've been more or less anesthetized emotionally. But I've been trying to 'feel' emotion by contemplating the difficult, often turbulent backgrounds of my parents, who came of age in an America mostly vanished now, very different from our own. At the heart of our family history there was a single act of violence that determined our subsequent lives. It may have had some simple explanation but to everyone involved, on the victim's side, it remains utterly motiveless and mysterious.

"'The Girl with the Blackened Eye' isn't about that act of violence but about another, obviously set in a contemporary time and fictionalized. The emotional connection must be the narrator's anesthetized state; yet her sense of having been given meaning, of an unspeakable kind, through her involvement with a serial killer who saw in her something 'special.' Aren't we pitiful in the rawness of our yearnings!"

DALE PECK is the author of the novels *Martin and John, The Law of Enclosures,* and *Now It's Time to Say Goodbye; The Garden of Lost and Found* is due to be published in October 2001. His reviews appear regularly in *Art-* and *Bookforum,* the *London Review of Books, The New Republic,* and *The Village Voice Literary Supplement.* His fiction has been published in *Conjunctions, Granta,* and *Zoetrope: All-Story.* He lives in New York City and teaches in the Graduate Writing Program of New School University.

"My first novel grew out of a series of linked short stories, but since that book I've largely avoided the form. I write a lot of one- and two- and three-page prose pieces, but 'Bliss' is only the third full-length story I've completed in the past eight years. For me, the challenge is avoiding that significant-day-in-the-life syndrome, which seems to suggest that epiphanies come with the same frequency as subscription-renewal notices. That, plus the fact that I'm pretty long-winded. Anyway, the germ of this story was a documentary I saw about a British organization that united the victims of violent crimes with the perpetrators, and the fertilizer was Mailer's beautiful, brilliant portrayal of the Nicole Baker–Gary Gilmore love affair in *The Executioner's Song.* The twisted outgrowth of the resulting product is entirely mine, except for the Monte Carlo, of course, which was my father's."

GEORGE SAUNDERS is the author of the story collections *CivilWarLand in Bad Decline* and *Pastoralia,* and of a children's book, *The Very Persistent Gappers of Frip.* He teaches in the Creative Writing Program at Syracuse University.

"'Pastoralia' came out of a dream I had, in which I was wearing a loincloth while trying to get a fax machine to work, while my coworker snarled at me and belligerently filed her nails, and also, we were in a cave, which should tell you something about the nature of my dream-life, and is pretty darn embarrassing, now that I see it all typed out. I'm honored to have the story included here, and grateful to the editor for including it, and also to you, dear reader, for buying and reading this book and thereby helping to keep writing alive in America."

DAVID SCHICKLER writes fiction and screenplays. In June 2001, The Dial Press will publish his first book, *Kissing in Manhattan,* which contains "The Smoker." He holds an M.F.A. in creative writing from Columbia University. His stories have appeared in *The New Yorker, Tin House, Seventeen,* and *Zoetrope: All-Story.* He lives in New York.

"'The Smoker,' like most of *Kissing in Manhattan,* takes place in the Preemption, a fictional apartment building in New York City. I created the Preemption because I wanted a gothic castle where all my characters— freaks, lovers, gun-toting stock brokers—could thrive and know magic while they chased sex or redemption. I wrote 'The Smoker' a few months after my father told me how, as a boy, he used to box on Friday nights and get cheap steaks afterward with his friends at some greasy dive. That's the only part of the story inspired by real life, despite the fact that I used to teach high school English. A colleague claims that the story is wish fulfillment on my part, but I believe *Kissing in Manhattan*—the book and the act—*should* offer impossible, hilarious, dangerous romance. Why shoot for anything less?"

MARY SWAN's stories have appeared in a number of literary magazines and anthologies, including *Ontario Review* and *Best Canadian Stories*. She works in a library in Guelph, Ontario, where she lives with her husband and daughter. A collection of stories is forthcoming from Porcupine's Quill Press.

"I have long been interested in the First World War, and when I was a child I desperately wanted to be a twin, so when a friend came across mention of the incident at the heart of this story, everything came together. I worked on the story in bits and pieces over nearly ten years, leaving it for long periods but always having it in the back of my mind. In the end, after all that time, I realized that the bits and pieces added up to something, and it came together rather painlessly."

Jurors

MICHAEL CHABON writes,"I was born in 1963, in Washington, D.C., and raised mostly in Columbia, an attempted utopia in the Maryland suburbs.

"I studied at the University of Pittsburgh, got an M.F.A. in creative writing at U.C. Irvine, and have spent most of the past fifteen years in California with brief sojourns in Washington State, Florida, and New York State. Since 1997, I have been living with my wife, Ayelet Waldman, a writer of mysteries, and our children, in Berkeley. Random House published my third novel, *The Amazing Adventures of Kavalier & Clay*, in September 2000. It followed *The Mysteries of Pittsburgh* (1988) and *Wonder Boys* (1995), as well as two collections of short stories, *A Model World and Other Stories* (1990) and *Werewolves in Their Youth* (1999). I have also written articles and essays, and a number of screenplays and teleplays, all of them thus far unproduced. My story 'Son of the Wolfman' was chosen for the 1999 O. Henry Awards collection and a National Magazine Award. *The Amazing Adventures of Kavalier & Clay* was selected by the American Library Association as one of the Notable Books of 2000, was a finalist for the National Book Critics Circle Award, and won the 2001 Pulitzer Prize for fiction."

MARY GORDON is the author of the novels *Final Payments, The Company of Women, Men and Angels, The Other Side,* and *Spending.* She has also published a memoir, *The Shadow Man;* a book of novellas, *The Rest of Life;* a short story collection, *Temporary Shelter;* two books of essays, *Good Boys and Dead Girls* and *Seeing Through Places;* and a biography, *Joan of Arc.* Her three O. Henry Award–winning stories include the 1997 first-prize winner, "City Life," and the 2000 third-prize winner, "The Deacon." She is a professor of English at Barnard College.

MONA SIMPSON is the author of the novels *Anywhere But Here, The Lost Father, A Regular Guy,* and *Off Keck Road.* She is working on a short story collection titled *Virginity and Other Fictions,* and has had stories included in *The Pushcart Prize* and *The Best American Short Stories.*

Short-Listed Stories

APPEL, JACOB M., "Counting," *Louisiana Literature,* **Vol. 17, No. 1**

A man takes a summer job with the Bureau of the Census, interviewing single women in Lawless County, Arizona. He and his partner, a sixties dropout, are initially turned away by a beautiful woman without legs, but she later agrees to answer their questions if her boyfriend fails to build a house of cards that reaches to the ceiling.

BANKS, RUSSELL, "The Moor," *Conjunctions,* **No. 34**

A middle-aged plumber encounters a woman who was his first lover, now eighty, in a restaurant after a performance in blackface at a Mason lodge. They talk and learn more about each other and recall their past encounters.

BEATTIE, ANN, "The Women of This World," *The New Yorker,* **November 20, 2000**

A woman prepares a nice pre-Thanksgiving dinner for her husband's stepfather and his girlfriend. But there's tension between the two guests and things do not go well. When the women go off to take a walk, leaving the men behind to polish off a bottle of expensive wine, they discover that a neighbor has been assaulted.

BOSWELL, ROBERT, "A Walk in Winter," *Colorado Review,* **Vol. XXVII, No. 1**

In the middle of winter, a man returns to the small South Dakota town where he grew up, for the purposes of identifying frozen remains that the police believe are his mother's. She disappeared when he was ten and he was left with his brutal father, who soon thereafter also disappeared.

BRENNAN, KAREN, "Secret Encounters," *Global City Review,* **No. 13**

Alternating titled sections tell the stories of three characters. In "Wreckage," a man slowly destroys his own house. In "Sleep," a woman spends the night in a sleep clinic. In "Face," a woman recovers from plastic surgery that she fears has made her look worse, not better.

BUSCH, FREDERICK, "Domicile," *Five Points,* **Vol. IV, No. 2**

After graduating from college, a young man maintains an impoverished existence in a trailer on an estate owned by a woman and her grown daughter, in exchange for labor he does around the property. His girlfriend has left him and he isn't sure what to do next with his life. In the meantime, he works at building a stone wall and sleeps with the daughter. Across the way, he notices a boy who appears to be living alone in one of the cabins of an abandoned motel.

CANTOR, RACHEL, "Minyan of One," *The Paris Review,* **No. 155**

The story of a Jewish advisor from the first century sent by the Sultan Harun with gifts for Charlemagne is alternated with the story of a woman in contemporary Italy who is considering doing relief work in Bosnia.

CARLSON, RON, "At Copper View," *Five Points,* **Vol. V, No. 1**

A seventeen-year-old boy, who plays football and is happy with his life, is asked to do a favor for the popular captain of the team. Though the boy has a girlfriend, he agrees to escort the friend of the football captain's girlfriend to a homecoming dance at another high school. This alienates him from his sweetheart and gets him into a fight at the rival school.

CHAPMAN, MAILE, "A Love Transaction," *Post Road,* **Vol. 1**

A woman with a "baby-thing" growing inside her, who works at some kind of a clinic or kennel or animal laboratory, tries to get the attention of a male coworker without telling him about her condition.

COHEN, MITCH, "Shadow Boxing," *DoubleTake,* No. 22

A man paid to be a sparring partner for boxers, who out of pride disdains protective gear and has taken a serious beating over the years, is asked to work with an up-and-coming boxing star and decides, for once, to try to fight back.

DAVIES, PETER HO, "Think of England," *Ploughshares,* Vol. 26, Nos. 2 & 3

During World War II, a Welsh teenager who works in a local pub becomes sweethearts with an English soldier. The soldiers are treated by the locals, many of whom are Welsh nationalists, as an occupying army and the romance is kept a secret. But the girl is in over her head.

DÍAZ, JUNOT, "The Brief Wondrous Life of Oscar Wao," *The New Yorker,* December 25, 2000 & January 1, 2001

An unattractive, bookish, overweight Dominican boy living in New Jersey spends his life searching for love. His efforts are in vain until, in his twenties, he accompanies his family on a summer trip to Santo Domingo, where he falls in love with a prostitute who has a dangerous and jealous ex-boyfriend.

DOBYNS, STEPHEN, "Part of the Story," *DoubleTake,* No. 19

A sixty-three-year-old waitress, who had five children and gave them all up for adoption, is found by all five, who want to meet her. They come to visit her in her trailer and she makes up elaborate stories about their fathers in order to please them, when the truth is that all of the fathers were more or less scoundrels whom she coupled with out of pure lust.

DOWNS, MICHAEL, "Ania," *The Georgia Review,* Vol. LIV, No. 1

A Polish couple emigrates to Hartford, Connecticut, just before World War II. They have a child. After her husband enlists in the army and goes off to fight in the war, the wife takes jobs cleaning houses. She steals two tickets to the circus that she finds on the desk of a wealthy woman and takes her son. There's a fire at the circus. The woman is disfigured, and the boy is badly burned all over. The husband comes home and at first she spurns him, but then she allows him back.

EGAN, JENNIFER, "Good-bye, My Love," *Zoetrope: All-Story,* **Vol. 4, No. 3**

A man travels to Naples to look for his twenty-two-year-old niece, who has been missing for five years. At first, he spends his days touring and doesn't make any real effort to find her. Then, by chance, they meet. He agrees to take her out to dinner and afterward she takes him to a club, steals his wallet, and disappears. He searches for her in earnest now and finds her once more.

EVANIER, DAVID, "Mother," *Southwest Review,* **Vol. 85, No. 4**

A man who has long had a difficult relationship with his mother goes to visit her in the hospital after not seeing her for two years, just in time to see her before she dies. He goes to her apartment after the funeral and organizes her things, finding a diary she kept when he was a baby, but he has few pleasant memories of her. His farewell to her and the apartment he grew up in is bittersweet.

EVENSON, BRIAN, "The Intricacies of Post-Shooting Etiquette," *Chicago Review,* **Vol. 46, No. 1**

A man fails in his attempt to kill his lover and instead blinds and disables him. The man claims it was an accident—he didn't know the gun was loaded or thought it was a lighter—and the lover absolves him of blame. After the victim's discharge from the hospital, the man who shot him becomes his caretaker.

FOUNTAIN, BEN, "Rêve Haitien," *Harper's Magazine,* **January 2000**

An American observer in Haiti becomes involved with a native who wants to smuggle great Haitian paintings to Miami, sell them, and use the money to buy arms. He seduces the observer into helping him.

GREER, ANDREW SEAN, "Cannibal Kings," *Boulevard,* **Vol. 15, No. 3**

A young man at loose ends gets a job accompanying a young Vietnamese boy on his prep school interviews. The man makes up stories to make the boy sound like a good candidate for each school. At the last school the man discovers that the boy has been making up stories of his own, stories that are guaranteed to keep him from being accepted at any of the schools.

HARMAN, MATTHEW, "Honeymoon," *The Gettysburg Review,* Vol. 12, No. 4

A man on honeymoon with his wife in a remote coastal Indian town starts to cavort with the locals, to his new wife's chagrin. Their guide takes them to a remote beach where they are attacked by thugs.

HASLETT, ADAM, "You Are Not a Stranger Here," *Bomb,* Issue 72

A deeply depressed man accompanies his wife to Scotland, where she is doing research at a university library. The man is paralyzed by his depression and is at the point where he is ready to kill himself to spare his wife living with him. He goes to jump off a cliff but is interrupted by an eccentric local who takes him home for tea. On a subsequent visit he meets her grandson who is debilitated by a terrible case of psoriasis. The depressed man talks to him.

HEULER, KAREN, "The Snakes of Central Park," *Mid-American Review,* Vol. XX, Nos. 1 & 2

An unlikable woman living in Manhattan scrapes by with marginal jobs because she can't get along with anyone and is down to her last friend. A dying man has released his exotic snake collection in Central Park and the woman encounters some of these creatures, even as her propensity to alienate others leads her on a downward spiral.

HOLLADAY, CARY, "The Broken Lake," *Five Points,* Vol. V, No. 1

A thirty-year old woman, living with her uncle, a former Confederate Army officer, in a rambling, mostly vacant hotel outside of Richmond in 1903, takes as a lover the president of a railroad who has come to inspect the damage to his line following a flood.

HOOD, ANN, "Total Cave Darkness," *The Paris Review,* No. 155

An alcoholic runs off with a minister nine years her junior whom she went to for counseling. They wander from motel to motel and end up touring a cave called the Endless Cavern.

JACKSON, YVONNE A., "Style," *The Kenyon Review,* **Vol. XXII, Nos. 3 & 4**

A woman who has been living outside and working in a health club so she has a place to shower, meets a man who belongs to the club and becomes his lover. He offers her a job and she takes it and moves in with him, but she misses the freedom of her old existence.

JOHNSON, GREG, "Last Encounter with the Enemy," *Chattahoochee Review,* **Vol. XX, No. 2**

In 1964, an eleven-year-old boy who wants to be a writer takes a trip to interview Flannery O'Connor, whom he thinks of disdainfully as "the peacock lady." The boy's questions become hostile. He claims to be a prophet and attacks her for her faith, but the peacock lady holds her own.

KLAM, MATTHEW, "European Wedding," *The New Yorker,* **May 8, 2000**

A couple goes to France for their wedding, in a house that is being restored by the bride's mother. Both the bride and groom have their doubts about the wedding plans and the marriage. The groom finds himself among only women, when his father, brother, and friends are kept from making their flights by a storm system. The only other man in the villa is a Frenchman who may or may not be the bride's father.

KOHLER, SHEILA, "Casualty," *Ontario Review,* **No. 53**

An American living in the French countryside is having an affair with a doctor. Her husband has a mistress, so things seem equal. But on a night her lover sneaks into the house to sleep with the woman, her teenage daughter has an accident, falling off a wild horse they keep and fracturing her skull. The husband rushes to the hospital and rebukes the wife, sending her home to take a bath.

LAVALLE, VICTOR D., "Trinidad," *Transition,* **Issue 80**

A ten-year-old boy from New York City is sent off to Trinidad for the summer after he is caught in a compromising position with his best friend for the second time. In Trinidad he feels more relaxed than in his old neighborhood, which is fraught with perils for a boy his age.

LEE, DON, "The Price of Eggs in China," *The Gettysburg Review,* **Vol. 13, No. 1**

A Japanese-American artisan, who makes a special custom-fitted chair out of a rare wood found only in Japan, gets caught in the crossfire between his girlfriend and a rival poet.

LEE, REBECCA, "Fialta," *Zoetrope: All-Story,* **Vol. 4, No. 1**

A young man interested in architecture goes to study with a famous architect and becomes involved in a web of entanglements with his fellow students and their teacher.

LENNON, J. ROBERT, "The Future Journal," *Harper's Magazine,* **December 2000**

A second-grade teacher flees after his ambitious plan for the upcoming school year is shot down by the principal. He calls his girlfriend, the school's art teacher, and tells her to pass along the message that he's quitting. He drives for several hours until he comes to a suburb, enters a house, and goes up to a little girl's room—his daughter's. The house is his ex-wife's and her new husband's. His daughter finds him in the room and falls asleep beside him and he slips out of the house and drives home again.

LEWIS, TRUDY, "Masked Ma'am," *Third Coast,* **Fall 2000**

A woman who works in a video store finds herself changed by her pregnancy. It makes her more assertive, but also testy and difficult to be around. Her submerged anger over the impending change in her life comes out in ways that seem beyond her control.

LOPEZ, BARRY, "The Mappist," *The Georgia Review,* **Vol. LIV, No. 1**

A geographer locates the author of an incredible series of books mapping major cities in complex and interesting ways. The mappist is now an old man, living in rural North Dakota. The geographer goes to visit him and sees some of the mappist's final project: a complex series of diagrams of the state of North Dakota.

MINOT, STEPHEN, "Hannah at Daybreak," *The Virginia Quarterly Review,* Vol. 76, No. 3

In 1849, a sixteen-year-old girl from a poor family in New England is sent off to live with a strange man and help care for the man's old, bedridden mother and dim-witted brother. Surprisingly, she takes to her new life. After a while, the mother dies, and the girl expects to be sent back to her family, but the man she works for proposes marriage. Though he is many years older, she eventually accepts and begins a new life with him.

MOODY, RICK, "Forecast from the Retail Desk," *The New Yorker,* June 12, 2000

The narrator claims to be able to foretell the future and proceeds to give examples from his past, but in each case his predictions seem not entirely accurate. He senses that his brother's son has leukemia and fears that it is true, but his prediction seems clouded by his past troubled relations with his brother.

MOSS, BARBARA KLEIN, "Rug Weaver," *The Georgia Review,* Vol. LIV, No. 2

A woman tries to coax her father-in-law, an Iranian Jewish exile, out of the smoky room he inhabits in his son's house in Los Angeles. In Iran, he had been a scholar and owned a carpet emporium, but was made a prisoner after the revolution. To keep his sanity, in his mind he wove a complicated rug, with a pattern of the Garden of Eden.

MUNRO, ALICE, "Post and Beam," *The New Yorker,* December 11, 2000

A young woman from a small Canadian town, married to a mathematics professor and living in Vancouver with their two small children, develops a friendship with a former student of her husband's that borders on infatuation. A cousin the woman grew up with, who was like an older sister, comes to visit but feels unwanted. When the young woman and her family return from a weekend away, they find the sister and the former student have become fast friends.

MURR, NAEEM, "Nude," *The Gettysburg Review,* **Vol. 12, No. 4**

An aging man, living in a rundown flat, considers a last attempt at becoming an artist, even as he starts to succumb to a series of mental lapses and seizures. He is haunted by his past, in which he was accused of carrying on with a sixteen-year-old student, an incident that led to his wife abandoning him.

OATES, JOYCE CAROL, "The Vigil," *Harper's Magazine,* **July 2000**

A divorced man, obsessed with his ex-wife, keeps a vigil outside her house nearly every night. He notices another man's car parked there. Under threat of a court order he withdraws, but starts watching the house again in a different car. He brings his hunting rifle one night and follows the other car home, but can't bring himself to shoot the man or to end his vigil.

PACKER, ZZ, "Drinking Coffee Elsewhere," *The New Yorker,* **June 19 & 26, 2000**

A black freshman at Yale withdraws to her room after exhibiting hostile behavior during orientation. The school has her consult a psychologist. She keeps to herself until another girl comes to her door and draws her out. A close friendship evolves.

ROTHROCK, JEANNIE, "I Am Not Like Nuñez," *Meridian,* **No. 5**

A teenage girl living with a single mother who's a stripper and a half brother in a trailer in a rundown neighborhood in Atlanta steals a bag of marijuana from her mother's latest boyfriend. The theft sets in motion a chain of events that nearly leads to tragedy.

RYDER, PAMELA, "Overland," *Conjunctions,* **No. 34**

Sir Richard Burton and his party search for the source of the Nile River, enduring great hardships and the pursuit of the Paca Bunta.

SNEED, CHRISTINE, "I Want to Marry You," *Third Coast,* **Fall 2000**

A woman pursues a crush on her college professor and takes for granted a nice man truly interested in her, offering him only friendship. After college, the two go their separate ways, but keep in touch. He marries into a rich family in Montana, and the woman flies out to visit him after she experiences a failed relationship. They fall into each other's arms and, eventually, he leaves his wife for her.

STEFANIAK, MARY HELEN, "The Turk and My Mother," *Epoch,* Vol. 49, No. 1

A man tells his daughter the story from his childhood of when he discovered that his mother had been in love with a prisoner of war in her native Croatia during World War I. The story was revealed by his grandmother, shortly after his mother punished his sister for getting pregnant by causing her to burn her hands by intentionally putting too much lye in a bucket of water.

UPDIKE, JOHN, "Nelson and Annabelle," *The New Yorker,* October 2 & 9, 2000

A man meets his half sister, the illegitimate daughter of his dead father, and tries to establish a relationship with her. But his mother and stepfather, whom he lives with while getting his life back together after a divorce and rehab, are suspicious of the woman and present obstacles to his plan. He moves out after they are rude to her at Thanksgiving. Over the course of Christmas and New Year's, he introduces his half sister to his son and ex-wife, with whom he ultimately reconciles.

VOLLMANN, WILLIAM T., "The Sleepwalker," *Conjunctions,* No. 34

Adolph Hitler courts his destiny, which he believes is tied to the myths immortalized in Wagner's Ring cycle.

WALKER, DALY, "I Am the Grass," *The Atlantic Monthly,* June 2001

A Vietnam veteran, who has become a plastic surgeon and lives in a wealthy suburb of Chicago, returns to Vietnam. As a soldier he participated in atrocities that he can neither talk about nor forget. He returns as part of Operation Smile, a charitable endeavor. While there, he meets a Vietnamese doctor whose thumbs were cut off during the war, and he tries to make amends for his past by performing an operation to restore the doctor's thumbs.

WALLACE, DAVID FOSTER, "Incarnations of Burned Children," *Esquire,* **November 2000**

A father working outdoors rushes into the kitchen when he hears the screams of his child, who has been accidentally burned by an overturned pot filled with boiling water. He and the mother respond as best they can, but it takes them a while to discover that the diaper has filled with scalding water.

WIDEMAN, JOHN EDGAR, "Sharing," *GQ,* **December 2000**

A black man knocks on a white neighbor's door, asking to borrow a jar of mayonnaise, and the two have their first real conversation in the seven years they've lived on the same street. Both reveal that they are in the process of painful divorces and they exchange other intimacies, still not knowing each other's names.

2001 Magazine Award:

The New Yorker

THIS YEAR'S winner of the O. Henry Award for the magazine publishing the best fiction in the past year is *The New Yorker*, on the strength of five O. Henry Award–winning stories: "The Love of My Life," by T. Coraghessan Boyle; "Revival Road," by Louise Erdrich; the third-prize-winning "Floating Bridge," by Alice Munro; "Pastoralia," by George Saunders; and "The Smoker," by David Schickler. *The New Yorker* also published seven of the fifty stories short-listed for this year's volume.

Other strong contenders for the magazine honor this year included *Harper's Magazine* and *Zoetrope: All-Story,* both with two O. Henry Award–winning stories. Congratulations are due to the editors of these magazines, as well as to the editors of *Epoch, Esquire, The Gettysburg Review, The Malahat Review, Ploughshares, Salmagundi, TriQuarterly,* and *Witness,* each of which published one O. Henry Award–winning story.

Over the course of eighty-one volumes of *Prize Stories: The O. Henry Awards, The New Yorker* has published 167 prizewinning stories, the most of any magazine by a sizable margin. When you consider that the first volume of this series was published in 1919 and the first *New Yorker* story wasn't included until 1935, this stacks up as an even more remarkable achievement—an average of more than 2.5 stories per O. Henry Awards collection over that period. A partial roll call of *New Yorker* authors who have had stories honored by this series is even more impressive: Thomas

Wolfe, John O'Hara, Carson McCullers, Irwin Shaw, Shirley Jackson, J. D. Salinger, Jean Stafford, Peter Taylor, John Cheever, Philip Roth, John Updike, Donald Barthelme, Mary McCarthy, Eudora Welty, Alice Adams, William Maxwell, Harold Brodkey, Woody Allen, Ann Beattie, Saul Bellow, Cynthia Ozick, Deborah Eisenberg, Raymond Carver, Lorrie Moore, Stephen King, and Annie Proulx, in addition to some of this year's prizewinners. *The New Yorker* has, over this time, been incredibly important to the short story. The magazine's ability to continually adapt and consistently find stories that truly matter has enabled it to maintain its preeminent position. Under current Fiction Editor Bill Buford, *The New Yorker* has broadened the range of stories it publishes and expanded its horizons with two fiction double issues a year, including, in recent years, an issue devoted to Indian writers, an all-fiction issue of writers under the age of forty, and last year's debut writers issue, which featured work by authors yet to publish a book, among them 2001 O. Henry Award–winner David Schickler.

Congratulations to Editor-in-Chief David Remnick, Fiction Editor Bill Buford, and Literary Editors Roger Angell, Cressida Leyshon, Meghan O'Rourke, Alice Quinn, and Deborah Treisman, as well as to other staff members involved in selecting, editing, and publishing the fiction that appeared in *The New Yorker* over the course of the past year.

Magazines Consulted

Entries entirely in boldface and with their titles in all-capital letters indicate publications with prizewinning stories. Asterisks following titles denote magazines with short-listed stories. The information presented is up-to-date as of the time *Prize Stories 2001: The O. Henry Awards* went to press. For further information, including links to magazine Web sites, visit the O. Henry Awards Web site at:

www.boldtype.com/ohenry

or

www.randomhouse.com/vintage/storylines/ohenry.html

Magazines that wish to be added to the list and to have the stories they publish considered for O. Henry Awards may send subscriptions or all issues containing fiction to the series editor at:

P.O. Box 739
Montclair, NJ 07042

All other correspondence should be sent care of Anchor Books or, via e-mail, to Ohenrypriz@aol.com. It is the responsibility of the editors of each magazine to make sure that issues are sent to the series editor. If none are received during the course of the year, a publication will not be listed as a magazine consulted for the series.

Note to writers who use these listings as a resource for submitting their fiction to magazines: The fact that a publication is listed in this section does not imply an endorsement of that magazine by the O. Henry Awards. It simply means that issues were received and the fiction published was read and considered for inclusion in this volume. Writers submitting fiction to a particular magazine are strongly advised to first examine a sample issue.

African American Review
English Department
Indiana State University
Terre Haute, IN 47809
Joe Weixlmann, Editor
web.indstate.edu/artsci/AAR
Quarterly with a focus on African American literature and culture.

Agni
236 Bay Street Road
Boston University Writing Program
Boston, MA 02215
Askold Melnyczuk, Editor
webdelsol.com/AGNI
Biannual.

Alaska Quarterly Review
University of Alaska Anchorage
3211 Providence Drive
Anchorage, AK 99508
Ronald Spatz, Editor
www.uaa.alaska.edu/aqr

Algonquin Roundtable Review
Room B336
Algonquin College
1385 Woodroffe Avenue
Nepean, Ontario
K2G 1V8 Canada
Dan Doyle, Editor
roundtable_review@
algonquincollege.com

www.algonquincollege.com/
roundtable_review
Biannual.

Alligator Juniper
Prescott College
301 Grove Avenue
Prescott, AZ 86301
aj@prescott.edu
Annual. Publication suspended. Next issue expected to come out Summer 2002.

Amelia
329 "E" Street
Bakersfield, CA 93304
Frederick A. Raborg Jr., Editor
amelia@lightspeed.net
Quarterly.

American Letters and Commentary
850 Park Avenue
Suite 5B
New York, NY 10021
Anna Rabinowitz, Editor
www.amletters.org
Annual.

American Literary Review
University of North Texas
P.O. Box 13827
Denton, TX 76203-1307

Lee Martin, Editor
americanliteraryreview
@yahoo.com
www.engl.unt.edu/alr/
main.html
Biannual.

Another Chicago Magazine
3709 North Kenmore
Chicago, IL 60613
Barry Silesky, Editor and Publisher
editors@anotherchicagomag.com
anotherchicagomag.com
Biannual.

Antietam Review
41 South Potomac Street
Hagerstown, MD 21740
Susanne Kass, Executive Editor
www.wcarts@intrepid.net

The Antioch Review
P.O. Box 148
Yellow Springs, OH 45387
Robert S. Fogarty, Editor
www.antioch.edu/review/home.
html
Quarterly.

Apalachee Quarterly
P.O. Box 10469
Tallahassee, FL 32302
Barbara Hamby, Editor

Appalachian Heritage
Berea College
Berea, KY 40404
James Gage, Editor
*Quarterly magazine of Southern
Appalachian life and culture.*

Arkansas Review
Department of English and
Philosophy

Box 1890
Arkansas State University
State University, AR 72467
Willliam M. Clements, General
Editor
delta@toltec.astate.edu
www.clt.astate.edu/arkreview
*"A Journal of Delta Studies."
Triannual. Formerly* The Kansas
Quarterly.

Ascent
English Department
Concordia College
901 8th Street South
Moorhead, MN 56562
W. Scott Olsen, Editor
ascent@cord.edu
www.cord.edu/dept/english/ascent
Triannual.

Atlanta Review
P.O. Box 8248
Atlanta, GA 31106
Daniel Veach, Editor and Publisher
www.atlantareview.com
Biannual.

The Atlantic Monthly*
77 North Washington Street
Boston, MA 02114
C. Michael Curtis, Senior Editor
www.theatlantic.com
*2000 O. Henry Award winner for
best magazine. The Atlantic
Unbound site features stories from
the magazine plus Web-only content,
including interviews with authors,
fiction not published in the print
version, a reader forum, and more.*

The Baffler
P.O. Box 378293
Chicago, IL 60637

Thomas Frank, Editor-in-Chief
thebaffler.org

The Baltimore Review
P.O. Box 410
Riderwood, MD 21139
Barbara Westwood Diehl,
Editor
Biannual featuring the work of writers "from the Baltimore area and beyond."

Bellowing Ark
P.O. Box 55564
Shoreline, WA 98155
Robert R Ward, Editor
Published six times a year.
Newspaper format.

Beloit Fiction Journal
Box 11
Beloit College
700 College Street
Beloit, WI 53511
Rotating editorship
www.beloit.edu/~libhome/Archives
/BO/Pub/Fict.html
Biannual.

Black Warrior Review
University of Alabama
P.O. Box 862936
Tuscaloosa, AL 35486-0027
Rotating editorship
www.sa.ua.edu/osm/bwr
Biannual.

Blood and Aphorisms
P.O. Box 702, Station P
Toronto, Ontario
M5S 2Y4 Canada
Sam Hiyate, Publisher
Quarterly.

Bomb*
594 Broadway, 9th Floor
New York, NY 10012
Betsy Sussler, Editor-in-Chief
bomb@echonyc.com
www.bombsite.com/firstproof.html
Quarterly magazine profiling artists, writers, actors, directors, and musicians, with a downtown New York City slant. Fiction appears in First Proof, *a literary supplement.*

Border Crossings
500-70 Arthur Street
Winnipeg, Manitoba
R3B 1G7 Canada
Meeka Walsh, Editor
bordercr@escape.ca
www.bordercrossingsmag.com
Quarterly magazine of the arts with occasional fiction.

The Boston Book Review
30 Brattle Street, 4th Floor
Cambridge, MA 02138
Theoharis Constantine Theoharis,
Editor
BBR-Info@BostonBook
Review.com
A book review that also publishes fiction, poetry, and essays. Published ten times a year—monthly with double issues in January and July.

Boston Review
E53-407, MIT
Cambridge, MA 02139
Joshua Cohen, Editor-in-Chief
bostonreview@mit.edu
bostonreview.mit.edu
"A political and literary forum" published six times a year.

Boulevard*

4579 Laclede Avenue
Suite 332
St. Louis, MO 63108-2103
Richard Burgin, Editor
www.boulevardmagazine.
com/boulevard.htm
*Triannual. Sponsors a short fiction
contest for emerging writers.*

The Briar Cliff Review

3303 Rebecca Street
P.O. Box 2100
Sioux City, IA 51104-2100
Tricia Currans-Sheehen, Editor
www.briar-cliff.edu/bcreview

The Bridge

14050 Vernon Street
Oak Park, MI 48237
Jack Zucker, Editor
Biannual.

Button

Box 26
Lunenburg, MA 01462
Sally Cragin, Editor and Publisher
*Biannual calling itself "New En-
gland's tiniest magazine of poetry, fic-
tion, and gracious living."*

Callaloo

English Department
322 Bryan Hall
University of Virginia
Charlottesville, VA 22903
Charles Henry Rowell, Editor
www.press.jhu.edu/press/journals/
cal/cal.html
*A quarterly journal of African
American and African Arts and
Letters.*

Calyx

P.O. Box B
Corvalis, OR 97339-0539
editorial collective
calyx@proaxis.com
www.proaxis.com/~calyx
*Triannual journal of art and litera-
ture by women.*

Canadian Fiction

P.O. Box 1061
Kingston, Ontario
K7L 4Y5 Canada
Geoff Hancock, Rob Payne, Editors
*Biannual anthology of contemporary
Canadian fiction, often with a
theme.*

The Carolina Quarterly

Greenlaw Hall CB#3520
University of North Carolina
Chapel Hill, NC 27599-3520
Rotating editorship
cquarter@unc.edu
www.unc.edu/depts/cqonline
Triannual.

The Chariton Review

Truman State University
Kirksville, MO 63501
Jim Barnes, Editor
Biannual.

Chattahoochee Review*

2101 Womack Road
Dunwoody, GA 30338-4497
Lawrence Hetrick, Editor
www.gpc.peachnet.edu/~twadley/
cr/index.htm
Quarterly.

Chelsea
P.O. Box 773
Cooper Station
New York, NY 10276-0773
Richard Foerster, Editor
Biannual.

Chicago Review*
5801 South Kenwood Avenue
Chicago, IL 60637-1794
Andrew Rathmann, Editor
humanities.uchicago.edu/review
Quarterly.

Cimarron Review
205 Morrill Hall
Oklahoma State University
Stillwater, OK 74078-0135
E. P. Walkiewicz, Editor
cimarronreview.okstate.edu
Quarterly.

City Primeval
P.O. Box 30064
Seattle, WA 98103
David Ross, Editor
*Quarterly featuring "narratives of
urban reality."*

Clackamas Literary Review
Clackamas Community College
19600 South Molalla Avenue
Oregon City, OR 97045
Jeff Knorr, Tim Schell, Editors
www.clackamas.cc.or.us/instruct/
english/clr/index.htm
Biannual.

Colorado Review*
Colorado State University
Department of English
Fort Collins, CO 80523
David Milofsky, Editor
creview@colostate.edu

www.coloradoreview.com
Biannual.

**Columbia: A Journal of Literature
and Art**
415 Dodge Hall
Columbia University
New York, NY 10027-6902
Rotating editorship
arts-litjournal@columbia.edu
www.columbia.edu/cu/arts/
writing/columbiajournal/
columbiafr.html
Biannual.

Commentary
165 East 56th Street
New York, NY 10022
Neal Kozodoy, Editor
editorial@commentarymagazine.
com
www.commentarymagazine.com
*Monthly, politically conservative
Jewish magazine.*

Concho River Review
P.O. Box 1894
Angelo State University
San Angelo, TX 76909
James A. Moore, General Editor
www.angelo.edu/dept/english/river.
htm
Biannual.

Confrontation
English Department
C. W. Post Campus of Long Island
University
Brookville, NY 11548-1300
Martin Tucker, Editor-in-Chief

Conjunctions*
21 East 10th Street
New York, NY 10003

Bradford Morrow, Editor
www.conjunctions.com
Biannual.

Cottonwood
Box J, 400 Kansas Union
University of Kansas
Lawrence, KS 66045
Tom Lorenz, Editor
cottonwd@falcon.cc.ukans.edu
falcon.cc.ukans.edu/~cottonwd/
index.html
Biannual.

Crab Orchard Review
Southern Illinois University at
Carbondale
Carbondale, IL 62901-4503
Richard Peterson, Editor
www.siu.edu/~crborchd
Biannual.

Crazyhorse
English Department
University of Arkansas at Little
Rock
Little Rock, AR 72204
Ralph Burns, Lisa Lewis, Editors
www.uair.edu/~english/chorse.
htm
Biannual.

The Cream City Review
University of Wisconsin–Milwaukee
P.O. Box 413
Milwaukee, WI 53201
Rotating editorship
www.uwm.edu/dept/english/
creamcity.html
Biannual.

Cut Bank
English Department
University of Montana

Missoula, MT 59812
rotating editorship
cutbank@selway.umt.edu
www.umt.edu/cutbank
Biannual.

Denver Quarterly
University of Denver
Denver, CO 80208
Bin Ramke, Editor
www.du.edu/english/DQuarterly.
htm

DoubleTake*
55 Davis Square
Somerville, MA 02144
Robert Coles, Editor
www.doubletakemagazine.org
*Beautifully produced quarterly
devoted to photography and literature.*

Elle
1633 Broadway
New York, NY 10019
Pat Towers, Features Director
*Monthly. Occasionally publishes
fiction.*

EPOCH*
251 Goldwin Smith Hall
Cornell University
Ithaca, NY 14853-3201
Michael Koch, Editor
www.arts.cornell.edu/english/
epoch.html
*Triannual. 1997 O. Henry
Award winner for best magazine.*

ESQUIRE*
250 West 55th Street
New York, NY 10019
Adrienne Miller, Literary
Editor

www.esquiremag.com
Monthly.

Event
Douglas College
Box 2503
New Westminster, British
Columbia
V3L 5B2 Canada
Calvin Wharton, Editor
Triannual.

Faultline
English and Comparative
Literature Department
University of California–Irvine
Irvine, CA 92697-2650
Rotating editorship
faultline@uci.edu
www.humanities.uci.edu/faultline
Annual.

Fence
14 Fifth Avenue, 1A
New York, NY 10011
Rebecca Wolff, Editor
rwolff@angel.net
www.fencemag.com
Biannual.

Fiction
English Department
City College of New York
New York, NY 10031
Mark Jay Mirsky, Editor
www.ccny.cuny.edu/fiction/
fiction.htm
All-fiction format.

The Fiddlehead
University of New Brunswick
P.O. Box 4400
Fredericton, New Brunswick
E3B 5A3 Canada
Ross Leckie, Editor

Fid@nbnet.nb.ca
Quarterly.

First Intensity
P.O. Box 665
Lawrence, KS 66044
Lee Chapman, Editor
leechapman@aol.com
members.aol.com/leechapman
*Biannual. "A Magazine of New
Writing."*

The First Line
P.O. Box 0382
Plano, TX 75025-0382
David LaBounty, Jeff Adams,
Coeditors
info@thefirstline.com
www.thefirstline.com
*Published six times a year. Stories all
begin with the same first sentence.*

580 Split
Mills College
P.O. Box 9982
Oakland, CA 94613
Rotating editorship
five80split@yahoo.com
www.mills.edu/SHOWCASE/F99/
580SPLIT/580.html
Recently established annual.

Five Points*
English Department
Georgia State University
University Plaza
Athens, GA 30303-3083
David Bottoms, Pam Durban,
Editors
webdelsol.com/Five_Points/
Triquarterly.

Florida Review
English Department
University of Central Florida
Orlando, FL 32816
Russell Kesler, Editor
pegasus.cc.ucf.edu/~english/
floridareview/home.htm
Biannual.

Flyway
203 Ross Hall
Iowa State University
Ames, IA 50011
Stephen Pett, Editor

Fourteen Hills
Creative Writing Department
San Francisco State University
1600 Holloway Avenue
San Francisco, CA 94132-1722
Rotating editorship
hills@sfsu.edu
userwww.sfsu.edu/~hills
Biannual.

Fugue
Brink Hall 200
University of Idaho
Moscow, ID 83844-1102
Rotating editorship
www.uidaho.edu/LS/Eng/Fugue
Biannual.

Gargoyle
1508 U Street NW
Washington, DC 20009
Richard Peabody, Lucinda
Ebersole, Editors
Published irregularly.

Geist
1014 Homer Street #103
Vancouver, British Columbia
V6B 2W9 Canada
Stephen Osborne, Publisher
geist@geist.com
www.geist.com
*"The Canadian Magazine of Ideas
and Culture." Quarterly.*

The Georgia Review*
University of Georgia
Athens, GA 30602-9009
Stephen Corey, Acting Editor
www.uga.edu/garev
Quarterly.

THE GETTYSBURG REVIEW*
Gettysburg College
Gettysburg, PA 17325
Peter Stitt, Editor
www.gettysburg.edu/
academics/gettysburg_review
***Quarterly. Published this year's
second-prize winner, "Big Me,"
by Dan Chaon.***

Glimmer Train Stories
710 SW Madison Street
Suite 504
Portland, OR 97205-2900
Linda Burmeister Davies, Susan
Burmeister-Brown, Editors
www.glimmertrain.com
Quarterly. Fiction and interviews.

Global City Review*
105 West 13th Street, Suite 4C
New York, NY 10011
Linsey Abrams, Founding Editor
*Nifty, pocket-size format. Biannual,
theme issues.*

GQ*
350 Madison Avenue
New York, NY 10017
Walter Kirn, Literary Editor
www.gq.com
Monthly men's magazine.

Grain

    Box 1154

    Regina, Saskatchewan

    S4P 3B4 Canada

    J. Jill Robinson, Editor

    Quarterly.

Grand Street

    214 Sullivan Street

    Suite 6C

    New York, NY 10012

    Jean Stein, Editor

    info@grandstreet.com

    www.grandstreet.com

    Quarterly.

The Green Hills Literary Lantern

    P.O. Box 375

    Trenton, MO 64683

    Jack Smith, Ken Reger, Senior

    Editors

    www.ncmc.cc.mo.us

    Biannual.

Green Mountains Review

    Box A 58

    Johnson State College

    Johnson, VT 05656

    Tony Whedon, Fiction Editor

    Biannual.

The Greensboro Review

    English Department

    134 McIver Building

    University of North Carolina at

    Greensboro

    P.O. Box 26170

    Greensboro, NC 27402-6170

    Jim Clark, Editor

    www.uncg.edu/eng/mfa/review/

    Grhompage.htm

    Biannual.

Gulf Stream

    English Department

    FIU Biscayne Bay Campus

    3000 NE 151 Street

    North Miami, FL 33181-3000

    Lynn Barrett, Editor

    Biannual.

Hampton Shorts

    P.O. Box 1229

    Water Mill, NY 11976

    Barbara Stone, Editor-in-Chief

    hamptonshorts@hamptons.com

    "Fiction Plus from the Hamptons

    and the East End."

Happy

    240 East 35th Street

    Suite 11A

    New York, NY 10016

    Bayard, Editor

    Two words: offbeat quarterly.

HARPER'S MAGAZINE*

    666 Broadway

    New York, NY 10012

    Lewis Lapham, Editor

    www.harpers.org

    Monthly.

Harrington Gay Men's Fiction Quarterly

    Thomas Nelson Community

    College

    99 Thomas Nelson Drive

    Hampton, VA 23666

    Thomas L. Long, Editor

Hawaii Pacific Review

    Hawaii Pacific University

    1060 Bishop Street

    Honolulu, HI 96813

    hpreview@hpu.edu

    Annual.

Hayden's Ferry Review
Box 871502
Arizona State University
Tempe, AZ 85287-1502
Rotating editorship
HFR@asu.edu
www.statepress.com/hfr
Biannual.

Hemispheres
1301 Carolina Street
Greensboro, NC 27401
Selby Bateman, Senior Editor
selby@hemispheresmagazine.com
www.hemispheresmagazine.com
The inflight magazine of United Airlines. Monthly.

High Plains Literary Review
180 Adams Street
Suite 250
Denver, CO 80206
Robert O. Greer Jr., Editor-in-Chief
Triannual.

Hudson Review
684 Park Avenue
New York, NY 10021
Paula Deitz, Editor
Quarterly.

Hurricane Alice
English Department
Rhode Island College
Providence, RI 02908
Maureen T. Reddy, Executive Editor
mreddy@grog.ric.edu
Feminist quarterly.

The Idaho Review
Boise State University
English Department
1910 University Drive
Boise, ID 83725
Mitch Wieland, Editor-in-Chief
english.boisestate.edu/idahoreview/
Annual.

Image
3307 Third Avenue West
Seattle, WA 98119
Gregory Wolfe, Publisher
and Editor
image@imagejournal.org
www.imagejournal.org
"A Journal of the Arts and Religion."
Quarterly. Note new address.

Indiana Review
Ballantine Hall 465
1020 East Kirkwood Avenue
Bloomington, IN 47405-7103
Brian Leung, Editor
inreview@indiana.edu
www.indiana.edu/~inreview/ir.html
Biannual.

Inkwell
Manhattanville College
Purchase, NY 10577
Rotating editorship
Biannual.

Interim
English Department
University of Nevada
Las Vegas, NV 89154
James Hazen, Editor
Biannual.

The Iowa Review
308 English/Philosophy Building
University of Iowa
Iowa City, IA 52242-1492
David Hamilton, Editor

www.uiowa.edu/~iareview
Triannual. Web site features additional fiction and hypertext work.

Iowa Woman
P.O. Box 680
Iowa City, IA 52244-0680
Rebecca Childers, Editor

Italian Americana
University of Rhode Island
Feinstein College of Continuing Education
80 Washington Street
Providence, RI 02903-1803
Carol Bonomo Albright, Editor
Biannual. A cultural and historical review with a focus on Italian Americans.

Jane
7 West 34th Street
New York, NY 10001
Jane Pratt, Editor-in-Chief
www.janemag.com
Six times a year. Publishes winner of annual fiction contest.

The Journal
Ohio State University
English Department
164 West 17th Avenue
Columbus, OH 43210
Michelle Herman, Fiction Editor
thejournal05@postbox.acs.ohio-state.edu
www.cohums.ohio-state.edu/english/journals/the_journal/
Biannual.

Kalliope
Florida Community College at Jacksonville
3939 Roosevelt Boulevard
Jacksonville, FL 32205
Mary Sue Koeppel, Editor
www.fccj.org/kalliope/kalliope.htm
Triannual journal of women's literature and art.

Karamu
English Department
Eastern Illinois University
Charleston, IL 61920
Rotating editorship
Annual.

The Kenyon Review*
Kenyon College
Gambier, OH 43022
David H. Lynn, Editor
kenyonreview@kenyon.edu
www.kenyonreview.com
Triannual.

Kiosk
State University of New York at Buffalo
English Department
306 Clemens Hall
Buffalo, NY 14260
Rotating editorship
eng-kiosk@acsu.buffalo.edu
wings.buffalo.edu/kiosk
Annual.

Krater: College Workshop Quarterly
P.O. Box 1371
Lincoln Park, MI 48146
Leonard D. Fritz, Managing Editor
Quarterly. Features work by writers currently enrolled in college writing workshops.

The Laurel Review
Department of English
Northwest Missouri State
University
Maryville, MO 64468
William Trowbridge, David Slater,
Beth Richards, Editors
Biannual.

Literal Latté
Suite 240
61 East 8th Street
New York, NY 10003
Jenine Gordon Bockman,
Publisher and Editor
Litlatte@aol.com
www.literal-latte.com
*Bimonthly. Distributed free to cafés
and bookstores in New York City.
Sold at bookstores elsewhere.*

The Literary Review
Fairleigh Dickinson University
285 Madison Avenue
Madison, NJ 07940
Walter Cummins, Editor-in-Chief
tlr@fdu.edu
www.webdelsol.com/tlr/
*Quarterly. An international journal
of contemporary writing.*

The Long Story
18 Eaton Street
Lawrence, MA 01843
R. P. Burnham, Editor
TLS@aol.com
www.litline.org/ls/longstory.html
Annual.

Louisiana Literature*
SLU-10792
Southeastern Louisiana University
Hammond, LA 70402
Jack B. Bedell, Editor
Biannual.

Lynx Eye
1880 Hill Drive
Los Angeles, CA 90041
Pam McCully, Kathryn Morrison,
Editors
Quarterly.

THE MALAHAT REVIEW
University of Victoria
P.O. Box 1700
Victoria, British Columbia
V8W 2Y2 Canada
Marlene Cookshaw, Editor
malahat@uvic.ca
web.uvic.ca/malahat
*Quarterly. Published this year's
first-prize winner, "The Deep,"
by Mary Swan.*

Mānoa
English Department
University of Hawaii
Honolulu, HI 96822
Frank Stewart, Editor
www.hawaii.edu/mjournal
*Biannual. "Pacific journal of
international writing" with a
special focus each issue.*

The Massachusetts Review
South College
University of Massachusetts
Box 37140
Amherst, MA 01003-7140
Jules Chametzky, Mary Heath,
Paul Jenkins, Editors
www.massreview.org
Quarterly.

McSweeney's
424 7th Avenue
Brooklyn, NY 11215
David Eggers, Editor
mcsweeneys@earthlink.net
www.mcsweeneys.net

Innovative quarterly. Original content also posted on Web site.

Michigan Quarterly Review
University of Michigan
3032 Rackham Building
915 East Washington Street
Ann Arbor, MI 48109-1070
Laurence Goldstein, Editor
www.umich.edu/~mqr
Often publishes issues with a theme or focus.

Mid-American Review*
English Department
Bowling Green State University
Bowling Green, OH 43403
Wendell Mayo, Editor-in-Chief
www.bgsu.edu/midamerican
review
Biannual.

Midstream
633 Third Avenue, 21st Floor
New York, NY 10017-6706
Joel Carmichael, Editor
Published nine times a year. Focuses on Jewish issues and Zionist concerns.

The Minnesota Review
English Department
University of Missouri–Columbia
110 Tate Hall
Columbia, MO 65211
Jeffrey Williams, Editor
Non-Minnesota based biannual.

The Minus Times
P.O. Box 737
Grand Central Station
New York, NY 10163
Hunter Kennedy, Editor
www.minustimes.com
Published irregularly.

Mississippi Review
Center for Writers
University of Southern Mississippi
Box 5144
Hattiesburg, MS 39406-5144
Frederick Barthelme, Editor
rief@netdoor.com
orca.st.usm.edu/mrw
Biannual. Maintains one of the best literary Web sites.

The Missouri Review
1507 Hillcrest Hall
University of Missouri
Columbia, MO 65211
Speer Morgan, Editor
www.missourireview.org
Triannual.

Nassau Review
English Department
Nassau Community College
1 Education Drive
Garden City, NY 11530-6793
Paul A. Doyle, Editor
Annual.

Natural Bridge
English Department
University of Missouri–St. Louis
8001 Natural Bridge Road
St. Louis, MO 63121
Steven Schreiner, Editor
natural@admiral.umsl.edu
www.umsl.edu/~natural
Biannual. Established in 1999.

The Nebraska Review
Writer's Workshop
Fine Arts Building 212
University of Nebraska at Omaha
Omaha, NE 68182-0324
James Reed, Fiction and Managing
Editor

www.unomaha.edu/
~fineart/wworkshop/nebraska_
review.htm
Biannual.

Neotrope
P.O. Box 172
Lawrence, KS 66044
Adam Powell, Paul Silvia, Editors
apowell10@hotmail.com
www.brokenboulder.com/
neotrope.htm
Annual featuring progressive fiction.

Nerve
520 Broadway, 6th Floor
New York, NY 10012
Susan Dominus, Editor-in-Chief
info@nerve.com
www.nerve.com/nerveprint
*Features literate erotica. Print spinoff
of the Web site, which features additional fiction. Published six times a
year.*

New Delta Review
English Department
Louisiana State University
Baton Rouge, LA 70803-5001
Rotating editorship
english.lsu.edu/journals/ndr
Biannual.

New England Review
Middlebury College
Middlebury, VT 05753
Stephen Donadio, Editor
NEReview@middlebury.edu
www.middlebury.edu/~nereview
Quarterly.

New Letters
University of Missouri–Kansas City
5100 Rockhill Road

Kansas City, MO 64110
James McKinley, Editor-in-Chief
newletters@umkc.edu
iml.umkc.edu/newletters
Quarterly.

New Millennium Writings
P.O. Box 2463
Knoxville, TN 37901
Don Williams, Editor
nmw@mach2.com
www.mach2.com/books/williams/
index.html
Biannual.

New Orleans Review
P.O. Box 195
Loyola University
New Orleans, LA 70118
Ralph Adamo, Editor
noreview@beta.loyno.edu
www.loyno.edu/~noreview
Quarterly.

New York Stories
La Guardia Community
College/CUNY
31–10 Thomson Avenue
Long Island City, NY 11101
Daniel Caplice Lynch, Editor-in-
Chief
Triannual.

THE NEW YORKER*
4 Times Square
New York, NY 10036
Bill Buford, Fiction Editor
www.newyorker.com
*Esteemed weekly with fiction
double issues in June and
December. 2001 O. Henry
Award winner for best
magazine. Published this year's
third-prize winner, "Floating*

Bridge," by Alice Munro. Also
won the O. Henry Award for
magazines in 1998 and '99. Web
site now temporarily posts complete stories and, occasionally,
interviews with writers.

Night Rally

P.O. Box 1707
Philadelphia, PA 19105
Amber Dorko Stopper, Editor-in-
Chief
NightRallyMag@aol.com
www.nightrally.org
*Triquarterly. Established in 2000.
Web site has a feature, the interlocu-
tor, that allows writers to report on
how their submissions were handled
by various magazines.*

Nimrod

University of Tulsa
600 South College
Tulsa, OK 74104-3189
Francine Ringold, Editor-in-Chief
www.utulsa.edu/NIMROD
Biannual.

96 Inc

P.O. Box 15559
Boston, MA 02215
Julie Anderson, Vera Gold, Nancy
Mehegan, Editors
*Annual. Sometimes features the work
of teenagers produced in workshops
sponsored by the magazine.*

Noon

1369 Madison Avenue
PMB 298
New York, NY 10128
Diane Williams, Editor
noonannual@yahoo.com
New annual.

The North American Review

University of Northern Iowa
1222 West 27th Street
Cedar Falls, IA 50614-0156
Vince Gotera, Editor
nar@uni.edu
www.webdelsol.com/
NorthAmReview/NAR
*Publishes five issues a year. Founded
in 1815. Note new editor.*

North Carolina Literary Review

English Department
East Carolina University
Greenville, NC 27858-4353
Margaret D. Bauer, Editor
BauerM@mail.ecu.edu
personal.ecu.edu/bauerm/nclr.htm
*Nicely produced and illustrated
annual.*

North Dakota Quarterly

University of North Dakota
Grand Forks, ND 58202-7209
Robert W. Lewis, Editor
ndq@sage.und.nodak.edu
Quarterly.

Northwest Review

369 PLC
University of Oregon
Eugene, OR 97403
John Witte, Editor
Triannual.

Notre Dame Review

Creative Writing Program
English Department
University of Notre Dame
Notre Dame, IN 46556
John Matthias, William O'Rourke,
Editors
www.nd.edu/~ndr/review.htm

Biannual. Web site offers additional content.

Now & Then
Center for Appalachian Studies and Services
Box 70556
East Tennessee State University
Johnson City, TN 37614-0556
Jane H. Woodside, Editor
cass@etsu.edu
cass.etsu.edu/n&t
"The Appalachian Magazine."
Triquarterly.

Nylon
394 West Broadway, 2nd Floor
New York, NY 10012
Gloria M. Wong, Senior Editor
nylonmag@aol.com
www.nylonmag.com
Edgy monthly women's magazine with occasional fiction.

Oasis
P.O. Box 626
Largo, FL 34649-0626
Neal Storrs, Editor
oasislit@aol.com
Quirky independent quarterly.

The Ohio Review
344 Scott Quad
Ohio University
Athens, OH 45701-2979
Wayne Dodd, Editor
www.ohio.edu/TheOhioReview
Biannual.

Ontario Review*
9 Honey Brook Drive
Princeton, NJ 08540
Raymond J. Smith, Editor

www.ontarioreviewpress.com
Biannual.

Open City
225 Lafayette Street
Suite 1114
New York, NY 10012
Thomas Beller, Daniel Pinchbeck, Editors
editors@opencity.org
www.opencity.org
Downtown annual.

Other Voices
English Department (MC 162)
University of Illinois at Chicago
601 South Morgan Street
Chicago, IL 60607-7120
Lois Hauselman, Executive Editor
All-fiction biannual.

Owen Wistar Review
University of Wyoming
Student Publications
Box 3625
Laramie, WY 82071
Rotating editorship
Annual.

The Oxford American
P.O. Box 1156
Oxford, MS 38655
Marc Smirnoff, Editor
oxam@watervalley.net
www.oxfordamericanmag.com
John Grisham–backed magazine with Southern focus. Bimonthly.

Oxford Magazine
English Department
356 Bachelor Hall
Miami University
Oxford, OH 45056

Rotating editorship
Oxmag@geocities.com
www.muohio.edu/
creativewriting/oxmag.html

Oyster Boy Review
P.O. Box 77842
San Francisco, CA 94107-0842
Damon Sauve, Publisher
staff@oysterboyreview
www.oysterboyreview.com
*Quarterly with full text available
online.*

The Paris Review*
541 East 72nd Street
New York, NY 10021
George Plimpton, Editor
www.parisreview.com
Esteemed quarterly.

Parting Gifts
3413 Wilshire Drive
Greensboro, NC 27408
Robert Bixby, Editor
rbixby@aol.com
users.aol.com/marchst/msp.
html

Partisan Review
236 Bay State Road
Boston, MA 02215
William Phillips, Editor-in-Chief
partisan@bu.edu
www.partisanreview.org
Quarterly.

Phoebe
George Mason University
4400 University Drive
Fairfax, VA 22030-4444
Rotating editorship
phoebe@gmu.edu
www.gmu.edu/pubs/phoebe
Student-edited biannual.

Playboy
Playboy Building
919 North Michigan Avenue
Chicago, IL 60611
editor@playboy.com
www.playboy.com
Sometimes takes on literary sheen.

Pleiades
English and Philosophy
Departments
Central Missouri State University
Warrensburg, MO 64093
R. M. Kinder, Kevin Prufer,
Editors
www.cmsu.edu/englphil/pleiades.
html
Biannual.

PLOUGHSHARES*
100 Beacon Street
Boston, MA 02116
Don Lee, Editor
pshares@emerson.edu
www.pshares.org
*Triannual. Writers serve as guest
editors for each issue.*

Post Road*
c/o About Face
853 Broadway
Suite 1516, Box 210
New York, NY 10003
Sean Burke, Publisher
www.aboutface.org
Biannual. Established in 2000.

Potomac Review
P.O. Box 354
Port Tobacco, MD 20677
Eli Flam, Editor and Publisher
www.meral.com/potomac
Quarterly.

Pottersfield Portfolio
P.O. Box 40, Station A
Sydney, Nova Scotia
B1P 6G9 Canada
Douglas Arthur Brown, Managing
Editor
www.pportfolio.com
Triannual.

Prairie Fire
423–100 Arthur Street
Winnipeg, Manitoba
R3B 1H3 Canada
Andris Taskins, Editor
prfire@escape.ca
Quarterly.

Prairie Schooner
201 Andrews Hall
University of Nebraska
Lincoln, NE 68588-0334
Hilda Raz, Editor-in-Chief
www.unl.edu/schooner/psmain.
htm
Quarterly.

Prism International
Creative Writing Program
University of British Columbia
Vancouver, British Columbia
V6T 1Z1 Canada
Rotating editorship
prism@interchange.ubc.ca
www.arts.ubc.ca/prism
Quarterly.

Provincetown Arts
650 Commercial Street
Provincetown, MA 02657
Christopher Busa, Editor
Annual Cape Cod arts magazine.

Puerto del Sol
P.O. Box 30001
New Mexico State University
Las Cruces, NM 88003-8001
Kevin McIlvoy, Editor-in-Chief
Biannual.

Quarry Magazine
P.O. Box 74
Kingston, Ontario
K7L 4V6 Canada
Andrew Griffin, Editor-in-Chief
quarrymagazine@hotmail.com
Quarterly.

Quarterly West
317 Olpin Union Hall
University of Utah
Salt Lake City, UT 84112
Margot Schilpp, Editor
webdelsol.com/Quarterly_West
*Biannual. Also publishes short shorts
and novellas.*

Rain Crow
2127 West Pierce Avenue #2B
Chicago, IL 60622-1824
Michael S. Manley, Editor
rcp@rain-crow.com
www.rain-crow.com
Established in 2000.

Raritan
Rutgers University
31 Mine Street
New Brunswick, NJ 08903
Richard Poirier, Editor-in-Chief
*Quarterly. Edited by former O.
Henry Awards series editor (1961–
66). Occasionally publishes fiction.*

Rattapallax
523 LaGuardia Place
Suite 353
New York, NY 10012
Martin Mitchell, Editor-in-Chief
rattapallax@hotmail.com
www.rattapallax.com
*Biannual. Issues include poetry
readings on CD.*

Red Rock Review
English Department, J2A
Community College Southern
Nevada
3200 East Cheyenne Avenue
North Las Vegas, NV 89030
Richard Logsdon, Editor-in-Chief
Biannual.

**(News from the) Republic
of Letters**
120 Cushing Avenue
Boston, MA 02125-2033
Saul Bellow, Keith Botsford,
Editors
rangoni@bu.edu
www.bu.edu/trl
*Appears irregularly. Publishes some
fiction.*

River City
English Department
University of Memphis
Memphis, TN 38152-6176
Thomas Russell, Editor
www.people.memphis.
edu/~rivercity
rivercity@memphis.edu
Biannual. Formerly known as Memphis State Review. *Themed issues.*

River Styx
634 North Grand Boulevard,
12th Floor

St. Louis, MO 63103-1002
Richard Newman, Editor
www.riverstyx.org
Triannual.

Rosebud
P.O. Box 459
Cambridge, WI 53523
Roderick Clark, Editor
www.rsbd.net
Quarterly.

St. Anthony Messenger
1615 Republic Street
Cincinnati, OH 45210-1298
Jack Wintz, O.F.M., editor
StAnthony@AmericanCatholic.org
www.americancatholic.org
*Monthly magazine published by
Franciscan friars with one story per
issue.*

Salamander
48 Ackers Avenue
Brookline, MA 02445-4160
Jennifer Barber, Editor
Biannual.

SALMAGUNDI
Skidmore College
Saratoga Springs, NY 12866
Robert Boyers, Editor-in-Chief
pboyers@skidmore.edu
Quarterly.

Salt Hill
Syracuse University
English Department
Syracuse, NY 13244
www.hl.syr.edu/cwp
Biannual.

Santa Monica Review
Santa Monica College
1900 Pico Boulevard
Santa Monica, CA 90405
Rotating editorship
Biannual.

The Seattle Review
Padelford Hall
Box 354330
University of Washington
Seattle, WA 98195
Colleen J. McElroy, Editor
Biannual.

Seven Days
P.O. Box 1164
255 South Champlain Street
Burlington, VT 05042-1164
Pamela Polston, Paula Routly,
Coeditors
sevenday@together.net
www.sevendaysvt.com
*Free weekly newspaper in the
Burlington area. Occasionally
publishes fiction.*

The Sewanee Review
University of the South
735 University Avenue
Sewanee, TN 37383-1000
George Core, Editor
www.sewanee.edu/sreview/home.
html
Quarterly.

Shenandoah
Troubador Theater, 2nd Floor
Washington and Lee University
Lexington, VA 24450-030
R. T. Smith, Editor
shenandoah.wlu.edu
Quarterly.

Songs of Innocence
P.O. Box 719
Radio City Station
New York, NY 10101-0719
Michael Pendragon, Editor and
Publisher
mmpendragon@aol.com
hometown.aol.com/
mmpinnocence/index.html
*Celebrates "the nobler, more spiritual
aspects of Man, the World, and their
Creator."*

Sonora Review
English Department
University of Arizona
Tucson, AZ 85721
Rotating editorship
sonora@u.arizona.edu
www.coh.arizona.edu/sonora
Biannual.

The South Carolina Review
English Department
Clemson University
Strode Tower, Box 340523
Clemson, SC 29634-0523
Wayne Chapman, Donna Jaisty
Winchell, Editors
Annual.

South Dakota Review
Box 111
University Exchange
Vermillion, SD 57069
Brian Bedard, Editor
sdreview@usd.edu
sunbird.usd.edu/engl/SDR/index.
html
Quarterly.

Southern Exposure

P.O. Box 531
Durham, NC 27702
Chris Kromm, Editor
info@southernexposure.org
www.southernstudies.org
A quarterly journal of Southern politics and culture that publishes some fiction.

Southern Humanities Review

9088 Haley Center
Auburn University
Auburn, AL 36849
Dan R. Latimer, Virginia M. Kouidis, Editors
www.auburn.edu/english/shr/home.htm
Quarterly.

The Southern Review

43 Allen Hall
Louisiana State University
Baton Rouge, LA 70803-5005
James Olney, Dave Smith, Editors
unix1.sncc.lsu.edu/guests/wwwtsr
Quarterly.

Southwest Review*

Southern Methodist University
307 Fondren Library West
Dallas, TX 75275
Willard Spiegelman, Editor-in-Chief
Quarterly.

Story

1507 Dana Avenue
Cincinnati, OH 45207
Lois Rosenthal, Editor
All-fiction quarterly. Ceased publication with the Winter 2000 issue.

StoryQuarterly

431 Sheridan Rd.
Kenilworth, IL 60043
M.M.M. Hayes, Editor
storyquarterly@hotmail.com
Actually an annual.

StringTown

93011 Ivy Station Road
Astoria, OR 97103
Polly Buckingham, Editor
Stringtown@aol.com
Annual.

The Sun

107 North Roberson Street
Chapel Hill, NC 27516
Sy Safransky, Editor
www.thesunmagazine.org
Spirited monthly.

Sundog

English Department
Florida State University
Tallahassee, FL 32311
Rotating editorship
sundog@english.fsu.edu
english.fsu.edu/sundog
"The Southeast Review." Biannual.

Sycamore Review

English Department
1356 Heavilon Hall
Purdue University
West Lafayette, IN 47907
Rotating editorship
sycamore@expert.cc.purdue.edu
www.sla.purdue.edu/academic/engl/sycamore/
Biannual.

Talking River Review
Division of Literature and
Languages
Lewis-Clark State College
500 8th Avenue
Lewiston, ID 83501
Student-run biannual.

Tameme
199 First Street
Los Altos, CA 94022
C. M. Mayo, Editor
editor@tameme.org
www.tameme.org
*Annual. "New Writing from North
America." Publishes bilingual fiction
in English and Spanish, the original
language and in translation.*

Tampa Review
University of Tampa
401 West Kennedy Boulevard
Tampa, FL 33606-1490
Richard Mathews, Editor
Biannual with hardcover format.

Tea Cup
P.O. Box 825
Ithaca, NY 14851-0825
Rhian Ellis, J. Robert Lennon,
Editors
Published "whenever possible."

The Texas Review
English Department
Sam Houston State University
Huntsville, TX 77341
Paul Ruffin, Editor
Biannual.

Third Coast*
English Department
Western Michigan University

Kalamazoo, MI 49008-5092
Rotating editorship
www.wmich.edu/thirdcoast
Biannual.

The Threepenny Review
P.O. Box 9131
Berkeley, CA 94709
Wendy Lesser, Editor
wlesser@threepennyreview.com
www.threepennyreview.com
Quarterly.

Tikkun
60 West 87th Street
New York, NY 10024
Thane Rosenbaum, Literary Editor
magazine@tikkun.org
www.tikkun.org
"A Bimonthly Jewish Critique of Politics, Culture, and Society."

Timber Creek Review
3283 UNCG Station
Greensboro, NC 27413
John M. Freiermuth, Editor
*Published quarterly or "whenever
there is enough material to fill a few
pages."*

Tin House
P.O. Box 10500
Portland, OR 97296-0500
Rob Spillman, Elissa Schappell,
Editors
Quarterly.

Transition*
69 Dunster Street
Cambridge, MA 02138
Kwame Anthony Appiah, Henry
Louis Gates Jr., Editors
Quarterly. An international review

with one or two stories per issue.
Founded forty years ago in Uganda.
Now published in the U.S.

TRIQUARTERLY
Northwestern University
2020 Ridge Avenue
Evanston, IL 60208
Susan Firestone Hahn, Editor
www.triquarterly.com
Triannual.

The Virginia Quarterly Review*
1 West Range
P.O. Box 400223
Charlottesville, VA 22903-4223
Staige D. Blackford, Editor
vqreview@virginia.edu
www.virginia.edu/vqr

War, Literature & the Arts
English and Fine Arts Department
United States Air Force Academy
Colorado Springs, CO 80840-
6242
Donald Anderson, Editor
donald.anderson@usafa.af.mil
www.usafa.af.mil/dfeng/wla
Biannual.

Wascana Review
English Department
University of Regina
Regina, Saskatchewan
S4S 0A2 Canada
Kathleen Wall, Editor
Biannual.

Washington Review
P.O. Box 50132
Washington, DC 20091-0132
Clarissa K. Wittenberg, Editor
www.washingtonreview.com
D.C.-area bimonthly journal of arts
and literature.

Washington Square
Creative Writing Program
New York University
19 University Place, 2nd Floor
New York, NY 10003-4556
Rotating editorship
Annual.

Weber Studies
Weber State University
1214 University Circle
Ogden, UT 84408-1214
Sherwin W. Howard, Editor
weberstudies.weber.edu
Triquarterly. "Voices and Viewpoints
of the Contemporary West."

Wellspring
4080 83rd Avenue North
Suite A
Brooklyn Park, MN 55443
Meg Miller, Editor and Publisher

West Branch
Bucknell Hall
Bucknell University
Lewisburg, PA 17837
Joshua Harmon, Editor
westbranch@bucknell.edu
Biannual.

West Coast Line
2027 East Academic Annex
Simon Fraser University
Burnaby, British Columbia
V5A 1S6 Canada
Roy Miki, Editor
www.sfu.ca/west-coast-line
Triannual.

Western Humanities Review
University of Utah
English Department
255 South Central Campus Drive
Room 3500

Salt Lake City, UT 84112-0494
Barry Weller, Editor
Biannual.

Whetstone

Barrington Area Arts Council
P.O. Box 1266
Barrington, IL 60011-1266
Sandra Berris, Marsha Portnoy,
Jean Tolle, Editors
Annual.

Willow Springs

705 West First Avenue, MS-1
Eastern Washington University
Cheney, WA 99201-3909
Christopher Howell, Editor
Biannual.

Wind

P.O. Box 24548
Lexington, KY 40524
Charlie Hughes, Leatha Kendrick,
Editors
Biannual.

Windsor Review

English Department
University of Windsor
Windsor, Ontario
N9B 3P4 Canada
Katherine Quinsey, General Editor
uwrevu@uwindsor.ca
Biannual.

WITNESS

**Oakland Community College
Orchard Ridge Campus
27055 Orchard Lake Road
Farmington Hills, MI 48334
Peter Stine, Editor
*Biannual.***

Worcester Review

6 Chatham Street
Worcester, MA 01609
Rodger Martin, Managing Editor
www.geocities.com/Paris/
LeftBank/6433
Annual.

Wordplay

P.O. Box 2248
South Portland, ME 04116-2248
Helen Peppe, Editor-in-Chief
Quarterly.

Words of Wisdom

8969 UNCG Station
Greensboro, NC 27413
Mikhammad bin Muhandis Abdel-
Ishara, Editor
*Published quarterly or "whenever
there is enough material to fill a few
pages."*

Writers' Forum

University of Colorado
P.O. Box 7150
Colorado Springs, CO 80933
C. Kenneth Pellow, Editor-in-
Chief
Annual.

WV: Magazine of the Emerging Writer

The Writer's Voice of the West Side
YMCA
5 West 63rd Street
New York, NY 10023
Publication suspended.

Xavier Review

Xavier University
Box 110C
New Orleans, LA 70125
Thomas Bonner Jr., Editor
Biannual.

Xconnect: Writers of the Information Age

P.O. Box 2317
Philadelphia, PA 19103
D. Edward Deifer, Editor-in-Chief
xconnect@ccat.sas.upenn.edu
ccat.sas.upenn.edu/xconnect
Pronounced "cross connect." Annual print version of triannual Web zine.

The Yale Review

Yale University
P.O. Box 208243
New Haven, CT 06250-8243
J.D. McClatchy, Editor
Quarterly.

The Yalobusha Review

P.O. Box 186
University, MS 38677-0186
rotating editorship
yalobush@sunset.backbone.
olemiss.edu
www.olemiss.edu/depts/english/
pubs/yalobusha_review.html
Annual.

ZOETROPE: ALL-STORY*

1350 Avenue of the Americas
24th Floor
New York, NY 10019
Adrienne Brodeur, Editor-in-Chief
www.zoetrope-stories.com
Quarterly. Published by Francis Ford Coppola. Web site provides full text of stories and allows for online submissions through its online workshops, provided users first read and rate five other stories.

Zyzzyva

41 Sutter Street
Suite 1400
San Francisco, CA 94104-4903
Howard Junker, Editor
editor@zyzzyva.org
www.zyzzyva.org
Triannual featuring west coast writers and artists.

Permissions Acknowledgments